# A KILLING GAME

## A CURTIS WESTCOTT THRILLER

Check out **Upcoming Releases** on www.JeffBuick.com
for all the details, and be sure to sign up for
Jeff's newsletter so you never miss a new title.

Published by Novel Words Inc. and Jeff Buick
www.JeffBuick.com

Cover and interior design by Lance Buckley
www.lancebuckley.com

ISBN: 978-1-999-5334-9-6

# A KILLING GAME

A CURTIS WESTCOTT CRIME THRILLER

# JEFF BUICK

NOVEL WORDS INC.

Dedicated to the memory of

# Michael Hartley-Robinson
## 1937—2019

A graduate of the Royal Academy of Dramatic Art in London, Michael was a true Renaissance Man. Over the course of his life he was:

An actor
A writer
A producer
A TV and movie reviewer
A master at radio drama in so many ways
A race car driver
A dragon boat racer
A photographer
A long distance runner
A SCUBA diver
A parachutist
A soldier
A paramedic
A sailor
A stage manager
A restauranteur
A newspaper consultant
A headmaster
A successful businessman
AND
A rabid Manchester United fan
And lastly, a Formula One racing enthusiast (Lewis Hamilton all the way)

Michael was a friend of mine. I miss him dearly.

# CHAPTER ONE

I t had been one hell of a night.

Renee Charlesbois glanced over the diminishing crowd. Sixty, maybe seventy guests were still milling about her new restaurant, finishing off the last of the free appetizers and liquor. Another two hundred had already left, most of them taking her by the hand and telling her how wonderful the evening had been. Success, they assured her, was in the cards. Her cheeks hurt from smiling and her feet were killing her. When she'd opened her first restaurant five years ago, working the room until two in the morning had left her invigorated and giddy. Not so much now.

*I'm only thirty-four*, she thought. *And this isn't getting any easier.*

She slipped in beside Hans Grummer, her maitre d'. "I've talked with most everyone, Hans. I'll be in the kitchen, helping with the cleanup."

"No, Renee," he said, his Austrian accent at home in the fashionable dining room. "You're exhausted. Go home, I'll handle whatever needs to be done in the kitchen."

She was going to object, but his stern look told her it wouldn't matter. "Okay, the leftover food goes to the shelter."

"As always. Don't worry. Go home and get some sleep."

She leaned over and kissed him on the cheek. "What would I do without you?"

"You would stop opening restaurants," he answered immediately. "And we don't want that."

She grinned and looked for the least populated escape route. After a few quick conversations and a handful more accolades, she slipped out the front door and took a deep breath of salty night air. She had chosen the location for this restaurant carefully, remembering the uphill struggle to gain a foothold when she opened her first place. Thinking her name alone would draw a steady clientele was a mistake. Bostonians, it turned out, were about as loyal as a total stranger.

The breeze off the harbor felt good after the artificial cold of the air conditioning and she slipped off her suit jacket as she walked, the August air pleasant on her bare shoulders. Her strides were long and confident, a benefit of being her father's daughter. Her inquisitive brown eyes and beautiful smile, those were courtesy of her mother.

The parking garage was less than a block away but to her feet, trapped in the high heels, it felt like a marathon. She swiped her access card in the reader, rode the elevator to P4 and hit the key fob. The lights on her Mini Cooper blinked, radiating like a strobe light through the deserted concrete structure, the acrid odor of gasoline lingering in the stuffy air.

She was almost at the car when she saw him. The man was in the process of unlocking a Porsche Carrera four stalls down, but was distracted by the flashing of her car lights. He stopped, looked up and smiled.

"Mini Cooper S," he said as she neared. "Now that's a fun car."

She hesitated a moment, then answered. "Yes, it is."

He looked back to the driver's door on the Porsche. For some reason, the key fob wasn't opening the lock.

Renee stared at his face, now positive she had seen him somewhere. Well dressed, average height and build, with dark hair and glasses with thick black frames. He was about her age, mid-thirties, with fair skin and clean-shaven. Then it clicked, she had seen him mingling earlier that evening at her opening. That was reassuring, but her fingers tightened on the small canister of mace in her handbag.

"You were at Chance tonight," she said. "The new restaurant up the street."

He looked up again from the key fob, which was refusing to work. "Yes, I was. You as well?"

"I own it," she said.

He smiled again, and walked around the Porsche toward her. "Then you must be Renee Charlesbois."

She nodded, and her grip on the mace loosened. "I am."

"I'm visiting from the west coast. A friend invited me—Doctor Bernard Rhonell. I'm sorry I didn't get an opportunity to personally thank you. The entire evening was fantastic. I think your new venture should do well." He had an easy smile that revealed even, off-white teeth.

She looked at him across the hood of her car. "You were Bernie's guest?" she asked.

"I was," he replied. "I'm a fellow anesthesiologist. We went to school together at UCLA."

"And you are?" She let go of the mace.

He tapped himself on his forehead and shook his head. "How rude of me. Liem Khilt." He took a couple of steps around the car so he was close enough to offer his hand. She felt a tiny prick as they shook, but a split-second later the sting was gone.

He glanced inside the Mini Cooper. "I had one of these for a couple of years. Everything about it was fun. Sometimes I wish I hadn't sold it."

"I took a quick test drive and bought it," Renee said, rubbing her hand. It felt like a tiny thorn had pricked her. "Love at first sight." She leaned against the car as her balance momentarily deserted her.

He watched her without speaking.

"Oh, my." Renee grabbed at the roof of the car. "I don't feel well." She started sliding down the driver's door and Khilt rushed in to catch her.

"Perhaps you had too much to drink." He steadied her by wrapping his arm around her waist.

She shook her head. It was a monumental task. "No, I didn't drink tonight."

Her eyes slowly closed and she collapsed into his arms. He lifted one eyelid gently, then let it drift shut. He fished her keys from the concrete where she had dropped them, lifted her up and walked around to the passenger door. He opened it and slid her unconscious body onto the soft leather. When she was propped up against the seat, he reached across and snapped the seat belt in place. Then he closed the door and jumped into the driver's side.

"That was easy," he said, taking a quick glance at the sleeping woman. "Almost too easy."

He started the Mini and pulled out of the parking lot, keeping to the speed limit while skirting the waterfront. After a few blocks he cut inland and headed east through the city, parallel to the Charles River, past Fenway Park and into Brighton.

Traffic was light and he made good time exiting the city, pulling up in front of an acreage just before midnight. He parked the car in the attached garage and pulled Renee's inert body from the front seat. Inside the garage a stairwell led to the basement and he hoisted her over his shoulder and started down. The air cooled slightly as he descended to the bottom where a short hallway led to a heavy wood door with a small, six-inch hole at eye height. He pulled the door open and entered the room.

It had been a wine cellar and the racks were still bolted to the walls. A toilet and sink had recently been installed, and it was sparsely furnished with a cot and a metal chair. The ceiling was low and made of poured concrete with metal I-beams to support the weight of the cars parked in the garage above. He laid her on the cot and smiled.

"Welcome home."

He left the room, locking the wooden door securely behind him.

# CHAPTER TWO

The day had been nothing short of a nightmare.

Curtis Westcott ran his hands through his dark hair and massaged his scalp, willing away the oncoming headache. It didn't work. He walked into his office and found the Advil bottle in the top right drawer. Two tablets and a glass of water would eventually push the pain away. Until then, he would have to suffer.

Stan Lamers, a mid-thirties black man stuck his shaved head through Westcott's partially open door and said, "I have the forensics on the Faber case."

"And…" Westcott said, downing the Advil.

"We have a DNA match on the blood stain on Anita Faber's shirt. It's the boyfriend's blood.

"What about the drops on the pavement near her body?"

"Not his, boss."

"Shit." Westcott sat in his chair. "So it's all circumstantial. Almara can come up with a hundred reasons why his blood could be on her shirt. We need to place him in the alley with her or we've nothing."

Stan nodded. "The lab techs ran the tests twice. It's definitely the boyfriend's blood on her shirt but the drops on the ground next to Faber's body belong to someone else."

Curtis closed his eyes, the details of Anita Faber's death running through his mind like a film. No witnesses had seen Louie Almara follow his girlfriend into the alley after they left the East Boston bar where they had been drinking since three in the afternoon. The alley was narrow, less than eighteen feet across, and dimly lit by a single forty-watt bulb above a boarded-up door. Her time of death was estimated at eleven o'clock, almost the same time they were kicked out of the bar for screaming at each other. The alley was less than a block from the bar and Almara had followed her onto the street. This was a no-brainer. What were they missing?

Curtis forced his mind to grind through the details.

The medical examiner had found fragments of brick in her hair and slight lacerations to her scalp, the type of injury that might have come from having her head smashed into the side of the building. There had been bruising above the hairline, but no discoloration on her neck or face. But the question was, how had Louie Almara gripped her head tightly enough to snap her neck without leaving bruises on her skin? He had unexplained scrapes on the back of his hand, but he could come up with any number of excuses for how they got there.

"We're screwed." Curtis opened his eyes. His sergeant was still standing by the door. "Unless…"

Stan waited for a few seconds, figuring Westcott had something, then said, "Unless what?"

Curtis put his hands out in front of him, as if holding someone's head between them, then twisted. "We're assuming he snapped her neck like that, but what if he rammed her head into something that would hold it immobile, then yanked her shoulders sideways."

"That would snap her neck," Stan said.

"Yeah, and it would explain the scrapes on his hands. When he twisted her body, the back of his hands could have hit the brick wall."

"We need to find a gap in the wall," Stan said.

"Exactly. Somewhere in that alley is an indent in the bricks where Anita's head would fit. He rammed her head into the crack, then twisted her torso. That's what snapped her neck. And that's why there is no bruising on her cheeks or neck."

"Just the tiny pieces of brick in her scalp," Stan said.

"Right, and I'll bet if you check the bricks around where he had her head jammed in the wall, you'll find traces of his blood. That's where he scraped his hand."

"We didn't see it because the color of the bricks and the dried blood were too close."

"It's there, Stan. Find it. That's how the son-of-a-bitch killed her." Eight hours of booze and one ugly argument had led to a corpse, and now the killer was going to pay.

"You got it," Stan said. He turned for the door and ran smack into another man entering Westcott's office. They both came to an abrupt stop in the opening.

Both were well over six feet and looking eye to eye. Stan, shaved head and tattoos, dressed in jeans and a t-shirt. The other, in his sixties with silver hair and expensive clothes. Both men held their ground.

"That's good, Stan," Curtis said. "Let me know what you find."

Reluctantly, Stan gave some ground and made his way around the older man and into the hallway.

Curtis peered up from his desk. "Can I help you?"

"Westcott, I'm Jacques Charlesbois."

Curtis leaned back in his chair. The Advil were doing the job and the throbbing behind his eyes was beginning to ebb. "I know who you are. I don't believe we have an appointment scheduled for today."

Jacques Charlesbois looked like he was going to erupt. Charlesbois was one of Boston's wealthiest men and anyone who read a newspaper or watched the news knew he was used to people jumping to attention when he arrived. He stared at Westcott for the better part of thirty seconds, then relaxed a notch and said, "My daughter has disappeared, Lieutenant."

Curtis motioned to one of the wingback chairs in front of his desk and Charlesbois sat. He was an unhealthy shade of red and Curtis could tell the lava was still simmering beneath the surface.

"Why not file a missing person's report? That's the proper procedure when someone is missing."

Charlesbois leaned forward in the chair. A vein on his forehead, near the hairline, was bulging and threatening to pop. "My daughter has been abducted. She is not just missing, she is in danger."

"You seem certain."

"I am."

"All right, let's assume that's true. Why homicide? And why are you so sure someone has taken her?"

"I was scheduled to have lunch with Renee today and she didn't show. I phoned everywhere—her house, her office, all of her restaurants. Nothing. And she didn't come home last night."

"Perhaps she has a friend with whom she spent the night. Your daughter is single, is she not?"

"My daughter is no more with some man than she is sitting in this room with us, detective."

Westcott leaned back in his chair, glad that he'd taken the Advil. "Your daughter is an adult, Mr. Charlesbois. Mid-thirties, I think. She's a wealthy woman, with resources. If she wanted to get out of the city and disappear for a couple of days, I'm sure she could do it."

Charlesbois stared at Curtis, his eyes burning. "You're not listening, Westcott. I know my daughter. She would never miss one of our lunches. Something is wrong."

Curtis shifted in his chair, aware Charlesbois was watching his every move. "You never answered my question, sir. Why homicide? We usually don't get involved until someone has been killed. At this point, there's no evidence any harm has come to your daughter."

"Homicide has the best resources, lieutenant. You have teams of detectives trained in investigative work. A full-blown investigation is what's needed here. Get a team working on what happened to my daughter." He paused for a moment, then added, "Before it's too late."

Curtis rubbed his forehead, wishing he'd taken three pills. Charlesbois was not a man to mess with, but allocating his department's resources to an investigation simply on the word of a distraught relative was not done. Especially when the person had been missing for less than twenty-four hours. All that taken into account, Jacques

Charlesbois could, and probably would, have the police commissioner and the mayor on the phone inside the hour. There was no upside to spouting official police procedure to this man.

Curtis texted one of his detectives and a few moments later a fit, mid-thirties woman was at the door. He motioned for her to come in. "Jacques Charlesbois, Detective Aislinn Byrne." They nodded to each other and Curtis said to Aislinn, "Mr. Charlesbois' daughter is missing."

Aislinn sat in the chair next to Charlesbois, took out a tablet and typed a few lines. Then she waited.

"Tell me what you know, Mr. Charlesbois," Curtis said.

"Renee and I have lunch once a week, every week, on Friday. Unless one of us is out of Boston on business or vacation neither of us has ever missed. I know she's in town. I spoke with her last night at six o'clock, just before the opening of her new restaurant."

"Which restaurant?" Aislinn asked.

"Chance. It's on State Street, just down from Sel de la Terre," he said. "She had about three hundred people at the opening. Lots of media types, restaurant critics, gallery owners, that sort of crowd. She worked the room from about seven o'clock until the crowd thinned out around eleven, then left for home."

"How do you know when she left the restaurant?" Curtis asked.

"Her maitre d', Hans Grummer, was at the restaurant today when I called. He was one of the last people to speak with her before she left."

"Did she catch a ride or does she drive herself?" Aislinn asked.

"She drives. When she bought the space for the restaurant she picked up a parking spot in an underground garage about a block away. She always parks there."

"What kind of car?"

"A white Mini Cooper S," Charlesbois said. "It's missing. Her parking spot is empty."

"Mini Coopers are popular," Aislinn said, looking over at Curtis. He gave her a nod and she continued. "I'll get the details from the DMV and have dispatch send the description and plate number over the radio."

"Do you know of anyone who would want to hurt your daughter?" Curtis asked. "Past business acquaintances or boyfriends with a grudge?"

"No," Charlesbois said tersely. "Renee was a good businesswoman, tough but fair. She does a lot for the community and donates a good deal of money to the children's hospital. No enemies, if that's what you mean."

Curtis nodded. "Is she dating anyone right now?" he asked, then continued when Charlesbois shook his head. "Obviously, you've had no word from her abductors? Providing, of course, that's what happened."

"Nothing."

"We'll need to look through her house and check her computer to see what appointments she had. Access to her cell phone records would be helpful."

"I'll arrange all of that," Charlesbois said.

"Does her car have a GPS tracker on it?"

"I don't think so."

"Okay, Mr. Charlesbois, leave it with us. We'll begin by speaking with some of the guests at the restaurant's opening and checking with Renee's friends. Please get us a list of her closest friends and email it to me. The sooner the better."

"Of course." Charlesbois nodded and looked at Aislinn. "I have a key to Renee's house. I could have someone meet you there."

"Please," Aislinn said. "I can be there at seven o'clock tonight."

"Seven is fine."

Aislinn said to Charlesbois, "Have whoever is meeting me bring a letter authorizing us to search the house. You can sign it."

Curtis handed Charlesbois a business card. "We're on this."

Charlesbois took the business card and slipped it into his wallet. "Find her, Westcott."

"We'll do our best." Curtis stood and shook the man's hand.

"Make sure your best gets my daughter back," Charlesbois said as he left the room.

# CHAPTER THREE

"Well, that was fun," Aislinn said as the door closed behind Jacques Charlesbois.

Byrne was in her fifth year with Boston Homicide, and being a cop was in her blood. Her father had spent his entire career with BPD, working a beat on the streets of Jamaica Plain. Her rise to detective had been unspectacular—time and hard work had got her there.

"Get the info on the car out to the uniforms," Curtis said. "Not that we'll get any hits."

"Of course not." Aislinn ran a chewed-to-the-quick fingernail through her short red hair. "It's already tucked away somewhere."

"Yeah. Wealthy woman disappears. He knows the heat will be on. There's no way he'll be driving around in an easily recognizable car."

"You're assuming it's a guy who grabbed her."

"It's a guy."

Aislinn nodded. "Okay, so the car's in a garage, somewhere out of sight. Does he move it when the dust has settled?"

"Maybe," Curtis said. "You might get more when you check the surveillance tapes in the parking garage."

"So we're going to spend time on this?" she asked.

Curtis nodded.

"What about your rule—*no special treatment for anyone*. We don't have a body. All we have is a rich white guy who thinks his daughter has been abducted."

"There's no special treatment here, Aislinn. Charlesbois and his daughter meet every Friday for lunch. They never miss. She opens a new restaurant on Thursday night and then doesn't show up on Friday. Something's wrong with that. If she *has* been taken, then we're out in front of this. Maybe getting a head start is the difference between someone grabbing her or someone killing her. I'm willing to risk a few hours of your time for that."

"Fair enough." She stood and stretched her five-ten frame. "An APB on the car, CCTV tapes from the parking garage and nearby businesses, then her apartment."

"Sounds like a plan."

His phone rang and he picked up the receiver as Aislinn left his office. "Westcott."

"LT., it's Stan. Guess what we found?"

"A wide crack in the wall and blood on the bricks next to it."

"Bingo. It's in a different alley, half a block to the west."

"Little wonder we missed it the first time," Curtis said.

"Right. It looks like there could be traces of skin residue mixed in with the blood. Louie Almara scraped his hand good when he twisted her body. We have a few hairs that look like they may be from the victim where he stuck her head in the crack. Must have carried her body over to where we found it."

"Good work, Stan," Curtis said. "Make sure the CSU techs are thorough, I don't want this piece of crap walking on some technicality."

"Sure, LT." The line went dead.

Curtis slipped the phone into its cradle and leaned back in his chair. His head felt better and that helped him to think more clearly. The Charlesbois thing bothered him. It was the sort of circumstance that had got him promoted to the top of the heap in Boston Homicide at thirty-five. His solve rate was high but what had won over the police commission was his proactive thinking and willingness to take calculated risks. The Charlesbois case, as he was beginning to view it, was a perfect example. Ignoring it was folly—if anything happened to the daughter and Charlesbois could prove he had given homicide a leg up, the whole department would feel his wrath. Assigning a senior detective, like Aislinn, was a drain on resources and flew in the face of the one rule he hated breaking. Nobody—regardless of financial status or social standing—received special treatment from his team. Still, if Renee Charlesbois was alive…

The phone rang and he checked the caller ID. It was Richard Westcott, his father. "Hi Dad, what's up?"

"Dinner. Tonight. Our place. Can you come?"

Curtis knew exactly why they wanted to see him. "Can it wait? Something has come up and it's important."

"And your mother's not?"

Curtis glanced at his computer screen and his schedule. "Okay, but it has to be early. I'm invited to a party at Chloe Harrah's place at eight."

"Well, you don't want to be late for Chloe. Let's say five o'clock. See you then."

Curtis hung up without saying goodbye. His father never did, so he had finally stopped as well. Maybe it was a habit that had come from being a busy lawyer. Maybe his father was just rude. He wasn't sure.

He stayed on task for the next two hours, checking the status of the homicide files all his teams were working on. Aislinn had already opened a case file for Renee and her notes from the meeting with Charlesbois were there, along with an email from him with Renee's contact list. It was extensive, but Charlesbois had flagged twenty-three names as being top priority. Curtis forwarded the file to a junior member of the team along with the case file Aislinn had prepared. They would know what questions to ask.

He packed up at four-thirty and headed for Brookline and Warren Street, back to where he had spent his youth. Driving through the heavily wooded neighborhood with its generous lots and elegant homes set back from the curb was calming. The office faded and visions of his younger years floated by. Racing friends on his bicycle at breakneck speeds on the winding roads, driving the car for the first time without his parents, drinking too much at Garrett Harrison's keg party. It all seemed so long ago now.

His parents' house fit in with its red brick exterior and sharply sloping slate roof barely visible through the trees. He pulled into the long, sweeping drive and parked in front of the garage. The August sun filtered through the branches and felt warm on his skin as he walked around to the backyard where he knew his parents would be sitting by the pool. He found them under the garden umbrella halfway through a game of Scrabble.

"Zeroed," he said, reading the board. "On a triple word score. Nice."

"Your father gets lucky every now and then."

Curtis leaned over and gave his mother a peck on the cheek. She was starting to look her age, he thought, wishing she would retire. Being a judge was, as she put it, still her life. *Why should I quit a legal career it took forty years to build?* she asked. *Because,* he told her, *all that stuff you see in your courtroom, it's tearing you apart.* He sat at the table and poured himself a glass of lemonade from the pitcher. It was cold and felt good on his throat.

"Chloe's." Richard Westcott said. "What's going on there?"

"She's having a party."

The elder Westcott glanced over at his wife. "Did we get an invite?"

Janis shook her head. "No."

He looked back at the Scrabble board. "We used to get invites to all her parties."

"You never wanted to go," Janis said.

"True, but at least we were invited."

Curtis sipped his lemonade, watching and listening. They were in their sixties, and younger men and women were taking over in his father's firm now. Neither of them were ready to retire, but their glory days were mostly in the past, and Curtis knew it was eating at them.

"She invites you because you're in the news," his father said.

"Probably. Why else would she bother?" Curtis didn't like being in the news, being invited to Chloe's parties, or this conversation.

"The camera is kind to you," his mother said.

"Kind my ass," his father snorted. "He's six feet, thin, and always looks tanned. And, he got my hair." His father winked at him.

Curtis rolled his eyes. His father's hair, silver now, had once been jet black like his, and was still thick and wavy. "Thanks, Dad. I do appreciate the hair."

His father looked pleased.

"I give them sound bytes,' Curtis said. "Ten to fifteen seconds of concise information on the case. They interview me because I make their job easier."

"Well, say hello to Chloe," Janis said.

"I will."

Kat poked her head out the patio doors and waved. Dinner was ready. The young chef cooked two nights a week for his parents, with the caveat that she could have dinner plated and be off to her night gig by five-thirty. It was an indulgence Curtis thoroughly enjoyed. The three of them filed into the house and sat at the dining table. Numerous plates with different kinds of tapas were on the table, along with a handful of ramekins with colorful sauces. They dug in as Kat waved and headed out the front door.

Halfway through eating, his father started in. "You haven't cashed the check."

*No surprise there*, Curtis thought. He knew the topic of joining his father's firm was the reason he'd been invited. "I haven't."

His father set his fork and knife on the plate. "Two years and you make partner."

Curtis sat back on his chair and studied the ceiling.

His father's face took on color. "Part of the reason I spent all those years building the firm was so you could take over when I retire. That was the plan."

"*I* never had a plan, dad. I went into law *because* I didn't have a plan."

"It's a waste of your degree," Richard Westcott continued.

Curtis remained silent.

"Jesus, Curtis. It's all there for you, and a fat signing bonus to boot."

Curtis set his cutlery on the table and focused on his father. "I like being a cop. I'm where I should be."

"Where you should be? You mean on a second-floor balcony trying to arrest a crazy naked guy who's waving a knife at you? Is that where you should be?"

"C'mon, dad, that was an exception."

"It happened. You went over the balcony with him and hurt your back. That sort of thing doesn't happen in a law office."

"No, it doesn't," Curtis agreed. Nothing much ever happened in a law office. Maybe that was part of the reason why it didn't appeal.

His mother chimed in, her voice calm and even. "Curtis has made his decision, sweetheart." Janis Westcott was a master at defusing her husband's anger. She beamed at both of them, and Curtis felt the ice in the room melting.

Curtis toyed with his fork, thinking of something to say that would let his father know why working homicide was so important. There was a methodology to tracking criminals, digging up clues, sorting through the chaff, interviewing the bad guys. Being lied to and figuring out what's true and what's not. Starting with a murder, and out of all those millions of people, finding the one person who did it.

"It's..." he paused, still searching for the right word. "It's rewarding."

"Rewarding?" his father snorted. "They stuck you in Jamaica Plain. That's hardly the country club."

His mother shot her husband a sideways glance. "Sweetie."

"Homicide." His father got up and went in search of an after-dinner coffee.

Curtis shook his head after his father left. "I like working homicide, Mom. I'm good at it."

She smiled. "Yes, you really are."

Curtis helped her clear away the dishes and they moved into the family room with their coffee, the conversation on easier subjects. After an hour, Curtis checked his watch. "I need to head for Chloe's. Traffic will be ugly." He kissed his mom on the forehead and nodded to his dad as he left.

He settled into his car and called Stan before turning over the ignition. "Is everything okay at the Faber crime scene?" he asked.

"Couldn't be better, LT. CSU is wrapping up and they were awesome. The report will be on the system sometime tomorrow."

"Okay, Stan, thanks. I'll be at Chloe Harrah's place. If I'm not in first thing Monday, come looking for me."

"You should film her party and send it in for a reality TV pilot," his detective said before killing the line.

Curtis chuckled and started his car. Chloe Harrah was waiting.

# CHAPTER FOUR

Aislinn Byrne leaned against her car and lit a cigarette. Whoever was meeting her was late and she was starting into a slow burn. Patience was not her strong suit.

She glanced up and down Beacon Street. This wasn't her world and as people walked by she felt a bit off. Her clothes were fine—snug dress pants and a crisply pressed dark blazer, but she felt their eyes on her. She tucked one foot behind the other, hiding one of the shoes she'd bought at Filene's Basement, then wondered why she cared. Her partner was walking the street, taking photos of the houses that bordered Renee Charlesbois' place as a silver Audi driven by a man in his thirties pulled up. When her sergeant returned, the Audi driver slipped out of his car, glanced at Aislinn, then approached her partner.

"Detective Byrne?" he asked.

"No, Sergeant Fleming. That's Detective Byrne." He motioned at Aislinn.

The man turned and headed toward her, his eyes moving from head to toe and lingering for a split second too long on her body. He held out his hand and smiled. "Scott Warner. Mr. Charlesbois asked me to drop by and meet you."

She briefly considered ignoring his hand, but decided not to be prickly. She shook and said, "Thanks for coming."

The smile widened. "I have a key. Let's go inside shall we."

"Please."

She'd seen it so many times before and it was getting lame. It wasn't uncommon when she and her partner met someone, for them to assume he was the detective. Then, when they took the time to look at her, they would turn on the charm. Aislinn owned a mirror and knew she was an attractive woman. She didn't need validation and she certainly didn't need anyone hitting on her when she was working.

Scott unlocked the door and started in, but Aislinn stuck her arm across the opening. "I'm sure you don't mind waiting out here," she said. It was obvious she wasn't asking. She slipped on a thin pair of booties and latex gloves, then said, "Did Mr. Charlesbois give you a letter for us?"

"Yes." He dug an envelope out of his suit pocket and handed it to her.

Aislinn opened it and scanned the contents. It was an authorization from Jacques Charlesbois for the Boston Police Department to search his daughter's townhouse, including any electronic devices they might find on site. It likely wouldn't hold up in court if it was contested but that was unlikely to happen. She folded it and slipped it into her pocket, then headed into the house and stood in the center of the living room and looked about.

The space was like a page out of a Restoration Hardware catalogue. It was clean, but not staged, with a handful of magazines scattered on the coffee table, some dishes in the sink and a MacBook Pro on the kitchen counter.

"Take the bedrooms, bathrooms, storage and garage," she said to her sergeant. "Look for any indication she recently packed—a suitcase set with one missing, no toothbrush on the bathroom vanity, stuff like that."

"Right." He headed up the stairs.

She walked over to the computer, which was open and plugged into the wall, and touched the power button, then ran her finger across the touch pad. The screen lit up. Renee hadn't signed out, so Aislinn didn't need a password to get in. An email from a restaurant supplier was open and she scanned the contents. It was a confirmation of a delivery to Renee's new restaurant, dated Thursday at four-eighteen. Aislinn glanced at the clock in the upper right corner of the screen. Seven o'clock. Less than twenty-seven hours later and now a homicide cop was checking Renee's messages. One day could certainly change things. Aislinn watched the screen as the emails started to pour in. There were over a hundred and most of them were congratulations on the launch of Renee's new restaurant. She waited until the influx stopped, then clicked on the Calendar icon.

Renee's daily calendar appeared on the screen and Aislinn took a careful look at the entries. There were numerous appointments with suppliers and quite a few slots set aside for meetings with the kitchen staff from Chance. Apparently, Renee used the calendar app to schedule everything. Aislinn closed the computer, unplugged it and slipped it into a large evidence bag. If Renee showed up of her own volition, she could pick up the laptop at the precinct. If not, then they had a snapshot of her life to work with.

There was movement in the front of the house. Scott Warner was in the foyer. Aislinn pointed to the door and walked directly toward him. "Please leave the house, Mr. Warner. Right now."

He took his time and stood outside the front door with an irritated look on his face. "I have better things to do than hang around here all night."

"No, you don't."

He wasn't going to back down. "I was the one who gave you the key," he said. "For all you know I was already in there."

She smiled. "You have a very good point."

"Thank you."

"About you being in the house." She crossed the threshold and stood within a few feet of him. She was an inch taller and in far better shape. "Where were you last night, Mr. Warner?"

He stared at her. "Are you serious?"

"I'm always serious." A few moments passed, then she said, "Where were you last night at eleven o'clock?"

"At home."

"Was anyone with you?"

"No."

"You weren't invited to the launch?"

His face took on some color. "No."

She moved closer, into his space. "Did that make you angry?"

He swallowed hard and licked his lips. "No, of course not."

She was only inches from him now and could feel his fear. "See that step? Sit down and be there when I get back."

Aislinn headed back inside, then upstairs to see what Brian Fleming had found. The sergeant was in the en suite bath going through the vanity. "Anything?" she asked.

"No missing suitcase, toothbrush is in its holder, hair dryer still plugged in. Nothing to suggest she had been thinking of leaving."

"Okay. Let's lock this place down and put some tape across the door handles. Keep it low key so the neighbors don't catch on."

"Got it."

"Tell Mr. Warner he can go, but we'll be keeping the key."

Aislinn walked through the master bedroom to the balcony doors and opened them. The MIT campus was directly across the river and she leaned on the wrought iron railing and wondered what it was like to be wealthy and privileged. Pretty nice, she imagined, until someone grabbed you.

She pulled out her cell and called Westcott. He answered and it sounded like he was in his car on hands free. "Not much here," she said. "I have Renee's computer and it's loaded with her entire life, so we should be able to piece together everything she's done and was going to do."

"Good," Curtis said. "Jacques Charlesbois called five minutes ago and there's been no activity on Renee's cell phone since Thursday night."

"Shit," Aislinn said. The gravity of that was substantial. No texts or calls for an entire day was the worst-case scenario when dealing with a missing person.

Curtis asked, "Any indication she was heading out for a few days?"

"None."

"That's not good. Her father might be right about this."

"It's starting to look that way." She reentered the bedroom and closed the doors behind her. The view and the opulence had lost its charm. "Are you around tonight if I get something off her computer?"

"Sort of. I'm at Chloe's place for a party. On my way there now."

"She's on Vernon Place, isn't she?"

"Yup."

"I'm about five blocks away. You need backup?"

Curtis couldn't help laughing. He could hear Aislinn on the other end of the line, laughing as well. "I'll manage, but thanks for the offer."

Aislinn killed the line and headed for the front door. She slowed, then stopped as she passed a grouping of photos on the sofa table. Every picture had Renee Charlesbois front and center—with friends, in front of Angkor Wat, in the mist at Machu Picchu, on the beach. Aislinn looked closer. There were at least fifteen pictures, and Renee had the exact same smile in every one. It was like a signature. Forced, almost, like it had to be that way. Aislinn wasn't sure why, but she found it unsettling.

She'd had enough of Renee Charlesbois' world for now. Her own world, the one with a meddling mother and a cop father, was looking better all the time.

# CHAPTER FIVE

The corporate offices of The Charles Group were a reflection of their founder.

Jacques Charlesbois had transformed two floors of the John Hancock Tower from a maze of cubicles into a hundred thousand square feet of chrome and leather furniture, potted palms and slate floors. The private offices had stunning views of Boston, which sat well with the wealthy clients who visited to discuss their investments. No matter which fund they chose, The Charles Group was there to collect a fee. Over the years, Jacques Charlesbois had collected a lot of fees.

Still, the majority of his wealth hadn't come from fees. His big break came when he bet on a drop in the British Pound in the '90s. The highly speculative gamble had paid off and Jacques Charlesbois became an extremely wealthy man.

His family life wasn't as fortunate. Charlesbois and his wife Irina had hoped for a handful of children but complications after Renee's birth left her barren. The news, at the time, was devastating, but over the next few years they accepted Renee would be an only child. Jacques and Irina watched some of their friends give their kids everything but they refused to do that with Renee. If she wanted something she had to work for it, just like they had. Her first car was used, purchased with money she saved from her summer job.

Her decision to open a restaurant after getting her MBA had bothered her parents, but their hands were tied. When Renee turned twenty-nine she had access to her trust fund and she used part of it to purchase and renovate a space. Renee hired Hans Grummer as her maitre d', paid him well and gave him a percentage in the restaurant. They put together a great team of chefs and servers and implemented a bonus system based on converting walk-in customers to regulars. The food was excellent and by the time Renee was thirty-four she was opening her third restaurant.

But now she was gone. Their daughter had disappeared into the mist off the Inner Harbor without a trace. He knew it for a fact and it was a punch in his gut like nothing he had ever experienced. She was a creature of habit and would never forget their Friday lunch. A light rap on the door caused him to turn from the window, lost in thought, his world at a standstill.

"Hello, Jacques." A mid-forties man with a military bearing walked across the office, his mouth set in a grim line.

"Amery," Charlesbois said. "Thanks for coming. Please, sit down."

Amery Kincaid sat on the couch and watched Jacques Charlesbois pour two cups of coffee. The financier added cream and sugar without asking. He knew how Kincaid took his coffee.

Kincaid was loyal, and collected his pay in cash. He was a shadow who worked behind the scenes to give Charlesbois an edge in the financial world. Charlesbois didn't care how Kincaid managed to get inside the hedge funds' computer networks. All he needed was some advance warning on what they were up to, and that had made both him and Kincaid wealthy men. Now, Jacques Charlesbois needed Amery Kincaid for a far more important reason. Finding his daughter.

"Renee," Charlesbois started as he slid into the chair behind his desk.

"I got your message," Amery replied. "Are you doing okay, Jacques?"

Charlesbois' face went vivid red. "Not fucking really."

"Of course. When and where did she disappear?"

"Around midnight last night. She was at the opening of her new restaurant and things were wrapping up. She said goodnight to Hans, then left through the front door. She was likely heading for her car, which was parked in a garage a block west on State Street."

"I'll pull the video from the parking garage," Amery said.

"The police probably already have it."

Amery raised an eyebrow. "You've already called the police?"

"I went in to see them a couple of hours ago. I spoke with Curtis Westcott and one of his detectives."

"Westcott. He's homicide."

"Yes."

"Jesus, Jacques." He was quiet for a moment, then asked, "Is Westcott putting anyone on it?"

"He is, but I want you working it as well."

Amery pulled out a small notebook. "The parking garage. Most CCTVs are digital. If that's the case, they'll copy the file for the police and the original will still be on their computer. I'll just borrow it."

"Okay," Jacques said.

Kincaid asked the tough question. "Do you think it's a kidnap?"

Jacques shook his head. "I don't know. What else could it be?"

"Have there been any demands for her return?"

"No, nothing." Charlesbois stared at his untouched coffee. "She's gone. Into thin air, Amery."

Kincaid knew all the stats on kidnapping. The percentages of getting the person back weren't good. "Anything else?"

Charlesbois leaned forward. "Find out who has my daughter, Amery. Do whatever is necessary."

Amery nodded. If he found Renee before the police, it would not go well for the kidnappers.

# CHAPTER SIX

L iem Khilt switched on the hall light and slipped the key into the lock. He glanced through the small opening in the door before turning the key. She was sitting on the bed, staring at the entrance. He unlocked the latch, gripped the pistol and swung open the heavy wood door. It groaned slightly, the well-oiled hinges complaining of the weight.

He glanced at the empty plate sitting on the serving tray. "I see you ate your dinner," he said. When she didn't answer, he added, "That's good. You should eat. Keep up your strength."

"Who are you?" Renee Charlesbois asked. Her voice was raspy, her throat dry from breathing the stagnant air for the better part of twenty-four hours.

"I told you who I was when we met in the parking lot. My name is Liem Khilt."

"I doubt that." She stared at him with unabashed hatred.

"As you wish," he said. She looked very different from the previous evening, with disheveled hair and smeared makeup. Purposely, he had not put a mirror in the room. "If you want something, I answer to Liem Khilt." He sat in the metal chair next to the door and watched her eyes as they focused on the gun. "I *will* use it if you give me reason."

"Why am I here?" She pushed her hair back from her face. Her eyes felt tired, and she was sure there were dark circles under the sockets. "Do you want money? I have money."

He crossed his legs and smiled. "Yes, I know about your trust fund. You're worth about sixteen million dollars. Which means I have more money than you."

Renee tried to read his eyes, and what she saw troubled her. He wasn't lying. "Then why kidnap me?"

"Kidnapping is an interesting word, don't you think?" Khilt said. "You're hardly a kid, and I didn't really 'nap' you. It's a very misused word."

"All right. Why abduct me if not for money?"

He used the gun barrel to rub an itch on his temple, then leveled it at her. "It's a game, Renee. I have you and they have to find you."

"Who is *they*?" she asked.

"Well, your father will be doing everything he can to save you and will get the police involved soon if he hasn't already. Amery Kincaid will already be looking for you as well."

"How do you know about Amery Kincaid?" she asked. Amery was one of her father's secrets. Few people knew he was on Jacques Charlesbois' payroll, and her father worked hard to keep it that way.

"Please, it wasn't that hard." Khilt toyed with the barrel of the gun for a minute, then said, "Your father will get Boston PD working on your disappearance. Personally, I'm hoping for Curtis Westcott."

"Westcott." Renee had heard the name. She closed her eyes and thought hard. It was on the television. She'd seen him interviewed on the news. A horrible thought hit her and she opened her eyes. "Westcott, he's homicide. I'm not dead."

"Not yet," he said quietly. "Not yet."

The coldness in his eyes chilled her. "What do you want?" she asked, surprised by the fear she could hear in her own voice.

"A worthy opponent," he said.

"What?" she asked. "I don't understand."

His checked his watch, then stood up and moved to the door. "I told you, Renee, it's a game. I have you and they have to find you. It's that simple, really."

Khilt opened the door and left the wine cellar, switching off the light after locking her in. A few hours of darkness would soften her up a bit. She was a feisty one and needed to be brought down a notch or two.

He took the stairs to the main floor two at a time and set the gun on the hall table, then made his way through the old estate home to the en suite bathroom. On the vanity was a variety of latex prosthetics, with a row of jars containing cake makeup and foundation cream. He applied a light coat of spirit gum to his nose and cheekbones, and a touch around his eyes. He waited until the glue was tacky then applied the latex, smoothing the edges carefully to avoid wrinkles. Fifteen minutes later, he looked in the mirror and a slow smile crept across his face. A completely different face stared back at him.

Khilt changed into clothes that were too large for him, then filled out the extra space by adding a few well-placed pieces of padding. It added the appearance of thirty pounds to his frame. He buttoned his shirt, slipped on his suit coat and took stock of his new look. It was perfect. He checked his watch and ran a last moment comb through his hair.

It was party time.

# CHAPTER SEVEN

Mount Vernon Place is half a block off Boston Common in the tony enclave of Beacon Hill, an area steeped in American history.

Chloe Harrah lived on Mount Vernon Place. Actually, Chloe Harrah ruled Mount Vernon Place. Nobody bothered calling in an illegally parked car if the owners were visiting Chloe. When Elton John visited Boston, he usually ended up at Chloe's at her grand piano, the door always open for the neighbors to drop by to listen. While not quite as well known as the tea party or Fenway Park, the charismatic seventy-something was a Boston icon.

Curtis Westcott knew that when she invited you to a party you were expected to attend. Her house was usually so jammed that he suspected he could skip and not get caught, but to date he hadn't dared try.

He left his car at his own house, in Back Bay, and walked over. He arrived a few minutes after eight, presented his invitation to the doorman and entered. There was nothing somber or dark inside the old Victorian house. Chloe had gutted the interior and now it was bright and full of granite and light-colored walls and trim. Curtis ran into her in the kitchen as he was getting a beer from the fridge.

"Curtis." She embraced him and kissed him on both cheeks. The scent of her perfume was faint and suited her. "How are things at the office? Do you have enough bodies to keep you busy?"

He couldn't help grinning. It wasn't the words, it was her droll delivery. "Sure, lots of dead people." He took a drink of beer from the bottle, wondering why she kept inviting him. "Lots of important people tonight—as usual."

She smiled and gave him the kind of look a kid does when she's planning some mischief. "You have a job that people find fascinating, Curtis. Tell me something interesting."

*And there she is*, Curtis thought, *fishing*. "It's gritty, Chloe. Dirty work with a lot of sad people. Lives torn apart. All that stuff."

"It sounds so intriguing when they interview you."

Curtis set his beer on the counter and moved closer to her. "Bodies are awful. They smell terrible. They look terrible. Every time I see one, I wonder what they would have done with their life if someone hadn't killed them."

She was inches from him and totally focused on his every word. "So why do you do it?"

He shrugged and backed off a bit. "I'm good at it, and they deserve a bit of retribution. The worst thing—ever—is seeing some bad guy walk when you know he did it, but you can't get the evidence to prove it."

She put her hand on his arm. "Boston needs you, Curtis."

"Well, thank you." He was starting to feel like maybe her parties weren't so bad after all.

She sipped her martini. "Are you dating anyone these days?"

He shook his head. "No. Wish I was though."

Chloe leaned in. "I could help."

Curtis tried not to, but knew he looked worried.

Chloe stared at him for a few seconds, then burst out laughing. It was a great laugh, contagious and full of life. "Never change," she said when the laugh had run its course. And with that, she left.

Curtis grinned and resigned himself to the fact that despite all her quirky traits, he liked Chloe. He decided to mingle, and moved about the house, beer in hand. He spent a few minutes discussing the yearly budget with a city councilor, then had twenty minutes one on one with a senator from Maine, talking about the crime stats in his state and what could be done to bring them down. He met a country and western singer with a top ten hit on the Nashville charts and was impressed with how down to earth she was. All in all, it was pretty normal for one of Chloe's parties.

Curtis tucked himself into a corner and took a break. The guests were standing in groups, or conversation pods as Curtis viewed them, and each pod seemed to have its own life force. Some were fun, others intellectual, some boring. He drifted from pod to pod, listening more than talking. He entered the library and joined a new group, which consisted of eight people. A man who Curtis vaguely remembered as playing for the New England Patriots was talking and motioning with his hands, his beer foaming over the neck of the bottle.

"…we were at the American ambassador's house for dinner when there was an attempted coup, and a Thai general stopped by and took all of us to his house. The coup wasn't successful and they took the ambassador and his wife back to their house the next morning, then dropped us off at our hotel."

"Come on, Barry," one of the listeners said. "That's unbelievable. No way."

"Seriously. It really happened. If the rebels had overthrown the Thai government, we would have been in some serious trouble."

"It sounds pretty wild," a brunette woman wearing a black pantsuit said. "I don't know…"

Another man, slightly overweight with dark hair, heavy eyebrows and thick glasses said, "I believe Barry is telling the truth." All eyes turned to him and he continued. "Think about it. Most of us have been through some pretty wild experiences. In fact, I'll bet that each one of us has a story that would seem unbelievable."

The woman in the pantsuit nodded. "That's a good point. I know I've got one or two stories that you would swear I made them up. I'll bet everyone here has one."

"Let's try it," the heavyset man said. "Everyone tells a story." He looked at the woman. "You first. Brevity is appreciated."

"Well, all right. It was about five years ago…" she started.

Twenty minutes later the group had made the rounds, with the exception of the man who had started the exercise. Most had managed a story that raised at least one eyebrow. The pod quieted as he cleared his throat.

"I was a suspect in a murder once," he said.

Curtis's hand tightened slightly on his beer bottle as the man launched into the event, apparently unaware a Boston homicide investigator was listening.

"My Uncle Al lived in a small town a few miles off the east coast of Florida. I can't even remember the name of the place now, it's been so many years. It was mostly a collection of mobile homes with retired people. My uncle's last name was Stoogs, like stooges without the e. Anyway, I'd been staying with him for about a week and decided to go rafting down a canal that runs between his town and the next one to the south. When I got back there were six cop cars out front. Turns out my uncle had been murdered. Run through with a pitchfork of all things. A few hundred dollars was missing. So I show up, in my early twenties with long hair and no alibi, except that I'd been on a raft by myself for the last three hours. No kidding I was a suspect."

"What happened?" someone asked.

"They threw me in jail and gave me some public defender about two weeks out of law school telling me to come clean and admit I did it. They threatened to charge me with first-degree murder when I insisted I was innocent. I sat in that cell for two days, not knowing what was going to happen. Nothing to do but read the personal ads in the local paper. Finally they opened the door and told me I could go. They'd caught the guy who had killed my uncle. No "sorry" or "can we give you a lift to the bus station," just "you're free to go." I was some kind of pissed. I'd even missed my uncle's funeral service."

"So what did you do?"

He shrugged. "I decided to head back home. Too much action in Florida for me."

The group eventually broke up, all eight people moving off to different parts of the house. Curtis floated about until he tired of the banter and searched out Chloe, who was talking with a published author. Curtis edged his way into the conversation, thanked her, got a perfunctory hug and then escaped into the August night.

A line of cabs was poised at the end of Chloe's street, but he strolled past them and turned toward Boston Common. Walking through Beacon Hill on a warm summer night was something he enjoyed. The darkened expanse of America's first public park loomed ahead and he jogged across Beacon Street and onto the sparse grass that bordered the road. He headed into the park and kept walking until he was two hundred yards from the street. It was quiet, the traffic noise muted, and only a few people on the dimly lit pathway. As he strolled along, he thought about Chloe's party, and all the people and the conversations.

The group he had met in the library was top of mind. Of the eight stories, the most interesting one, to him at least, was the one told by the murder suspect. There was an underlying tone and cadence to the man's delivery that had tweaked some sixth sense. He wasn't sure why, but there was no denying it. Perhaps it was an occupational hazard. The moment the guy had said *murder*, Curtis had felt his senses perk up.

Curtis's thoughts turned to Renee Charlesbois as he walked. Where was she? Was her father right? Had she been abducted? Would her body end up on a cold slab at the morgue in the next few days? If it did, Jacques Charlesbois would be more than distraught—he would be furious. That wasn't a great thought. Charlesbois was highly connected and enraging him would cause no end of problems. In fact, it wouldn't surprise him if Charlesbois could somehow manage to get the FBI involved. The best thing for everyone, especially Renee Charlesbois, was to find her and do it quickly. He just needed to do it while she was still breathing.

*If* she was still breathing.

# CHAPTER EIGHT

The weekend slipped past with no new angles on Renee Charlesbois' disappearance. Aislinn and her assistant had gone over the last three months of Renee's cell phone records line by line, then cross-checked the numbers against her contact list. Ninety-eight percent of her incoming and outgoing calls were made to someone on the list. They ferreted out who owned the other two percent and eliminated them one by one. Her emails were easier, as they could read the correspondence between Renee and the person on the other end. Nothing suspicious popped up. Almost everything Renee had either talked or emailed about had to do with her existing restaurants or the upcoming opening. They had no leads and nothing promising on the horizon. The first call Curtis took on Monday morning was her father, and his tone was anything but civil.

"It's been over seventy-two hours. What have you got?"

"Nothing new since you called last night," Curtis replied.

"You had nothing then." Charlesbois wasn't even trying to hide his dissatisfaction. "My daughter is missing, detective."

"Yes, we've established that and we've opened a file and are working it with everything we have."

"I expect to be kept up to date with your progress."

"Of course. I'll be back to you before end of business today."

"There *is* no end of business until you find Renee." Somehow, that simple statement came across as threatening.

Curtis made a conscious decision not to fight that battle now. "I understand."

He hung up and texted Stan Lamers and Aislinn Byrne. They were in his office in less than a minute.

"It's been over seventy-two hours since Renee Charlesbois disappeared. We have an open file and we need to run it like we have a murder without a body. We've already looked at her cell phone and email records, now I want you to trace her movements over the past two weeks. Check out friends, acquaintances, work associates, and anyone else who crossed her path. The barista who served her coffee at Starbucks. The bank teller who took her deposit. Anyone. Get the invite list for the restaurant's opening. Pick fifty people at random from the list and set up interviews. Find out what went on that night. Did anyone see anything suspicious."

"Any preference on who we interview?" Aislinn asked.

"Start with names that aren't on her contact list. Skip over anyone who has a high profile—football players, basketball stars, that sort of thing. We can come back to them later. This isn't looking like it was someone who is going to stand out."

"We'll start with people who have good observation skills—lawyers, judges, and writers," Stan said.

"Good idea," Curtis agreed. "Canvas the bars and businesses near her restaurant and see if she stopped in for a drink after the opening. She may have wanted to wind down a bit."

"Should we get a tap on her father's phone, in case it's a kidnapping?" Aislinn asked.

"Yes, do it."

Aislinn continued. "We didn't get the surveillance tape from the parking garage. They stonewalled us for a full day, then finally admitted they don't have coverage for Thursday night. The system was on the fritz. I pushed hard and the parking attendant finally remembered seeing a guy on P4 just before the system went down. The description is generic—white guy, average height, average weight, well dressed and wearing glasses."

Westcott froze, then slowly leaned forward in his chair. "When did the system go down and how long was it out for?"

Byrne checked her notes. "The system crashed about nine-thirty Thursday night. They couldn't get a tech out until Friday morning."

"No video." Curtis said softly. "That's a bit of a coincidence, don't you think."

Aislinn shrugged. "These things go down all the time. It could be legit." She saw the look on her boss's face and said, "I'll find out what happened to it."

Curtis nodded. "Yeah, do that. You know what we think of coincidences."

"Sure do. We don't like them."

"No, we don't," Stan said.

"Okay, what else," Curtis said. "Let's get a couple of warm bodies out there to canvas the surrounding streets and see if anyone saw Renee walking to or from the parking garage. While they're out there they can locate every CCTV that covers the sidewalks and roads, note the location and business name and fill in the paperwork so we can get the archived footage."

"See if we can follow her car using the cameras," Aislinn said.

Curtis tapped his pen on his desk. "Exactly."

"We're on it." Stan flipped his notebook shut and stood.

Aislinn gave her notes a quick check, then retreated with Stan to the collection of desks and computers in the bullpen. "Nasty one, this," she said.

Stan dropped into his chair and put his hand on the phone. "What do you think?" he asked.

Aislinn sat on the edge of his desk. "I'd feel better if we had a ransom demand. All this quiet when she's missing isn't good."

"She alive?" Stan asked.

Aislinn gave the question some serious thought. "If she is, then this was planned. Chances are this was random, which means she's likely dead. But, then there's the CCTV in the parking garage going down like that. Could mean it was a setup." She weighed the options for a minute, then said, "I think she's alive. How about you?"

Stan nodded. "I'm on the fence."

"Let's get an Incident Room up and running."

"I'll set it up," Stan said. "You can dole out the assignments."

"Done."

She waved at Brian Fleming as she walked to her desk and he headed over. "Stan's setting up an IR, we need to get on these." She pointed to her notes and he scanned them.

"We'll need at least two more people. I can get them from the pool."

Boston Homicide was the top of the heap in Investigative Services and junior staff members in other departments were usually willing to set aside what they were doing to get a chance at working a homicide file. It was a good way to get noticed.

Aislinn sat in her chair and stared out the window. The main offices of Boston Homicide were on the top floor of a six-story granite building on New Sudbury Street and the view was excellent. A few clouds drifted over the harbor against a brilliant blue sky. She wondered if Renee Charlesbois would ever see a cloud again.

Amery Kincaid was standing nearby, waiting for the results from his boss's conversation with Curtis Westcott. Jacques Charlesbois didn't waste any words after he hung up.

"Nothing new," he said. "We need to keep our own avenues open. What did you get from the video in the parking garage?"

"The system was down. There is no video."

"Shit," Charlesbois said. "Rotten timing."

"Maybe not," Kincaid said.

Charlesbois caught the tone in Kincaid's voice. "What do you mean?"

"I'm going to find out what happened to the CCTV system. Why it went down. Maybe it wasn't an accident."

Ever so slightly, Charlesbois started to nod. His lower jaw pushed forward and through clenched teeth he said, "Good idea."

"Has Westcott set up surveillance on your phone?" Amery asked.

"Not yet."

"He will," Kincaid said as he headed for the door. "Make sure you answer every call, especially if you don't recognize the number or if it's blocked."

"Amery," Charlesbois said. "Pick up additional help if you need it. Whatever you need. Cover all the angles."

"Sure." Kincaid closed the door quietly behind him.

A woman passed him in the hallway, dressed in a well-cut skirt and blazer. Their eyes met for a moment, but neither one acknowledged the other. They lived in different worlds, hers in these hallways where hundreds of millions of dollars moved about as easily as water running downhill. His, off the books—one of corporate espionage with the ever-present threat of doing time in a federal penitentiary. It was a ruthless game where corporate secrets were mined and exploited. But it was that game that had allowed Charlesbois' daughter to be raised in a world of privilege.

Now she was gone. Renee Charlesbois had disappeared into thin air. Amery had the gut feeling that from the moment she left the restaurant she was a marked woman. No readily apparent clues, the CCTV cameras on the fritz, and her car missing. Everything pointed to a carefully planned abduction, but there had been no ransom demands. Nothing was making sense. Still, someone with an agenda had abducted Jacques Charlesbois' daughter and he needed to figure it out.

He knew one thing from his experience with kidnappings. They don't often end well.

# CHAPTER NINE

Tuesday morning at District A-1 was a zoo. Aislinn Byrne had arranged for twenty-three of the guests who had been at Renee Charlesbois' restaurant to come in for interviews. She had allowed fifteen minutes per person and the result was a steady stream of people entering and leaving Homicide.

Some of them knew each other, and they stood in small groups talking quietly as they waited for their turn in the interview room. The story had already hit the *Boston Globe*, which was no surprise as one of the women who had been in for an interview was Angela Burton, a writer for the paper. Aislinn and Curtis had hoped that once the story ran it might spark a memory in a reader. It was pushing ten o'clock and so far the phones were quiet.

Curtis sat in on most of the interviews. One of his strengths was questioning suspects, and although none of the people they had asked to come in fit that description, he still liked to watch for the subtle things even seasoned detectives like Aislinn and Stan might occasionally miss. The small things that told him if the subject was telling the truth or lying. He returned to the interview room from answering some emails, coffee in hand, just as Aislinn was wrapping up with a middle-aged woman.

"What do you think happened to her?" the woman asked as Aislinn escorted her to the door.

"We're not sure, Ms. Turcotte. That's why we had you come in today."

"Right. Well, I hope I was some help."

"You were."

She nodded and headed down the hallway as the next person was led in. He was sharply dressed, in freshly pressed black pants and a white dress shirt. It was open at the neck, the tabs on the collar buttoned down. His blazer was jet black and matched his highly polished shoes. He had an olive complexion, common to those who live near the Mediterranean, with black hair and dark-framed glasses. His cheeks were a touch exaggerated and his nose slightly bulbous, his eyes were dark brown and intelligent. Curtis pegged him in his late thirties, perhaps early forties. He motioned to an empty chair at the metal table and the man smiled and sat, his posture straight.

"I'm Detective Westcott," Curtis said, then motioned to Aislinn and Stan. "Detectives Byrne and Lamers. If you could state your name for the record, please."

"Certainly." The man glanced at the recording device on the table. "Liem Khilt." He spelled both his first and last names.

"Interesting name," Aislinn Byrne said. "Irish?"

"Gaelic, Detective Byrne," Khilt said. "Liem should have been spelled with an a not an e, but from what I'm told, the hospital made a clerical error. Now I get the lifelong curse of having to spell my name when such things are important."

"Well, it's certainly different," Aislinn said. "You were at the restaurant's opening on Friday night, Mr. Khilt?"

"I was. And it's Dr. Khilt, detective. I'm an anesthesiologist."

"Pardon me." Aislinn glanced back at her notes. "How did you come to be at the party?"

"As Dr. Bernard Rhonell's guest."

"Are you a resident of Boston?" Aislinn asked.

"No. I know Bernie from our younger days. We went to medical school at UCLA together. I'm in Dallas now, but we've stayed in touch over the years."

Aislinn nodded. "What can you tell us about the evening, Dr. Khilt? Did you speak with Renee Charlesbois at any point?"

"Yes, I spoke with her twice. Once, just after I arrived. That would be about six-thirty. We both enjoy wine, in particular from Napa Valley, and we spoke at some length about the different vintages and cellars. I think she mentioned that Frog's Leap was one of her favorites. She seemed to have a genuine love for the valley and knew the years when the grapes were good and the years when they faltered. She made the off years sound like they were nothing short of the apocalypse."

"Was your conversation limited to wine?" Aislinn asked, her notebook handy but idle.

"No, we discussed Chance, a normal conversation to have considering we were at the opening. I remember her saying that despite her success, she really felt tied down by the business." Khilt crossed his legs and smoothed his pants, careful of the crease.

"Did Ms. Charlesbois say anything to you that you feel may be important to our investigation?"

"How so, detective?"

"Did she mention where she was going after the party was finished?"

He smiled, revealing even white teeth. "No, nothing like that. I had never met the woman before, although Bernie talked about her a few times. Our conversation never got that deep."

"You said that you spoke with her twice, Dr. Khilt," Curtis said. "What did you talk about later in the evening?"

"Sports," Khilt said, shifting slightly to face Westcott. "I saw her at the bar getting a drink at about nine-twenty. Ms. Charlesbois is a dedicated Red Sox fan. She told me that during the playoffs she lives and dies on every pitch. Hates New York. She had a dessert in one hand and was waving her fork around with the other. Damn Yankees, she said. She hated the years when she had to drown her sorrows when New York went on and Boston hung up their gloves. Things got better in 2004, of course," he added, referring to the year when the Red Sox had finally won the World Series.

"She left shortly after you spoke with her the second time. Did you see her leave?"

Khilt shook his head. "No. In fact, I left almost immediately after we talked."

"Where did you go?" Aislinn asked.

"I caught a cab back to my hotel. I'm staying at Fifteen Beacon."

"Nice digs," Stan said.

Khilt smiled. "It's not cheap. But then, what in life truly worth having, *is* cheap?"

"Anything else you can think of, Dr. Khilt?" Stan asked, and when Khilt shook his head he stood and offered his hand. "Thanks for coming in."

"You're welcome." He started for the door, when Curtis' voice stopped him.

"How long are you in Boston, Mr. Khilt?" he asked.

Khilt swiveled to face Westcott. "Until my business is concluded. A few more days." He moved to the door, then turned back. "It's doctor, Detective Westcott, not mister."

"Sorry," Curtis said. The door closed behind Khilt and Curtis grinned. "It's doctor, not mister," he said, mimicking the man's smooth voice. He stood and stretched. "Who's next?"

Liem Khilt strode down the crowded corridor, moving confidently through the uniformed and plainclothes police. His eyes shifted back and forth over the eclectic mixture of men and women who worked for the Boston Police Department. So many, and all of them unimportant. This game involved only three people. Himself, of course. Renee Charlesbois, still securely locked in the wine cellar, and Curtis Westcott. Khilt was delighted, Westcott was the best Boston had to offer, and what was a game if it didn't have the best players? Now Westcott had the clues he needed to solve the crime. They were right in front of him and he just had to see them. It was something that none of the detectives in the previous cities had been able to do. Maybe Westcott would be more astute.

Things couldn't be better. He reached the front doors of District A-1 and gave them a gentle push, smiling as he passed two uniformed officers. They smiled back.

"Oh, my," he said as he walked down the worn cement stairs under the hot August sun. "It seems the person you're looking for just walked out the front door of the police station."

# CHAPTER TEN

Twenty-three people had passed through the interview room without shedding much light on Renee Charlesbois' disappearance. Most had spoken with her at some point during the evening and a few had seen her leave. Once she was through the front door, though, she was gone. Just another person out for a walk on a beautiful August night. But this person hadn't made it home, and the building pressure to find her had fallen directly on Curtis Westcott and his team.

The mayor had called Westcott's direct line at two o'clock. With the *Globe* story running, Renee's disappearance was the hot topic of conversation on the street. Curtis brought him up to date on things, which was that they didn't have much of anything. He promised the mayor that when they had something new he would be in the first volley of calls.

Downstairs, newspaper reporters were camping out in the precinct lobby, but so far Curtis had limited his comments to Angela Burton at the *Globe*. Over the years, he and Angela had established a relationship that allowed him to control the flow of information. He would have to call a press conference soon, but with little to report, he was reluctant. He could talk about the interviews they had conducted and say that they were now sorting through the pile of information, but reporters had a way of seeing through the fluff and homing in on the facts. Right now, the fact was, they had nothing.

Jacques Charlesbois was getting more impatient by the hour. He had called three times, wondering what they had managed to dredge out of the interviews. Net zero wasn't acceptable, and he was threatening to phone the police commissioner. Curtis assured him that the mayor and the commissioner were already on his speed dial and there was nothing that could be done to raise the urgency on the file.

It was almost three o'clock when he called Stan and Aislinn to his office. "Are we monitoring the phones at Charlesbois' house and office?" he asked.

"We're up and running," Stan said. "We have a man at the house and his office."

"Did you get any hits when you ran the list of known offenders?"

"A handful of possibilities," Aislinn said. "I pulled two guys from the pool to work on it and they're about halfway through the list. Nothing so far."

"Anything from VICAP?" Curtis asked. It was the online system the FBI used to share information about violent offenders and their Modus Operandi with police departments across the country. Many a serial killer or repeat offender had been tripped up by the FBI's willingness to share this information.

"The feds input everything we gave them about Renee, then ran the MO through their computers, but it's too vague. The numbers that came back from the search are huge. They need to narrow things down. We need to give them some sort of profile on this guy before they can generate a manageable list."

Curtis nodded. What Aislinn said made sense. The VICAP database was huge and without some limiting parameters it would spit out thousands upon thousands of possible suspects. "Stan, did you check recently released inmates who fit the MO?"

Stan nodded. "There were eighteen men released over the last sixty days who may fit the profile. All of them have reporting conditions on their release, and we've managed to get addresses and phone numbers from their parole officers. I have two men working it right now, but so far nobody stands out."

"Okay." Curtis rubbed his temples, willing away the pain. "Any new leads from the website and phone line we set up for the public?"

Stan checked his notes. "The calls are starting to come in, but so far nothing with any promise."

"Surveillance tapes from the parking garage?" Curtis asked Aislinn.

"You're not going to like what we found. It's a digital video recorder system, with sixteen dome cameras that report back to the hard drive. The drive is in the operations manager's office on the second level, which is powered by a single 110V line that comes up from the electrical room on the main level. It was a power failure at the electrical panel that took out the system. It looks like it was tampered with."

"Get someone from forensics to look at it," Curtis said.

Aislinn made a note in her book.

"So this was premeditated," Curtis said. "But no ransom note. Curious." He leaned back in his chair and ran his hands through his hair. "Renee appears to be a pretty ethical person, but what about her father? He didn't get to where he is without stepping on some toes."

"It's no secret that he's run over a few competitors in the past," Stan said, making a quick note in his book. "I'll check and see if he's pissed off anybody in the last few months."

"Look hard at everyone who could be holding a grudge," Curtis said. "Privacy laws are going to be a hurdle. If you need to, get one of the department's legal staff on it." Curtis stood and walked to the window and stared at the imposing façade of the JFK Federal Building. "Ex-boyfriends?"

"The most recent one was months ago, and he was at a Red Sox game on Thursday. There are plenty of witnesses."

"Any other guys in her life?"

"Not that we've been able to dig up. We've talked with all her close friends and it looks like she was working 24/7. Run off her feet opening the new restaurant."

"Who inherits her fortune if she *is* dead?" Curtis asked.

Stan flipped over a couple of pages in his book. "Most of it goes to charity, including two million to the local animal shelter." Stan glanced up at Curtis. "Isn't that where you got Barclay?"

"It is." Curtis rubbed his hand across his chin, figuring the more he learned about Renee the more he liked her. She was an animal lover and suffering through the tyranny of being married to the job. All things he could relate to.

"She has seven cousins and her will leaves a few hundred thousand to each of them," Stan continued. "Another five hundred thousand to Hans Grummer, her maitre d', and then a sprinkling of a few thousand here and there."

"Nothing that leaps out?" Curtis asked.

"Nothing. She has a three million life insurance policy that gets paid into her estate and split up evenly among her charities, so nothing there either."

"All right," Curtis said, sitting on the edge of the window jamb. "We've got ourselves a strange one. No witnesses, no apparent motive, and no body, *if* she's dead. No ransom note or demand, and a victim with no enemies. Not our average case."

"Not even close," Stan said, running his hand over his shaved head. "And like you said, we don't even know *if* she's dead."

"Well, Stan," Curtis said thoughtfully. "If she's not dead, where the hell is she?"

He didn't have an answer.

# CHAPTER ELEVEN

Renee Charlesbois looked up at the sound of a key turning in the lock. A moment later the door opened and Liem Khilt entered. In his hand was a pistol and his finger was inside the trigger guard. He pulled the metal chair away from the wall and sat down, careful not to crease his pants.

"How are you doing?" he asked her.

"What do you care?" She pushed her matted, dirty hair back from her face. "I've been rotting in here for four days now. If you really gave a shit about me you'd let me go."

He smiled. "That's not possible, Renee. And you've been here five days, not four. Today is Tuesday."

"I would like to have a bath," she said. "It's impossible to stay clean in here."

"Use the sink."

"I want to shower or bath."

"It's simply not possible."

She eyed him up, in her mind rushing him and taking the gun, then pistol-whipping him and kicking him square in the balls. She knew if she tried she would likely die. "Why am I here?"

"I told you, this is a game. So far, everything is going splendidly. You're the prize and, lucky for you, Curtis Westcott is the cop on the trail. I hoped he would be." Khilt was relaxed in the chair now, his legs crossed and the gun resting on his knee. "I had a nice conversation with him this afternoon."

"What?" Renee said. "You talked to Westcott?"

"Face to face."

"So you're a suspect."

"Hardly. He and a couple of his detectives were interviewing some of your guests from Thursday night. I made sure I got on the list."

"You *wanted* to meet him?" Renee asked incredulously. "Why?"

"Without a few clues, the police will never find you. Even with the clues, your chances aren't great. Westcott is savvy, but I'm not sure he's smart enough to see what this is all about."

"You kidnapped me as part of a game? What sort of bullshit is this?" She felt her fury rising and could barely contain it.

He leaned forward on the chair. "Look around. It's not bullshit. It's real. This is where you get to live while the police search for you. And there are consequences if they fail to find you."

"What sort of consequences?" she asked, her throat suddenly dry.

"I kill you."

"Why?" she asked, her voice barely a whisper. "Why would you want to kill an innocent person?"

"Innocent." His voice seemed distant, like he was somewhere else. "That's a subjective word." He snapped out of it and stared at her. "I've been fair. If Westcott can figure it out, he'll find you. However, there's a bit of a wrinkle to all this."

"What's that?" She streaked dirt across her face as she wiped the wetness from her eyes.

"There are time constraints. Westcott doesn't know that, of course. He may never figure that out. No one else has yet."

Renee's eyes widened, her breath shallow and fast, her chest heaving in and out. The reality of it was finally setting in. This man—this monster—had every intention of killing her. This was the room where she would die. She had to make a move on him.

"What do you mean, no one else has yet? Have you done this before?" Desperation was in her voice as every muscle in her body tensed.

"I've said too much, Renee." He glanced at his watch. "Oh, look at the time. I really must be going."

She came off the bed and across the floor at a dead run. At the last second he dodged her and swung the pistol down on her head, driving her into the wall. She crumpled on the dirty floor and lay there, moaning with pain. Khilt walked around her and opened the door. He gave her a quick smile as he left.

"I'll be back in half an hour with your dinner," he said. "Try to clean up a bit. Your personal hygiene is awful."

The door clicked shut and she did something she had not done in years.

She cried.

# CHAPTER TWELVE

Curtis Westcott needed a suspect.

Murders were seldom solved without a suspect and right now he had nothing. In fact, he didn't even know if he *had* a murder. He had pressure from every side, but nothing tangible to explain why Renee Charlesbois was missing. Nothing. He slipped out of bed and turned on the shower, waiting for it to warm up before stepping in. The water stung as it hit his skin and it felt good, invigorating. He finished showering, then slipped on his robe and padded downstairs to make coffee.

Barclay, his black Labrador, appeared at the entrance to the kitchen, then walked to the back door and waited while Curtis poured his coffee.

"Want to go out?" he asked, and Barclay wagged his tail. Curtis opened the door and stood watching as Barclay sniffed about, looking for the right spot to do his business.

A suspect. The word kept pushing its way into his mind. Curtis used the remote to turn on his television. Highlights from the Red Sox game were on and he sat on the couch and watched as the announcer talked about how the team had blown a two-run lead in the ninth on a wild pitch.

Pitch. The word stuck with him. Along with suspect, it was the second word this morning. Suspect—that was a normal word for him to key in on, but pitch, that was different. The highlights finished and he got up to let his dog in.

"What's going on, Barclay?" he asked. The dog came over and set his head on Curtis's leg, looking to be petted. "Why are these words sticking in my head?" He rubbed the dog behind his ears and was given an appreciative look. "There's a reason, Barclay. I probably heard the words recently."

He sipped the coffee and closed his eyes, replaying the last few days of his life. Something was there, stuck in the recesses of his mind and trying to surface. His subconscious stored data and let it sit dormant until some trigger brought it to light. His mind worked that way, piecing together disjointed bits of information and unraveling them like a rebus. Clues were often just dots that needed joining. But right now, with the words floating about in his mind, the connections weren't happening.

He finished his coffee and poured one more. The hardwood floors were cool on his bare feet as he climbed the stairs to the second floor. It was time to get on with his day. He shaved, combed his hair, dressed and returned to the main floor where Barclay was curled up on the couch, preparing for a full day of sleeping.

Images from the weekend were coming back and Chloe's party was foremost. He closed his eyes again and retraced his steps through the evening, moving through the different conversation pods. When he reached the library, the images sharpened and he could visualize the overweight man with heavy eyebrows and thick glasses. The one who had said he was once a suspect in a murder. What else had he said? What? Something was there, trying to get through. He opened his eyes for a minute, then closed them again and concentrated on replaying the scene. It came to him like images from a PVR.

*I was a suspect in a murder once…somewhere in Florida…uncle had been murdered… staying with him for about a week…run through with a pitch-fork…public defender.*

Curtis opened his eyes and picked up the pad of paper and pen he always left on the end table. He clicked the ballpoint and started making notes—key phrases at first, then filling in the blanks. Working in homicide had honed certain skills and recalling events was one of them.

His mind sucked in what people said and did, then filed it. Unimportant stuff disappeared after a while, freeing up space for what he considered more important. While the memories were still fresh, he could remember most of a specific conversation. And now, with the words starting to flow, he was filling in the blanks.

*... cops threw me in jail ... first-degree murder ... nothing to do but read the personal ads ... caught the guy who had killed my uncle ... I'd missed my uncle's funeral service.*

*Pitchfork.*

He stared at the word. It wasn't one that came up in normal conversations very often. Yet something else was tugging at him. He'd heard it recently. In a different setting. But where?

Curtis checked the clock. Seven forty-three. He set the pen and paper on the end table, gave Barclay one more quick rub and left for the office. Summertime Boston slipped by as he drove. The Public Garden and Boston Common were green and inviting and the morning walkers already out in force. He took Tremont into the core, pulled into the underground parking garage and swiped his card key in the reader. A uniform cop held the elevator door for him and he punched six. As he stepped out, it hit him.

Pitch. Fork. Two separate words. One of the interviewees from Renee Charlesbois' restaurant's opening had used both words. He pushed open the doors into BOSTON HOMICIDE and motioned for Aislinn and Stan to join him. He poured a cup of coffee and by the time he reached his office they were waiting.

"What's up?" Stan asked. "You look like you've got something."

"One of the men we interviewed who was at the restaurant's opening said something interesting. Two words. Pitch and fork. Do either of you remember?"

Stan shook his head and Aislinn offered a simple, "No.

"He was visiting Boston from out of town. Staying at Fifteen Beacon, I think," Curtis said.

"Yeah," Aislinn said. "Stan commented on how expensive the rooms are. He was a doctor."

"Bernard Rhonell's guest," Stan said.

"That's him," Curtis said. "Aislinn, pull the transcript and the video. Something's off with him."

"Sure," Aislinn said, moving for the door.

"And get Dr. Rhonell down here for an interview. Find out how he knows this guy, why he invited him, the whole nine yards."

"Done." Aislinn was out the door and moving.

"Stan, we need to take some time and go over everything else we have on our plate. This Charlesbois thing is starting to eat away at our resources a bit too much. I don't want the other cases suffering."

"Okay. We've got three unsolved and two cold files."

"Three?" Curtis asked. "I thought we had two."

"We had a domestic last night. Wife shot the husband six times at point-blank range. First shot was probably fatal."

"CSU work the scene?" Curtis asked.

"Yeah. It looks pretty cut-and-dried. She killed him."

"Any history of violence?"

"Uniforms had two previous calls to the house. She was beat up bad one of the times. Pictures are in the folder. No charges ever filed. She refused."

Curtis was silent for a minute, then said, "Talk to the neighbors, find out if she was seeing anyone else. You know these ones, Stan. Wife gets smacked around, eventually has an affair and the boyfriend ends up pulling the trigger. Let's make sure she did it."

"She had powder on her hands," Stan said, flipping through the file and reading the CSU report.

"All right," Curtis said. "Check the trajectory of each bullet. Playing the devil's advocate here, but what if there *is* a boyfriend and he shoots the husband once or twice, then gives her the gun when he's bleeding out on the floor and she fires another few rounds into him."

Stan shook his head. "You have a devious mind, LT."

Curtis grinned. "Product of the job."

Stan flipped the file shut and left the office, leaving Curtis alone with his thoughts. He sipped on the coffee, now lukewarm. *Pitchfork.*

*Pitch. Fork.* What was going on? Why was this sticking in his mind? He closed his eyes, rewinding the tape and playing back the scene at Chloe's party. The overweight man with the glasses. His story. Then the interview at District A-1 with Bernard Rhonell's guest.

Something wasn't right.

# CHAPTER THIRTEEN

"Anything new to report?" Jacques Charlesbois asked. He and Amery Kincaid were alone in Charlesbois' office.

Kincaid sat in one of the chairs that faced the desk. "I talked with the parking attendant after his shift last night and offered him a bit of cash. Then I made sure he wasn't holding anything back."

"I don't want to know." Charlesbois waited a moment, then asked, "What did he see?"

"A well-dressed man on P4 about the time the cameras failed."

"What did this guy look like?" Charlesbois asked.

"Caucasian, with dark hair and glasses. Middle age, probably late thirties or early forties. The same description the attendant gave to the police."

"Do you think he's the one who grabbed Renee?" Charlesbois asked.

Kincaid shrugged. "Maybe. The description is generic, almost useless. White male, dark hair, glasses, with average height and build. Who knows if the glasses are even real."

Charlesbois slammed his fist on the desk. "Christ, Amery, what the hell is going on? It's Wednesday. She disappeared almost a week ago and we don't have a clue who took her or where she is. I want some goddamn answers."

"What does Westcott have?" Kincaid asked, deflecting the anger.

"Jack shit. I spoke with him an hour ago and he was reviewing a transcript from an interview. Someone who attended the restaurant's opening. He admitted they didn't have anything new."

"He's not going to be happy about us meddling with the parking attendant," Kincaid said.

"I don't give a shit what Westcott thinks right now, Amery. This isn't working. I want my daughter back." He leapt up from his desk and stormed over to the window, his body convulsing with rage. "Get the word out on the street that the reward for her return is one million dollars. Cash. No questions. Whoever brings her in alive gets the money. I don't give a shit what happens to the scumbag who has her." He turned to face Kincaid. "One million dollars, Amery. Someone, somewhere, knows something. They'll surface for the money."

"I don't think Westcott's going to like *that* either, Jacques."

"Like I said, Amery, I don't give a shit what Westcott thinks about anything right now. There's one goal here. Only one."

Kincaid nodded and rose from the chair. "Okay, Jacques. I know a few people who can get the word on the street real quick. I'll speak with them. But you need to understand that you're unleashing every street-level punk and junkie on whoever took Renee. Westcott is going to find out you've got a bounty on this guy's head. This move could have a definite downside."

"The downside is that my daughter is dead, Amery," Charlesbois snapped. His eyes narrowed. "Do it. Get the word out."

"When did Liem Khilt check out?" Curtis asked, his mouth suddenly dry.

"This morning, about two hours ago," Stan said. "He paid the bill in cash. The hotel still had the VISA number. I've got one of the guys running it right now."

Curtis nodded. "Seal the room. No one is allowed in until CSU has been through."

"Already done. Management wasn't happy. That room rents for over twelve hundred a night. They want us in and out in a hurry or they'll send the city a bill."

"We'll keep the room as long as we want," Curtis said in a curt voice.

Aislinn Byrne appeared in the doorway and Curtis asked, "Dr. Bernard Rhonell. Have we found out why he invited Liem Khilt to be his guest at the restaurant's opening?"

"He's coming in later today."

"Good work."

"I have the interview with Khilt cued up and ready to run," Aislinn said.

"Let's have a look."

Curtis jumped out of his chair and followed his detective to a small windowless office with a large screen on one wall. They often used it to replay the footage from interviews and crime scenes, looking for clues in the tiniest details that might have eluded them the first time through. Six chairs faced a long narrow table with notepads and pens in front of each seat. They sat down and Aislinn started the feed from the hard drive.

"*I'm Detective Westcott. Detectives Byrne and Lamers. If you could state your name for the record, please.*"

"*Certainly. Liem Khilt. L-I-E-M K-H-I-L-T.*"

The images played on, Curtis, Aislinn and Stan watching without speaking. Khilt consistently made eye contact with the person who asked him the question, and answered without hesitation. His attention to detail when he crossed his legs and smoothed his pants was not lost on the detectives. The interview finished and Curtis motioned for Stan to queue it up again. They watched the interview four more times before any of them commented on the conversation. This was normal procedure and ensured no one watching would be influenced by another person's take on what they had seen. By the fifth time through, idiosyncrasies started to show and the detectives were beginning to form opinions.

"He's too smooth," Stan said as they finished watching. "Too composed."

"It's almost like he knew what questions we'd be asking him," Curtis agreed. "Watch the part where he talks about the sports teams. His language patterns change slightly. They're more contrived."

"They're a bit stilted all the way through," Aislinn said.

"Like he's reading from a script." Stan added.

Curtis mulled that over for a few moments. "Sort of, but not quite. It's more like he knows what he wants to say and he's manipulating the conversation to move in the direction he wants it to. Like he's delivering a message."

Stan ran a large mitt over his shaved head. "Message? What do you mean?"

"I don't know. I get the feeling that this guy is telling us more than it appears."

The door opened and a uniform cop entered and handed Aislinn a sheet of paper. When she read it, her face hardened. "It's from Dr. Bernard Rhonell. He's still coming in later today to answer questions, but he called a few minutes ago and left a message that he did not bring a guest to the opening. He RSVP'd by email that he would be attending alone."

Curtis stared at the image frozen on the screen. Liem Khilt, sitting in the chair at the start of the interview. Calm, ready for the questions. Staring directly at the hidden camera.

"Aislinn, find out how Khilt submitted his reply that he would be attending. My guess is that there was a second e-mail from Dr. Rhonell advising the restaurant that he would be bringing a guest. See if they still have that email. If they do, trace it to its origin. He probably spoofed the IP address, but it's worth a try."

"I'm on it," Aislinn said, shutting the door behind her.

"Is he our guy?" Stan asked as they both stared at the screen.

Curtis was silent for a minute, locking eyes with the image, trying to see inside the mind. "Not sure, but he's a possibility."

One thing Curtis had learned early in his homicide career was never to let his suspicions set the direction for the investigation. The evidence, and only the evidence, did that. Suspects floated to the top as the investigation moved ahead—some of them stayed relevant and others fell away. He figured homicide cops were like a juggler with balls in the air. And right now, Liem Khilt was a big fat ball in the air.

Curtis glanced at Stan. "If he *is* our guy, what the hell is he up to?"

# CHAPTER FOURTEEN

Curtis took the elevator to the tenth floor of Fifteen Beacon, one of Boston's most prestigious hotels. The hallway carpets were soft underfoot and the lighting muted, almost seductive. He reached the door of the suite where Khilt had stayed and flashed his creds to the on-duty uniform. The hotel manager, a stately looking black man in his fifties, was waiting outside with a woman, who Curtis figured by her uniform was one of the cleaning staff. Hovering another thirty feet down the hall was the forensics team, waiting for access to the room.

"Barry Bronconnier," the man said. His dress was semi-formal, and the attention to detail the hotel was so famous for was evident on the man. His clothes were properly pressed, his nails manicured.

Bronconnier didn't look like he wanted to waste time and Curtis certainly didn't either. "Thanks for meeting me." He glanced about. "Has the room been cleaned?"

"No. Maria hadn't started on the room today and we locked it down immediately when you called. It's untouched, as you asked."

"Thank you," Curtis said. "Do we need a warrant?"

Bronconnier was careful with his response. "That depends, detective. If you can be done this afternoon, then I'll sign a consent. If you need to tape it off for longer than that, then you'll need a warrant."

Curtis was impressed. Bronconnier was handling the situation masterfully. He knew the law—once a guest checked out there is no expectation of privacy and a warrant would not be required. But if the hotel insisted on a warrant, the police could take their time and keep the room locked up for a good length of time, which was bad for the hotel. Bronconnier had offered immediate unfettered access to the room if Curtis could expedite the process.

"We can be in and out this afternoon," he said.

Bronconnier was prepared and produced a signed consent order from his inside suit pocket. "Thank you." He motioned at the mid-fifties woman in the uniform. "This is Maria, she cleans this side of the tenth floor. Maria, this is Lieutenant Detective Westcott of the Boston Police. Please answer any questions he has for you." Bronconnier backed off a few feet and stood silently, his eyes attentive, his posture rigid.

"Hello, Maria," Curtis said. "What can you tell me about the guest who was staying here over the last few days?"

"Well," she said. Her voice was soft, with a thick Spanish accent. "I never see him, and I don't think he sleep here."

Curtis cocked his head slightly, taken aback by her comment. "Why would you say that?" he asked.

"I clean rooms for many years. I never see a bed like this one. It was like he pull the covers down and mess them up, but never lay down. The bottom sheet, the fitting one, has no wrinkles. And the bathroom. Always the towels on the floor, but not wet like most. I'm sorry, my English is not so good."

Curtis smiled. "Your English is fine. You noticed some very important details. Can you think of anything else?"

She shook her head. "No, I don't think so."

"Thank you," Curtis said, and she left after getting a quick nod from the manager. Curtis turned to Bronconnier. "Let's get the crew in the room so we can finish as soon as possible."

"Do you want me to wait here?" Bronconnier asked as he slid a card key through the slot and opened the door.

"Please. I'll step out if I need to speak with you."

Curtis slipped on a pair of latex gloves before entering the suite. Immediately behind him were the forensics team, already suited up in booties, white body suits and gloves. The suite was large, as expected, with a great room that featured a wall-mounted sixty-inch television with surround sound. The curtains were open and sunlight flooded in from the dazzling view of downtown and the financial district.

He spent a minute giving the forensics team an idea of what they were looking for and they split up and started working the room. Curtis walked around, taking in the feel of the space. He stood with his back to the window, thoughtful and quiet. After a few minutes he walked down the hallway to the bedroom. A king-size bed was the main piece of furniture. The sheets were in disarray, but he looked closer and could see what Maria meant. There was no depression in the mattress, and the fitted sheet was still pulled tight to the corners. The pillow was slightly askew, but still fluffed. *I never see him, and I don't think he sleep here.* Why would someone do that?

A dresser, an armoire and gentleman's valet completed the set, and there appeared to be no smudges on the highly polished surfaces. It would be unlikely that CSU would find fingerprints. A second television, also with a stereo sound system, hung on the wall opposite the bed. The remote control sat on the night table, most likely untouched.

Curtis walked about, not touching anything. He had been here. Liem Khilt. He had stood in this exact spot, Curtis thought. The man had been here for a reason. But what? He walked into the bathroom and looked about, taking in every detail. Everything was in its proper place. The shampoo and conditioner bottles all lined up on the marble vanity. The individually wrapped soap. Little bottles of mouthwash and some black polish for shoes. Towels on the floor. He opened the shower door carefully and looked at the marble base. Wet, but no sign of body hair. Khilt had probably run the water for a few seconds, then turned it off without ever getting in.

Again, why?

Why would someone rent a room for twelve hundred dollars a night and not use it? Why would he voluntarily show up at police headquarters for an interview?

His cell phone vibrated and Curtis checked the incoming call. Stan Lamers. He touched the screen and said, "What have you got?"

"You're not going to like this, LT," Stan said.

"What am I not going to like?"

"A couple of things. It seems someone visited the parking attendant where Renee Charlesbois' car was parked. They beat the guy up pretty bad. He's scared shitless and won't say who did it, but our money's on Jacques Charlesbois."

"What else?" Curtis said tersely.

"Charlesbois has put the word out on the street that he's offering a reward for the safe return of his daughter."

"What?" Curtis said. "What kind of reward?"

"A million dollars. Cash. No questions asked."

Curtis was silent for a few moments, then said, "Get Charlesbois in my office this afternoon, three o'clock. I don't care if he's busy, tell him to be there."

"It's two o'clock now."

"Find Charlesbois and have him in my office at three." He killed the call, took one more glance around the bathroom and re-entered the bedroom. A photographer was working the scene and Curtis told him to get good shots of everything in the bathroom as well. CSU was looking for trace evidence on the bed, but the technician shook his head when they locked eyes.

Bronconnier was waiting in the hallway. Curtis shook his hand and said, "My guys will be done in the next hour or two. Thanks for keeping the room intact."

"No problem," Bronconnier said, looking pleased the room would be ready for the next guest.

Curtis retraced his steps to the elevator and punched the button. He had anticipated problems with Jacques Charlesbois, but this was beyond expectations. Her father had unleashed the ultimate in vigilante justice on his daughter's captors and created an unmanageable monster. Human nature was predictable and Curtis knew exactly where this would go. Hearsay and innuendos would lead to violent accusations and confrontations. Even the slightest hint of Renee Charlesbois' whereabouts would cause total chaos. The elevator arrived and Curtis hurried on and headed down from the tenth floor. He had a very short window of time to find Renee Charlesbois before someone got hurt or killed.

# CHAPTER FIFTEEN

Liem Khilt watched Curtis Westcott leave Fifteen Beacon with a newfound appreciation of the man's abilities. That had been much closer than he had calculated. He had only briefly considered checking out the night before, thinking he had ample time before Westcott pieced together the clues. But because he disliked the heavy evening traffic, he had decided to wait until the morning. He needed to come in today anyway, to drop something off at the *Globe*. It was a decision that had almost put him face-to-face with the police. Westcott was proving himself a worthy opponent.

He sipped on his cappuccino and motioned to the waiter to bring the check. This was his last trip to the *Globe*—Boston PD either caught the clues or they would continue to get recycled with the rest of the paper.

Regardless, Westcott was the fastest yet out of the gate. If he was at the hotel, it meant that he knew Dr. Bernard Rhonell had not brought a guest with him to the restaurant's opening. Which meant Westcott already suspected Liem Khilt was his man. Well done, but that was all window dressing, unless Westcott looked beyond the obvious and saw the clues.

That was what the game was all about. He was giving Westcott everything he needed, either through their conversations, or by the written clues in Boston's daily newspaper. The question was, would the homicide cop see what was sitting in front of him? It was so painfully obvious once the veneer was stripped away. Yet, to date, not one ho-micide detective had even come close. Not one. What a pathetic lot. They took courses in human behavior and investigative techniques, had access to databases piled with information and basically had every possible advantage, including a string of clues that would lead them di-rectly to the missing women. Yet not one had even figured out the most basic part of the game. He had briefly considered making the link to the starting point a little easier, but had decided against it. Just because the police were too thick to see what was happening was no reason to reduce the playing field to their level. This was his game, played by his rules, and he had decided they were not to be altered.

Why should he? Curtis Westcott had just breezed through the first stage. He suspected Khilt was the person who had abducted Renee Charlesbois. Westcott may have even figured out Liem Khilt and the man at Chloe Harrah's party were the same person. If he had, then he knew Khilt was disguising himself. That would account for him not issuing a physical description. Westcott was moving quickly now, but whether it was fast enough remained to be seen.

The clock was ticking.

Khilt paid the tab with a twenty and left a reasonable tip. The CCTV cameras at the restaurant and the *Globe* offices didn't bother him—he had on a short blond wig and wire frame glasses. It was doubt-ful Westcott would recognize him even if he was across the table, let alone across the street. Khilt walked to his car, then drove through the congested streets to the main offices of the *Boston Globe*. Luck was with him, as he pulled into the lot another car was backing out. He parked and strode through the front doors, head angled down to escape the camera as much as possible, breezed past the receptionist and headed directly to the advertising department. His message was in an envelope on standard twenty-pound bond paper with no distinguishing marks. He handed the clerk the envelope and she removed the paper.

"Oh," he said. "Could I have the envelope back? I can reuse it."

"Of course."

He took it and slipped it into his pocket. Now he had the only piece of paper with his fingerprints.

"The ad will appear in tomorrow's paper and run for one day," she said. "That'll be forty dollars and forty-three cents, please."

He paid with two twenties and a dollar bill, not worrying about prints. Money was wonderful that way, it all looked the same. With the amount of cash the paper took in every day, there was no chance of determining which bills he had handled. He took the change, thanked the clerk and returned outside to the afternoon sunshine.

It was after two o'clock and Renee would be hungry soon. Every day, twice a day. Khilt figured having Renee locked in the wine cellar was a bit like owning a pet—lots of daily maintenance. But killing her right out of the gate was not the way things worked. That would ruin everything.

What if they *did* figure it out? What if Westcott managed to piece everything together? Boston Homicide would charge him with murder. In fact, if the cops were smart enough to solve the case using the trail of clues he had planted, he would be facing a number of murder charges. Something occurred to him for the first time. They would label him a serial killer. He had never seriously considered the possibility of the police actually catching him.

"Well, that's not going to happen," he said quietly as he clicked his key fob and slid into his car. The leather was hot against his legs. He opened the calendar app on his phone and stared at the day marked with a large red X. "You were reasonably fast getting started, Lieutenant Westcott, but you don't have enough time." He pulled out into the afternoon traffic.

"Too bad," he said, then turned on the radio.

# CHAPTER SIXTEEN

Curtis left the quiet opulence of the hotel, slipped on his sunglasses against the mid-day glare and walked briskly down Bowdoin Street. He yanked a parking ticket from under the wiper blade, crumpled it and threw it on the passenger seat. A Boston Police parking permit hung from his rearview. He started the car and pulled into traffic.

He was almost convinced the man using the name Liem Khilt was responsible for the disappearance of Renee Charlesbois. But what the hell was he up to? And why? Motive was necessary when abducting or murdering someone. Money, rage, and infidelity—the list was long and varied—but there needed to be a trigger. People didn't kidnap or kill others without motive. Figuring that out would go a long way to getting them on track with finding Renee.

What was boggling his mind above all else was why be so brazen?

Why go to the effort of forging an invitation to the restaurant's opening when he knew where she parked her car? Appearing at the restaurant, knowing the police would be looking at everyone who was there, was risky. So was showing up at the station for the interview. That was either monumentally stupid or another calculated risk. Once he had Renee, why not just fade away?

Curtis ran back over the interview at the precinct. Khilt had deliberately showed up where he knew a camera would be recording everything he said, along with his physical description. Aislinn was in the process of extracting a clear image from the footage and saving it to a shared drive. Every cop in Boston would have the photo and be on the lookout for him.

He slowed the car and pulled over to the curb so he could think. This was all wrong. Khilt, or whatever his real name was, wasn't stupid. He disabled the video surveillance system in the parking garage, abducted Renee and sat through a police interview without flinching. He rented an expensive hotel room, but didn't stay there. He had somewhere else to sleep, which showed premeditation and careful planning. No, stupid was not a word to describe him. What, then?

Curtis got out and leaned against the car in the warm afternoon sun. What was he missing? He closed his eyes and let his mind wander. Nothing dawned and eventually he forced his thoughts off Renee Charlesbois and onto other things. Barclay would need letting out soon and he plotted out the best route home to avoid afternoon traffic. He could just envision his dog staring up at him with those big, brown eyes. Glad to see him, happy to get out and looking for a treat. How could he resist those eyes?

Then his own eyes flew open. "Oh, my God," he whispered.

A fleeting image had raced through his head, and stuck. It was the over-weight man at Chloe's party, the one who had been a suspect in a murder. Purposely taking off his glasses and polishing them. Looking directly at Curtis. The eyes. The same eyes that had stared at him when they were interviewing Liem Khilt. The two men—they were the same person.

Christ, what was going on? He touched the screen on his cell phone, found Chloe's private number in his address book and dialed. A moment later she answered.

"Detective Westcott. What a pleasant surprise." She sounded intrigued.

"Hi, Chloe. Sorry, but this is a business call."

"Oh, my, how exciting. Am I a suspect or a witness?"

He couldn't help laughing. "Chloe, do the two cameras over your front door work?"

"Of course, dear," she said. "Why else would they be there?"

"Do you still have the recordings from last Friday's party?"

"I don't know. I could check with Allen. He handles all my security." She took a rasping breath. "This sounds serious, Curtis. What's going on?"

"One of my cases. I have a hunch, that's all. I need the footage from those cameras."

"All right. I'll see if we have them on file and have him call you."

"Thanks. The faster the better."

"Does this have to do with Renee Charlesbois?" she asked.

"Strictly between you and I, Chloe?"

"Of course."

"Yes, it does. Not a word to anyone."

"I understand. Allen will be in touch with you within the hour." The line went dead.

Curtis dialed another number, this one from memory. Aislinn Byrne answered. "Aislinn," he said, "hold onto that picture of Khilt. Don't release it yet."

"Okay, boss." She sounded puzzled but didn't ask why. "Oh, I just finished the interview with Dr. Bernard Rhonell. He has never heard of Liem Khilt and didn't invite anyone to the opening."

"Big surprise there," Curtis said.

"I asked him if one of our computer guys could have a look at his email to see how Khilt latched onto him, and he agreed. I'm searching through everyone registered in medicine at UCLA when Rhonell was a student. Khilt definitely wasn't a student at that time, or any other. Still, I'm looking for anywhere Khilt and Rhonell might have crossed paths."

"Good work."

There was a short break in the conversation, then Aislinn said, "It's almost three, LT. Are you going to be here when Jacques Charlesbois arrives?"

"I'll try. If I'm late, tell him to wait."

"Wonderful," Aislinn said. She didn't sound happy.

"Give him something to read." He killed the call, imagining the look on Aislinn's face. Guaranteed she wasn't smiling.

He slipped back into his car and gunned the motor. Khilt and the overweight man were possibly the same person. What the hell was going on?

# CHAPTER SEVENTEEN

Jacques Charlesbois was sitting in a chair in Westcott's office, waiting, but not patiently. He glared at Curtis as he walked in at ten minutes past three.

"I trust you have news on my daughter's case," he said in a clipped voice. The look in his eyes matched his voice.

"Not really," Curtis said. "I asked you to come down for a different reason."

"This better be good, detective. I'm a busy man."

"Word on the street has it that you're offering a million dollars to anyone who brings your daughter in alive." Curtis sat on the edge of his desk so he was looking down at Charlesbois.

"I told you from the outset, Westcott, that I would do whatever is necessary to get my daughter back."

"So you're admitting to the million-dollar bounty?"

"I never said that." He stood up, using his height and size to intimidate. "There is nothing illegal about offering a reward for the return of a lost item. People do it all the time. Check the personal columns."

Curtis took two deep breaths before replying. "Let's not get into semantics here. A million dollars for someone to find your daughter is not the same thing as a hundred bucks for finding a stray cat. What you're doing will turn this city into a pack of vigilantes. My mandate is to find your daughter, not spending time sorting out all the problems your reward is going to cause."

Charlesbois shrugged. "Same game, different rules," he said.

Curtis's voice hardened. "Don't think your wealth or position carry any extra weight in this office. If your actions endanger others, I'll be the first one on your doorstep."

"And what will you do, detective?" Charlesbois asked. "Arrest me?"

Curtis slowly raised himself off the desk, the two men only a foot apart. "If I have to, yes." They stared at each other, neither man blinking. "I strongly suggest you retract the reward before someone gets hurt."

Curtis could actually hear Charlesbois' teeth grinding. "You're messing with the wrong guy, Westcott."

"Keep something in mind. You came to me, I didn't come to you." They stared at each other for a few seconds, then Curtis added, "The parking attendant who worked the night Renee was abducted was roughed up last night. Do you know anything about that?"

"Of course not."

"That's a good thing, Mr. Charlesbois, because our jails are full of people serving time for assault." Curtis walked around his desk and sat in the chair. He scanned the paperwork on his desk for a few seconds, then looked up. "You still here?" he asked coolly.

Charlesbois spun on his heels and stomped from the room, slamming the door as he left. A minute later, Stan Lamers peeked in.

"Holy, shit, did he look mad."

"He was," Curtis said, pointing at the thumb drive in his sergeant's hand. "Is that from Chloe?"

"Yeah, it just arrived."

"Let's have a look. And queue up the interview with Khilt again. Set up two screens, side by side. I want images from Chloe's security footage on one and Khilt's interview on the other."

Ten minutes later they had Liem Khilt's image frozen on one screen and were watching the guests arrive at Chloe Harrah's house on the other. Curtis pointed at the screen as a pudgy man puffed up the front stairs. As he reached the top stair, he stopped to catch his breath. Then he pulled a handkerchief from his pocket, removed his glasses and gently rubbed the lenses. But before he placed them back on his face, he looked directly at the camera. Then he was gone.

"Stan, rewind it to where he's staring into the camera."

Stan touched the rewind function for a second and the image of the overweight man rubbing his glasses reappeared. When he looked up, Stan stopped the tape. "Want me to zoom in on his eyes?" he asked.

"Please," Curtis said, leaning forward.

The face grew larger as Stan worked the zoom, until the man's eyes were front and center on the screen. Stan made sure the eyebrows were visible and in focus. Few things on a person's face were as individual and telling as their eyebrows. Change them, change the face. Immediately adjacent to the man's eyes, on the second television, was another set of eyes—those belonging to Liem Khilt. Curtis leaned back in his chair and thoughtfully rubbed his chin. The shape of the eye sockets was definitive, deep without being sunken, the eyelids tucked up and the lashes average length. At the far edges, tiny crow's feet creased the skin. The face housing the eyes had been altered—the cheeks, jowls and chin enlarged, and the lips fattened. But two things were constant. The eyes and the eyebrows.

"Christ, LT," Stan said softly. "They're the same guy."

"Yeah, they are. Stan, get a sketch artist to look for similarities between the two faces. Maybe they can come up with some sort of a composite of what this guy looks like without the prosthetics and makeup."

"So, that's why you told Aislinn not to release Khilt's picture," Stan said as he wrote *suspect was disguised* on his pad.

"Looks like it was a good idea to hold onto it," Curtis said.

Stan glanced sideways at his boss. "What's going on?" he asked.

Curtis shook his head. "I'm not sure. He wanted us to see this. He altered the shape of his face and his weight, but he didn't change his eyes or his eyebrows. Anyone who can apply makeup like this guy would know that if you don't want to be recognized, you alter your eyes. Plus, he took his glasses off and looked directly at the camera."

"Is he taunting us?"

Curtis shrugged. "There's a reason he showed up at Chloe's party and at the interview. We need to figure it out. If we can do that, we'll stand a better chance of finding Renee Charlesbois."

"And if we don't?" Stan asked.

"Not an option, Stan," Curtis said, staring at the eyes in the darkened room. "Not an option." He glanced at his watch and cursed. "Shit, Barclay is going to be a very unhappy dog."

# CHAPTER EIGHTEEN

"No wonder the phones are ringing," one of the uniformed cops said as he doctored his coffee. "That Charlesbois guy putting a million bucks on the table for his daughter. This is crazy shit."

"Yeah," Tommy Strand said. "Crazy shit indeed."

Tommy headed back to his desk, gathered up the mail and started on his rounds. The squad room around him was bustling with extra bodies working the Charlesbois case. Every landline was busy as the public called in with leads and Strand picked his way through the chaos until he found Aislinn Byrne. A black and white headshot of a man lay front and center on the detective's desk. It was a face that he knew. He pointed to the picture.

"Who's that?" he asked.

Byrne glanced up, then slid the glossy into a file. "A suspect in one of our investigations." She paused and smiled at Tommy. He looked frail and uncomfortable. "You know him?"

"Can't say I do," he said.

"How's the leg."

"Sore, you know," Tommy said, handing her an envelope.

"Yeah, I can imagine." Aislinn took the envelope and signed for it. "Thanks, Tommy."

He took the sheet with Byrne's signature and limped out to the hall. His heart was beating fast and his mouth was dry. The name on the file was *Renee Charlesbois*. He had just seen a picture of a suspect in her disappearance, and he knew that face. He closed his eyes and tried to remember where from. Not lately, and not in Boston. Then it hit him. It was from his old precinct in Newton. The guy was a lawyer, a total nobody who surfaced every now and then with some drug dealing scum in tow. Still, a lawyer kidnaping a rich woman? It was a stretch. Tommy leaned over and rubbed his leg, mulling it over, then slowly straightened up. It was definitely him.

Tommy found a quiet spot in the hallway and pulled out his cell. Maybe, just maybe, he was finally going to get a break. He called a number from memory and waited as it rang.

Thomas Strand was twenty-eight and going nowhere, the result of a bullet wound he had suffered chasing down a teenage suspect. It was a beat cop's worst nightmare, and a risk they all took every shift. The bullet had carved a hole through his thigh muscle, then shattered his femur before embedding itself in a mess of bone fragments, tendons and muscle. Strand had gone down hard on his side, shrieking as he saw the blood spurting from his severed artery, his life turned upside down in an instant.

The former Texas A & M halfback teetered between losing his life, or at the very least, his leg. In the end the doctors had even managed to save the limb, but with a steel plate holding the bone together and a pound of muscle sliced out, every day was a struggle. Tommy Strand, still six-two, with blond hair and a quick smile, was damaged goods.

Regular police work was out of the question, and they found him a desk job. But something darker was happening under the surface. Tommy had become dependent on the drugs that took the edge off his pain and upset. His athletic body and easy smile were fading, and his personal life was coming apart as fast as his career.

He was charged with possession of a prohibited narcotic, but his court-appointed lawyer managed to find a clerical error that spared him the embarrassment of facing criminal charges. No one wanted to see him off the force, but the writing was on the wall. For Tommy, simply knowing his time was limited was tearing him apart, but today, it appeared, a way out may have fallen in his lap.

A voice answered the phone. "I told you, man, I don't like you calling me from the big house." The person on the other end of the line sounded like Barry White. It was Joey McGinley, a street-level dealer who got Tommy the opioids he needed to keep the pain in check. "Get that through your fucking head."

"Don't hang up," Tommy said in a hushed voice. "I have something big for you. It could be worth half a million in your pocket."

"What?" Joey said. "What the fuck are you on?"

"Listen. I may know who grabbed that Charlesbois woman."

"You serious?" Joey asked.

"Absolutely serious."

"That guy's ass is worth a million bucks," Joey said.

"Exactly. Half for you, half for me. I'm telling you, Joey," he paused as a sergeant passed by. "I'm not shitting you. I saw his face."

"Who?" An eagerness had crept into Joey's voice.

"No, not now. Later, the usual place. Eight o'clock."

"I'll be there."

Tommy hung up and wiped his palms on his pants, sweating with anticipation. If anyone could wring the truth out of the piece of crap lawyer it was Joey.

Tommy headed back for his desk, shuffled a few papers about and tried to look busy, but his mind had already left the precinct. He was with Joey, in the seedy hole-in-the-wall where the dealer sold his drugs. And Joey was listening, intent on every word.

Half a million each. Maybe there was a payday just around the corner.

# CHAPTER NINETEEN

Aislinn Byrne printed a copy of the interview with Liem Khilt in large font and posted it on the corkboard in the Incident Room. They arranged three chairs facing the board and Stan handed out notepads and pens. It was after six and the room was much quieter than earlier in the day. The temporary bank of phones that had been set up to monitor incoming calls on the Charlesbois case was on the far side of the room and they could just hear a slight drone of voices. Aside from that bit of white noise it was almost silent.

Aislinn checked her notes. "We ran *Liem Khilt* through every conceivable database without getting one hit. As suspected, the name is made up."

"No surprise," Curtis said. He pointed at the printed copy of Khilt's interview. "Let's see what we can get out of this."

"There has to be something there," Stan said.

"Khilt, or whatever the hell his name is, says that he and Rhonell went to medical school at UCLA together. We know from Aislinn digging into the UCLA registry that Khilt is lying."

Stan said, "Khilt says he's a guest of Dr. Bernard Rhonell, then two lines later he calls him Bernie. I mentioned that to Chloe Harrah when I was picking up the surveillance footage and she got a horrified look on her face. She told me nobody ever refers to him as Bernie. He hates it. I don't think Khilt knows him."

Aislinn checked her notes from the interview with Bernard Rhonell. "I agree. Rhonell took his undergraduate work at UCLA, but his medical schooling was at Stanford University. Our guy didn't do his homework."

Curtis shook his head. "No, that kind of thinking will get us in trouble. We have to take every phrase, every word this guy says, seriously. We're not throwing out parts of the conversation because they don't seem to fit. Let's assume that if he mentioned the medical facility at UCLA, he did it for a reason."

"Okay." Stan rubbed his shaved head. "So we put UCLA on the board?"

"Right, keep it in mind. I don't know if it means anything, but he came in and interviewed for a reason." Curtis stood and plucked a yellow hi-liter from a small table and ran a few strokes over the words *pitch* and *fork*. "I think he used these words specifically so I would tie Liem Khilt back to the overweight man I met at Chloe's party." Curtis pointed to a separate sheet of paper on the right side of the board where he had written six words and phrases. "Those are some of the key words Khilt used when he was at Chloe's. It could be as important as what he said in the interview, but I'm going strictly from memory. There's a lot of what he said that I can't remember."

Stan repeated the words aloud. "*Florida, pitchfork, rafting down the canal, personal ads, eight days in jail* ... Shit, LT, he's all over the map.

"Yeah, no kidding." Curtis stared at the writing. "Back to the interview. What other words seem forced?"

"*Dessert. Drowning.* Those are both very specific words," Aislinn said. "He could have said food instead of dessert or used a different colloquialism rather than drowning her sorrows."

Curtis nodded. "Both good points, Aislinn." He used the highlighter on the words. "Stan?"

"We never asked him what time he spoke with her. He volunteered that information two separate times."

Curtis read the script aloud. "*Yes, I spoke with her twice. Once, just after I arrived. That would be about six-thirty.*" He made a few swipes through the words and continued. "*I saw her getting a drink at about nine-twenty.*" Again, he used the hi-liter. "Excellent, Stan. There's absolutely no reason for him to be so exact about the time. "What about the reference to New York? The Yankees don't win the division every year."

"Yeah," Stan grinned. "2004 was the best. 2007 and 2013 were icing on the cake. World Series champs, baby."

Curtis grinned. Bostonians still talked about the team that, in 2004, broke the eighty-six-year curse. "Back to New York," Curtis said. "Highlight it?"

Aislinn nodded. "He definitely took the conversation on a tangent there."

Curtis highlighted the city name. "The same thing happens when he talks about them both liking wine." He read the text aloud. "*Yes, I spoke with her twice. Once, just after I arrived. That would be about six-thirty. We both enjoy wine, in particular from Napa Valley, and we spoke at some length about the different vintages and cellars. I think she mentioned that Frog's Leap was one of her favorites. She seemed to have a genuine love for the valley and knew every good and bad year. She made the bad ones sound like the Apocalypse.*"

Aislinn was nodding, her head moving up and down like a bobble head. "Why Napa? Why Frog's Leap? And why so specific on the time? You're right, LT, this guy is telling us something."

Curtis waved over Art Friesen, one of the junior detectives. "Art, call the restaurant and talk with Hans Grummer, the maitre d'. Find out what kind of wine Renee likes. Get the details. Red, white, country, specific wine cellar."

"Okay."

Curtis highlighted Napa and Frogs' Leap. "What else do you guys see?"

This time Stan read from the text. "*I remember her saying that despite her success, she really felt tied down by the business.*"

"Tied down," Aislinn said. "That draws a picture."

"It does, doesn't it," Curtis said. He highlighted the words. "Okay, so he was schooled in medicine in California, likes to talk about wine and baseball and gave us two very specific times. He mentions New

York, Boston and Napa Valley. Places and times, all clues?" It was a rhetorical question.

Stan said, "Then he tells us where he's staying. Fifteen Beacon. Nothing mysterious about that. Other than he paid for an expensive hotel room but didn't sleep there." Stan grabbed the file CSU had given them from their investigation of the room. Inside were three typewritten pages and a thin stack of glossy photos. He leafed through them. "Nothing here, LT." He handed the photos to Curtis and scanned the report a second time.

Curtis flipped through the photos and set them on the desk. Then, a few seconds later, he picked them up and pulled out the photo of the bathroom vanity. He stared at it for a minute, then handed it to Aislinn. "Look at the bottles," he said.

Stan leaned across and peered at the photo, which had been shot holding the camera exactly at the height of the vanity top. On the marble top were seven bottles of varying size and content. Shampoo, conditioner, body lotion, hand cream and liquid soap. Three of the bottles were hotel inventory, the other four standard brands found in any local drug store. Both detectives concentrated on the array of bottles for a minute, then Aislinn shrugged her shoulders.

"I'm not sure what you mean, LT," she said. Stan shook his head.

"That photo was taken directly facing the bottles. Look again."

Aislinn saw it first. "Jesus," she said. "He's set the bottles at specific angles so only certain letters show. Like the two o's in shampoo."

"L-o-o-k-b-a-c-k," Stan read, one letter at a time.

"Exactly," Curtis said. "Look back. That is not a coincidence."

"*Look back*. What the hell does that mean?" Aislinn said.

"Not sure," Curtis answered. "But it's there for a reason."

Friesen returned, a piece of paper in his hand. He read the contents out loud. "According to Hans, Renee Charlesbois likes red wine, with her tastes leaning toward a Cabernet Sauvignon or a Merlot. And her favorite wineries are Lindemans, from South Australia, and numerous of the Reserva and Gran Reserva Cabernets from the Maipo valley in

Chile. She occasionally drinks Napa Valley wines, but she's not a huge fan of them."

"Thanks, Art," Stan said. He turned to Curtis and Aislinn. "So he's definitely making up the conversations. They never happened."

Curtis snapped his fingers. "The surveillance footage from the restaurant. Let's go back over them and check what's happening at six-thirty and nine-twenty."

"The cameras only cover the front entrance and the bar, LT," Aislinn said. "And we've been over them twenty times. Khilt kept himself out of camera range as much as possible."

Curtis shook his head. "That's not what I'm thinking. I want to know if Renee was on the tapes at either of those times. If she was, and Khilt isn't with her, then we know he's lying about the times as well."

Aislinn made a note in her book. "Good thinking."

Stan was fixated on the board and Curtis asked, "What is it, Stan?"

He shrugged. "Maybe he's talking about kidnapping a rich person when he says, *It's not cheap. But then, what in life truly worth having, is cheap?*"

"Perhaps," Curtis said. "But that doesn't tell us anything we don't already know." Curtis was silent for a minute, running his hands through his hair, then he said, "Not one word about this to Jacques Charlesbois. He'd use it to fuel his vigilante efforts."

"Okay," Stan said and Aislinn nodded.

"And let's check VICAP for perps who use multiple disguises, taunt the local police or attend police interviews. It's a long shot, but it'll narrow down the parameters for the computer search."

"Good idea," Aislinn said.

"Okay, I think this is our only suspect. This scumbag, whoever he is, has Renee Charlesbois." Curtis stared at the corkboard.

"We just have to find him," Aislinn said.

"Well, that sounds easy," Stan said.

"Maybe it is," Curtis said. "We need to figure out what he's telling us. It's all here. I can feel it."

"She still alive, LT?" Stan asked. "You got any feelings on that one?"

Curtis shook his head slowly. "Not sure."

# CHAPTER TWENTY

"Chicken tonight," Khilt said, closing the door behind him. He set the tray on the foot of the cot and retreated to the chair by the door. She didn't move, just stared at him from where she sat at the other end of the bed, her knees pulled tight against her chest. Her hair was like straw and her face had traces of smeared dirt from washing in the small sink. Her cheeks resembled dry creek beds where water had once trickled down in tiny rivulets.

"Not hungry?" he asked. "Maybe you're not getting enough exercise. I could bring you a treadmill if you like."

"You know what I want." Her voice was little more than a croaking whisper. It hurt just to talk and her lips were cracked and peeling.

"You probably want to go home." He adjusted the sleeves on his shirt so they were exactly the same length. "Who knows, maybe that's possible."

A tiny spark lit her eyes. "What do you mean by that?"

"Lieutenant Detective Curtis Westcott." Khilt leaned forward and lowered his voice, as if he were telling her a secret. "He almost caught up with me today. We missed each other by a couple of hours. He knows what I look like."

The spark grew. "He'll find you."

"Perhaps," he said. "But there are still so many layers to peel back. I don't think he's grasped the fundamentals of the game yet. He needs to do that before he has any chance of success."

"Everyone in Boston will be looking for you," she whispered. "Someone will see you."

He smiled, took the safety off his pistol and set it carefully on his lap. Then he reached up and tugged on the even white teeth. They pulled away, revealing slightly stained, smaller teeth with numerous irregularities. He repeated the procedure on the bottom set. Then he ran his fingers down his right eye. His nails caught an edge and a portion of his face began to peel away. He continued to pull and the entire cheek came away in his hand. Beneath the spirit gum and latex was an uneven surface, pockmarked with deep purplish scars. He repeated the procedure on the other cheek, then stripped the latex off his forehead and chin. His entire face was a mass of the hideous scars. He set the pieces of thin, soft plastic on his lap.

She stared at him with terrified eyes. The man was a monster, hideous and unrecognizable. Whatever picture of him the police were using, it was useless. She felt the hope drain away, like water.

"I don't think their description of me is going to help them very much, do you?"

The tears were welling up again and she closed her eyes to block the vision of his real face from her mind. "Westcott will find you."

"Maybe. The clues are all there, but here's the thing. They need to outsmart me. I don't think that's possible."

"Get out," she said quietly. She opened her eyes, wiped the tears away and swallowed. "I've had enough of your ego for today."

Khilt cocked his head slightly and gave her an intrigued look. "Spunky little bitch, aren't you?" he said.

"I'm no one's bitch. Now get the fuck out." She wanted desperately to tell him he was ugly and she was losing her appetite, but she looked at the gun on his lap and kept her mouth shut.

His face changed, color flushing into his cheeks and his yellow teeth grinding together. "You're pushing your luck," he hissed. "That's not very smart."

"What are you going to do?" Something inside snapped and she leaned forward. "Kill me? I don't think so. Not yet anyway. Or you would already have done it. You're waiting, and there's nothing I can do or say to change your plans. We both know it's up to Westcott whether I live or die. So you give me one good reason why I should be civil to you, you fucking freak."

"Shut up," he yelled, springing from the chair.

"One reason, asshole," she yelled back. "And if you don't have one, then shut up and get out."

Khilt teetered between leaping on her and choking her to death on the spot or leaving the room. The rage bordered on uncontrollable, then the anger began to dissipate and he relaxed. She was just goading him on. If he were to kill her now, the game would be a disaster. Everything for naught, and he couldn't let that happen. He picked up the various prosthetics he had stripped from his face and left without saying another word.

He locked the door, tried the handle just to be sure, then headed back upstairs. She was right about one thing. Whether she lived or died certainly did depend on Curtis Westcott.

But until then she *was* his bitch.

Renee listened to the footsteps as her captor retreated to the main floor and felt a wave of relief that he was gone. She glanced at her dinner, sitting on the other end of the bed. The chicken looked edible, as had all the meals he had served her. She had no appetite, but knew she had to eat to keep her strength. Her lips were cracked and bleeding from the hot dry air, but it was preferable to a damp, cold prison. That would lower her body temperature and she'd be much more susceptible to the mold and spores that thrived under those conditions.

Her health was good and she was still alive. Every hour she survived was one more hour that the police had to work the case. She had read a few articles in *The Globe* where the reporter had interviewed Curtis Westcott, but aside from that she knew nothing about the man.

Now she sat in a locked room, waiting. Waiting for someone to solve the sick game that Liem Khilt had devised. She reached over, picked up her dinner and set it on her lap. Then she did something she seldom, if ever, did. She said a short prayer.

# CHAPTER TWENTY-ONE

The street was a mess of overflowing garbage cans and a powerful stench hung in the still air. A '96 Lincoln Town Car with a dented front quarter panel was parked at the curb in front of a low brick building. Tommy Strand pulled up behind the Lincoln and shut off the motor. He locked the car and limped to the front door, checked both directions on the street, then slipped in through the front door.

Inside, four old wooden tables sat on the hardwood floors, blackened by years of dirt and grease. Three walls were covered with old album covers—The Beatles, Def Leppard, Black Sabbath, and the stale odor of bacon and coffee lingered from the morning. A lone candle burned on the table occupied by a large man dressed entirely in black. Tommy approached the table and sat down.

"Hi, Joey," he said. "How are things?"

"Always good, Tommy," the man said in his deep baritone.

Joey McGinley was second generation Irish-American. He had pale skin and dark red, tightly-curled hair that hung to his shoulders. The scales topped two-forty and his wide face was creased with two long scars, sloppily stitched. His dad had come across from Ireland in his early teens, a wharf rat who drank the hard stuff and ran with cheap women. He died of stab wounds from a bar fight when Joey was four and his mother didn't attend the funeral.

Joey grew up in Jamaica Plain, a tough-looking kid with rock-hard fists and the quickest knife on the block. He liked his life and had no inclination to rise above it. Selling drugs and collecting debts was fun. He'd seen the inside of a cell a few times, but that didn't deter him. It was a cost of doing business.

He took a slug of beer, his huge hands dwarfing the mug. "You shittin' me about this Charlesbois thing?"

Strand shook his head. "No, Joey, this is the real thing. I saw the suspect's photo on one of the detective's desk. She stuck it in the folder really quick, like she didn't want me seeing it. I haven't heard anything about the department releasing the picture to the public, so I figure they're keeping this one close to their chest. It's real for sure."

The bar owner came by and set a beer on the table. Strand took a long drink with a hand he was trying hard to keep from shaking.

Joey leaned forward, his eyes alert. "Who is it?"

Strand fidgeted in his seat, shifting his weight about, trying to get comfortable. "How are we going to do this, Joey? The money, I mean."

Joey shrugged and leaned back in his chair. "You said fifty-fifty on the phone."

Strand nodded. He was shaking worse now, and the head on the beer foamed up and ran down the side of the mug. "Yeah, Joey. Fifty-fifty."

"Who is it?" Joey asked. The tone of his voice left no doubt he wanted an answer.

Strand wet his lips. "You remember when Manny got charged in Newton?"

"Yeah, three pounds of coke."

"That's it. Remember that piece of shit lawyer who managed to get him off?"

"Vaguely."

"That's him. That's the guy."

"The lawyer?"

"Yeah, the lawyer."

Joey scratched the side of his head for a few seconds. "You mean the one who kept showing up for court drunk?"

"That's the one."

"Okay, I remember him. Brian somebody. What the fuck was his last name?"

"Newman," Strand said.

Joey picked a piece of food from his teeth with his fingernail. "Why would a lawyer kidnap someone? Lawyers make shitloads of money."

Tommy leaned forward. "This guy? He's a bottom feeder, Joey."

"Yeah, he is." McGinley thought about it for a minute. "I saw Manny a while back and he said the guy was in trouble. Might even get himself disbarred."

"Wouldn't surprise me. Could be he needs money."

Joey sort of nodded, then stopped. "Something's not making sense."

"What's that?" Strand asked.

"If Newman's picture is in the file and they suspect he's the guy, why haven't they picked him up?"

Tommy shrugged. "I don't think they know who he is. I've never seen him in any of the Boston courts."

"Yeah, maybe."

Tommy kept pressing him. "The picture was grainy, like it came from CCTV footage." He didn't want to lose Joey, and added, "He's only a suspect right now. They need definitive proof. Beyond any doubt, for the court."

There was a long silence as Joey finished his beer and motioned to the bartender. He lit a cigarette, his eyes locked on Tommy Strand. The man was a cop, and that held some water. Still, he was an addict, and to Joey that severely diminished credibility. The bartender arrived with another mug of beer. "You better be sure about this, Tommy. This guy might be an alcoholic piece of shit, but he's still a lawyer. If you're wrong this could backfire big time."

"No, Joey, I'm sure. I'm real sure."

Joey McGinley smiled. It was anything but pleasant. "Okay, Tommy, you did good. I'll take it from here." The large man dug in his pocket and pulled out a baggie. It was half full of pills. He set it on the table. "Consider it a bonus."

"Sure. Thanks, Joey." He scooped the baggie off the table, finished his beer and left the bar. He twisted the key in the car's ignition and the motor turned over. Maybe he'd finally get rid of this piece of shit and pick up a decent ride.

All he needed was his half of the reward.

# CHAPTER TWENTY-TWO

Sleep wouldn't come.

Curtis watched television, read a dry book for an hour, sipped chamomile tea, but nothing worked. He paced about his house, just as he had done a thousand times before, his mind alive, his body spent. All his life he had suffered from a hyperactive mind, but recently it was getting worse. Night after night without sleep, ugly memories pushing their way to the surface. Memories of murder victims, their bodies, the torment of everything gone wrong. So many of them. So much death.

He could get through the days, there was enough to distract him. It was at night, when the city was sleeping and the activity about him slowly ground to a halt—that was when his brain went into overdrive. He couldn't stop it. And now, Renee Charlesbois joined the stream, like a dripping tap he couldn't turn off.

He whistled and Barclay appeared. Curtis sat on the floor next to him and rubbed the dog behind its ears. "How about a walk?" Barclay was all for it and Curtis slipped on his collar and leash.

Back Bay was quiet and beautiful, the elegant brownstones warm and inviting under the soft yellow glow of the streetlamps. He let Barclay, who took sniffing the latest pee spots seriously, set the pace. It was slower than usual—apparently an enticing newcomer had happened by—and that gave Curtis time to think.

His gut feeling was that Renee Charlesbois was still alive—that Khilt had her locked up somewhere for some unknown reason. Why else would he have made himself so visible and gone out of his way to leave a series of clues? Nothing would make sense until they figured out what Khilt had embedded in the precinct interview and the conversation at Chloe's party.

"It's all purpose driven," he said to the dog. "Khilt is doing this for a reason." Barclay stared up at him and Curtis rubbed the top of his head. At least Barclay was getting some satisfaction out of his insomnia. He thought back to his younger days, when a decent night of sleep was the norm rather than the exception. He couldn't remember when that had changed, but it was in the past and this was his new reality.

They walked on and Barclay got back to sniffing, returning home a little after four o'clock. Curtis sat on the living room floor, petting Barclay and kicking around a word that had stuck in his mind. *Past.* Something was clicking. What? Why would past, present or future matter? Something someone had said. He closed his eyes and blocked out everything, then replayed his banter with Aislinn and Stan. The stilted, antagonistic conversations with Jacques Charlesbois. The footage from Chloe's CCTV. The interview with Liem Khilt. When he hit the interview, he stopped, one line catching his attention.

*I saw her at the bar getting a drink at about nine-twenty. Ms. Charlesbois is a dedicated Red Sox fan.*

He hugged his dog. "*Is,* Barclay. He said she *is* a Sox fan, not *was.* She's alive." He ran his hand over the dog's fur. "Yes, it's all in the tense he uses. That's the key." He closed his eyes, his mind slowed, and his spent body finally took over. He was asleep in seconds.

Light was streaming through the living room window when he opened his eyes, and Aislinn Byrne was staring down at him.

"Nice," she said. The key to his front door dangled from her hand. Both she and Stan had a key in case Curtis crashed and the phone couldn't wake him. They knew he seldom slept, and when he did it was like he was in a coma. "So now you're sleeping on your living room floor."

"I'll take whatever I can get." He sat up and massaged a few sore muscles. "What time is it?"

"Almost nine."

"Shit."

Barclay showed up and stuck his nose a few inches from his face, then padded over to the back door and gave Curtis a look. Aislinn headed over to let him out and stood by the door, waiting. Curtis joined her in the kitchen and poured some coffee beans into the grinder. He loaded the coffee machine and turned it on, then leaned against the counter, still trying to wake up.

"Curtis, what the hell is this?" She was pointing to a check stuck to his fridge with a magnet.

He squinted at where she was pointing. "It's from my parents."

"Two million dollars?" She stared at him. "Holy shit."

"Yeah."

"Why don't you cash it?"

"There are some conditions attached." He was going to leave it at that, but she was giving him a look that he knew well from watching her interview suspects. "My dad wants me to join his law firm. He doesn't think much of me being a cop."

"C'mon, you're the commander of homicide."

"Yeah, well..."

She let Barclay in and said, "You're not actually considering it."

He rolled his eyes. "Me in a suit, working in an office?"

She grinned and headed for the front door, then turned and said, "It looks good on your fridge. It'll be a hell of a conversation starter if you bring a date back to your house."

"Never thought of that."

"See you at the office," Aislinn said.

"Thanks for stopping by to wake me up."

There was a soft click as the front door shut behind her. The coffee machine beeped and he poured a cup, added some cream and sugar and sat on his couch, coffee in one hand, scratching Barclay's head with the other. He didn't move until he'd finished the entire cup, then he headed upstairs, had a quick shower and dressed.

Barclay was not going to be placated by a quick break in the backyard and stared at Curtis until he gave in. "No dawdling," Curtis warned. "I need to work if you want to live in a nice house."

Dawdle he did, and Curtis had to half drag him away from the choicest sniff-spots and back home. Curtis refilled Barclay's water bowl, then grabbed his car keys and backed out of the garage. The drive to work was quicker than usual, rush hour long over. He parked and took the elevator to the sixth floor. Stan glanced up when he entered.

"Rough night, LT?" he asked.

Curtis just smiled. Aislinn had already told him.

He headed for his office, Stan in tow. "Get Aislinn. I might have a new angle on Khilt's interview. I'll meet you in the Incident Room."

Stan veered off to find Aislinn and Curtis powered up his computer and checked his email. Nothing of consequence. He had three new messages on his voice mail. He listened to them and jotted notes on a loose sheet of paper. One from the police commissioner, one from the mayor and one from Jacques Charlesbois. All wanting him to return their call and bring them up to speed on the investigation. He dropped his pen on the paper and headed down the hall. Right now he had an idea, and that meant all three could wait. He found his two detectives in the IR.

"Aislinn, bring me up to speed."

"We have the results from the VICAP search."

"What are they?"

"Not one hit. Nothing came up when the profile ran through the FBI computers. Either we're being too specific, or he's not in there. One or the other."

"Shit," Curtis said. "I really thought we might get something on that."

"No luck with the sketch artist either, LT. The eyes, eye sockets and eyebrows are the only part of the face he didn't alter. The prosthetics are so good they can't find the seams where his real face starts."

"Damn," Curtis said, scowling. "So, no composite."

"No sketch."

Curtis glanced at Stan. "Any other good news?"

Stan shrugged. "We dug hard for someone Jacques Charlesbois might have pissed off enough to abduct his daughter. Nothing. The revenge angle appears to be a dead end."

"Well, no big surprise there," Curtis said. "It was a long shot."

Aislinn chimed in. "The VISA number Liem Khilt used to rent the room at Fifteen Beacon was registered to Ismail Khadi, who lives in Columbus, Ohio. Khilt must have scammed the number somehow and had a fake card made up. Not that difficult to do. And since Khadi hadn't received his monthly bill yet, he had no reason to suspect someone was using his card."

"Khadi's clean?" Curtis asked.

"We think so. He's an accountant, works nine to five, home every night. We're positive he's not our guy."

"Why Khadi?" Curtis asked.

"It looks like random identity theft," Aislinn said. "Khadi uses his credit card for online purchases and Khilt probably just picked him from a long list he lifted from some pay site."

"Okay, well, so much for all the good news." Curtis pointed at the corkboard. "I had an idea last night. See here where Khilt says *saw her at the bar getting a drink at about nine-twenty. Ms. Charlesbois is a dedicated Red Sox fan.* Check out the tense he uses. He doesn't say she *was* a fan, he says she *is* a fan. What does that tell you?"

"She's alive," Aislinn said.

"That's what I'm thinking. So let's go back over what he said and concentrate on the tense he's using. See if that gives us anything else."

Aislinn used an orange hi-liter to mark the words. "At the start he says, *We both enjoy wine, in particular from Napa Valley, and we spoke at some length about the different vintages and cellars. I think she mentioned that Frog's Leap was one of her favorites. She seemed to have a genuine love for the valley and knew the years when the grapes were good and the years when they faltered. She made the off years sound like they were nothing short of the*

*Apocalypse.* He uses *spoke* and *was.* Both past tense. The whole reference to Napa is in the past tense."

"Right, then he shifts to present tense when he says that she's a Boston fan and *she lives and dies on every pitch.*" He pursed his lips. "Interesting choice of words, *lives and dies.*"

"Then he moves to future tense," Curtis said. *"Every year she got to look forward to drowning her sorrows when New York went on and Boston hung up their gloves.* Napa in the past, Boston in the present and New York in the future."

Stan was nodding and scratching his head at the same time. "Okay, but what does that tell us? Napa is a bit north of San Francisco. Maybe he's from the bay area. Why mention Frog's Leap?"

"Who are they?" Curtis asked.

Aislinn returned to her seat and keyed it into her phone. She scrolled through the hits, looking for hints of scandals. "It's a vineyard that produces a few good mid-range wines. There doesn't appear to be any intrigue in their history. So why did he mention Frog's Leap?"

"Why indeed?" Curtis stood and started pacing. "Napa. Boston. New York. What do you think? Boston is what's happening right now? He uses Boston in the present tense and he's here now. Renee Charlesbois is missing. Present tense. That fits. If we assume he's playing around with the tenses he's using, then Napa in the past and New York in the future could be indicative of other crimes."

"Remember what he left us in the bathroom at Fifteen Beacon. The bottles lined up to spell *look back.* I think we've got something here, LT."

"The tense he speaks in is important," Curtis agreed.

"*Look back,*" Aislinn said. "Look back to Napa?"

"Maybe," Curtis said.

"Do you think he's a serial killer?" Stan asked.

"Oh, Christ." For a moment Curtis felt the wind go out of his sails. "Don't even mention those words. If you think we have a mess on our hands right now with Charlesbois' insane reward, just wait for the reaction if *that* gets out. Those words are not to be repeated. Got it?"

"Got it, boss," Stan said.

Aislinn nodded, not a strand of her short red hair moving with the motion. "So what's all this about Napa? Has he been there? Up to no good in the valley?"

"Nothing this guy is up to is good." Stan rubbed his bald head.

"So what are we saying here?" Curtis got up and walked to the board. "That everything points back or ahead in time, not to the present? Napa has already happened. Boston is happening now, and unless we stop him, New York will happen. Is that it?"

"Could well be," Stan said.

Aislinn smacked her hand on the table. Both Curtis and Stan jumped at the sharp sound. "Christ." She jumped up and stood beside Curtis at the board, then used a green hi-liter to color over the times Khilt had given them. "The times he gave us in the interview. Six-thirty and nine-twenty are dates."

"Six-thirty and nine-twenty," Stan repeated. "June 30th and September 20th."

Aislinn glanced at the calendar. "Today is eight-ten. August 10th."

Curtis shook his head. "WTF. One in the past, one in the future."

They were all silent for the better part of a minute, then Curtis said, "We're on a short fuse."

"And it's been lit," Aislinn said.

# CHAPTER TWENTY-THREE

Jacques Charlesbois' house was set on eight heavily wooded acres in the affluent bedroom community of Chestnut Hill. An ornate wrought iron gate, always closed, was the only part of the estate visible to passing traffic.

Charlesbois stood on the balcony overlooking the south gardens, coffee in hand. His stomach was churning, and he felt like he was going to be sick. His daughter was gone. It had been a week and still nothing. It was starting to sink in that he may well have lost her. He turned at the sound of footsteps as Amery Kincaid arrived for their morning meeting.

"It's a week today, Amery," he said. "Tell me something."

His corporate spy looked grim. He leaned against one of the thick concrete pilasters that supported the railing and shook his head. "I've hacked into the BPD mainframe, which was no small feat, and I'm watching everything the homicide team is putting on their shared drive."

"And…"

"It's not encouraging. They set up a bank of phones to handle calls relating to Renee's abduction, but the calls are all shit. A lot of them are people asking what they need to do to get the reward. Some are from nutbars confessing to taking her, but every time the police follow up it's a dead end."

"What else are they doing?" Charlesbois asked. The sinking feeling in his gut was getting worse.

"They accessed VICAP, checked all recent prison releases, talked with parole officers, and pulled up every abduction file in and around Boston, then looked for similarities in the MO. Westcott put three detectives on reviewing all abduction and murder cases in D.C., New York, and Philadelphia, looking for similarities. So far there's nothing concrete."

"What does that mean?"

"The details in these files can get pretty gruesome," Kincaid said. "Lots of grisly details. The problem they have is no one knows where Renee is or anything that's happened to her since she went missing. They have nothing to cross-check against the existing files, so that leaves them guessing."

"You mean things like collecting pieces of clothing or cutting off body parts," Charlesbois said, his face taking on color.

"Exactly. Stuff like that. Say he moved her just before the police managed to find them, and there were newspaper clippings pasted to the wall, then they could look at previous cases with the same MO."

Charlesbois recovered his composure. "What about people calling us concerning the reward?"

Kincaid nodded. "We're busy. We've had a lot of calls, most of them asking if the reward is real. We've had a few promising ones. We got a call about ten o'clock last night that might be something."

"What?" Charlesbois asked, leaning forward on the railing.

"A guy called and wanted to know if he had to deliver Renee's abductor alive. He asked what would happen if the bad guy gets killed while they're getting her? That's pretty specific. That caller might be onto something."

"Did you get a phone number?"

Amery shook his head. "Blocked call."

"Do you think this guy knows who has her?"

"It's possible."

Charlesbois nodded. "Okay, good work. Just wondering, how did you answer that question?"

"It's a million dollars either way, as long as Renee is safe."

Charlesbois set his empty coffee mug on the railing. "I'll try Westcott again and see if he has anything new."

"Okay. I'll keep the hack into their system open as long as possible. At least you'll know if Westcott is keeping you up to date." Kincaid retreated across the balcony and disappeared into the house.

Charlesbois spent a few minutes staring at the gardens, thinking about the times he and Renee had leaned against the railing and talked. Sadness poured over him, and he tried to shake it off. It was too thick, too overpowering. He shuffled back into the house and stared at the phone. Why didn't it ring? What did they want? Where was his daughter? Right now it was all questions and no answers.

There was a low sound behind him and he turned to see his wife enter the room. She was pale, almost white, her eyes little more than sockets in a skull. It was the first time she had ventured out of the bedroom since Sunday. He moved quickly to her side and she fell into him, shaking. She stared into his eyes and he shook his head. Tears washed across her sunken cheeks and she buried her head in his chest.

"Our baby," was all she said.

# CHAPTER TWENTY-FOUR

The mayor couldn't be ignored any longer. At some point he would come looking for the head of homicide, and if that happened his mood would be more than just a little sour. Better to initiate the contact. It was just before noon on Thursday when Curtis dialed his direct line and waited.

"Westcott." Franklin Stone did not sound happy. "You and I, we've been dealing with each other for a while now."

"We have." Curtis wasn't sure where this was going.

"You've always been quick to return my phone calls. What's changed?"

"We're focused on the Renee Charlesbois case," Curtis said, thinking it would be prudent to bring it up first.

"What's your progress so far?" he asked.

*So much for idle chit chat*, Curtis thought. "We've opened a bank of phones for the public to call in on, and we're monitoring them 24-7. I've brought in additional detectives to work with my team and they're running down every possible lead we get. We've accessed VICAP, the FBI database, and we're checking the results of the searches very closely, looking for a similar Modus Operandi."

He continued with the spiel, but left out anything to do with Liem Khilt. It was a calculated risk, but one he was willing to take. Stone was a politician, and if he felt releasing certain information would help keep the city calm, he would do so. If their suspicions hit the six o'clock news, Khilt would know they were looking for him and he might do something rash. He finished running through their progress and waited for Stone's reaction.

"So you have no idea where she is," Stone said.

"At this time, no sir."

"Jacques Charlesbois is all over me on this," Stone said. "He doesn't think you're working the case hard enough."

"Right now, we have no definitive proof that Renee Charlesbois has been murdered, yet the full resources of Boston Homicide are on the case. With all due respect, we're working her disappearance with everything we have."

There was a long silence as Franklin Stone evaluated his reply. Finally, he said, "I want to know the minute you get anything new."

"Of course, Mr. Mayor. Your office is first on my list."

"Let's get this resolved before it hits the fan, Curtis."

"Yes, sir."

Curtis set the phone on his desk and sucked in a deep breath. Franklin Stone was a fair man, but he had his limits. Those limits would be sorely tested if he found out his homicide team was holding back information on the case. But Curtis was firm on it, Liem Khilt was off limits for now.

Napa was a key to Renee's abduction, he was feeling more and more certain about that. Following the trail back to the wine-producing valley just north of San Francisco was their best course of action. Renee didn't seem to have any connection to the region—Aislinn said there was no Frog's Leap wine in her fridge, she hadn't traveled there in years, and there was no mention of Napa anywhere in her calendar. It was Khilt who wanted them to look at Napa, and if Aislinn was right, they had a specific date to key in on. June 30th. No year associated with the date—it could be forty days ago or a year and forty days. Or more. Who knew? It should be easy enough to have the local police pull up their logbooks for that date and check for disappearances or murders. Pressure was mounting quickly and Stan was already working that angle. Curtis headed for the staff room and was pouring coffee when Stan appeared, breathless.

"Holy shit, LT, I think we've found the Napa case." Stan held out a single sheet of paper. "Successful businesswoman, abducted without a trace in mid-June, and her body showed up on the 30th, in a ditch alongside a secondary road."

Curtis dropped his coffee cup in the sink and grabbed the paper. "How was she killed?"

"She had a rope tied around her feet and pulled tight along her back, then looped around her neck. The way the ropes were rigged up, she slowly strangled herself."

Curtis scanned the page, taking in the details. "What did Khilt say in his interview? *…she really felt tied down by the business.* Ropes. Past tense. What do you think? Is he telling us that's how he killed her?"

Stan sucked in a quick breath. "Jesus, that's possible."

Curtis felt the energy pulsing between them. "Get everything you can on the Napa case." He read the victim's name. "Erica Klein. Have whoever handled the investigation forward copies of what they have to us. Maybe we can help them put this one in the books."

"Yeah, we have a bit of a problem there," Stan said.

Curtis stopped breathing. "What sort of problem?"

"They've already arrested someone for Klein's murder. He's in custody awaiting trial."

Curtis sucked in a long, deep breath. "And how did they respond to you asking questions?"

"Not well. Not well at all," Stan said. "I was lucky to get that out of them." He pointed to the single sheet of paper.

"Shit," Curtis said. "How successful was Ms. Klein?"

"Very, and she comes from money. Big money."

"Napa was under some pressure for an arrest."

"Yeah. Remind you of anyone?"

Curtis raised an eyebrow. "Sure, but we're not putting an innocent guy in jail."

High profile cases usually raised the bar for the investigating officers, and if the dead person was influential enough, it would land on a politician's desk. That escalated things even further, and news coverage could get citizens in the area clambering for an arrest. It was like a self-perpetuating problem that sometimes led to the police forcing the pieces of the puzzle to fit. Which in turn could lead to a wrongful arrest. Whether that had happened in Erica Klein's murder was uncertain, but there was one thing Curtis was sure of. If the Napa cops had a suspect languishing in a prison cell, and a grateful public, they were going to be less than hospitable to another cop flying in from the other side of the country and dredging up facts that might reopen the case. This was not going to be easy.

"Who did you speak with?" Curtis asked.

"Brent Keely. He was the lead investigator on the file."

"Homicide detective?"

"Yes."

"Okay, jot his number down and I'll call him. You didn't give anything away, did you?"

"You mean that we think they might have the wrong guy?" Stan asked and Curtis nodded. "Christ, no." He took the sheet of paper from Curtis, wrote down a number prefixed with a California area code, and handed it back.

Curtis headed for his office, then stopped and said, "Stan, get Corrine Wheeler on the phone. It's time I talked with her, but for God's sake, don't let anyone know." Corrine was the department psychologist, and she knew what made serial killers tick.

"Yeah, no shit."

Curtis closed his door and sat in the leather chair, staring at the phone. He had to make the call, but even before dialing Brent Keely's number, he knew what the outcome was going to be. There was no way the Napa cops were going to share information on an active file over the phone or by email. There was only one way to get that information, and that was to fly out to San Francisco. And if he *was* to mention that he thought they had the wrong guy in prison, the files could snap shut tighter than a frog's sphincter.

Flying out to the west coast while the heat was on at home risked bringing the brass to his door, demanding to know why he had left the city. Right now though, he was reticent to lay his cards on the table. He could send Stan or Aislinn, they were more than competent, but he wanted to handle this himself. Khilt was playing them, and cornering this guy was going to take more than just deductive reasoning. No, if someone was going to Napa to speak with Brent Keely and look over the Klein file, it was him.

He reached for the phone and dialed the number, starting with the California area code.

# CHAPTER TWENTY-FIVE

Brian Newman totaled the bill and smiled. Ten hours of legal work would buy him a couple of weeks at the Grand Flamenco in the Dominican Republic. Half of the hours were coded as *meeting with the client* and *research*, the other half for a quick court appearance. Billable hours were a touchy subject with lawyers, but Newman wasn't overly concerned. Most of his clients were drug dealers who came in with wads of cash, peeled off a handful of hundreds and threw the bills on his desk like poker discards. That was the upside of representing that sort of clientele. The downside was when he couldn't beat the charges and they blamed him. He had three capped teeth and two nasty scars as a testament.

Newman opened his top drawer and pulled out a bottle of Jack Daniels. It was well after noon, almost two o'clock, and time for a drink. He tipped the bottle and guided the smooth brown liquid into the glass, took a sip and looked back to his paperwork. God, this one was good.

Some schmuck had brought his teenager in, hoping a criminal defense lawyer could use a loophole to get the kid off. What he got was five court appearances leading to a guilty plea and a bill in the thousands, but what the hell, giving someone a break was the Salvation Army's job. Brian Newman was living proof of why a lot of people hate lawyers.

There was a sharp rap on his outer door and he took a quick glance in the mirror. He was tired and his face was beginning to get lines, some from the strains of the job, but mostly from the alcohol. He smoothed his hair and pulled on his suit jacket. "Come in."

The door swung open and a large man stood framed in the doorway. He looked street wise and tough, and Newman immediately pegged him as Irish and into drugs. The man strode into the room, his body relaxed and fluid.

"You Brian Newman?" he asked.

"Yeah, I'm Newman." He took off his glasses and wiped them with a Kleenex. "What can I help you with?" Another drug dealing lowlife, he figured, who'd got himself caught with a handful of crack.

Newman barely saw the man move when he came straight across the desk, scattering files and pens on the floor. He bowled over the lawyer and sent him flying back into the wall. His neck snapped forward from the impact and there was a blinding flash of light, then nothing.

When he woke it was dark and there was an odor, irritating at first, then almost unbearable. It reminded him of rotting meat, and he thought he might be sick to his stomach. He tried to raise himself but his wrists were bound and he couldn't move his arms more than an inch. His head throbbed and there was a weird metallic taste in his mouth. The floor beneath him was concrete, damp and slimy. He felt the bile rising and was powerless to stop it. He vomited, again and again, until all that was left was the dry heaves. A heavy metal door opened and a stream of light flowed into the room. He glanced up at the person entering and shuddered. It was the man who had come across his desk at him.

"You're awake." Joey McGinley's baritone resonated off the stone walls. "That's good. I've got a few questions for you."

"What do you want?" Newman asked, trying to sit up but slipping in his own vomit.

"What do I want?" McGinley asked. "I want a million dollars. And you're going to help me get it."

"What the hell are you talking about?" Newman said, his head threatening to come apart.

McGinley squatted down so his face was only a couple of feet from Newman's. "You have Renee Charlesbois. And when I get her from you, I get a million dollars. So, I just need to know where you're keeping her."

"What? You're fucking crazy. I have no idea where she is."

McGinley smiled. It sent a shiver through Newman's body. "Yeah, that's what I thought you'd say. I've got a few tricks up my sleeve to make you talk."

Newman was almost hysterical. "I didn't have anything to do with her disappearance. Nothing. You've got to believe me." His voice was close to a scream.

McGinley opened a plastic case and pulled out a cordless drill. He fitted a small-bore drill bit in the chuck and tightened it. "You're going to have to convince me, you piece of fucking lawyer trash."

Newman heard the sound of the drill, then an excruciating pain shot up from his knee to his brain. He screamed but the bit kept boring into his bone and tendons. And every time he stopped screaming long enough to suck in more air, he heard Joey McGinley laughing.

# CHAPTER TWENTY-SIX

Corrine Wheeler called at three-fifteen. Curtis closed his door and took the call in private.

"I want to fly something by you," he said. "What we'll be talking about has to be kept in the strictest confidence."

"Of course, Curtis. As always."

Corrine Wheeler was the resident shrink for the Boston Police Department. She preferred not to be called a profiler, but it was the catchphrase that prime time television had made popular, and that's what she was. Wheeler was a couple of years into her sixties and had a world of experience. She was all business when a detective came to her with the profile on a perp.

"It's the Charlesbois case, Corrine. I'm getting some ominous rumblings here. The investigation is going a direction that worries me."

"How so?" she asked, her voice even but obviously intrigued.

"It's starting to look like the guy who grabbed Renee has done this before. If I'm right, he killed the last woman he abducted." Curtis spent the next ten minutes filling Wheeler in on the details. The man at Chloe Harrah's party and Liem Khilt turning out to be the same person, and the embedded clues in his conversations and at the hotel. She interrupted on occasion to ask him a question, but mostly let him speak. When he was finished there was silence on the line for a few moments.

"You suspect you might have a serial killer on your hands," she said.

"Yes," Curtis responded. "That's what it's starting to look like."

"I don't know. I made some notes while you were talking and this is like nothing I've ever seen or heard. If your guy is a serial killer, he's outside the box. Before I speculate on what you might be dealing with, I'd like to see a written text of Khilt's interview when he was at the precinct. Write down whatever you can remember from the conversation at Chloe's party and have Aislinn or Stan run it over to my house later tonight. I'll look at it when I get home."

"Thanks, Corrine. You're the best."

"No problem. I'll call when I have something."

"Call my cell. I may not be in Boston."

"Napa?" she asked.

"Yup, Napa."

He hung up, leaned back in his chair and stared at the pictures on the wall. Aside from one of his parents, every picture was of his dog. Barclay chasing a ball, Barclay with a rope toy in his mouth, Barclay ready to shake a paw. Not even a picture of a girlfriend. The truth was, he was reluctant to draw a woman into his life. He dealt with death every day, and that wasn't something easily shared. Street cops dealt with violence—robberies, rapes, domestic disputes—but homicide cops crossed the line into an entirely new realm of insanity. Curtis tried to leave work at the office, but for someone in his position that was almost impossible. For a moment he felt a wave of loneliness. He sat up and shook it off. Finding Renee Charlesbois was what mattered right now.

He opened the contacts icon on his cell phone and dialed his travel agent. She booked him a flight for San Francisco, departing at six-eighteen that evening, and she knew an excellent hotel in Napa she'd try to get him in. Curtis paid a premium and left the return flight open. He hung up, made sure his cell phone was charged, and stopped by Aislinn Byrne's desk on the way out.

"You off to California?" Aislinn asked.

"Yeah. I'll probably be back by Sunday at the latest. That puts me out of the office tomorrow and Saturday. I just talked with the mayor, and he'll likely call the police commissioner and Renee's father. They should be okay for a day or two. You guys can hold the fort while I'm gone."

"Not a problem."

"And if the mayor calls or stops in, don't mention Khilt. That's one thing we need to keep close to our chest right now. He's getting desperate for something to release to the media."

"What about Angela Burton?" Aislinn asked, referring to the *Globe* reporter Curtis had been keeping in the loop. "What should I tell her?"

"That I needed a break." He grinned. "A little west coast sunshine."

Aislinn glanced out the window at the clear, summer sky. "I don't think that'll work."

"Deal with it," Curtis said. "Angela's not so bad, Aislinn."

"She's a barracuda."

"And you're not?" He checked his briefcase for the Charlesbois file and snapped it shut. "It's one day out of the office. If anyone asks, tell them we're working other cases."

"Okay."

"Oh, one more thing. I want you to drop off transcripts of Khilt's interview and my conversation with him at Corrine Wheeler's house."

"We don't have email?"

"No way this stuff is going online," Curtis said.

"You have her address?"

"I'll text it to you."

Curtis ducked out before anyone could get their hooks into him and rode the elevator to the parking garage. He thought back over his conversation with Brent Keely, the lead investigator on Erica Klein's murder. Keely was tight-lipped, but seemed a reasonable sort, especially when Curtis had told him he needed to piggyback on Klein's investigation with one of their own. He made no mention of the fact that they might have the wrong man in jail.

Which, in turn, got Curtis to thinking. *Did* Napa Homicide have the wrong man in jail? Right now it was complete speculation on his part that Liem Khilt was tied to Erica Klein's death. The entire Napa

connection was based on a conversation with a man they strongly suspected had abducted Renee Charlesbois. But again, with no concrete
proof this trip to Napa could be a total waste of time. As he thought
about it, he began to wish it *was* off course, because if he was right they
had a serial killer on their hands.

And he had Renee Charlesbois.

Curtis felt a chill creep down his backbone.

# CHAPTER TWENTY-SEVEN

Curtis Westcott left his car in the underground lot at District A-1 and caught a cab to the water taxi that serviced Logan International. He was in plenty of time for his flight and used his laptop to check his email. There was a confirmation for his room at the Napa Valley Lodge, close to the precinct where Brent Keely had led the homicide investigation on Erica Klein.

His travel agent had provided information on a second hotel, this one in the vicinity of Frog's Leap Winery. Shady Oaks Country Inn, on Zinfandel lane, was her recommendation. Google maps showed it was close by, which was good as the traffic through the valley was slow. That should work nicely. He planned on starting with the police report in Napa, then moving north up the valley to see if he could find a connection to Frog's Leap.

The flight boarded and he found his seat and tucked himself in for the ride. He was tired and leaned his head against the bulkhead and closed his eyes. Maybe, by some miracle, he would get some sleep.

His mind wandered and eventually landed on what sort of evidence the Napa police had on the suspect they arrested for Erica Klein's murder. It could well be their case was airtight and he would end up flying back to Boston feeling foolish. But somehow, he doubted it. There was a connection between Boston and Napa. Khilt, or whatever his real name was, was manipulating them like a puppeteer. Every time he pulled a string, it suggested a direction to take the case. What they needed, was to figure out why. Liem Khilt was likely a lot of things, but he was no fool. Curtis had learned quickly in his career that the most dangerous thing to do in police work was to underestimate your opponent's abilities. There was not a chance that would happen here.

He felt the jet shudder as it left the ground, the plane's engines humming as they propelled countless thousands of pounds to thirty-five thousand feet. About twenty minutes into the flight, the pilot throttled back and they settled in for five hours at cruising altitude. He kept his eyes closed and prayed for sleep.

Aislinn Byrne and Stan Lamers were handling things at A-1, as they had many times in the past. This time, things were different. The wheels would come flying off if something went wrong with Charlesbois' insane reward. There was also the possibility the mayor could go off the deep end if he found out his lead detective was in Napa. None of that could be helped and he pushed it to the back of his mind. He thought of Corrine Wheeler, sitting at home drafting a profile on Renee's abductor. She had sounded convinced that Khilt was outside the usual parameters for a serial killer. On the other hand, she hadn't seen the entire contents of the file. He had taken a few courses on psychotic behavior, and even with the limited knowledge he had of how serial killers think and act, he had to agree with her. But if his guy *was* involved in Erica Klein's death and Renee Charlesbois' disappearance, and he *wasn't* a serial killer, then what or who the hell was he?

Khilt had showed up at the restaurant's opening, disabled the video surveillance system in the parking garage and snatched Renee Charlesbois without leaving a solitary clue. He had crashed Chloe Harrah's party, steered the conversation in exactly the direction he wanted while disguised, then disappeared without a trace. He reappeared at the precinct, sat in a locked room with three of Boston's top homicide detectives and told them exactly what he wanted to without any of them realizing who he was or what he was saying.

Why?

That was the question on Westcott's mind. Why go to all this trouble? It must have been a logistical nightmare to arrange everything with such perfection. And to what end? Crimes, especially kidnappings and murders, have motive associated with them. Always. There had to be a motive tucked away in this quagmire somewhere.

Khilt's cold eyes appeared in the blackness, dark, cruel, and focused on him. Slowly the image faded until there was just darkness. He tried to pull more pictures from his mind's archive, but there was only the drone of the plane and an impenetrable screen of black.

He heard a voice in the distance. Someone was calling to him. They didn't know his name and he ignored them, wishing them away. They wouldn't leave. Finally, he simply asked them what they wanted.

"Well, sir," the voice said. "We would like you to wake up and collect your luggage. We've arrived in San Francisco and we're waiting for you so the crew can deplane."

Curtis opened his eyes, sat up and shook his head. A flight attendant was leaning over the seat, a worried expression on her face. Two more were standing in the isle, watching. When he stood up, he banged his head on the overhead bin. He glanced back through the plane's fuselage. It was completely empty. He squeezed between the seats and grabbed his carry-on.

"Sorry," he said. "Thank the pilot for the smooth flight."

"I'll do that, sir," she said.

Curtis made his way into the terminal, his mind and body now waking up. He felt rejuvenated, and relaxed. He glanced at his watch. He had slept for almost five hours without a break. It was the best sleep he'd had in days. A smile crept across his face as he picked up his luggage. He couldn't remember the last time he had felt this good.

Alamo had his reservation and he steered the car out of the parking lot and headed north for the bay area. It was a quarter after ten and the sun had already set. The freeway was a blur of lights, but his senses were heightened, his mind whirring. Traffic was moving well and he made good time through the city, stopping for a quick bite at a restaurant in San Rafael. It was after one in the morning when he finally arrived at the Napa Valley Lodge. The lights were on in the main lobby and the night clerk, an elderly man with a full head of silver hair, was waiting when he walked in."

"Mr. Westcott?" he asked.

"Yes," Curtis said.

"You're the only guest not checked in yet," the clerk said. "I assumed it was you."

"Of course," Curtis said. "You'll need a credit card?"

"Yes, please. We have a fine room for you and a complimentary breakfast is included. There is a pool if you like to swim, but it's not open until six."

Curtis signed the credit card authorization and smiled. "Thanks." He declined the man's offer of help with his single suitcase and went in search of his room.

The clerk hadn't oversold things. The room was large and sparkling clean, with a comfortable sofa and a fifty-inch flat screen television. Curtis glanced at the bed, figuring at this point sleep was the last thing he needed. He set his bag on the floor and returned to the car. Napa's streets were deserted and he drove around for a few minutes before merging onto Highway 29 and heading north through Yountville and Oakville, then east on Rutherford Cross. He missed the turn for Frog's Leap on the first pass and turned around at Silverado Trail, then drove slowly on the reverse trip, watching for the signage. Even at a crawl he almost missed it again. Finally, he turned and drove slowly up the winding drive.

Curtis had visited Frog's Leap once in the past on a wine tour. The name had sparked a memory when Khilt mentioned it in the interview, and he was questioning the coincidence. He didn't like or trust coincidences. Of all the wineries in Napa, or the world for that matter, why Frog's Leap? Perhaps it was nothing. Still, Khilt had mentioned Frog's Leap specifically, and he didn't appear to waste words. Curtis figured that somehow, Frog's Leap would fit into Khilt's puzzle.

There was a brightly painted red barn that housed the tasting room at the top of the road, and he pulled up and switched off the motor. An eerie silence settled in as Curtis got out of the car and walked across the drive, the gravel crunching under his feet. He stopped at the edge of a field of old, withered vines, gnarled and twisted from years of exposure to the hot sun. The moon was in its last quarter, and he could see the Napa hills silhouetted against the night sky. There was no wind and he stood alone in the darkness, with only his thoughts to fill the void.

What had brought him here? What had happened to Erica Klein? And how did her death relate to Renee Charlesbois' disappearance?

He needed some answers.

Tomorrow he would look in the Klein file and talk to the man charged with her murder. Tomorrow, hopefully, the answers would begin to worm their way out of Liem Khilt's labyrinth.

# CHAPTER TWENTY-EIGHT

The Napa Police Department was on First Street, two short blocks south of the town center. Four cruisers were parked diagonally outside the white stucco building and Curtis pulled in next to one of the squad cars and made his way to the front door. The air conditioning was a welcome relief from the heat, even at eight-thirty in the morning. He glanced about the precinct, absorbing the sights and sounds of yet another police station.

Without fail, they all showed the wear and tear from the steady flow of foot traffic through the main door to the offices and holding cells. The grey carpets were beginning to wear and paint was rubbed bare in a few places around the chairs in the waiting room. The interior of the building was a large bullpen with about fifteen desks, surrounded by private offices. There was no receptionist, just a uniformed officer who approached the front counter when Curtis rang the bell. He listened to Curtis's request, checked his ID, then buzzed him through and pointed to the back of the precinct.

"Corner office," he said.

Curtis found Brent Keely in his office, hunched over a pile of paperwork. The detective was wearing a long-sleeved shirt, which Curtis found odd. It was already eighty-five degrees outside and the mercury hadn't topped out yet. Keely glanced up as Curtis approached. He closed the file, stood up and offered his hand.

"Brent Keely," he said. "You must be Curtis Westcott."

"Guilty," Curtis said, accepting the hand. They exchanged business cards.

"Have a seat," Keely said. He was average height and build with a slight paunch. Curtis put his age at thirty-eight, give or take a year. His hair was sun-dyed blond with slightly darker roots and he sported a bushy mustache on his thin face.

"So what brings a Boston homicide cop out to Napa Valley?" He glanced at Curtis' business card. "Commander of Homicide, in fact."

"Just a title, Brent. I'm interested in the Erica Klein file," Curtis said, easing into the conversation with the man's first name. "By the look of things, we have an open file with some similarities to the case involving the Klein woman. I thought having a look through your files might help our investigation."

"What have you got?" Keely asked.

"A woman disappeared, never turned up. A couple of things led us to the valley and one of the wineries just east of St. Helena." Curtis was careful with his words. He wouldn't lie to Keely, but wasn't about to spill the details of the Charlesbois case either. Not unless he had to.

"You think Arnold Baker was involved in your gal's disappearance?" Keely asked.

Curtis shrugged. "Don't know. Like I said, we've got a couple of clues pointing this way. Nothing more right now. It may be a dead-end, but I'd like to check it out."

"What do you need?" Keely asked, taking a sip of coffee. "Sorry, you want a cup?" he asked, pointing to his mug.

"No, had three with breakfast. I'm already wired. But thanks for asking." He sat thoughtfully for a minute, then said, "I'd like to leaf through your file and then maybe talk with your perp. Find out his whereabouts when our crime was committed."

"Well now, I don't see that as being possible," Keely said.

"Why not?" Curtis was struggling now to control his emotions. Coming all this way from Boston was going to be a complete waste of time if Keely slammed the book shut on the Klein case.

"Baker isn't a traveling kind of guy. He's lived all of his life in the valley. I don't think he's ever been to the east coast."

Curtis felt a wave of relief, but kept his face a mask. Keely's comment was about Arnold Baker. The murder book might still be on the table. "Sometimes these guys have lives we don't know about. I don't have to tell *you* that," Curtis said.

Keely chuckled. "No kidding. Christ, we see some stuff, don't we?"

"We certainly do."

Keely leaned over and grabbed a thick yellow file from the edge of his desk. "Here it is, all ready for you. Even got a place for you to sit."

"Thanks," Curtis said, accepting the file. He followed Keely through the bullpen to a scratched-up oak desk in the corner. There was an older computer and a phone, and a window next to the desk that provided some natural light.

"This is great." Curtis sat in the chair and opened the file. "Thanks again."

"Not a problem." Keely headed back to his desk and the mound of work.

Curtis slipped the thick elastic off the yellow folder and opened it. Inside was a bio sheet on the victim with all her background information, the Medical Examiner's report and notes on persons of interest. Curtis read the particulars. Erica Klein had been driving home from a wine tasting at Sutter Home, one of the more noted wineries in the Napa region, when she disappeared. Her BMW was found abandoned on Zinfandel Lane, an east west road that cut through the valley, linking Highway 29 and Silverado Trail. Her estate was east of Silverado Trail and she had been driving home on her usual route. That had them thinking her abduction may have been planned.

She had gone missing late on June 16th, and her body had turned up in a ditch on the 30th. Two weeks to the day. Her stomach contents indicated she had been well fed and hydrated, but her body was filthy. The CSU team dug some dirt out from under her fingernails, which were mostly broken off, but were unable to pinpoint its origin. Because the soil composition varied considerably in the valley, nailing an exact location wasn't possible. They were pretty sure that Erica Klein had been held somewhere in Napa for at least part of the two weeks she was missing. With that information, the investigation began to focus on the possibility that her abductor was a local.

They had few other clues to work with. The rope that strangled her was garden variety, available at any home improvement store. There were no witnesses, except one woman who had come forward with the license plate number off a red 1995 GMC Jimmy. The SUV was seen driving eastward on Zinfandel Lane just before Erica Klein's body was discovered. The driver of the truck was Arnold Baker, an employee with Zeuker's, a local store specializing in paint and lumber. They also stocked the same rope that was used to kill Erica Klein.

Arnold Baker was brought in for an interview, grilled for almost three hours, then released. Processions of other people, many from the wine tasting at Sutter Home, were brought in for routine questioning. Nothing. Then the police got a break. A friend of Erica's identified Arnold Baker as the man who she had seen parked in a red SUV at the intersection where Erica's private drive left the main road. Brent Keely had secured a search warrant for his house, and during the search they had uncovered a utility knife with traces of rope on the blade that matched the rope wrapped around Klein's neck. A further search of the garage turned up a length of rope identical to that which had been used to kill Erica Klein. Baker was unable to provide an alibi for the night Klein was abducted, other than he was at home watching television. Despite the evidence being entirely circumstantial, they charged him with second-degree murder.

Curtis leaned back in the chair and rubbed his hands across his temples. There was no other evidence. They had no witnesses who could put Baker at the scene of the crime, no idea where he had kept her for the two-week period, and no motive. What they had was a marginal suspect and a public clamoring for someone's head. What they had, Curtis thought, was a wrongful arrest.

He leaned forward and delved into the thickest part of the file—interviews with potential witnesses. He concentrated on the conversations with the guests who had attended the wine tasting at Sutter Home. He was two and a half hours into the pile when he hit pay dirt.

Brent Keely had personally interviewed a male Caucasian, late thirties, described as average build and height and well dressed. He had dark hair and wore black-rimmed glasses.

"Holy shit," Curtis whispered. "Sounds like you. Is it?" He read the entire interview, from the top, barely stopping to breathe.

Keely: State and spell your name, please.

Response: Keith Mill. K-e-i-t-h M-i-l-l.

Keely: Were you at Sutter Home Winery on the evening of June 16th?

Mill: Yes.

Keely: Were you invited, Mr. Mill?

Mill: Sort of. I attended as Patrick Ashley's guest. Patrick was a personal friend of Erica Klein.

Keely: Had you ever met Erica Klein prior to the evening?

Mill: No. But I did get a chance to speak with her that evening.

Keely: Perhaps you can tell me what you talked about.

Mill: I arrived early, at five minutes after five. I remember, because I checked the time as I was walking up to the main doors. I had just flown in from Chicago and I reset my watch to local time. There were only a handful of people at such an early hour, and I milled about for a bit, then went for a walk in the garden behind the main building. I spent the better part of two hours in the gardens, south of the little river that runs through the property. They're very beautiful, you know. Reminded me of the setting for an Alex Haley novel. One of the gardeners was working, taking cuttings of the flowers. When I returned to the main building it was quite crowded and very loud. I found Patrick, talked with him for a bit, then mingled, tasting the new Cabernets and talking with the other guests. I was introduced to Erica Klein at seventeen minutes after eight…

Keely: How can you be so sure about the time?

Mill: It was getting on, and I had just glanced at my watch before another guest I was talking to introduced us. She was a very interesting woman, from a long line of vintners and well traveled. We talked at length about lots of things, but ended up spending a bit of time discussing Boston. The fellow who introduced us was from some suburb just outside the city. Anyway, he was a bit of a jerk. Made a stupid remark about one of the wines and Erica moved on. As did I. He moved around the room like a chicken with its head cut off, and ended up talking with a couple of shady looking characters. Rather a motley crew for such an upscale tasting.

Keely: Did you recognize any of these men?

Mill: No. But that's not unusual. I'm from south of San Francisco so I don't know a lot of the locals. You'd do better asking the other guests about them. Some of the locals may know who they are.

Keely: Did you speak with Ms. Klein again?

Mill: No.

Keely: Did you see her leave?

Mill: No.

Curtis stared at the words, the hairs on the back of his neck standing on end. "*Boston*. It's a location. *Seventeen minutes after eight*. That's a date." He could barely believe what was in front of him. "It *is* you."

He dug in and reread the interview two more times, then sat back and rubbed his eyes. Curtis was feeling sure of one thing. Keith Mill and Liem Khilt were the same person.

"Ahh, shit," he said, throwing the papers on the desk.

Corrine Wheeler was wrong. They had a serial killer on their hands.

# CHAPTER TWENTY-NINE

Stan Lamers parked just off Decatur Street, twenty feet shy of the yellow crime scene tape, and hung his detective's badge over his belt so it was visible. He nodded to the uniforms manning the perimeter as he ducked under the tape. Another homicide detective, Jay Robertson, was already working the scene. Robertson was mid-thirties, eight years with the force and Stan knew him from previous cases. He looked the same as he had a year ago when they had worked together—goatee and light blond hair cut short. Robertson steered Stan toward the water as he approached.

"What have you got?" Stan could see a lump under a sheet on the edge of the dock. Across the harbor, a world away, was the upscale neighborhood of Charlestown.

"Floater," Robertson replied. "We figure he's only been in the water a few hours, tops."

"Ah, damn," Stan said. "I hate floaters. Fucking gross—all bloated to shit."

Robertson gave Stan a grim look. "This one's not too far gone, but he's not pretty either. Someone tortured the poor bastard before they killed him."

"Tortured? Seriously?" Stan said and Robertson gave him a curt nod.

They arrived at the corpse, the off-white sheet stained red where blood had leached through. The morning sun was warming the body and the familiar stench of death hung in the air. Robertson leaned over and pulled back the cover. Dead eyes, still open, stared up. Even in death, the agony the man had endured was still there. The victim was naked and the first thing Stan noticed was the man's genitals. Or, more specifically, the lack of them. The entire package had been cut off, but not with any sort of surgical instrument. Jagged shards of skin hung down, evidence that a serrated knife had been used to remove the organ.

"Aww, shit," Stan said, swallowing back bile. "What a fucking mess."

"They did a job on him all right," Robertson said.

Cigarette burns peppered the fleshy areas, many of them burned through to the bone, and dozens of small round holes covered the man's joints.

"What the hell?" Stan said, leaning closer to look. "Are those from a drill bit?"

"That's what we think," Robertson replied. "Whoever did this drilled right into his bones."

"Got a positive ID yet?" Stan asked, motioning for the attending uniform to cover the body.

"Yeah. One of the uniforms who responded recognized him from court. His name is Brian Newman, and he's a criminal lawyer whose clients are mostly drug dealers."

"Guess someone wasn't happy with the verdict." Stan moved back from the scene and lit a cigarette. He felt sick to his stomach. "Any idea where they worked him over?"

"CSU hasn't done their thing yet. Could be close by, there's not much current in the harbor."

"Yeah, and lots of vacant warehouses around the waterfront," Stan said, staring at a handful of pleasure craft from the Chelsea Yacht Club that were sailing past, heading for the Inner Harbor. It was another normal summer's day for them. Not so normal for Brian Newman. At least he was dead now. What he had gone through must have been unbelievably cruel.

"Guilty verdict," Robertson said. "I guess shit like this happens."

Stan gave the younger man a sideways glance. He was bigger, meaner and had been on the force a lot longer than Robertson and he didn't appreciate being told what happens. He already knew what happens. Robertson caught the look and interpreted it correctly. He shut up and waited for Stan to give him directions.

"Wait for CSU," Stan said. "I doubt if they'll need any babysitting on this one. Hang around until they get going, then back to the precinct and file a report. Check on next of kin and if they're in Boston, make the trip personally."

"You got it," Robertson said, glad the uncomfortable moment was over.

Stan took a last glance at what was left of Brian Newman and ambled slowly back to his car. Christ, as if they didn't have enough to do with the Charlesbois case on their hands. He had one thought as he tucked away his badge and slipped into his ride, and that was at least this one would be pretty straightforward.

He had no idea how wrong he was.

# CHAPTER THIRTY

Curtis knew there was nothing to be gained from speaking with Arnold Baker. At least, nothing for him. For Baker, the visit might be a life saver. The man was incarcerated for a crime he didn't commit, and average guys who find themselves in prison sometimes think of suicide. It would be cruel not to let Baker know that there was at least one person on the outside who thought he was innocent.

The Napa police were holding him in the remand cells adjoining the station, and Brent Keely authorized the visit and escorted him back to the holding area. It was a typical set-up, with an administration desk for booking in new prisoners and three locked metal doors leading to the cells. Keely and Westcott checked their weapons and moved through the series of sliding doors, waiting for the one behind them to close and lock before the one ahead would open. They reached a long hallway with cells on either side, and Keely walked past six empty ones before stopping. A solitary man sat on the concrete bed, a thin mattress between him and the unforgiving stone. He glanced up as Keely relayed the message through his two-way radio to open the door. Keely waited until Curtis was in the cell and the door closed before heading back to the admin area.

"Just yell down the hall when you're finished," he said. "There's a microphone above the entrance doors. The guards will come and get you."

Arnold Baker watched Curtis with scared eyes as the visitor sat on the other end of the bed. Curtis glanced about the room. It was small, with off-grey walls and a stainless-steel toilet and sink crammed in the sixty square foot space. An innocent man in hell, Curtis thought.

"I'm Curtis Westcott," he said, not bothering to offer Baker his hand. "I'm with the Boston Police Department."

"Boston?" Baker said. A tiny light briefly lit the man's eyes, then flickered out. He was an average man in every part of his makeup. The kind of man you would walk by on the sidewalk and not even notice. Curtis estimated him to be about five-eight, one-sixty, with thinning sandy-blond hair and no distinguishing facial features, save for slightly thicker eyebrows than most people.

Curtis leaned over so he was close to Baker. "What I'm going to say to you must remain between you and me. It can go no further. If it does, it could be very bad for you. Do you understand?"

Baker straightened up and nodded. His eyes were locked on his visitor. "Okay," he said.

"I know you didn't kill Erica Klein," Curtis said. "I'm going to do everything I can to get you out of here. If Keely and the other cops find out I'm trying to dig up evidence that would jeopardize the case they're building against you, they'll shut down any access I have to the file. It would be bad if that were to happen."

A suspicious look crept across Baker's face. "This is weird," he said. "A cop from Boston shows up and tells me he knows more about Erica's death than the local cops. You got any ID?"

Curtis slipped out his badge and a business card. "My being here isn't by chance, Arnold." He handed him the card after Baker had scrutinized the detective's badge. "Erica Klein's death may be linked to a woman's disappearance in Boston. Evidence is starting to point toward the same guy being involved. And from what Detective Keely has told me, the evidence they have against you is circumstantial. They don't have anything linking you directly to her death."

"That's 'cause I didn't do it," Baker said. "I never even met the woman."

"Were you sitting in a red SUV near her driveway the night she was abducted?"

"Yes."

"Why?"

"I was meeting a friend and we were heading into Rutherford for a few drinks. We often met at that intersection. It's got a place where you can pull off the road and park."

"And the rope and exactor blade they found in your house?"

"I bought that gear from Zeuker's, where I work. I kept the rope for doing stuff around the house. Nothin' suspicious about that."

Curtis nodded. "Okay. Did you see anything the night she went missing that might be able to help me? Did any vehicles drive by? Anything at all."

"There's a bit of traffic on that road. It services the entire east side of the valley. Mostly locals, not as many tourists as the west-side highway. I was parked there waiting for Gus for about twenty minutes. Probably thirty or forty cars and trucks went past."

"Any of them stand out?"

"Yeah. Zack drove by in his plumbing truck. He's got a paint job you can't miss. Looks like the incredible hulk with a plumbing wrench."

Curtis was silent for a few seconds, then quietly said, "Arnold, I'm going to get you out of here. You need to hang in there until I can figure out who did this. When I do, I'll make sure that Detective Keely gets all the evidence so he can release you. Okay?"

There was no smile, but Baker's eyes held a glimmer of hope. "Yeah, that sounds good."

Curtis patted the man on the knee, then rose and leaned against the bars and yelled for the guard. A few seconds later the door clanged open and a young deputy in a starched brown uniform walked crisply down the corridor and opened the door. Curtis followed the man from the holding cells and found Keely waiting for him at the admin desk.

"Well, did you get anything useful?"

Curtis shrugged. "Maybe. Baker's just one small piece of the puzzle. I've got a lot of ends to try and tie together. I'll let you know if anything comes of it."

"Sure, you do that," Keely said. They shook hands and Curtis returned to the parking lot and the burning afternoon sun.

He sat in the rental, the air conditioner on full blast. Boston was warm in the summer, but nothing like this. The superheated air trapped next to the ground was harsh on his throat and he swallowed some warm water to keep from coughing. He put the car into gear and started north on the highway.

First some lunch, then a trip to Frog's Leap, followed by taking time to review Keely's notes from the Erica Klein case. He had a lot to go through today. He wondered how Stan and Aislinn were faring in his absence. His key people were both very capable, but if the mayor or Jacques Charlesbois decided to cause trouble, they would be put to the test. Liem Khilt, or Keith Mill, or whoever the bastard was, had led him here. The clues were starting to pile up, and if Khilt thought he could keep disgorging information and not get caught, he was sorely wrong. To Curtis, there were only two options for how this could end.

With Khilt in jail. Or dead.

# CHAPTER THIRTY-ONE

Tommy Strand was shuffling papers from Admin to Vice when the call came through on his cell. The number was blocked, and his heart quickened slightly. Joey McGinley always blocked his number. He sidled into an alcove in the hallway and took the call. It was McGinley's voice on the other end.

"Tommy, we've got to meet," the drug dealer said.

"I'm working," Strand said quietly. "Can't get away until after five."

"Okay. Five-fifteen at the warehouse on Condor," McGinley said. "Be on time."

"Everything okay, Joey?" Strand asked. "You find that guy we were talking about?"

"Yeah, I found him. Everything's fine. I'll see you at a quarter after five."

"Good, Joey. Quarter after five." The line clicked over to a dial tone and Tommy Strand leaned against the wall for support. He couldn't cope with the job anymore and he felt a massive weight come off his shoulders. Five hundred thousand dollars. Christ, he was set for life. He'd say good-bye to the guys at BPD and head somewhere warm. Thailand, maybe. He'd heard you could live on the beach with a local to help out for two thousand US a month. It would be the new start he needed.

His hands were shaking as he went back to delivering documents. He gave the Vice desk sergeant a smile, and the man smiled back, but Tommy was somewhere else. He had his ticket out.

Aislinn Byrne stopped in her tracks and stared at the computer screen on Jay Robertson's desk. Robertson slowly turned and glanced at her.

"Hey, Aislinn," he said. He turned back to the screen, where a photo of Brian Newman was staring back at them. "You know him?" he asked.

Aislinn looked closer. At first glance she had thought it was Liem Khilt, but a second look dispelled that. The shape of the face was similar, the hair and the glasses almost identical, but the chin was larger, the cheeks sallower, and the eyes definitely different. "Thought I did. Who is he?"

"Some defense lawyer who got himself killed and dumped in the Inner Harbor. Whoever did it tortured the crap out of him before they offed him. Never seen anything like it. Cut off the poor bastard's nuts."

Aislinn moved back toward the screen, her mind whirling. "When did he die?" he asked.

"Sometime last night. He'd only been in the water a couple of hours when someone spotted him floating next to one of the piers off Decatur." Robertson stroked his goatee, studying Byrne's face. "What's up?" he asked.

"Can you print that on the color LaserJet?" she asked.

"Sure."

"And Jay, whatever you've got on this Newman guy, I'd like to have it."

"Yeah, no problem."

"Thanks."

Aislinn returned to her cubicle and pulled the file on Liem Khilt. A grainy, but usable, color picture was front and center. She stared at it. The likeness to the dead lawyer was unbelievable. And so was the timing. Robertson appeared at the edge of her desk with a sheet of paper and Aislinn held the two photos side by side. No doubt about it, they were almost carbon copies. Liem Khilt, the suspect with a million-dollar bounty on his head, and Brian Newman.

But that line of reasoning brought a chilling thought with it. The picture of Liem Khilt had never been released to the public. In fact, to the best of her knowledge, aside from herself, no one but Curtis and Stan had seen Khilt's picture.

"What's going on?" Jay Robertson asked, looking at the two pictures.

Aislinn gave Robertson a quick glance. "Nothing good, Jay," she said. "Nothing good."

# CHAPTER THIRTY-TWO

Curtis knew a bit about Napa's history and as he drove north toward Yountville he wondered what it would look like now if the Wappo tribe still ruled the valley. Or the Mexicans, who had pushed them aside, only to be overthrown by the Anglos. There were still a few places where prickly pear cacti were the only signs of life, but nowadays much of the land was covered by vineyards, a practice started by a group of padres at Mission San Juan Capistrano. It was all about wine now.

"Well, it is what it is," he said to himself. Boston had changed a lot over the past two hundred years as well. Hell, everything had.

He passed the wooden structure of Trefethen Vineyards, the Tuscan-red building shimmering in the mid-day sun. The freeway traffic was moving fast, but Curtis knew that would end quickly once he hit Yountville, where the highway narrowed to two lanes. He reached the town, continued through and stopped for lunch at Mustard's Grill. He finished eating and headed north, crawling with the traffic.

About halfway between Yountville and Rutherford, he called Aislinn on her cell. She picked up on the third ring and wasted no time bringing Curtis up to speed.

"We plucked a floater out of the river today," she said. "Stan and I figure it could be tied to the Charlesbois case."

"How's that?" Curtis asked.

"This guy looked like Liem Khilt. Hair, facial shape, glasses, teeth, everything but the eyes. His picture was on Robertson's screen when I walked by and it stopped me in my tracks. I thought it was Khilt. Whoever killed him worked him over good first. Cigarette burns, drill holes in his knees and elbows. Sick bastard even cut off the guy's package."

The level of violence took even Curtis by surprise, and he felt his stomach turn. "You think he was tortured because someone thought he had Renee Charlesbois?"

"That's my guess."

"You and Stan and I are the only ones who have seen Khilt's picture."

"Yeah, I know, but it's the only thing that makes sense. I mean, there's a million dollars waiting for whoever gets Charlesbois' daughter back and this guy is an absolute double of Liem Khilt. Somehow, Khilt's picture got out on the street."

"Shit," Curtis said. They had a leak, but where, or who? "You said he was a floater. Do we have a crime scene?"

"Not yet. There isn't much current in the harbor where he was found and he'd only been in the water a short time. We have some units searching the nearby warehouses."

"Okay. In the meantime, I want you to have a chat with Jacques Charlesbois. Let him know that if this guy's murder is linked to his reward, we're going to be looking at laying charges against him. I want that reward canceled. Now."

"I'll make the call," Aislinn said. "But you know Charlesbois. He's not just going to go away. He wants his daughter back."

"We all do," Curtis shot back. "Try to get that through his thick head."

"I'll try."

Curtis shifted the conversation. "Aislinn, this thing in Napa is related to Renee's disappearance. I'll forward you everything I have on Erica Klein. Look for a common thread between her and Renee. Somehow, these two women are linked."

"Okay. I'll wait until I get the info before I call Charlesbois. He'll take an ass-chewing a little better if I can dangle a carrot."

"That's dangerous," Curtis said. "I don't want you to give Charlesbois too much."

"I understand," Aislinn said.

She spent the next few minutes running over where they were in the investigation. Not much had changed in Boston over the last twenty hours and most of the update was on procedure, not new leads. Curtis hung up and dialed another number. Corrine Wheeler answered.

"Do you have anything for me?" Curtis asked the psychologist.

"Maybe," she said. "But first, tell me what you found out in Napa."

Curtis gave her the full update, ending up with his speculations. "I'm sure the guy they have in jail for Erica Klein's murder didn't do it. And I think Liem Khilt was in Napa when Klein was killed. He came into the precinct for an interview, like he did in Boston."

"What makes you think it was him?" the profiler asked.

"He used exact times, like five after five and seventeen minutes after eight. And he mentioned Boston. He's taking care of the linkage blindness for us. He knows Napa and Boston don't share common databases, so he's giving us the connection."

There was a long silence on the line, and Curtis waited, figuring she was thinking things through. Finally, she said, "Yes, I agree. That's what he's doing. He's making sure the trail between his crimes doesn't end with police jurisdiction. He's giving you the connection to the previous crime, and by the looks of things, the next one as well. When he mentioned Napa, he said six-thirty. And Erica Klein was killed on June 30th. So if that is what he's trying to tell us, Renee Charlesbois is still alive. At least until August 17th. If that's what he means by seventeen minutes after eight."

"That's what I was thinking," Curtis said. "So we've definitely got a serial killer."

There was a brief silence, then the profiler said, "I'm not so sure about that. You have a man who is killing women, but these are not random. These murders are extremely well planned and not sexually motivated. Serial killers can be organized, although the vast majority of them fall into the disorganized category, but invariably the killings are sexual in nature. Was there any evidence that Erica Klein was raped?"

"No. Nothing showed up in the autopsy."

"As I suspected. Your guy has killed in the past, and will probably kill again. And if our assumption that seventeen minutes after eight means August 17th, and today is the 11th, then you have six days to find him."

"So there is a motive. Something connecting these women to our killer."

"My best guess would be yes. I think there's a reason behind what he's doing."

"Okay, Corrine, thanks. Call me if you get anything else."

"I will. Good luck, Curtis."

"Thanks."

He set the phone on the passenger's seat, his eyes on the car in front of him, his mind two thousand miles to the east. Erica Klein was dead, but if both he and Corrine Wheeler were correct, Renee Charlesbois was still alive. For the next week. The pieces of the puzzle were beginning to surface, but they were coming too slowly. Time was something he had precious little of.

Corrine's words rang true. *He's making sure the trail between his crimes doesn't end with police jurisdiction. He's giving you the connection to the previous crime, and by the looks of things, the next one as well.* Khilt wasn't stopping after Boston. Someone in New York was on his radar. It wasn't just Renee Charlesbois who would die if he failed to stop Khilt.

Curtis concentrated on driving, and headed east when he reached the town of Rutherford. He found the turn to Frog's Leap with no problem and drove up the access road, dust spewing up behind the rental. He pulled in by the red barn and checked his watch. Three o'clock. A few cars were in the parking lot and a couple exited the wine tasting center as he locked the car. The winery was open, which was a good thing, as many had odd hours and he hadn't called ahead. As he hurried to the building, a thought raced through his mind. Today was the 11th and the day was almost over. If Khilt decided to kill Renee Charlesbois early on August 17th, then they didn't have six days to find her.

They had five. He felt a wave of panic.

# CHAPTER THIRTY-THREE

Tommy Strand cursed the afternoon traffic jamming the Sumner Tunnel. Why did Joey McGinley have to pick East Boston to meet, especially in rush hour? Christ, the traffic under the Inner Harbor was already thick with cabs and shuttle buses heading for the airport before adding commuters to the mix. He finally reached the end of the tunnel and took the first off ramp. A couple of turns later and he pulled up in front of a derelict warehouse and cut the engine. It was almost five-thirty. He hoped Joey wouldn't be pissed.

Tommy pulled on the scarred brass handle and the door opened easily. He entered the building, the warmth of the afternoon sun replaced by a damp chill and darkness. He waited for a few seconds as his eyes adjusted, then made his way to where he knew Joey would be waiting.

He would have Renee Charlesbois. Joey wouldn't want his name involved and needed him to take the woman to the precinct. Yeah, that was it, Tommy thought as he walked through the cavernous space, his footsteps echoing off the empty racks. Joey needed him to deliver the woman. Then, when the money was paid out, he would take his five hundred large and give the rest to the drug dealer. Perfect.

He rounded a bank of shelves and saw a light in the office, barely visible through the dirty windows. He knocked on the door and entered. The room was empty except for a table and four chairs set in the middle. McGinley was sitting in one of the chairs and motioned for Tommy to join him.

"Thanks for coming, Tommy." He crushed out his cigarette in the overflowing ashtray. Smoke continued to drift up from the pile of butts. He ignored it. "Sit down. Make yourself comfy."

"Sure, Joey," Tommy said. He sat across the table from Joey. "You find her okay?"

"Well, I got a little bit of a problem there," Joey said. He folded his arms across his chest. "That lawyer didn't seem to know what I was talking about."

Tommy felt a slight movement of air in the room and turned back towards the door. Two men, both with guns in their hands, had entered the room. They shut the door behind them. Tommy looked back to Joey.

"Give me your gun, Tommy," Joey said, holding out his hand.

"I'm a cop, Joey. I can't just hand over my gun. It's against regulations." Sweat beaded on his forehead.

"Okay, Tommy. I understand."

A second later Strand's arms were pinned behind his back by one of the two men. The other slipped his hand inside Tommy's windbreaker, unsnapped the harness and removed the service pistol. The man tucked it in his belt, then bent over and frisked Tommy's ankles and legs for a second weapon. He shook his head and when Joey nodded both men backed off.

"I relied on you, Tommy." Joey McGinley leaned forward and the harsh light reflected off the scars that cut across his face. "And you gave me the wrong guy."

"No way, man. I saw the guy's picture into the Charlesbois file. It had to be him." Tommy saw where this was going and began to panic.

Joey leaned forward another few inches, his voice soft, but menacing. "It wasn't him, Tommy. Nobody could take what I gave him and not crack. Nobody." He leaned back in the chair. "You fucked up, Tommy."

Strand was visibly shaking now. "I'm sorry, Joey. I thought…"

"You thought," Joey cut in, his voice rising. "You fucking thought. I tortured a guy and then killed him because you thought. You fucking moron. I should kill you, Tommy."

"I'm a cop, Joey. Killing me is a very bad idea. I can make it up to you." He could feel vomit in his throat.

"Yeah, maybe," Joey said.

Strand swallowed back the bile and took a few shallow breaths. "Yeah, Joey, I can get you information on cases. I can make sure evidence disappears. There are lots of things I can do for you."

"Maybe," McGinley said slowly, letting both syllables roll off his tongue. "Then again, maybe not."

A gun appeared in his hand and in one motion Joey targeted Tommy Strand's head and fired. The bullet caught the cop directly between his eyes, crushing his frontal lobe and blowing a six-inch hole in the back of his head. The impact jerked Strand back in the chair and sent his body crashing to the floor. Blood pooled on the floor around the corpse.

"Aw, shit," one of the men said. "This motherfucker's blood is all over my jacket. Fuck, Joey, I just bought it."

McGinley set the gun on the table. "Go get another one." He stood up and moved towards the door. "And get rid of this sack of shit."

# CHAPTER THIRTY-FOUR

Brandy Eagleson spotted the new arrival from the air-conditioned interior of Frog's Leap wine tasting room. She liked looking out the window, watching the cars as they drove up and imagining who the people were and what they did for a living. It was a game that passed the time and she was getting quite good at it. She could nail the engineers almost every time. This one was different. She could tell that immediately.

He was well tanned, with thick black hair that swept back naturally from a sharply defined face. He wasn't wearing sunglasses, and even from a distance she could tell he was focused on something. This one wasn't a tourist sightseeing in the valley. He was here for something specific. She glanced in the mirror as he approached the main doors, smoothing her blouse over her waist and hips and pushing an errant strand of hair from her high forehead.

Brandy Eagleson was a local in every sense of the word. She had been born in the valley, schooled in the valley and married and divorced in the valley. Her birthday was in two weeks and she sure wasn't looking forward to turning thirty-five. She checked her look again in the mirror as the door opened and decided she looked fine.

Curtis entered and glanced about, his gaze meeting hers. She moved forward and smiled as it hit her—he was a cop.

"Welcome to Frog's Leap," she said.

"Thanks," Curtis said.

"What can I help you with today?" They were about six feet apart and she could feel his intensity.

Curtis withdrew his shield from his pocket and held it out. "I'm with the Boston police department," he said. "I'd like to speak with someone who knows the area."

"Boston? You're a ways from home, Mr..."

"Westcott. Curtis Westcott." He extended his hand and they shook.

"I'm Brandy Eagleson. I can probably help you. I grew up here," she smiled, "and I know the valley as well as anyone." She pointed to a quiet corner of the room and Curtis followed her. They stood in front of the window, the California sun radiating through the glass.

Curtis leaned against one of the display cases. "The name of your winery came up when we were interviewing someone."

"During an interview. That sounds dangerous," Brandy said.

Curtis grinned. It was a silly thing to say, but the way she said it made it work. "This fellow said that Frog's Leap was someone's favorite winery. Is there anything about Frog's Leap that would make a person say something like that?"

"Oh, we're very different," Brandy said. "We don't cater to the Robert Mondavi crowd. We're a small winery with a more intimate touch. No huge tasting rooms filled with hundreds of people." She glanced at the tasting area, which was only a few hundred square feet, to make her point. "We don't have a large selection of wines, but what we do have are very high quality. We're niche. I think our slogan says it all." She pointed to some writing on the wall.

*Time's fun when you're having flies.*

"That's cute," Curtis said.

"I think we have a little more fun here than most of the wineries."

"What about the caves where you store your wine while it ferments? Do you have any abandoned ones?"

She stopped smiling and gave him a long, hard look. "You mean, like a place where you could hide a body?"

"What makes you say that?" Curtis asked.

"Your badge says homicide on it."

Curtis was impressed. Brandy Eagleson, with her intense, deep teal colored eyes, was observant. "Okay," he said. "Why not? Some place where a person could hide a body."

She shook her head. "Nothing like that here, but there are probably a hundred wineries in the valley with unused caves. Hundreds, even. That was a problem when the police were searching for Erica Klein. There were too many abandoned wine cellars to check all of them. They still don't know where Arnold Baker kept her before he killed her."

"You know about the Klein murder?"

She raised one eyebrow. "Who doesn't? Everyone in the valley was talking about it. Erica Klein disappearing was big news. When they found her body I thought some of the locals were going to lead a lynching party. Erica was really nice. Everyone who met her liked her."

"Did you know her?"

"A bit. We'd met a few times, mostly because we were both in the wine business. I wouldn't say we were friends, but I did have coffee with her, one on one, about six months ago. We ran into each other in Napa and she asked if I had time to talk for a few minutes."

"What did you talk about?"

"Nothing in particular. Guys. Wine. Living in the valley. That sort of stuff." She was silent for a moment, then said, "Does your investigation have anything to do with Erica's death?"

Curtis shrugged. "I don't know. Maybe. Maybe not. As I said, when we interviewed this guy in Boston, he spoke of Frog's Leap. Would you mind reading over the transcript from the interview and seeing if anything stands out?"

She shook her head. "No, I wouldn't mind at all."

"I'll get the file," Curtis said. He walked to his car and brought his briefcase back into the winery. He handed her the interview with Liem Khilt. "Do you have a scanner I could use? I need to send something to my detectives in Boston."

"Police business?" Brandy asked.

"Yes." He held up his notes on the Klein file.

"We can send them from the office," she said. "I know the owners won't mind."

"Is it okay if I scan them myself?" Curtis asked. "The information in the file is confidential."

"Sure." She led him to an office on one side of the building. A multi-purpose printer sat on the desk. "Help yourself."

"Thanks." He nodded at Khilt's interview, which she was clutching. "How about you read through that while I send the file?"

"Sounds good."

Brandy retreated back to the wine tasting room, leaving Curtis alone with the scanner. He watched her lean against one of the counters and start reading the notes, a serious look on her face. Not many clients were out braving the afternoon heat and the winery was quiet. She glanced up as a fresh face walked through the door, but another employee was speaking to the newcomer and Brandy returned to the report. Curtis fed the final page into the machine and returned it to the file folder. He saved the file, sent it to both Stan and Aislinn's email, then deleted the file from the computer. Brandy was just finishing the interview as he approached.

"It sounds pretty generic," she said, shrugging her shoulders. "Nothing leaped out at me. He mentions Napa and Frog's Leap, but other than that, I don't think there's anything I could help you with."

"I'm going to give you a bit of an insight to our case, but it's extremely confidential. Are you okay with that?" he asked.

"I guess. Don't you guys usually keep this stuff under wraps?"

"Usually, but right now I don't think I have much time. If I'm right, the woman who's missing in Boston is still alive, but the clock is ticking. I need to connect the dots, and I need to do it quickly. If that means asking for help, then that's what I'm going to do. Okay?"

She nodded and Curtis continued. "I don't think what this guy says is what he means. There's a message in the conversation that goes beyond what it appears to be. For example, he says he arrived at six-thirty, and then talks about Napa in the next sentence."

"I don't see what you mean," Brandy said, looking puzzled.

"Erica Klein's body was found on June 30th. Thirtieth day of the sixth month. Six-thirty."

Brandy's hand went to her mouth. "Oh, my God," she said. The color drained from her face.

"In his next response to our question, he says our woman in Boston felt *really tied down*. He uses the past tense, and Erica Klein was strangled. Again, it appears that what he's saying is not what he means."

Brandy glanced at the interview. "I see, he shifts to the present tense when he says, *Ms. Charlesbois is a dedicated Red Sox fan*, then to the future tense when he talks about New York." She looked up at Curtis. "Is this the guy who killed Erica?"

Curtis nodded. "He could be. Right now the Napa police have Arnold Baker sitting in a jail cell for a crime he likely didn't commit. That's why I need you to be tight-lipped on this. I need time to figure out exactly what he's saying. But I'm sure of one thing. He didn't just stick Frog's Leap in here for fun. This winery is one of the keys to solving Erica Klein's murder."

She looked back to the pages in her hand and read the portion of the interview that touched on Napa. "*Yes, I spoke with her twice. Once, just after I arrived. That would be about six-thirty. We both enjoy wine, in particular from Napa Valley, and we spoke at some length about the different vintages and cellars. I think she mentioned that Frog's Leap was one of her favorites. She seemed to have a genuine love for the valley and knew every good and bad year. She made the bad ones sound like the Apocalypse.*" She pursed her lips and remained thoughtful for a moment. "I don't know. Strange he should use *Apocalypse*. The word is a little out of context."

Curtis nodded. "I agree. Does it tie in with the valley at all?"

She shrugged. "Not that I know of."

Curtis looked out the window at the fields and toward the hills in the east. "Do you think anyone would mind if I walked about a bit?"

"No, not at all. I'll come with you if you want. Answer questions if you have any."

"Are you sure that's okay with your boss?"

She grinned. "My uncle owns the winery. He's pretty easy going."

They walked out and Brandy led him to the Red Barn, a restored building built in 1884 that served as Frog's Leap's home base. It took the better part of an hour to walk the forty acres of surrounding farmland, and they arrived back at the Vineyard House just before four-thirty. Their conversation had been easy and varied, but always reverting to the issue at hand. That Curtis was looking for a murderer.

They reentered the main tasting building and he rubbed his temples, then ran his hands through his hair. "Is there anything in what he says that might tie in with Napa?"

Brandy spread the papers on one of the counters and reread the entire interview, her eyes pausing at times to let the words sink in. Finally, she said, "No. Nothing at all." She handed him the pages. "Sorry."

He dug in his pocket and pulled out a business card. He jotted his cell phone number on the back and handed it to her. "Thanks, Brandy. If you think of anything else, give me a call."

"Sure," she said. "I know this is important. I'm sorry I couldn't help more."

He shook her hand. "It's okay. And thanks for letting me use the scanner. Are you sure I don't owe you anything?"

"No, it's fine."

He nodded and walked through the exit into the late afternoon sun. He slipped into his car, started the motor and adjusted the air conditioning. Nothing. He hadn't expected much, but nothing was disappointing. As he drove down the winding road toward Rutherford Cross, he had a thought. And it wasn't about the case. It was about Brandy Eagleson. He was thinking that, perhaps, she had the most beautiful eyes he had ever seen. And for a moment, the murdered bodies and gruesome crime scenes were gone and there were just her eyes.

He grabbed that moment and held it. He had so few.

# CHAPTER THIRTY-FIVE

Aislinn picked through her inbox until she found the email Curtis had sent from Napa about Erica Klein. Napa was a world from the historic streets of Boston, yet Curtis felt the two women were somehow linked. She looked over the printouts, then tucked them in the Charlesbois file and headed for Chestnut Hill.

Aislinn had reluctantly called Jacques Charlesbois and set an appointment to speak with him. The financier was at home and she muttered a few choice words about him and his sprawling estate outside the city. That life was far removed from hers and the tiny apartment in South Boston she called home. Still, here she was, the daughter of an Irish beat cop, heading off to meet with one of Boston's richest and most powerful men to threaten him with jail time.

She had just cleared Boston Common and was merging onto Columbus Avenue when her phone rang. She checked the incoming number. It was Stan Lamer. "It's almost seven o'clock, Stan," she said. "You should be home having dinner."

Stan's voice was serious. "We got a problem, Aislinn. A big problem."

"What?" Aislinn asked. She knew Stan too well. He wasn't playing games.

"You know Tommy Strand?" Stan asked.

"Yeah, sure. Everyone knows Tommy. He shuffles papers around 1-A."

"That's him," Stan said. "He's dead. Execution style shooting. One bullet between the eyes. It must have been some kind of mushroom shell. It took out the whole back of his skull."

"Shit." Aislinn pulled over to the curb lane and stopped. The car behind her laid on the horn until she hit the lights and gave the siren a quick squawk. The driver gave her the finger as he pulled around and merged back into the traffic. She ignored him and said, "Okay, Stan, I'm parked. Go ahead."

"A passerby found him hanging out of a dumpster on Eagle Street and called it in. A patrol car responded and one of the guys recognized him."

"Eagle. That's in East Boston," Aislinn said. "Same place as that lawyer they pulled out of the harbor."

"Right."

"Shit, that ties them together, but there's something else." Aislinn's trip to see Jacques Charlesbois was looking grimmer by the minute. "You know that picture of Liem Khilt that we never released?"

"Yeah. What about it?" Stan asked.

"The Charlesbois file was sitting on my desk when Tommy Strand dropped off some inter-office mail on Wednesday afternoon. Khilt's picture was on top, in plain sight. Tommy asked me who it was."

"And now he turns up with a bullet in his head," Stan said.

"Yeah, that." Aislinn gripped the steering wheel hard enough that her knuckles went white. Charlesbois and his stupid, fucking reward. "Looks like we found the leak."

"Yeah."

Aislinn's fingers were aching and she let go of the wheel. "Any idea who the shooter is?"

"There are a few names being thrown around. Joey McGinley is at the top of the list."

Aislinn opened the door and stepped out on the curb. She liked Tommy, but it was common knowledge at the precinct that he had a drug problem. No one wanted to be the one who fingered a shot-on-duty cop, and it sure as hell wasn't going to be her. "McGinley is Tommy's dealer, isn't he?"

"Yeah," Stan said. "Listen, we all know Tommy wasn't the best cop on the force, but he was still a cop. We need to come down heavy on whoever did this."

"Yeah, I know." Aislinn took a deep breath. "And it starts with Charlesbois. His reward triggered this mess."

"We'll handle things on this end. You take care of Charlesbois."

"Yeah, thanks for that." She punched end on the phone and got back in the car. Curtis was away and this one was her call. She took a few deep breaths, reminded herself to keep her emotions in check, then pulled out into traffic.

Rich and powerful or not, Jacques Charlesbois was about to be reined in.

# CHAPTER THIRTY-SIX

There was a spring in his step as Liem Khilt glided down the stairs to the basement. Things were going very well. He stopped in front of the door, had a quick peek through the opening and slipped his key in the lock. Renee Charlesbois was curled up in the fetal position on her mattress and didn't move when he entered. He placed her dinner on the floor beside the bed and sat in the chair next to the door, his pistol in his right hand.

"Curtis Westcott is doing a good job," he said. Her eyes were open but she didn't respond. She lay on the bare mattress staring at the wall. "He's in Napa, you know. I phoned the precinct, told them I was his dog sitter and they believed me. Told me Westcott flew out to California last night."

"So." Renee's voice was just a whisper.

"So Napa is the key, Renee. He has to understand that. If he doesn't, then he won't stand a chance of finding you."

"And if he does?" she asked. She sat up slowly, leaned over and picked up her tray and began to eat. The food tasted good. Pork chops in gravy tonight.

"Then he's on track. Think of it like a bobsled run. If your sled is on the course, you're eventually going to hit the finish line. It's getting on the course to begin with that's tough. Westcott is on course and starting to piece things together."

"That seems to make you happy." She poked her plastic fork into the salad. "Which is strange, because if he figures this out and he finds you, you'll be convicted and spend the rest of your life in jail. Is that what you want?"

"Westcott won't figure it out in time. Not in a million years. It's too complicated. The fact that he's moving in the right direction is good. It provides a little drama and makes things more exciting. Gets the adrenaline flowing, so to speak."

She glowered at him over her dinner. "You're sick," she said. "I hope he gets you and you rot in some small cell."

"Are you trying to push my buttons?" Khilt asked. "It's not going to work. I'm in too good of a mood tonight."

Renee returned to eating her dinner. The vegetables were fresh and steamed, still crunchy and green. She ate quickly, knowing he was watching her but not caring. When she was finished, she set the plate aside and leaned against the wall. He was dressed in a crisp white shirt and dark colored dress pants with black loafers. As usual, his face was made up to look like the Liem Khilt character who had abducted her from the parking garage.

"Why are you doing this?" She brushed back a strand of dirty hair. "Why me?"

He was silent for a moment, then leaned forward. "We met once before, Renee. It's obvious you don't remember."

Her eyes narrowed slightly, taking in his features. "You're always disguised," she said. "I don't remember what you look like without the prosthetics."

He smiled. It was anything but warm. "Oh, you remember. You just don't remember *me*. Why would you? I was an insignificant speck in your privileged life. The one in the group who didn't matter."

"What? What are you talking about? I was never in any group with you."

Khilt rubbed his leg with the barrel of the gun. "Yes, Renee, you were. A long time ago. A time of crisis in your life."

She stared at him, dumbfounded. There was nothing in her memory of this man. Not the slightest hint of a long-lost moment in her life. And what crisis? In her life a crisis was when she was young and having a bad hair day. She searched the far reaches of her memory, looking for something that would tie this monster into her life.

Nothing.

"I don't know you," she said.

"No, you don't," Khilt responded, rising from the chair. He collected the plate from where she had set it and moved to the door, the gun still leveled at her chest. "You never did know me. None of you did. As I said, I was the one who didn't matter."

He unlocked the door and stood in the open doorway for a few seconds. "Looks like I matter now." He closed the door and was gone.

# CHAPTER THIRTY-SEVEN

Curtis drove back to Rutherford, then turned north toward St. Helena. Signage to wineries was everywhere—Grgich Hills, Inglenook/Niebaum-Coppola, Beaulieu, all trying to entice visitors to their tasting rooms. It was late afternoon and the traffic was lighter now, with many of the tourists parked and eating supper. He reached St. Helena and drove slowly down Main Street, taking in the quaint sun-bleached stone buildings that were a throwback to the valley's early days.

Curtis found a spot in the public lot on Railroad Avenue and walked back to Ana's Cantina, tucked into the corner of Main and Spring. He chose an empty table against the front window where both the view and the light were good and ordered dinner and a glass of Merlot. He set the contents of both the Charlesbois and Klein files on the table, then flipped through the papers until he found the interviews with Liem Khilt in Boston and Keith Mill in Napa. Next to the typed text were handwritten notes from his meeting with the man at Chloe Harrah's party. His wine arrived and he pulled out a pen and a fresh piece of paper so he could make additional notes.

When Liem Khilt spoke about Napa, it was in the past tense and he specifically mentioned six-thirty. Curtis was now sure that referred to June 30th, the day they found Erica Klein's body. Khilt was specific about the winery, naming Frog's Leap in particular, but his visit to the winery had turned up nothing to indicate Khilt had held Erica Klein captive there. Frog's Leap didn't have old caves and tunnels like so many of the nearby wineries, and there were hundreds of old buildings in the valley that would be a better place to keep a live hostage for two weeks. The ditch where they had found her body was a short distance from Frog's Leap, but there was no other reason to think Frog's Leap was where he had kept her or killed her. So why mention it?

Curtis dropped the pen on the paper and sipped his wine. It was excellent, and he motioned for the waiter to bring another glass. He went back over the interview again, then wrote a single word on his paper. *Apocalypse.* Why did Khilt use that word? There were hundreds of other words that would have fit the sentence equally as well, or better. It didn't make sense. He spent a few minutes thinking about what connection the word might have, but came up empty. His food arrived and he pushed the papers aside so the waiter could drop the plate. As he ate, he moved on to the interview with Keith Mill, making more notes.

Mill, like Khilt, had been very specific about the time of day, and had mentioned Boston. If the times were dates, then eight-seventeen became August 17th, which would be two weeks to the day after Renee Charlesbois had been abducted. Curtis was feeling confident that the 17th would that be the day the Boston police would find her body. June 30th was the day the Napa police had found Erica Klein's body, exactly two weeks from the date she had been abducted. Using that logic, Mill's mention of Chicago, in the past tense, could be a clue to another murder. In the same paragraph where he mentioned Chicago, he said he had arrived at the wine tasting at five minutes after five. Did that translate to May 5th? If he was consistent in his methodology, then someone would have disappeared on the 21st of April and that body would have shown up on May 5th. Chicago homicide could provide that information easily enough. But what did it all mean?

Khilt, or Mill, was offering clues to past crimes, while being very careful to leave little or no evidence at the existing crime scene. They had nothing to go on in Boston, just as the Napa police had absolutely no evidence in the Klein murder. It made no sense, to plan the current abduction so carefully that not a trace of the crime existed, then drop clues tying together all of the killings.

Curtis reread the interview and stopped on Mill's mention of Alex Haley. What made the gardens at Sutter Home Winery look like a setting out of an Alex Haley novel? Haley had written numerous bestsellers, but *Roots*, his most read work, dealt with his African heritage. Danielle Steele would probably be a more apt author to use if you wanted a writer who penned stories of rich people, wineries, and intrigue. He circled other parts of the text; *south of the little river, taking cuttings* and *garden behind the main building*. Somehow, these were probably related to what had happened in Chicago. He moved on to the paragraph about Boston.

*Some suburb just outside the city.* Curtis stared at the words, thinking that Khilt could be giving them the location where Renee Charlesbois was being held. If she was in a suburb, then which one? Boston, including all the bedroom communities, was huge. If that was all they had to go on, finding her would be next to impossible.

The server stopped by with his meal and he dug in, taking a few minutes to clear his mind before going back to the paperwork on the table. He read on, jotting down two more phrases. *He moved about the room like a chicken with its head cut off* and *rather a motley crew for such an upscale testing. Motley crew.* Out of context. But there for a reason? Perhaps Tommy Lee's rock band, *Motley Crue*? Again, that made no sense. *A chicken with its head cut off.* He had met Liem Khilt, and the man was not one who butchered the English language. He was articulate and intelligent. That phrase did not fit. He circled it, staring at the last three words. Christ, he hoped he was wrong.

Boston. Head cut off.

Renee's fate?

He glanced back at the phrases and words he had jotted down from the paragraph about Chicago. One of the gardeners was taking cuttings of the flowers. Cuttings. Chicago. May 5th. Cuttings.

He finished his meal and tucked the papers back in the file. After paying the bill he walked down Main Street until he found a travel agency. The agent was closing for the day, but powered up her computer and booked him a flight out of San Francisco for Chicago, departing in four hours. He paid with his VISA card, thanked her and walked quickly back to his rental.

Chicago. Cuttings. May 5th.

God, how he hoped he was wrong.

# CHAPTER THIRTY-EIGHT

Aislinn turned off the main road and stopped at the gate outside Charlesbois' Chestnut Hill estate. She looked directly at the security camera and a few seconds later heard a click and the iron bars slowly swung open. She headed down the winding drive, lined with mature white oaks and freshly trimmed lawns, and wondered what his monthly gardening bill ran. When she rounded the last bend the house came into view and she sucked in her breath at the sight.

The house, if it could be called that, was at least twenty thousand square feet spread over two stories. Stone pillars framed an entry portico the size of a normal bungalow, and a man dressed in a blue suit was standing on the front steps, waiting for her. She pulled up near the front door and made a point of locking her car. He looked amused by that and she felt like punching him.

"I wouldn't want someone stealing the shotgun," she said as she walked up the stairs.

"Detective Byrne?" He was large, and thick across his chest, with close-cropped hair. Aislinn thought he looked like a GI-Joe doll dressed for church.

"Yeah."

"Follow me, please." He moved into the house, across the tiled foyer and down a long hallway to a study at the rear of the house. The walls were lined with neatly filed books on dark-stained wood shelves, and a series of floor-to-ceiling windows looked over the rear gardens. Jacques Charlesbois was sitting in a grouping of heavy leather chairs, and he made no move to rise as the homicide detective entered.

"You have news on my daughter's disappearance?" he asked. His tone was anything but civil.

Aislinn walked across the room and without invitation sat down next to the financier. She leaned forward slightly as she spoke. "We're moving ahead with our investigation and I have a few questions. Do you know a woman named Erica Klein?"

"What?" Charlesbois sat up, leaving only a few feet between them. "Who? What are you talking about?" There was bewilderment on his face.

"Erica Klein, do you know her? It's important you try to remember."

Charlesbois' expression didn't change. He stared straight at Aislinn and said, "No, I don't. You said your investigation was moving ahead. What do you have?"

Aislinn leaned back in the chair, struggling to keep her panic under control. She was in Charlesbois' comfort zone and they both knew it. Her Glock was between her and the sofa cushion, and she could feel it pushing into her back. It was ridiculous, but having a gun gave her a feeling of control.

"I asked about Erica Klein because her death may be linked to Renee's abduction." She enunciated every word carefully.

"I don't know her," Charlesbois snapped. "Tell me you have something of value, Detective Byrne."

"Everything in a homicide investigation is of value," she said calmly.

He shifted squaring himself to her. "Why are you here?"

"I'm here for two reasons, Mr. Charlesbois," Aislinn said. "First, to find out if you know Erica Klein. That's taken care of. The second is to tell you to get the word on the street that the reward is no longer in effect. Immediately."

Charlesbois' face took on color, all of it red. "And if I refuse, Detective Byrne?" Emphasis on *detective*.

"I'm not asking, sir. I'm telling."

Jacques Charlesbois started forward in his seat, then stopped. His breathing was shallow and fast and his teeth were grinding so hard Aislinn could hear them. "Who do you think you are, coming in here and *telling* me what I'm to do? My daughter is missing, you can't find her, and now you walk in my house and order me to stop searching for her. Not a chance. Not a chance in hell."

Aislinn stood up, any feelings of inadequacy gone. "Who am I? I'm the cop who has every right to haul you down to the precinct and charge your rich ass with murder. And when the guys find out you're the one responsible for a cop being killed today, you'll receive some special attention all right. Real special."

"What cop? I had nothing to do with any cop getting offed."

"Actually, you did. Your reward got a lawyer tortured and killed. Then one of our guys had his head blown apart because he gave the killer the wrong man. If we can tie your reward back to the murders, and I don't think that will be much of a stretch, then you will likely get charged as an accessory. Which means you go to jail for murder, just like the shooter. You, sir, you do not have the right to incite people to murder." Aislinn stared down at him. "You have twenty-four hours to get the word out. The million dollars is off the table."

"And if I don't?" Charlesbois said.

"I'll be back," Aislinn said. "And you'll find out that there are some things that money can't buy."

Aislinn turned toward the door and eyed GI-Joe. The man didn't move a muscle as she passed. She didn't look back, just kept moving to the front door, down the stairs and to her car. As she drove down the road to the gates, a bead of sweat trickled down her temple and she wiped it away. Jesus, that was not fun. If there was one thing she was sure of right now, it was that she didn't want to have to go back.

No, a return trip to see Jacques Charlesbois was not on her bucket list.

Charlesbois called Amery Kincaid's cell phone and told him to drop by his house. An hour later, Kincaid walked into Charlesbois' study.

Charlesbois closed the file on his computer and set the mouse aside. "What do you have for me?"

Kincaid shook his head. "Nothing. I'm not getting anything from my hack into the police computer, it's like they're being careful and not sharing information online. If they think they have a ghost in the machine, they could find me."

"Shut it down," Charlesbois said. "What about the calls on the reward?"

"They've slowed down to a trickle. The ones that are coming in now are pretty much useless. Crack heads and addicts trying to get their hands on a bit of the money."

"Well, that didn't work."

Kincaid shrugged. "It's still an incentive. The right person might see something and call. We should leave it for now."

Charlesbois stood and walked over to the window. Aislinn Byrne was an extension of Curtis Westcott and Boston Homicide. If they had sent her, then they were getting royally pissed at him over the reward. The logic of keeping it on the table needed to be addressed.

"Detective Byrne was here today. She's Homicide, and told me the reward got a lawyer and a cop killed."

"What? How?"

"I'm not sure, but they're really angry about it. They threatened me with accessory to murder charges."

"That probably wouldn't stick," Kincaid said.

"That's not the point," Charlesbois shot back. "What we're doing is pissing off the people who are looking for Renee."

"You'd rather do nothing?"

Charlesbois gave the man a withering look. "Careful, Amery. You're treading close to the line."

Kincaid remained quiet, waiting. Finally, Charlesbois said, "Leave it for now, but be ready to pull it the minute I give you the word."

"Okay."

"How long will it take?"

"To pull back the reward?"

"Yes."

"A few hours, tops. Word gets around fast on the street."

Charlesbois returned to his desk and picked up the mouse. His screen lit up and he glanced over at Kincaid. "Keep your cell on."

Kincaid knew he'd been dismissed and headed for the door. When it clicked shut, Charlesbois leaned back in his chair and closed his eyes. Amery Kincaid was an excellent resource when it came to stealing corporate secrets or hacking into systems, but he was nothing compared to Boston Homicide. The police had resources no one else had, or could ever hope to have. They were linked to databases with DNA profiles, fingerprints, known offenders, and a host of other crucial information. Angering Westcott and his team was foolish. He could fight any trumped-up charges they came up with, but he couldn't replace them if they decided to stop looking for his daughter. He had to tread carefully.

# CHAPTER THIRTY-NINE

Westcott's flight arrived at O'Hare at three-fourteen in the morning. Chicago's airport was almost deserted, a welcome change from its usual bustle. Curtis waited for his bag to arrive on the carousel, then slipped into the back seat of the first cab in the queue and asked to be dropped off at the Renaissance on Wacker Drive. The hotel catered to business travelers and since it was Saturday he knew there would be vacancies. That, and it was close to the main Chicago police station. When he arrived, he requested a room on the twentieth floor or higher where the views of the lake and the Chicago River were the best. The desk clerk offered Curtis a special weekend rate for a suite when he mentioned he was with BPD and in town on police business. Sometimes there were perks for being a cop.

Curtis settled in and wandered over to the window and stared out over Lake Michigan. The moon was almost full, its light reflecting off the water's smooth surface. He stood motionless until the morning sun began to creep up over the eastern horizon. Curtis brewed some coffee and checked his watch. Six-thirty. Too early for him to visit the precinct. Too late for any attempt at sleep.

It had been almost thirty hours since the flight attendants had wakened him on the tarmac in San Francisco, and he was starting to crash. He poured the coffee and added some chemical creamer and a touch of sugar. It tasted awful, but right now he needed his senses about him. He finished the first cup in a few gulps and poured a second, then sat on the edge of the couch and watched the sun rise against the lightening sky.

Boston to Napa to Chicago. Liem Khilt, or whoever the sick bastard was, had him on the move. Khilt had left a trail that could be followed if discovered. It was purposeful, and if Curtis was right, would eventually lead to Renee. Brent Keely's chance to see the clues had come and gone—he'd missed them. Then the Napa Valley cop had panicked and grabbed the first suspect out of the gate and sold the public on it. Arnold Baker, the poor bastard, was sitting in a stark jail cell because Keely needed an arrest. If Brent Keely had done his job, he would have noticed the innuendos in Mill's interview.

Or would he?

Curtis thought back to the first time he had linked the evidence to Liem Khilt. If it weren't for the man at Chloe's party mentioning the incident with the pitchfork, he might not have tied Khilt to the abduction. Khilt, disguised as the overweight man, had told the story of being a suspect in a murder for one reason. To give Curtis what he needed to start looking at Liem Khilt as a suspect in Renee's abduction. What if he had done the same thing with Brent Keely? Curtis doubted Keely would remember the connection this long after the fact, especially if he hadn't recognized it at the time.

Curtis walked back to the coffee pot and poured one more cup. He was beginning to shake slightly from the combination of no sleep and too much caffeine, but ignored it. His briefcase was on the couch and he pulled out the interviews and laid them on the coffee table, this time concentrating on the handwritten notes from the night at Chloe's. Pieces of what the man had said, filed in a distant part of his memory, were coming back and he wrote what he could remember on a sheet of hotel stationery.

Khilt, disguised as the overweight man, had said he was visiting his Uncle Al in Florida. Some nondescript town—Curtis couldn't remember the name. He had given his uncle's last name. What was it? Probably just a name Khilt had manufactured, nevertheless remembering it could be important. He closed his eyes, replaying the video of the party, the conversation pod, the man speaking. Then it came to him. Stooges. No, not quite. Like Stooges. What had he said? Stooges, without the e. That was it. *Stoogs.* Curtis underlined the name. *Al Stoogs.* He stared at it, but nothing clicked. What else had he said? He had been rafting down a canal, and when he had returned to the house, his uncle had been murdered, skewered on a pitchfork. Not skewered. Run through. That was it. Run through. He jotted down *pitchfork* and *run through* and underlined them as well. *He had been in his early twenties, with long hair.* Curtis studied that line and went on without underlining any words. Khilt had said the cops had made him sit in the jail cell for a few days. How many? He couldn't recall. Damn. He poured the last of the coffee and added some sugar. There was no chemical creamer left, which was probably a good thing.

His hands were shaking. He needed to eat, and even more, he needed sleep. His eyes felt heavy and the bed looked too inviting to ignore. He set the papers on the table, then lay down on top of the covers and closed his eyes. For a minute or two there was a peaceful darkness, then the images came. Bodies of murder victims, mutilated and bloated with dead eyes staring back at him. His eyes flew open and he stared at the ceiling. Christ, was this the legacy of his career? Forever haunted by the victims whose lives had ended violently? He got off the bed, paced about the room for a few minutes, then had a quick shower. The pounding water helped, refreshing him and clearing his mind. He wrapped a towel around his waist and walked back to the coffee table, where he stood and stared at his notes.

There was something else. Khilt had said something about reading while he was in jail, waiting for the police to lay charges in his uncle's murder. The newspaper. That was it. But what part? He had been specific. A certain part of the paper. Not the sports section or local news, it was something specific. And different. Not a part of the paper someone regularly read. He racked his brain but it wouldn't come. He called down to the front desk and asked for a newspaper to be delivered to his room, then returned to the bathroom, shaved and brushed his teeth. By the time he was dressed there was a low knock on the door.

Curtis tipped the young man and returned to the coffee table with the newspaper. It was the Saturday edition of the *Chicago Tribune*, and it was thick. He leafed through the various sections, scanning the international and local news, the sports and entertainment sections, until he hit the personal ads. That was it. Khilt had said he had *nothing to do but read the personal ads*. He was sure.

Personal ads. What the hell was with that? Personal ads was too specific not to be of some importance. He checked the time, then put a quick call through to Aislinn Byrne's cell. A tired voice answered.

"Aislinn," Curtis said. "Got a couple of things for you. Need you to be quick."

"What?" Her voice was more awake now.

"Go back through the personal ads in all the local Boston papers. Look for key words, like abducted, kidnapped, holding her, stuff like that. Start date is August 3rd, the day Renee Charlesbois disappeared." He glanced at the paper, there was ad after ad of meaningless drivel, often in what appeared to be some sort of abbreviated code. Most were signed simply with initials. "And Aislinn, watch for anything signed by the sender as LK. Get back to me on my cell."

"I'm on it," Aislinn said. "Which paper is the priority?"

Curtis answered without even thinking. "The *Globe*. I'd put money on it. But check the others as well."

"Okay. What else?"

"Khilt mentioned his uncle by name at Chloe's party. Stoogs. Al Stoogs. He lived in a small town a few miles inland of the east coast of Florida. See what you can dig up."

"Got it. By the way, your dog sitter called. Barclay's out of food. He wanted to know where you get it."

"Aislinn, my dog sitter is a woman. And Barclay has lots of food."

"Aw, shit," Aislinn said. "Khilt?"

"Probably." Curtis was instantly furious that Khilt knew that much about his personal life, and that he had dragged Barclay into it. If the bastard touched his dog...

"Fucking guy," Aislinn said.

Curtis settled a bit, but he was still seething. "What did you tell him?"

"I didn't take the call. Jacoby did. He mentioned you were out of town."

"Did he say I was in Napa?"

"I don't know."

"Find out," Curtis snapped, then added. "Please."

"Right, and I'll see if he made the call from a traceable number."

"Good luck there," Curtis said.

Aislinn signed off and Curtis set the phone on the coffee table. Not one mention from her that it was Saturday morning. No griping. All action. Curtis had trained his team well. Right now, Aislinn Byrne would already be on the phone and on the task. It wouldn't take long. The newspapers could run a simple search on the personal ads over the last ten days. And looking for Al Stoogs was easy. A scan for a person by name, complete with correct spelling, was a no-brainer. Computers made their jobs so much easier. Millions of people live up and down the Florida coast, but if Al Stoogs was a real person, the computers would find him in less than ten seconds.

He checked his watch. It was after seven. Time to visit the Chicago police. He had specific questions to ask them, and if he was right, he already knew the answers.

# CHAPTER FORTY

Curtis had a quick breakfast, then caught a cab to the main Chicago police station. He arrived a few minutes after eight-thirty, the shift change was finished and the desk sergeant on duty smiled pleasantly as he approached.

"Good morning, I'm Curtis Westcott, Boston Homicide." He held up his badge and put a business card on the desk. "Is there anyone from homicide in today?"

"Sure," the sergeant said. "I'll ring them that you're coming up. They're on seven." He pointed to the elevator. "Kevin Shipton is in this morning."

"Thanks." Curtis slipped his badge back in his pocket. He rode the elevator to the seventh floor and glanced both ways in the deserted hall. There were no signs and he went left, past a series of doors until he reached the end of the hall and a single door marked HOMICIDE. Inside was a long counter topped with a Plexiglas window running from wall to wall and some guest chairs. The door next to the reception counter opened a moment after Curtis entered and a man looked out.

"Westcott?" he asked.

"Yes."

"C'mon in." He motioned for Curtis to follow him and the door clicked shut behind them. They walked through a bullpen area, filled with battered desks and well-used chairs. A few detectives were in, but for the most part, the room was empty. "I'm Kevin Shipton." He offered his hand as they reached his office.

Curtis shook his hand. "Curtis Westcott, Boston Homicide."

Shipton sat and Curtis dropped into one of the rickety wood chairs facing the desk. Shipton was early forties, with wire-rim glasses and a serious face. Curtis glanced at the family photos that covered his desk and felt a small tug of loneliness. He couldn't ignore the pictures of Shipton's wife and girls, and said, "Nice family."

"Kids," Shipton said. "I've got three of the little buggers. Expensive, they are. Especially the thirteen-year-old. Let me tell you, thirteen-year-old girls need all the new fashions." He was smiling at the picture. "What can I do for you, Curtis?"

"I've got a situation in Boston," Curtis said. "Woman abducted about nine days ago, but so far, no body. I've picked up a trail that led to Chicago through Napa."

"Same MO?" Shipton asked.

Curtis nodded. "I think so. He killed the woman in Napa, but he hasn't done that yet in Boston. At least, not that we know of. I'm looking for a pattern, but I've only got Napa so far. I think he may have been active in your backyard about four months ago. If he was, then that would confirm or negate his MO."

"What details can you give me?" Shipton asked, setting his laptop on the desk.

"Victim would be female, probably abducted on or about April 21 of this year. If he's consistent, her body would have shown up on May 5th. Death may have been from stab wounds, some sort of sharp instrument."

Shipton's fingers froze over the keyboard, then he slowly set them on his desk and gave Curtis a long hard look. "That's the Shelby case. You never looked up any of this information in the papers?"

Curtis shook his head. "No. This is all from evidence we've gathered while working the Charlesbois case. What can you tell me about Shelby?"

"Annette Shelby. Thirty-one, white woman, married with two children and a successful medical practice. She disappeared in the early morning while jogging near her home. Not a trace. We didn't have a single clue to work with. One moment she's having a run on a quiet residential street, the next she's gone. Then two weeks later her body shows up on the ninth fairway of the Diversey Golf Course."

"Solve the case?"

"Nope. It's still open."

"What was the cause of death?" Curtis asked. He had never thought he'd be glad to hear a case had gone without an arrest, but in this instance it allowed him to be upfront with Shipton and the Chicago police.

Shipton steepled his fingers and leaned back in his chair. "We never released that information," he said. "One of the groundskeepers found her when he headed out to cut the grass, and we made sure he kept his mouth shut. Cause of death was from numerous cuts with a very sharp knife, possibly a surgical scalpel. She bled out somewhere, then the killer moved her to the golf course." He was quiet for a minute, then asked, "How did you know she was killed with a knife?"

Curtis went back to the restaurant's opening and Renee Charlesbois' abduction to bring Shipton up to speed. He tied Chloe's party and the interview with Khilt together, hoping that would stimulate Shipton's memory in the case that Khilt had done the same thing in Chicago. Shipton removed his glasses, cleaned them with a napkin while he thought about it, then shook his head.

"Nothing comes to mind."

"Okay, the perp also used word association to lead us in a specific direction. Maybe he did that with you as well." Curtis showed the Chicago cop what he considered to be the key words from the two times he had met Khilt, then explained how he had based his guess regarding the Chicago case on what Khilt had said.

"He's giving us the clues we need," Curtis said. "But not to the crime in front of us at the time. The clues seem to point to a crime he's previously committed, and maybe even to one he plans to commit in the future. In the interview we had with him in Boston, he talked about New York in the future tense. If the tense he uses is important, then he may have been giving us an insight to his future plans. I think the trick is to follow the chain back to the start."

"And that's Chicago?" Shipton asked.

Curtis shrugged. "Who knows? We need to find the interview you guys had with him and see what he said."

"How do we find the right one?" Shipton asked. "We must have five hundred to a thousand interviews in the file."

"Look for one with some mention of Napa Valley. If I'm right, he'll talk about Napa in the future tense and some other place in the past. Whatever place he speaks of in the past tense is the direction the chain moves."

"And if there is no mention of a previous place?"

"Then maybe Chicago is the start. I don't know. We need that interview."

"Christ," Shipton said. He gave Curtis a searching look. "How the hell did you put this together?"

"Bit of luck, I think," Curtis said. "Our guy gave me some word association and I caught it."

"What about the Napa guys who were working that file. Did they pick up on what was going on?"

Curtis shook his head. "No. In fact, they've got the wrong guy in jail. Small community, prominent citizen, and they needed a collar. They grabbed some poor sap who happened to be near the area where the Klein woman disappeared."

"I'm surprised they opened the file for you," Shipton said. "This could derail their investigation."

"They don't know what I'm doing. If they knew, the files would snap shut."

Shipton nodded. "No shit. Well, one thing is for certain, our files are open. If you're right and you get this bastard, we get to close the Shelby file. Win-win." He glanced at his watch and reached for the phone. "Better tell the wife I won't be home for a while. We have a lot of interviews to look through."

"Thanks," Curtis said.

He got up and walked to the window while Kevin Shipton explained to his wife that his Saturday morning stop at the office wasn't going to be so quick. Curtis knew it all too well—life on the job. Outside, the morning sunlight was reflecting off the buildings that formed The Loop, the nickname for the downtown core. It was large and congested, like any major US city. Millions of people in close proximity, most of them living within the constraints of the law. It was a small percentage that ever stepped outside those boundaries and committed a crime, and of those, very few were violent offenders. When they were, the cops were there. Waiting, with resources at their fingertips, and most times, the cops won. They tracked down the rapist or the killer and the prosecutors put them in jail. The system, as flawed as it was, worked.

It was seldom, if ever, that the police ran up against something like this. Khilt was methodically killing women and if their resident psychologist, Corrine Wheeler was right, he had a reason. These murders were not random. Perhaps that would make tracking the man down a bit easier. Perhaps, but then again Khilt had given them no clue to his true identity, except that he had committed similar crimes in the past, and that he intended to continue.

Curtis watched as Kevin Shipton placed the phone in its cradle and rose slowly from his desk. It was obvious by the look on Shipton's face that his wife was disappointed they wouldn't be spending the day together. Instead, today would be spent in a windowless room full of carefully filed boxes, helping a cop he didn't know from a city he'd never visited, search for the interviews from the Shelby case. And somewhere in those boxes they would find the next set of clues.

# CHAPTER FORTY-ONE

The second-floor apartment was a disaster. Empty pizza boxes and beer cans littered the stained carpet and a cheap radio blasted out AC DC. The sound was tinny and irritating, but Joey McGinley didn't notice as he packed his Nike bag.

"Why we leaving?" the girl asked. She was young, not yet twenty, and totally hooked on the drugs Joey sold at street level. She looked anorexic, with her clothes hanging off her skinny frame, and stringy, thin hair. Her face was a pasty, unhealthy white.

"Because I got business in Florida. Now move your ass or I'll leave you here," Joey snapped back.

She pulled herself off the couch and sauntered into the bedroom, returning a minute later with a plastic bag from a nearby grocery store. One leg of a pair of blue jeans stuck out the top. "You got anything for the trip?" she asked, lighting a cigarette with her free hand. She was shaking and it took three tries with the lighter to connect the flame to the tobacco.

"Yeah, baby, I got shit. Now let's go." McGinley grabbed her by the arm and pulled her with him. He locked the deadbolt and they started down the creaky stairs. "C'mon, hurry up," he said as he reached the door that exited onto the street.

Joey's Lincoln Town Car was parked next to the curb a few yards from the door. It was still early on Saturday morning and the street was quiet. He jumped in and gunned the motor as the girl slipped in beside him, then Joey rammed the car into drive and pulled away from the curb. When he reached the corner, two police cruisers screeched into position, blocking the road in front of him, and officers from both cars leaped out and pulled their guns.

"Fuck." Joey slammed on the brakes and threw the car into reverse. He floored it and the car careened backwards down the road, swaying from side to side as Joey struggled to control it. Through the rear window he saw two more squad cars blocking his exit. He was trapped on the street. He hit the brakes hard and the car went up on two wheels then crashed onto its side and rolled. Neither of them had seatbelts on and they flew about the car, smashing into the roof and seats as the car skittered down the street. Eventually, it came to a rocking stop.

"Joey," she moaned. Her face was covered with blood and she'd knocked her front teeth out on the dashboard.

He ignored her and kicked at the driver's door, which was jammed shut from the force of the crash. It groaned, then creaked open. He slid out of the car, pistol in hand, and made a run for a door a few feet from where the car had stopped. He tried the handle, but it was locked. He spun around, looking for options. There were none. He leveled the gun at the closest cruisers and opened fire. Joey got off three shots that punched holes in the cruiser the officers were hiding behind before the snipers opened fire.

The shooters were positioned on the roofs of the surrounding buildings and had been waiting for the okay before firing. They had him pinned down on the street and away from the car with the girl, and now they had him in their crosshairs. He was a cop killer, and their shots weren't meant to wound, they were meant to kill. Three rifle bullets slammed into his head in quick succession and Joey dropped to the pavement like a sack of cement.

The wail of approaching ambulances sliced through the air as the gunfire ceased and the police moved from behind the protection of their cars into the street. They approached Joey's car with guns drawn.

"Get out of the car," one of the officers yelled at the girl, his gun leveled at her. "Hands where I can see them."

"I'm trying," she said, pushing on the door. The metal was twisted and she shoved it harder until it groaned and finally popped open.

Four cops were moving in on her in a semi-circle. "On the ground. Spread-eagle. Now."

She was bleeding and in tears as she hit the pavement. The police were on her in seconds, checking for weapons and cuffing her hands behind her back. She was clean and they hustled her into the back seat of a squad car.

Stan Lamers arrived fifteen minutes later and surveyed the scene. The yellow tape was up, cordoning off the entire street, and residents who lived in the apartments above that section of the street were being asked to clear out for a while and let the forensics teams do their job. Stan walked up the street, glancing at the buildings on either side, wondering which one of these slums Joey McGinley had dealt his drugs from. What a waste of skin. Some piece of crap who had never done one beneficial thing for society, was now responsible for two other people dying. One of them a cop.

He reached the squad car and looked in. The girl in the back seat was in rough shape. She had on a short-sleeve shirt and he could see the track marks on her arms. McGinley had worked his magic on her. At least she wasn't dead, he thought. Maybe this would shock her back to reality and give her a chance to kick the drugs. Maybe.

He looked down the street at the bevy of news crews, their cameras filming the scene. This was going to run first on the local channels tonight. Christ, what a mess. Then he had another thought, and his temperature rose.

Jacques Charlesbois had caused this.

The million-dollar reward had resulted in three deaths, if you included Joey McGinley. That was too much. Stan turned his back on the carnage and walked to his ride, a grim look on his face. Charlesbois had better have taken Aislinn's advice and called off the reward, or there was going to be hell to pay.

# CHAPTER FORTY-TWO

The file rooms were exactly as Curtis had imagined them, dusty and windowless with dim lighting. Racks of boxes lined the walls, each row almost sixty feet long and piled to the ceiling. The boxes all had three codes—case name, department, and date. Chicago PD digitized all the conversations between cops and suspects using a voice recognition program, but Kevin Shipton and Curtis opted to use the computers in the storage room, as the software sometimes made mistakes. That way, they had the hard-copy files nearby.

Going through the files, even though they were digital, was onerous. Each file was separate and had to be opened, then searched by keywords. They used Napa, valley, wine, wineries, Frog's Leap, and another eight words they considered important. The two men were more than halfway through the files when Shipton hit pay dirt. He called Curtis over to the computer and they looked at the contents. The man being interviewed mentioned Napa in the future tense. Curtis asked the Chicago homicide cop to pull the hard copy of the interview and they sat down at one of the long, wooden tables and went through the interview line by line.

The man's name was Timothy Kehill. He was a local resident who lived on one of the streets that Annette Shelby used for her morning jog. He had called the precinct and offered to come in for an interview, on the off chance that he could provide something of interest to the police. They had accepted, hoping he may have seen the perp hanging about, familiarizing himself with Shelby's morning route. Nothing had materialized from the interview and it had been filed and forgotten. Curtis read the entire conversation from the beginning. The interviewing officer was John Abbot, a newly assigned detective who had come over from major crimes.

Abbot: Thanks for coming in today, Mr. Kehill. My name is John Abbot.

Kehill: No problem, John. You can call me Tim. Nobody calls me Timothy. Ever.

Abbot: Well, sir, I'm more comfortable with Mr. Kehill. If you don't mind.

Kehill: Whatever works for you.

Abbot: You indicated that you live in the area where Ms. Shelby routinely jogs.

Kehill: Yes. I'm on Belmont Avenue, between Halsted and Broadway. I recognized her from the picture in the newspaper when she disappeared.

Abbot: Did you see her every day?

Kehill: No. I'm not an early riser, and she jogged early. Very early. I remember one morning when I was awakened by a dog barking at three-ten. It didn't stop, and at three twenty-four I looked out the window to see which house the dog belonged to. I planned on visiting the owners the next day and giving them a piece of my mind. That's when I saw her jogging.

Abbot: : It would have been dark, Mr. Kehill. How can you be sure it was Annette Shelby?

Kehill: There's a streetlight just outside my house. I love electricity. It brightens up our lives. So her features were quite clear. I know it was her. I'm originally from Los Angeles, and it's not unusual to see people jogging at all hours of the morning. I didn't think anything of it.

Abbot: Were there any other times you saw her jogging?

Kehill: No. That was the only time. She was up and about too early for me. I usually have a glass or two of wine with dinner, and tend to

sleep late some days. American wine, detective. From Napa mostly. I refuse to get roped in by the slick marketing the European and Australian
wine producers employ. Do you drink wine?

Abbot: No, not often, Mr. Kehill.

Kehill: You should. They say a glass a day is good for you. I'm planning a trip to Napa Valley soon. Think I'll visit Frog's Leap while I'm
there. It's my favorite. They have the most delicious Merlot.

Abbot: I'm sure they do. Did you see anyone parked on the street or
loitering about, Mr. Kehill?

Kehill: You mean, like, casing out the street?

Abbot: Yes. Someone watching Ms. Shelby to get a feel for her
routine.

Kehill: Well, like I said, I sleep late some days. Even my early days
are nowhere near the time Ms. Shelby jogged. I set my alarm for six-sixteen and am up by six-thirty. And I can't recall seeing anyone parked in
a car. No, can't say I can help you there.

Abbot: That's about it then, Mr. Kehill. Thanks for coming in. If we
need to be in touch we'll call.

Kehill: Goodbye, then.

Shipton glanced at Curtis and said, "What do you think? This
your guy?"

Curtis nodded. "Oh, yeah, that's him. Everything is here." Curtis
picked up a yellow hi-liter and worked the text. When he was finished,
he used the pen to point at the words. "He starts out in the past tense,
saying he was originally from Los Angeles. He gives two specific
times—three-ten and three twenty-four. I think what he's doing is giving us the previous crime. Los Angeles, abducted his victim on March
10th and dumped her body on March 24th. That's how I knew the dates
your victim disappeared here in Chicago."

"You knew how he killed her. What's in here that gives you that?"

Curtis pointed to *electricity.* "He didn't need to use that word. There
was absolutely no reason for him to say that. Yet he did. It comes across
as rambling, but it's anything but that. My guess is that he electrocuted
his LA victim."

"Holy shit," Shipton said. "Who the fuck is this guy?"

"I don't know," Curtis said. "Sure wish I did."

"No kidding."

Curtis continued on with the text. "Then he shifts to the future tense, saying he is planning a trip to Napa. He mentions Frog's Leap and gives two more dates. Six-sixteen and six-thirty. June 16th and June 30th. The exact dates Erica Klein went missing and when her body was found in a ditch. And, *roped in* could point to how he killed her. She was strangled with a length of rope from a local hardware supplier."

"He dumped Annette Shelby's body on a golf course," Shipton said. "It was a very visible spot. In Napa he left the body in a ditch. Again, very visible. He wants the body to be found the same day he dumps it."

Curtis nodded. "He abducts them, keeps them somewhere for two weeks, then kills them and leaves the body in plain sight. All on a time-table. *His* timetable."

"When did he abduct your woman?" Kevin Shipton asked.

"August 3rd."

"So if he's consistent, you've got until the 17th to find her."

Curtis swallowed hard. "The body has to show up on the 17th, and he can't dump her in broad daylight. That means he's going to kill her just after midnight, then leave the body somewhere highly visible."

"So you've got until the 16th."

"Yeah. The 16th."

"And today's the 12th. Jesus, that's not much time."

Curtis shook his head. "No, not much at all. Right now, I have ab-solutely no idea who he is or where he's keeping her."

Shipton tapped his pen on the thin stack of paper. "We'll check everything we've got on this Timothy Kehill guy. I know we'll have an address and phone number on file. If he's left anything for us to work with, we'll find it."

"I don't think you'll find much, Kevin. It looks like our guy is giving us clues to where he was and where he's going, but nothing to use to solve the current case. There is a possibility though. He's used the per-sonal ads in the past to pass along information. You might want to scan the newspaper personals using TK, or any key words he gave us from the Napa or Los Angeles interviews."

"Right. His initials when he was using Tim Kehill." Shipton was quiet for a minute, then said, "Do we have a serial killer?"

"Not exactly. I had our resident shrink look at the case and she thinks this guy is highly motivated and very specific about who he's killing. He's on a mission, and he knows exactly who he's going to kill."

"Like an assassin with a list?" Shipton said.

"Yeah. Like that."

Kevin Shipton leaned back in his chair and rubbed his eyes. "Well, Curtis, whatever you need from us, you've got it. You get your perp, we get ours."

"Thanks, Kevin."

"What now?" Shipton asked.

Curtis pointed at the words he had marked with the yellow hi-liter. "Los Angeles. That's where the trail leads."

# CHAPTER FORTY-THREE

"What's the word on the street?" Stan Lamers asked. He was visiting Vice, using his connections to track what was happening at street level.

"Nothing new," Leah Atkinson replied. Leah was young, black, and very attractive. It was her fifth year working undercover in the tough world of Vice, often posing as a prostitute on one of Boston's many strolls. She knew the streets, the players and the latest gossip the second it hit the grapevine.

A couple of Vice cops walked by with a hooker in thigh-high shiny patent boots. Vice was different from Homicide—dirtier, more street-level. It was the kind of place where you didn't want to take your gloves off. Even in summer.

"Charlesbois hasn't taken the million dollars off the table?"

She shook her head, her long kinked hair flying about her face. "Nope. There's still a feeding frenzy out there. Everyone's digging around, trying to find something that might lead to Renee. A million is a lot of money to someone dealing dime bags."

"A million dollars is a lot of money. Period." Stan sat on the edge of her desk. "What's the word on Joey McGinley going down?"

"No secrets there. It's common knowledge that McGinley did that lawyer. Lot of speculation he killed Tommy Strand too. But no one wants to point the finger at a cop killer. I don't think it surprised anyone when our guys were waiting for him."

Stan's face turned sour. "We thought taking him on the street in front of his house would be best. Man, did we fuck up."

"You couldn't have known he'd start shooting," Leah said. She leaned back in her chair, chewing on a swizzle stick. She smoked, and the non-smoking policy in the station drove her crazy. "Pity about the girl with him."

"Yeah. She was nineteen for Christ's sake," Stan said.

"What are you going to do now?" she asked. "Captain was telling us that you guys in Homicide gave Charlesbois a deadline to call off the reward."

"Tonight at dinner time, but we'll give it a few hours to percolate out. Sunday morning. That's it."

Leah nodded. "You want me to check the word on the street and call you?"

"Yeah. You mind?"

"No. But most of the types I need to ask won't be up until after noon. Give me until about three in the afternoon. By then I'll know if he's pulled it."

"Thanks, Leah," Stan said, rising from her desk and winking. "Why, if I wasn't married…"

"You'd what? You're too old for me, Stan."

"Thought you liked older men," he said, grinning as he left Vice. Leah Atkinson was a sexy woman who played the vixen very well. It drove the guys around the precinct crazy when she was dressed for undercover, looking at her in tight jeans and low tops. Everyone knew you could tease her, but there was a line no one stepped over.

Stan returned to Homicide and headed straight to Aislinn Byrne's desk. She was on the phone, scratching something on a pad of paper. She motioned for Stan to wait. Finally, she dropped the pen on the paper and hung up.

"That was Jacoby. He was the one who talked to the guy who said he was Curtis's dog-sitter."

"Right. What did he tell him?"

"Curtis was in California."

"That was really fucking stupid," Stan said.

"Yeah, and it makes you wonder."

"Wonder what?"

Aislinn set her pen on the pad of paper and stretched. "How much does Khilt know about us? You and me and Curtis. He knew about Barclay, for Christ's sake. Is he watching us? I gotta say, I'm feeling really creeped out by this."

"He getting under your skin?" Stan asked.

"Yeah, but it's more than that. We keep missing him. He's given us every chance to collar him and we don't see what's going on until it's too late."

"It's damn frustrating all right."

"No kidding." Aislinn looked back to the paper on her desk. "Curtis called this morning. Wanted info on a name he remembered from his conversation with Khilt at Chloe's party. Al Stoogs. There's nobody in the Florida registries by that name. Total dead end."

"Not a surprise. What else?"

"I have the daily newspapers downloading their personal ads from August 3rd onward. Curtis thinks Khilt might have stuck an ad in somewhere."

"In the personal ads?" Stan asked. "Where did *that* come from?"

"Dunno. It was early when he called. I was still half asleep. He said to watch for any ads signed LK."

"Got anything yet?"

"I'm waiting for the download to come through on my e-mail. I have a program ready to scan them when they arrive." She took a sip of coffee and asked, "What's happening with Jacques Charlesbois? Did he pull the reward?"

"Just checked with Leah in Vice. Doesn't look like he did."

"Fuck." Aislinn shook her head. "I went hard on him. Thought he'd get that we were serious."

"Not your fault," Stan said.

"We need to drag his ass down here." Aislinn's face was almost the color of her hair.

There was no hesitation from Stan. "Let's check with Curtis and see if he wants us to bring him in and charge him. The bastard might be hurting with his daughter missing, but he's not above the law."

"I completely fucking agree with that."

Stan said, "Leah needs until three on Sunday to find out if he's pulled it, so not until after that."

Aislinn grimaced. "Okay, but this time it's your turn. I took the first shot, you get to haul his ass in."

"Yeah," Stan said, envisioning Monday's headlines. "Lucky me."

# CHAPTER FORTY-FOUR

Curtis reset his watch to Pacific Daylight Time as he disembarked at LAX. It was a quarter after nine on Saturday night. The flight from Chicago was delayed and air traffic into LAX was atrocious, adding another delay in his search for Renee Charlesbois. He knew the key personnel he needed wouldn't be working, but he asked the cab driver to take him to the main police station. It was well after ten when they arrived.

The central precinct was down to a skeleton staff and the best Curtis could do was leave his business card with the name of his hotel on the back. They promised a call first thing Sunday morning and Curtis returned to the cab and gave the driver the name of his hotel. His eyelids were heavy, the cadence of the tires on the pavement and the regular interval of the streetlights lulling him into a trancelike state. Everything began to blur—the lights, the traffic, the buildings. It had been almost forty-six hours since he slept. Too long. If he crashed in the cab he would only get twenty minutes of sleep. Then, refreshed by the catnap, the rest of the night would be spent staring at the ceiling. Finally, with everything going black, he pulled out his cell and dialed Aislinn Byrne's home number. It was after one in the morning in Boston, but without something to keep his mind active, he was going to drift off.

"I've been calling you," Aislinn said when the call connected.

"I was on a plane. I'm in Los Angeles now. What's up?"

"Well, there's no one by the name of Al Stoogs in the state of Florida. I don't think that's going anywhere."

"Big surprise," Curtis said.

"The thing with Barclay. Jacoby took the call from your supposed dog-sitter and he told them you were in California."

That news had the effect of being thrown in a cold shower. Curtis was awake now and seething. "I want to talk with Jacoby when I get back." He couldn't imagine how a detective could make a mistake like that. "Khilt is making this personal and I'm getting really fucking angry."

Aislinn tried to diffuse things a bit. "I knew you'd be worried about Barclay, so I took him to my parents' house. He knows them, and Khilt won't think to look there."

Curtis considered whether Khilt would go as far as to harm his dog and couldn't come up with an answer. "Good thinking. Thanks."

"It's like he's watching us," she said.

"That's entirely possible, Aislinn. I want you to be extra careful until we nail this guy. He seems to be able to grab women at will."

"Yeah, well, none of those women were me."

That comment drew a picture for Curtis of the look on her face. She was right, none of the women Khilt had taken were anything like Aislinn. "So he knows I found the Napa connection."

"Probably."

"He knows," Curtis said. "What do you think, will he panic and move things up if he figures we're getting close?"

There was a long pause, then Aislinn said, "I don't think so. He planned this and he's methodical to the point of being obsessive. And, he probably still doesn't believe we can find him."

Curtis kicked around her comments. They pretty much matched his. "Yeah, I agree. Let's hope we're right."

Aislinn cleared her throat. "The personal ads were interesting."

"How so?" His grip on the phone tightened.

"Two entries between August 3rd and now, both from LK to CW."

"What the fuck. Seriously?"

"Seriously. On August 4th, this one appeared. *CW. It's not difficult. Everything makes sense. Just look back. LK.* And on August 10th he ran a second one. *CW. Just missed you at the hotel. Good work. But you were too slow out of the gate. Not enough time. LK.*"

"Oh, for Christ's sake, the son-of-a-bitch is taunting us," Curtis said angrily. Khilt had been at Fifteen Beacon, watching them when they searched the room. He tried to figure out where Khilt might have been, but couldn't put it together.

The cab turned off the freeway onto a palm-lined street and for a second Curtis wished palms would grow in Boston. LA was so pretty, until you scratched away the façade. Then it was just as gritty as Boston. Curtis decided LA could keep their palms.

"He was watching us," he said.

"Yeah, just when you thought this couldn't get any creepier," Aislinn said.

"Can you email that to me," Curtis asked.

"Already did."

"Thanks." A moment of silence, then, "Check with the newspaper and see if you can get anything on who placed the ads."

"Already done. The purchaser paid cash and there are no CCTV cameras at the advertising desk."

"Yeah, okay."

"What are you doing in LA?" Aislinn asked.

"Exactly what he told us to do. Looking back. So far I've tied him in to murders in Napa and Chicago. It looks like the trail heads from Chicago to Los Angeles."

"Christ, how many women has he killed?"

"I don't know," Curtis said. "I'm hoping this is the end of the line. No idea, though. Did Charlesbois take the reward off the table?"

"Not yet. Stan has Leah Atkinson in Vice watching what's happening on the streets. She'll know by mid-afternoon tomorrow."

"What the hell does he think he's doing?"

Aislinn sensed Curtis's anger and cut in. "Stan's going to visit him tomorrow afternoon. We're thinking that if it's okay with you, we'll arrest his ass and throw him in jail."

Curtis actually grinned. "I'd like to be there for that."

"Not me."

"Tell Stan it's okay to go ahead, just make sure he follows exact procedure on this one. Charlesbois has expensive lawyers."

"Stan knows that."

"Okay, Aislinn. Thanks. Sorry to call so late on a Saturday night."

"It's okay, boss. When are you back?"

"Hopefully before Wednesday."

"Right, Wednesday." She didn't say it, but they were both thinking the same thing. Wednesday was when Renee's body would show up somewhere.

Curtis continued. "I'll send you and Stan an email with what I've figured out since I left Boston."

"I'll watch for it." Aislinn was quiet for a moment, then said, "We've really got a sick one here."

"Yeah, we do. Talk later."

Curtis sat quietly in the back seat until the cab pulled up to the hotel. He paid the driver, shouldered his laptop and pulled his suitcase behind him into the lobby. The Figueroa Hotel was his favorite in LA—potted palms, hand-painted furniture and soft music on the house system. Everything normal. Just another day.

Except for Renee Charlesbois. She was somewhere in or around Boston, either waiting for someone to kick down the door and save her or waiting to die. Those were her options, and which one played out was up to him.

Some days he wondered if he should just cash his parents' check and be done with it.

# CHAPTER FORTY-FIVE

The cold crept into Renee's bones and chilled her. At first it had been hot and dry, but now she couldn't seem to get warm. She was an optimist, but she was beginning to worry about her health. She had a constant cough, and pneumonia wasn't far off.

She had diligently kept track of the days that had passed since Liem Khilt had grabbed her, and the count was up to ten. Ten days in solitary, not feeling the sun or fresh air on her skin. Ten days of listening to his footsteps on the stairs, wondering if this was the time he would be intent on killing her. She was a strong woman, but she had her limits. Her hair was filthy, hanging in greasy strands about her sallow face. Other than the tiny sink, there were no facilities for her to bathe, and her captor hadn't given her any soap. Splashing water on herself was not an effective way of keeping clean. Although she was acclimatized to her odor, she knew it was bad.

Renee stared at the door. It was little more than a simple piece of wood with hinges and a lock, but it kept her a prisoner with no chance of escape. She had searched everywhere, looking for one weak spot in the room's armor. There was none. Her survival depended entirely on the Boston police. It was that simple. Every day she hoped for the good guys and thought of Curtis Westcott and his team, and urged them to do the impossible. To find her. To save her.

How would he kill her? She tried to push it from her thoughts, but couldn't. Would he torture her or simply shoot her? It was like being in a slow-motion car crash, watching the front of the car crumple and the engine pushing the steering column into her chest. Every passing moment closer to death. Sometimes she thought it would drive her mad.

She turned her head slowly and stared at the ceiling. How was she connected to her captor? It was a total mystery. The man was adamant he knew her, and that if she dug deep enough she would remember where they had met. But to date, any memory of him had remained elusive, filed away in some dark recess of her mind. There had been so many young men milling about while she was in college. Was he one of them? A shapeless body in a sea of eager faces, all anxious to date the attractive, rich girl. What made it even more difficult, was that he was always in disguise. She had only seen him once without the prosthetics. His hideously scarred face was not one she would easily forget. Unless she had met him before he had been disfigured.

Renee closed her eyes and thought about her parents. Her father would be his usual self, stomping about and threatening anyone and everyone that if anything happened to his daughter there would be hell to pay. It was not only his nature, but his defense mechanism as well. He would get through this. It was her mother she worried about. She didn't cope well with problems and over the years Renee and her father had developed a habit of shielding her mother from things. She knew nothing of Amery Kincaid or her father's questionable business practices. She was completely in the dark about the rampant drug and alcohol abuse Renee had seen growing up in affluent circles. Her mother was beautiful, and delicate. It was entirely possible this could destroy her health, and Renee constantly worried for her.

The sound of footsteps on the stairs resonated through the small room and she sucked in a couple of deep breaths to keep her pulse in check. Was this the time? Did he have dinner in his hand, or a knife? The key slipped into the lock.

# CHAPTER FORTY-SIX

Curtis arrived at the crime scene fifteen minutes after Stan Lamers. His detective was already in control of the situation. The area surrounding the body was cordoned off and a forensics crew was suiting up near their van. Curtis flashed his creds at one of the uniforms working the perimeter and slipped under the tape. Stan watched him as he approached.

"Not good, LT." His left hand was on his hip, his right hand rubbing his bald head. "Not good at all."

"Is it her?" Curtis asked, glancing about. It was early morning and the dew was still burning off the grass. A white sheet lay on the wet grass, covering a body.

"I think so. It's hard to tell."

Curtis gave him a sideways look, then continued on to the sheet, careful where he was stepping. He tucked his hair behind his ears, reached down and pulled the sheet aside. What had been an adult woman was now a headless torso. Her head had been severed midway up the neck by a dull knife or axe. The cuts were more like hacks than slices and skin hung in jagged globs. Her spinal vertebrae were bright white against the splash of red.

"Where's her head?" Curtis asked, his mind replaying Khilt's words in the interview. ...*like a chicken with its head cut off*. "You find it yet?"

"Over here." Stan pointed to a tiny shed about twenty yards from the torso. He picked his way through the grass, disturbing as little as possible. Another uniform stood by the door to the shed and he nodded as Stan and Curtis entered. Curtis could smell death as he ducked through the low door and left the sunshine behind. Another sheet, this one smaller, lay in the middle of the floor. Stan tiptoed over to it and pulled it back. Renee Charlesbois stared back at them, her eyes frozen open in death. They bored into his soul, asking why he had been so slow. Why hadn't he found Liem Khilt before he killed her? Why?

*This could have ended differently, Lieutenant Westcott. You could have done your job and found him before he sliced off my head. Why were you so slow?*

Curtis sat bolt upright, his heart racing, his mouth dry, his body drenched in sweat. Around him, the hotel room was dark and quiet. A low red light glowed from the alarm clock on the night table, and Curtis dropped his head back on the pillow and sucked in air. He could barely breathe. It took a couple of minutes to calm down enough to have a drink of water. He sat up and took a cautious sip, but it caught in his throat and he coughed it up. Eventually, he managed to keep some down.

He was used to dreams, but that one had been more jarring than anything he had experienced. Renee Charlesbois had been so real, her eyes so pleading. He slid out of bed and checked the clock. Almost eight Sunday morning. He had slept for nine hours. His mind was clearing now, the vivid images dissipating as he headed for the shower. He turned on the tap and slipped in, the cool water invigorating.

By nine o'clock Curtis had downed two cups of coffee and placed a call to the Los Angeles police. Steve Armitage, a lieutenant in the homicide department, was on duty and took the call. Curtis quickly explained the reason for his visit and gave Armitage the dates he had found in the Chicago interview with Timothy Kehill. He explained that he felt those dates were tied to a crime in Los Angeles. After they spoke, Armitage agreed to meet with him, and they settled on ten o'clock. Curtis hung up and took some time to review his notes.

Liem Khilt had left a string of bodies across the country, and if Corrine Wheeler was right, there was a connecting thread. He enjoyed taunting the police, although neither of the investigators in Napa or Chicago had noticed. It remained to be seen whether the LAPD had been any more diligent. He wasn't holding his breath on that one. The key, at least in the Boston crime, was to catch the word association and tie the two together. If you missed that, you missed the entire exercise. Khilt had not mentioned the personal ads in any interviews, so maybe he hadn't used that medium in any of his previous crimes. If he was consistent, and Curtis felt he was, Khilt would have met with someone from the investigating unit in LA, and that was when he would have dropped the clues. But why?

That simple question was driving him crazy. Why would Khilt take the time to create such an intricate web? Why not just kill the women and be done with it? If Khilt hadn't shown up at Chloe's party and steered the conversation in the direction he wanted, there would be no trail. Khilt had left no clues in Boston for them to work with, and was almost perfect in his execution of the crime. He could simply have killed Renee Charlesbois and walked away. Yet he had shown up at both Chloe's party and the precinct with the sole intent of giving the police a trail to follow. Once Curtis had made the connection, the trail was clear. Boston to Napa to Chicago and now Los Angeles.

Curtis jotted down the key words from the interview with Timothy Kehill. *Electricity. Three-ten* and *three twenty-four*. All in the past tense. Moving back from Chicago. Had Khilt abducted the woman on March 10th and dumped her body on the 24th? His meeting with Steve Armitage would tell. Curtis packed up his files and laptop and headed for the Lobby Café, where he ordered breakfast and another coffee. He finished eating and caught an Uber to the police station, arriving at three minutes to ten. A uniform at the main desk put a call through to Armitage's local and a minute later the man appeared. He was a very fit, mid-forties African-American with intelligent eyes. He smiled and Curtis noticed one tooth was slightly crooked, enough to be noticeable. He offered his hand and they shook.

"Come on in," he said after they introduced themselves. His voice was a stereo system with full bass, no treble. "My office is down the hall."

"Thanks." Curtis followed Armitage through the sea of desks. It didn't seem to matter that it was Sunday, the precinct was busy. At least twelve cops were at their desks working the phones or typing on their computers. They made their way through the bullpen and entered a wide hall, walking side-by-side.

"I only found one case that matches the dates you gave me," Armitage said as they entered his office. It was a small space, made more cramped by a large desk and a filing cabinet. Armitage sat in the recliner behind his desk and waved at an empty chair. "Here's the file. Unsolved. Cold, and getting colder."

Curtis flipped through the contents and glanced up at Armitage. "You sure this is the only one?" he asked.

"Yeah, why?"

"The other women he killed were high profile in the community. This gal, Kelly Moran, was pretty down and out."

Armitage nodded. "Yeah, she was living with addictions. She had a shitty little bachelor apartment on Skid Row."

"Skid Row?" Curtis asked. "You've got to be kidding me."

"Nope, it's real, around 5th and San Pedro. There are rectangles painted onto the cement sidewalks. Designated sleeping zones between 7: 30 at night and six in the morning."

"Only in LA," Curtis said.

"Anyway, she was in a handful of porn movies a couple of years ago and from what we could gather, dealing meth and crack cocaine when she was abducted. Not a lot of waves on this one, Curtis. Dealing is a risky business."

"She was electrocuted?" Curtis asked.

"Uh huh. Fried good. Coroner suspected she got hit with a couple of thousand volts. But there were no high voltage lines near where we found her. That's how we knew she was either murdered or she had died accidentally and then someone moved her body."

"Oh, I don't think she died accidentally," Curtis said. He took a few minutes to bring the LA cop up to speed on his investigation. When he had finished, Armitage let out a deep breath and scratched his head.

"So we need to go back through the interviews," he said. "See if we can find one that might be your guy."

Curtis nodded. "Yup. Do you have time?"

Armitage smiled. The large, slightly crooked tooth suited him. "Sure. Why not?"

They rode the elevator to the basement and Armitage filled out the necessary paperwork requesting access to the murder book on Kelly Moran. The uniform working the desk was a pleasant man, late fifties, who knew Armitage. They joked around for a bit, then when everything was in place, he buzzed the two homicide cops through into the records room. Curtis followed Steve Armitage down a long hall, their shoes clicking emptily on the worn tiles. They reached an unlocked, nondescript door and Armitage entered, holding the door for Curtis. He flipped on a light.

Curtis stared, open-mouthed. The room was crammed with more paper and files than he would have thought possible. The lighting was horrible, the air thick with dust, and the aisles between the rows of files narrow.

Curtis glanced at Steve Armitage. "I sure hope you know where this stuff is," he said.

Armitage scanned the paper he had been given by the cop working the desk. He studied it for a minute, then said, "Over there." He pointed to one side. "I think."

"Oh, my God," Curtis whispered under his breath, following Armitage into the labyrinth.

# CHAPTER FORTY-SEVEN

Jacques Charlesbois sat in his den, staring at the family pictures above the fireplace. Renee, his wife and him, they had spent so much time together. Christmas portraits taken with fresh snow weighing heavy on the evergreen branches. Vacation photos from a beach in Hawaii, parasailing in Costa Rica, climbing the ruins at Macho Picchu. Only on a very rare occasion had he thought about life without his wife or his daughter. The very idea of either woman disappearing was unthinkable. And yet, the unthinkable had happened.

What sort of sick bastard had taken his daughter? And why? He had received no ransom note, no demand of any sort for money. Nothing made sense. The police were working hard to find Renee, but to date they had come up empty. That confused him. Criminals almost always left clues when they committed crimes, yet the Boston police had been unable to find anything. Not even the smallest bit of forensic evidence pointing to who was responsible. Were they incompetent, or was the person behind this that brilliant?

He feared the latter was the answer.

He had been aggressive with Curtis Westcott from the onset, and in retrospect he wondered if alienating the man in charge of finding his daughter was a smart move. His tenacious nature—the drive that had seen him succeed where others had failed—was working against him here. These were new, uncharted waters. As was relying on someone else to get things done. Like trusting Curtis Westcott to find Renee.

Westcott had come under intense fire when he assumed the top position in the homicide department, but he had silenced his opponents by proving he could do the job. He was well respected by his peers, the media, and Boston's public in general. He was intelligent and creative and his track record for solving unusual crimes was common knowledge. He should feel lucky that this was the man who was searching for his daughter.

Charlesbois stood and paced slowly about the room. The rich mahogany and teak furniture. The thick carpets and expensive tapestries. The bookshelves filled with first editions. They all meant nothing without his daughter. He leaned against a built-in wall unit, filled with his golf trophies and did something he hadn't done in many years. He cried.

For five full minutes he stood without moving, his hands at his sides, refusing to acknowledge the tears by wiping them away. His breathing was slow, his metabolism and pulse relaxed. He made a decision. He knew what he had to do. Slowly, he walked to his desk and picked up the telephone.

He dialed a number and waited for the other party to answer.

# CHAPTER FORTY-EIGHT

Steve Armitage was an optimist to the core. He refused to see the records room as a sea of indistinguishable papers. Rather, he viewed finding the Moran interviews, which had been improperly filed, as a challenge. On one hand, Curtis applauded his vigor. On the other, he thought Armitage was a bit crazy.

"It's not the first time," Armitage said, taking a third careful look at where the files should be.

Curtis glanced about the fire hazard. There were at least a thousand dead redwoods in the room. "I can't imagine," he said.

The sarcasm wasn't lost on Armitage. "This is central LA, Curtis," he said. "We just try to keep up with things. Getting ahead isn't an option. We've got gangs killing gangs, husbands killing wives, locals killing tourists, and on a really bad day we even get the tourists killing each other."

Curtis smiled. "Imagine how bad it would be if it snowed here. That would *really* piss everyone off."

Armitage laughed. "Yeah, at least we've got the weather. But, you know, that's what attracts all the nutcases. That and Hollywood."

"Everyone's a star," Curtis said.

"Yeah, everyone's a star." Armitage glanced at what he had on the Moran file. "Okay, stuff gets misfiled all the time. Cases filed by first name rather than last, married rather than nee, that kind of thing. We can track them down, you'll see."

"Okay, how about I watch, you think. I'm not sure my brain works that way."

Armitage grinned. "This is LA, baby. Your brain's gotta work that way."

Ninety minutes later, Steve Armitage pulled a thin file from the shelf and held it up like a trophy. It had been filed under Crown Valley Parkway, the location where her body had been found. The two men retreated to Armitage's office, where the light was better and spread the contents of the investigation across the desk. Aside from the perfunctory particulars and autopsy results there wasn't much of any substance.

"Seven interviews," Armitage said. "Not a lot of willing witnesses when most of them are either selling drugs or trying to score. We know she had friends and acquaintances in Skid Row, but they didn't surface. This is what we've got."

Curtis glanced through the file, reading the ME's report first. Kelly Moran had died from a lethal jolt of electricity, administered to her back, between the shoulder blades. A large round burn mark was evidence of where the killing voltage had entered, and the soles of her feet were both split open where the electrical charge had exited. According to the ME, she had died quickly. Her body was covered with scarring, predominantly in the crooks of her arms and on her legs. Track marks from intravenous needles. Drugs. The tox scan showed a heavy concentration of cocaine and heroin. Her stomach contents indicated she had eaten about six hours before death. Her overall health was poor, as were her teeth. Curtis spent an extra minute or two looking at the dental records. He set them on the table in front of Steve Armitage.

"Check out the older dental work," he said. "At one point, her teeth were properly cared for. In fact, I'd say she had orthodontic work when she was younger."

Armitage studied the photos and attached records. "Yeah, she had good teeth at one time. What are you thinking?"

Curtis leaned back in the chair and cupped his hands behind his neck. "The women in Boston, Napa and Chicago were all successful, and they all had rich parents and privileged lives. I wonder if Kelly Moran ever had that sort of life."

Armitage shrugged. "According to the files, both her parents are dead. Looks like they died at the same time about four years ago. No cause of death given. She had no other family, so we didn't spend any time looking in that direction." Armitage leaned forward, his elbows on the desk. "Where she lived, Curtis, it's a war zone. Drugs, gangs, prostitution, porn, violence—it's all there. When a woman with no family, no friends, and track marks up and down her arms ends up on a slab, the case doesn't get the attention it should. It can't. We've got limited resources, and when the people who knew her don't want to be interviewed, everything grinds to a halt."

Curtis gave the man a hint of a knowing smile and nodded his head ever so slightly. "Yeah, we get them too, Steve," he said. "Just not the volume you guys see."

Armitage's voice and face were sad, and he said, "We just can't do it."

Curtis saw the hurt in the man's eyes. A decent man in a job that witnessed so much sadness. So many good, young lives wasted. And time after time, watching the scenes play out, powerless to stop it. Curtis knew the feeling, just not on that scale.

"Where was she from before she came to LA?" Curtis asked. "Maybe I'll poke around a bit and see if she had a better life before the drugs got her."

Armitage studied the file. "Seattle," he said. "Her parents' names were Peter and Joyce." He jotted that on a piece of paper and handed it across the desk.

Curtis slipped it into his pocket and began reading through the thin stack of interviews the police had conducted after her body had appeared next to the parkway. Three were with women, and he scanned them quickly, reading enough to get the idea that Kelly Moran was a woman with problems. Men problems, drug problems, money problems. The fourth interview was with a young black man, described by the interviewing officer as approximately twenty-two. Not his guy but Curtis perused it anyway. Same stuff, just a different slant. He went on to the next one. Immediately, the warning lights went off.

The man's name was Michael Thill, white male, about thirty-eight years of age. His general description fit Liem Khilt to a T, including the black-rimmed glasses. And the interview was more than a little interesting. Curtis found the coffee station, poured a cup, added cream and sugar and retreated to Armitage's office to read the contents. The date and time on the first page indicated Michael Thill had come in voluntarily on March 8th, five days after Kelly Moran had disappeared. The interviewer's name was Alec Brand, a twenty-year veteran of homicide central.

Brand: What brings you in today, Mr. Thill?

Thill: Please, I hate formality. Call me Mike. Even Michael is too formal. Right from the beginning, I've always preferred Mike to Michael.

Brand: Okay, Mike. Did you know Kelly Moran?

Thill: Yes, I knew her. She cleaned my house every two weeks. She did a great job, especially in the winter months when I was always rolling wood into the house for the fireplace. You ever have to get large chunks of wood up a hill from the forest by the lake? It's hard, and it makes a real mess. Chopping the trees. Wood chips everywhere. She cleaned them up, every last one of them.

Brand: That's nice, Mike. Did Kelly ever talk to you about her friends? Where she hung out, what she did when she wasn't at your place.

Thill: A bit. Most of the time she stayed around the area where she lived. She said some of the guys had been really rough on her. I think they beat her. And I know she was still using drugs. She was unsteady with the vacuum cleaner, like the way a plane sometimes yaws back and forth on landing.

Brand: She admitted to you she was into drugs?

Thill: Sure, I knew it. She wore short-sleeve shirts sometimes when she cleaned. I could see the track marks on her arms. I talked to her about it. Asked if she would like to try and clean herself up.

Brand: You saying you reached out to her? Tried to help?

Thill: I tried, yes, but she didn't accept. I try to steer clear of the OG in my personal life and help the people who really need it. But even though she declined, she was polite about it. Told me she had plans to get out of LA. I think she said she was going to Seattle or Chicago. Going to get off the drugs and go clean and sober. Figured it would probably be Chicago. Said it rained too much in Seattle.

Brand: I'm a bit lost, Mike. What's the OG?

Thill: The overly gregarious. You know, the happy-no-matter-what-happens-type. They drive me nuts. I cut them out, keep real people in my personal life. Normal people.

Brand: I see. When was the last time you saw her alive?

Thill: On March 2nd, the day before she disappeared. She stopped by, it was her regular cleaning day. Everything seemed normal. I always made her lunch, a good hearty meal, and when she left, she was in good spirits. She left about five after five. No, I think it was five-nineteen. I looked at the kitchen clock after she went out the front door. I wasn't the last person to see her alive, was I?

Brand: No, she was at a club near her house in the evening. We've spoken to a couple of people who saw her. What else can you tell us?

Thill: She liked to read. Asked to borrow one of my Alex Haley books once. *A Different Kind of Christmas*. And when that Star Trek show was on, she'd watch it while she worked. Said her favorite character was Patrick Stewart, that Captain Picard character. Liked his bald head. You know, she was a good person. But I don't think she liked to remember the past, and she looked forward to the future as a real challenge.

Brand: That's common, Mike. Listen, we'll need your address and phone number. And thanks for coming in.

Thill: Not a problem.

Curtis finished his coffee, had Steve Armitage show him to the photocopier and made two copies of the interview. He worked the hi-liter on the text. When he was finished, the page had numerous yellow marks. Steve Armitage watched, and when Curtis had gone through the entire text he turned it so the LA cop could see.

"I'm just guessing at some, but I think these are the words he wants us to see. *Beginning. Chopping. Seattle. Chicago. Personal. Five after five. Five-nineteen. Hearty lunch. Alex Haley.* These are for sure. There's probably more in there somewhere."

Armitage looked puzzled. "What the hell. I don't get it. What does all this have to do with your investigation?"

"This guy does not say what he means. There's an underlying message in all his interviews. I think when he says *beginning*, he means that Kelly Moran was his first victim. *Seattle* is easy, that's where Kelly Moran was from originally. *Chicago* is easy too. Unfortunately. *Five after five* and *five-nineteen* are dates. Annette Shelby disappeared on May 5th and they found her body on a golf course on May 19th. And she had been cut up pretty bad. So that ties in with *chopping*. *Personal* is a bit of a stretch, but I think he's referring to the personal ads column in the local papers. We found two in the *Boston Globe*, both directed at me personally. Taunting more than anything else."

"You want me to have a couple of my detectives to look through the personal ads at that time?"

"Do you have the manpower?" Curtis asked.

"I'll find it," Armitage said. He made a note in his day timer.

Curtis continued on the words he had hi-lighted. "*Hearty lunch* I'm not so positive should be there, but maybe. Moran's stomach contents, had she been well fed while captive?"

Armitage checked the autopsy report. "Yes. Evidence of meat, vegetables, and dairy products."

"He was particular about what he fed Annette Shelby and Erica Klein as well. May be important, may be that he likes to cook."

"What about *Alex Haley*?" Armitage asked.

Curtis shrugged. "No idea. But he mentioned Haley by name when he was interviewed in Napa."

"But Napa and Erica Klein—she was his third victim. What about Chicago?"

"If he's consistent, then he's giving us clues to both the previous crime and the next one. With LA being his first, he only shows us the clues to Chicago. When he's interviewed in Chicago, he points to LA and Napa. In Napa, he looks back at Chicago and ahead to Boston. There's a definite pattern. That said, he's being very careful not to give the investigating police any clues to the current crime. So if you don't pick up on what he's doing, and you look at the murder in your own jurisdiction as a single crime, you miss everything he gives you."

"Holy shit," Armitage said. "Are you sure Kelly Moran was his first one?"

"Not a hundred percent, but I think so. He doesn't refer to any city or time in the past tense. And he uses the word *beginning*. I think Kelly Moran is the start of the trail. He got going in your backyard."

"Lucky us," Armitage said.

Curtis was silent for a minute, then he said. "If I'm right, I've only got until Wednesday midnight, maybe early morning Thursday, before he kills Renee Charlesbois. I need to find the link between these women."

"Anything stand out? Same schools, universities, social clubs?"

"Nothing so far. I've sent everything back to Boston that I unearthed in Napa and Chicago and they're looking to see if the women's lives are connected somehow. So far no common threads, but we haven't had enough time to dig deep. We've only just discovered the LA connection—that Kelly Moran was one of his victims. Each time we discover a new murder it expands the amount of time we need to search through their past lives and see if there are any commonalities."

Armitage shook his head. "Jesus, Curtis. Four women in four different cities with totally different lives. You're running out of time."

"We are."

"Well, good luck."

Curtis glanced at the words he had hi-lighted with the yellow marker. "We're going to need it."

# CHAPTER FORTY-NINE

Stan Lamers checked the clip in his pistol and slipped it into his shoulder holster. The last thing he expected was for Jacques Charlesbois to oppose his arrest, but stranger things had happened. He nodded to the three officers who were escorting him to the Charlesbois estate and they all headed for the parking garage.

Sunday afternoon and he had the privilege of arresting one of Boston's most prominent citizens. He wondered how long it would take the press to get wind of this. They were like sharks at sensing the slightest trace of blood in the water and in about an hour it would be churning red. Stan put a last call through to Leah Atkinson in Vice, hoping to hear Charlesbois had pulled the reward.

"Nothing yet," Leah said, her voice commingled with static. "But I've only talked with a couple of my contacts. I need more time. These guys sleep late."

"Wake them up," Stan said as he got in his car and started the motor. "I need to know before I go kicking down Charlesbois' door."

"Okay, I'm on it." The line went dead.

Stan pulled out of the parking garage, two patrol cars following him. It was only fair that Aislinn got to hang back at the precinct and run computer searches on Kelly Moran and her deceased parents. She had already visited Charlesbois once and it was his turn. This time though, he was bringing a few uniforms with him.

Curtis was constantly updating them as he unraveled the threads Khilt had left. Curtis suspected Los Angeles was the end of the trail of bodies. Boston to Napa to Chicago to LA—Curtis had uncovered the links between the murders in less than a week. Impressive, but not shocking. Catching the nuances and twists of the case was Curtis's trademark, and by the look of things, this one was all about double meanings and hidden clues.

Stan stared out the window as he drove, the congestion of the city giving way to the leafy green of Chestnut Hill. Groves of white oaks flashed by and the scent of freshly cut grass hung in the air. They reached the gates for the Charlesbois estate and he punched the intercom button. There was a buzzing sound and the gates slowly swung back. He pulled ahead, surprised at how clear headed he felt. Charlesbois had been warned, and was about to find out he was not above the law.

Stan tried Leah's number one more time, but her cell rang busy. This was going to happen. Christ, Charlesbois was going to be hot. Stan slipped the phone back in his pocket and touched the handle of his gun. This one was going to be by the book.

An extremely fit security guard was standing under the portico and behind him the front door was open. Stan pulled in a bit too fast and slammed on the brakes. He jumped out of the car and headed straight for the bodyguard, the uniformed officers in tow.

"Boston Police," he said as he took the stairs two at a time. "Check him for weapons and one of you stay with him."

He moved fast into the house with the remaining men, their footsteps echoing through the massive foyer. Stan headed for Charlesbois' office and was just outside the door when his phone rang. He checked the number on his call display, then stopped and answered. It was Leah.

"Give me some good news," he said, staring at the door.

"He pulled the reward," the Vice cop said. "The word's getting out fast now. There are a lot of real pissed off people."

Stan let out a long breath. "Thanks, Leah. You sure made this a lot easier."

"Glad I could help."

Stan motioned for the other cops to stay in the hall, then walked into the office. Jacques Charlesbois sat by the window with his back to the door. Fifteen seconds passed, then he turned to face Stan. His face was haggard, his eyes like an old prizefighter who knows he's been beaten. The two men remained silent for a minute, and when Charlesbois finally spoke, his voice was cracked with emotion.

"I am deeply sorry about the loss of life," Charlesbois said. "I regret my decision to offer the reward."

Stan just nodded. He had what he'd come for.

"It's in your hands," Charlesbois said quietly, his humanity on his sleeve. "Please find my daughter."

"We'll find her, sir. We'll get your daughter back."

There was nothing else to say and Stan turned and left the room. As he walked back to the entrance he realized all he had given Jacques Charlesbois were empty words. Despite all their efforts they had nothing that would lead them to the man who held Renee Charlesbois.

Nothing but a trail heading in the wrong direction through three distant cities.

# CHAPTER FIFTY

C urtis checked the caller ID on his phone. It was Aislinn.
    "What have you got for me?" Curtis asked, cutting into his
steak at the café in the Figueroa Hotel.

"Nothing to connect the women yet, but I have some info on the
Moran family," Aislinn replied.

"And..."

"Peter and Joyce Moran, both born and raised in Seattle. High
school sweethearts, married twenty-two years, one daughter, Kelly, and
what appeared to be a perfect life."

"Wheels come off?" Curtis asked.

"Big time. Peter had a successful construction company that
specialized in neighborhood malls. In addition to building them, his
company owned three. The company revenues were in excess of forty
million a year. They had twenty-five full-time employees and lots of
sub-trades. Anyway, about five years ago the contracts began to dry up.
I can't see any reason for the downturn, but they definitely cratered. A
year later his corporation was filing for bankruptcy protection. That's
when things came apart at home."

"What happened?"

"Murder-suicide. Peter shot his wife, then killed himself. Kelly
found them when she came home for a visit. They'd been dead about
three days. She moved to LA about two weeks after the funeral with just

the shirt on her back. No insurance, house mortgaged to the nines, and a long line of creditors ready to jump on whatever was left. Six months after she buried her parents she started appearing in night court. Charges were dealing drugs, theft, and lots of other misdemeanors. She didn't take their deaths well."

"So Kelly Moran came from a wealthy family," Curtis said. "That's consistent with the other three women."

"Yup. She'd only been on the skids for the last three and a half years."

"I wonder," Curtis said, pausing for a moment, "what caused their business to fail. Aislinn, see what you can find out about Peter Moran's construction company. Something's not right with that. It sounds like this guy built his business from the ground up, and the fact that he owned three strip malls points to him being in for the long run. He sounds cautious and calculating, and not the kind of guy to overextend himself."

"I'll see what I can find, but it'll take some time."

"Time, Aislinn, is what we do not have. Light a fire under your ass, then do the same to every person you talk with."

"Okay. Hey, Leah got word that Charlesbois pulled the reward."

"Thank God for small miracles. Stan didn't have to bring him in, did he?"

"Nope. Charlesbois was just sitting at home when Stan arrived. Stan said he looked like shit. That he had no fight left in him."

"That's not a bad thing, Aislinn. We're the ones in the trenches. It's our fight, not his."

"Are we going to find this guy?" Aislinn asked. It seemed like a silly question, but she knew her boss well enough to know whatever answer he gave would be an honest one.

"Yeah, Aislinn, we'll get him. I just don't know if we'll find him in time."

"That's kind of important."

"No kidding."

"When are you coming back to Boston?"

There was a brief silence, then Curtis said, "The answer's here, Aislinn. I'm not sure how to read what he's giving us. I need to get everything out of these clues. Khilt does everything for a reason. The key to this whole thing, and ultimately to finding Renee Charlesbois, starts in LA. I'm not leaving here until I figure it out."

"There are a lot of people expecting you back tonight. The mayor and the police commissioner to name a couple. They'll be calling tomorrow morning."

"Then talk to them," Curtis said.

"All right. I'll call to you when I get something on why Peter Moran's business tanked."

"Talk to you tomorrow," Curtis said.

Curtis hung up and stared at his steak. It was rare and he had ordered it medium. He waved over the server and handed it back, nicely, then pulled out the stack of interviews Liem Khilt had provided to the various police departments. This time he made a list, noting all the hilighted words in columns, headed by cities and victims.

| Boston | Napa | Chicago | LA |
|---|---|---|---|
| Renee Charlesbois | Erica Klein | Annette Shelby | Kelly Moran |
| Six-thirty | Five after five | Three-ten | Chopping |
| Napa Valley | Chicago | Three-twenty-four | Overly gregarious |
| Frog's Leap | Eight-seventeen | Electricity | Personal |
| Tied down | Alex Haley | Wine, from Napa | Chicago |
| Apocalypse | cuttings | Frog's Leap | Hearty meal |
| Pitch—fork | Boston | Roped in | Five after five |
| New York | Chicken/head cut off | Six-sixteen | Five-nineteen |
| Drowning | Motley crew | Six-thirty | Alex Haley |
| LA | Patrick Stewart | | |

Curtis studied the list. No doubt about it. Khilt was giving them clues to crimes he had committed or was about to commit—on either side of the abduction he was being interviewed for. When he was going to kill the women, how, and in what city. Even looking ahead from Boston to New York, it was all there. And Los Angeles was the start.

He added *beginning* to the LA column, then went back through each interview again. There had to be more, he was just missing it.

LA was the first, and he reviewed that interview. *Michael Thill. Call me Mike.* He knew Kelly Moran, or so he said. Curtis read slowly, looking at each word. *She cleaned my house every two weeks.* Two weeks. Probably giving the interviewer the length of time between when he abducted the women and killed them. He added *two weeks* to the list. *She did a great job, especially in the winter months when I was always rolling wood into the house for the fireplace.* Curtis reread the text. *Rolling wood.* That didn't make any sense. You didn't roll the wood, you chopped it then carried it. He jotted *rolling wood* at the bottom of the list. *You ever have to get large chunks of wood up a hill from the forest by the lake?* What the hell was that? Wood came in logs, not *chunks of wood*, and where was this *forest by the lake?* More words made the list.

His steak arrived, freshly cooked and to his liking. He thanked the server, slid the paper aside and ate his meal, his mind still focused on the interview. *She was unsteady with the vacuum cleaner, like the way a plane sometimes yaws back and forth on landing.*

Curtis stopped, his fork an inch from his mouth. *Yaws.* That wasn't right. A plane could rock sideways, and that was called yaw or yawing. The word was yaw, not yaws. Khilt was too particular with his words to make a mistake. And why use that particular word? Why yaw or yaws? Curtis grabbed his computer from its case on the floor and powered it up. He opened a link to an online dictionary and searched for the word. It appeared on his screen.

*Yaws. An infectious tropical disease marked initially by red skin eruptions and later by joint pain. It mainly affects children and is caused by the bacterium Treponema pertenue.*

Curtis was quiet. *Yaws.* A tropical disease. Where was this going? Did it mean something?

He grabbed his cell phone and called Aislinn.

"LT," Aislinn said, reading Westcott's name on his call display. "What's up? I didn't expect to hear from you until tomorrow."

"I might have something," he said. "Talk to Jacques Charlesbois. It's a long shot, but find out if Renee ever had yaws."

"Yaws?"

"It's a tropical disease."

"Okay, and if she did?"

"I'm not sure. It might be nothing, but Khilt used the word in his LA police interview."

"I remember reading it," she said. "Struck me as a strange word, like it didn't belong."

"Agreed. Let me know what Charlesbois says." He hung up.

Curtis returned to his dinner and the interviews. He retraced his steps through Boston, Napa and Chicago, and came up with some new words and phrases that Khilt may have inserted for their benefit. From the Boston interview, he added *UCLA*. From the Napa interview, when Khilt had been talking about Boston, Curtis jotted down *some suburb just outside the city*. *I'm from south of San Francisco* made his Napa list. He added *Belmont*, *Halsted* and *Broadway* from Chicago, although it was likely these were simply necessary street names that Khilt had used to make his interview believable.

The server arrived with his bill and he left her a good tip. The improperly cooked steak wasn't her fault. He shouldered the carrying case for his laptop and headed for the elevator and his empty hotel room. The next ten hours would be sleepless. Just him and his demons.

# CHAPTER FIFTY-ONE

There was a hint of a smile on Liem Khilt's face. He was hunched over his computer, on-line and inside the LAPD database. He was there for one reason only, and when he had his answer, he left immediately. He had spoofed his IP address, effectively blocking the LA police from tracing him, still, he didn't like to tempt fate. He powered down the computer and leaned back in his chair, his hands running over the silky-smooth surface of the prosthetics covering his face.

Curtis Westcott was good. In fact, the man was very good. In the last seventy-two hours, there had been hits on the Klein file in Napa, the Shelby case in Chicago and finally that scaggy bitch's file in Los Angeles. He had linked Boston to Napa, Napa to Chicago, and Chicago to Los Angeles. Westcott had forwarded everything he found to Aislinn Byrne and Stan Lamers, who were doubtless working with a team of detectives to try and unravel the clues. All that remained to be seen was whether Westcott or his team could piece together the information from the LA interview. If he could, the race would be on. Khilt glanced at his watch. It was nearing midnight on Sunday, August 13th, and time was running out.

By now, Westcott was surely aware of the deadline, which meant he knew they only had three days before Renee Charlesbois showed up without her head. Slowly, his smile disappeared. If Westcott could actually piece things together from the disjointed string of clues, there was little doubt he would eventually key in on the killer's identity. Khilt stared at his reflection in the empty screen, thinking all his plans would be in disarray. The woman in New York would live, and even worse, his life, with all its privileges, would be gone. This was not something he had foreseen.

He had never really expected the police to follow the trail of clues. He certainly hadn't thought they would ever uncover his identity. The edges of his mouth curled down into a sadistic sneer. Christ, how could he have underestimated them so badly? Westcott in particular. He had suspected, hoped even, that the Charlesbois file would end up on Westcott's desk. Most of Boston's high-profile cases did. He knew Westcott was a good detective, and he was anticipating a bit of fun with the man, but this was unacceptable.

First these women had destroyed whatever normal life he could have had, and now simply ridding the planet of them was going to cost him everything—his house, his wealth, his freedom. That couldn't happen. They couldn't win. Not after all these years. The reality of what he'd done by leaving all the clues was beginning to set in. He should have just killed them and been done with it. His actions had been monumentally stupid. He had no one but himself to blame.

Khilt gripped the computer mouse so hard his fingers turned white, and then he hurled it against the wall. Pieces of plastic and metal showered down on the floor and the furniture. The destruction only fueled his rage and he grabbed the screen and yanked it off the desk, ripping the cords from the back of the computer. With a scream he sent it flying across the room and smashing into the window. Glass flew in every direction and embedded in the walls, the ceiling and his face. Most of it hit the prosthetics, but one piece sliced into his skin, a fraction of an inch above his eye. He screamed in pain as blood poured from the cut, momentarily blinding him. When he tried to wipe it away from his eye, his hand grazed the glass and it cut deeper into his face.

He stopped and took a few breaths. This was going in the wrong direction very quickly. He had made some serious mistakes, but losing his cool and destroying things was not the answer. A minute or two passed and he glanced down at his hand. He had an inch-long slice between his index finger and thumb. It should have stitches, but a trip to a hospital would only invite questions. Not a chance. He had enough to worry about with Curtis Westcott sniffing around Los Angeles. He didn't need to open any more doors for the police. He'd done enough already. He'd done far too much.

Khilt retreated to the bathroom and splashed some cold water on his face. He found a pair of tweezers, got a grip on the shard of glass and pulled. It came out easily enough, and he slowed the bleeding with a few pieces of toilet paper, then cleaned his hand and pushed the cut together as best he could and covered it with a bandage. A few minutes of carefully dabbing the cut above his eye stopped the blood and he put on another bandage. He glanced at himself in the mirror and shook his head. What an idiot.

Khilt walked to the living room and sat down in one of the over-stuffed chairs. A massive river-rock fireplace covered one wall, and a bank of shuttered windows covered another. Three more days and he'd be leaving Boston. Right now, that couldn't happen fast enough.

He sat in total silence, going back over the clues he'd given the police, and what his next move should be. They had everything they needed to solve the crimes, but only one clue to link the murders back to his true identity. It was so insignificant, so tiny, that Westcott would never catch it. *Al Stoogs*. Westcott would have to be at the top of his game to catch that one. Maybe things weren't so bad.

He closed his eyes and thought how to proceed. First off, he'd have to finish his business in Boston, get back home and lay low for a while. Westcott had found the links between the murders, and understood the times in the interviews were actually dates. That meant heading for New York now was questionable, as they would be watching. Still, chances were Westcott and his detectives hadn't figured out his reason for killing the women, and if that were the case then they would have no idea as to the identity of the woman in New York. Keep on schedule or let things cool down? He kicked it around for a bit, and decided to wait. The final woman would live a little longer, but she would still die.

He managed a small grin at that. The goal was still in sight, just not as he had planned it.

He was not so flexible on Renee Charlesbois. She was going to die, and on schedule. He briefly contemplated heading down to the wine cellar and killing her now. Westcott was still in Los Angeles, and there was no way he could find what he needed in Chicago and Napa in time. Then a sense of calm returned. Even with Westcott moving at full speed, the chances of him showing up before Thursday were next to impossible. There was no reason to change his carefully planned timetable. Renee Charlesbois would die in the early morning hours of August 17th. Just after midnight. And it would be a grisly, well-deserved death.

# CHAPTER FIFTY-TWO

Curtis lay on the bed as day broke outside his hotel room, staring through the open curtains at a deep blue sky. Traffic noise picked up about six o'clock and he slipped out of bed and into the shower. His last recollection of Sunday night was about two in the morning, when he stopped pacing and lay down on the bed for a nap. Somehow, that had turned into four hours of good sleep and he felt refreshed, even before the shower or coffee.

Monday morning. Less than seventy-two hours until Renee Charlesbois' body would show up somewhere in or around Boston, and here he was a world away in Los Angeles. The phone was ringing when he stepped out of the shower and he wrapped a towel around his waist and jogged across the room. It was Aislinn Byrne.

"Not too early for you, is it?" Aislinn asked.

"Hey, you're on Eastern time. It's only six o'clock here, but I'm up."

"Yeah. When *do* you sleep?"

Curtis ignored her. "What have you got?"

"I talked to Jacques Charlesbois about that yaws thing. He couldn't recall if Renee had ever had it, but after he talked to his wife he called me back. She said that Renee had come down with some weird tropical disease when they were in Costa Rica, about eighteen or nineteen years ago. She thinks it was yaws."

"Really. Eighteen or nineteen years. That's a long time."

"Sure is. They're pulling out the old photo albums. He's going to try and pinpoint the date of the vacation and where they stayed."

"Okay. Good work."

"Do you think it ties in?"

"I don't know," Curtis said slowly. "Right now it's a bit of a long shot, but I think we should follow up. Contact with Annette Shelby's parents in Chicago and Erica Klein's in Napa. Find out if their daughters ever had yaws or any other strange tropical disease. And ask them if they were in Costa Rica eighteen to twenty years ago. Let's say around 2000, give or take. Like I said, it's a long shot, but you never know."

"I'll need contact numbers," Aislinn said.

"I have them right here," Curtis said, digging into the files in his briefcase. He gave Aislinn the information she needed, then asked, "Anything on Peter Moran's bankruptcy?"

"It's only eight o'clock in Boston, boss. I need some time."

Curtis chuckled. Aislinn was right, the agencies she needed to contact weren't even open yet. "Let me know when you get something. Oh, and now that we've got a bit more on this guy's MO, let's run what we have through VICAP again and see if the new information gets any hits."

"Now *that* I can have back to you before noon." Aislinn and Curtis both knew how fast the FBI's computer could run through the criminal records and MO's of all known violent offenders.

"Thanks." Curtis hung up.

He repacked the case files, made some coffee and took some time to read the newspaper that had been left just outside his door. The time constraints on the case were beginning to tell on him, but there was little he could do other than wait until Armitage arrived for work at the Southeast Community precinct. He shaved and brushed his teeth, then grabbed his bag and headed for the lobby. He ate breakfast, downed another cup of coffee and caught a cab to the precinct. With a few hours sleep and some caffeine in his system, he was feeling empowered. It was just after eight when he walked through the front doors and was shown through to Steve Armitage's office. Armitage was on the phone and waved Curtis in when he saw him in the hall. Curtis sat in the same chair he had the day before, and watched the man get animated as he argued for three new computers for his department. By the end of the call he was waving his arms about like a wild man. He hung up and grinned.

"We'll get them," he said. "One thing I know how to do is get around departmental budgets. How are you doing this morning?"

"Great. Got some sleep," Curtis said.

"That always helps. Any new ideas?"

"I have one of my detectives running some new stuff through VICAP. And we're chasing down that *yaws* thing."

"What *yaws* thing?" Armitage asked, leaning back in his chair.

"The interview with Michael Thill. He talked about the way a plane yaws. Planes are sometimes subject to yaw when they land, but the word doesn't work in the plural. Our guy doesn't make mistakes with his English, and he's been consistent in meaning something different from what he's saying."

"So what is *yaws*?"

"Some kind of tropical disease."

Armitage shook his head. "Jesus, Curtis, this whole thing is one big mind fuck."

"Excellent description," Curtis said. Exactly what he had been thinking. "One of my detectives checked with Renee's parents and they think she had some tropical disease about twenty years ago while they were vacationing in Costa Rica."

"Twenty years?"

"Something like that. It was a long time ago. Any chance we could find out if Kelly Moran had been in Costa Rica way back when?"

"Parents dead and no relatives. I don't think so."

Curtis nodded. "What about the personal ads? Any luck?"

"Jim Strickland is working that. He's talking with the papers, getting the files downloaded."

"Excellent."

"What else do you need?" Armitage asked.

"Some kind of a break. This thing is driving me nuts. It's all there, but I'm missing it."

"How about a quiet corner?"

"Naw, I'd rather be outside. Maybe if I'm surrounded by palm trees it will kick start my brain. I think I'll go for a walk. You have my cell number."

"It's on your card?" Armitage glanced at the business card Curtis had left with him.

"Yeah, it's there. Call me if you get anything."

"Do you need a ride?" Armitage asked.

Curtis thought about it. The area around the precinct wasn't the nicest. Maybe if he took the offer he'd end up in a friendlier part of town. "Sure, why not."

The LA cop called down to the front desk and arranged for a uniform and a squad car for Curtis while he was in town. Generous, but he wanted Kelly Moran's killer, and Curtis was proving an excellent ally in the hunt.

Curtis met his driver in the lobby, a young Hispanic officer with two years under her belt. Anna Rodriguez had grown up in LA, her father a maintenance man with the local school board and her mother a teacher. She was intelligent and articulate with a shy grin, and knew LA like she was reading the streets off a map. Curtis liked her.

"I need a beach, Anna," Curtis said. "A stretch of sand where I can sit back and think. I don't function very well inside a box."

"Got it. Long Beach it is. Close by and lots of places to think. It's perfect." She tromped on the gas and for a moment Curtis thought she was going to turn on her lights and siren. Rodriguez settled for weaving in and out of cars on the 710 until they hit Ocean Boulevard and turned east. When they reached the shore, Rodriguez pulled up in a restricted parking zone and switched off the ignition. "We're here."

"You'd never be late delivering pizzas." Curtis already had a firm grip on the door handle, and pushed down.

"Nice place right over there." Anna pointed to a section of beach with a storm wall. "It's about as quiet as it gets in LA."

Curtis slipped out of the car with his bag over his shoulder and walked along the oceanfront for a bit. Couples, families, teenagers with great tans—the beach belonged to everyone. The sun was warm, the surf was low and people bobbed in the water. He walked by two men, concentrating on a Scrabble board, oblivious to the activity about them. It reminded him of his mother and father, sitting in their backyard playing the same game. It had been a while since he had seen them and he made a mental note to give them a call once this case was over. He found a place to sit a hundred yards farther down the shoreline and set his laptop on the table.

Liem Khilt.

What was his real name? Where was he from? Why was he killing these women? Why was he taunting the police?

More questions with no answers.

Why was he Liem Khilt in Boston, Michael Thill in Los Angeles, Keith Mill in Napa and Timothy Kehill in Chicago? Why not just use the same name? In two instances the name could be shortened and he had taken the time to tell the interviewer he preferred the short version. Never Michael or Timothy. Too formal, use the abbreviated version. Mike or Tim. Good Scrabble letters, Curtis thought. What was the letter count for a K? Five. And an M was three or four. Lots of vowels. Curtis gazed at the beach, watching a game of volleyball, then he then sucked in a fast, shallow breath.

The letters. He visualized them as best he could, like they were Scrabble letters. LIEM KHILT. MIKE THILL. KEITH MILL. TIM KEHILL. All names had nine letters, with one K, one M, and two L's. He scooped up his bag and hurried back to where the two men were playing Scrabble. He flashed his badge.

"Police emergency. I need some of your letters."

"What?" one of the men said. "Are you serious?"

"I'm not kidding." Curtis waved at the police cruiser. Rodriguez was out of the car and moving toward him at a dead run in seconds. Curtis picked up the bag containing the remaining letters. "If you've got a problem, tell it to her," Curtis said as Anna arrived.

The Scrabble player checked out Rodriguez, her gun in full view. "No problem. Help yourself."

Curtis dumped the letters on the table and sorted through them. He picked out the nine letters that made up Liem Khilt, then rearranged them into the other three names. Perfect fit. No coincidences here. Then he started rearranging the letters into different combinations. In less than two minutes he had it. He stared at the nine letters, wondering how he hadn't seen it before. It all made sense.

Curtis turned to Anna Rodriguez. "Let's get back to the precinct. Maybe Armitage has something for me."

"Sure." Rodriguez took one last glance at the letters on the table. They left, leaving two very puzzled men in their wake, both staring at the words formed by the letters.

I KILL THEM.

# CHAPTER FIFTY-THREE

After her conversation with Curtis, Aislinn signed onto VICAP and entered the new information they had on Khilt. Some of it was generic and likely of little use—that he moved about from one location to another and that he used different methods to kill the victims. Other things—he arranged to come in for an interview with the investigating police and killed his victims exactly two weeks after abducting them—were specific and likely to be more helpful. She finished and signed out. The system would alert her by email if it had any hits.

She searched through the papers on her desk, found the contact numbers for the parents of the other murdered women and made the first call. Annette Shelby's parents were first on the list and she crossed her fingers. Calling Erica Klein's mother and father risked exposing their belief that Khilt was the perp to the Napa police, and that could result in a total lack of cooperation going forward.

A woman answered the phone, her voice refined and calm. Aislinn asked to speak with Doris Shelby.

"This is Doris. Who's calling?"

"Mrs. Shelby, this is Detective Aislinn Byrne. I'm with homicide in Boston, and I'm calling concerning your daughter, Annette."

There was a long pause on the line, then the voice returned. It had changed, and now sounded hopeful. "Have you found who killed her?"

"Not yet, but we think we're getting close."

"You're in Boston? Is the person who did this from Boston?"

"The investigation is ongoing Mrs. Shelby, and I can't speak to the details. I do have a question for you, if that's okay."

"Yes, of course. What is it?"

"Did Annette ever suffer from a disease called yaws? It would likely have been quite a while ago, around 2000 perhaps."

"Yes, she did."

Aislinn sat bolt upright in her chair. "You sound sure of that."

"I am. It was in June of 2000 and we were vacationing in Costa Rica. We stayed at the Condovac la Costa Resort. Annette got very sick. We were extremely worried about her."

"Can you give me the exact dates you were at the resort?"

There was no hesitation. "June 15th to the 30th."

"You sound positive of that."

"Detective Byrne, it was a nightmare. Our daughter could have died or been horribly disfigured. It was a terrible experience that we never forgot."

"Were there other women about Annette's age at the resort who were sick?"

"Yes, but I can't remember any names or details. We were focused on Annette."

"You mentioned Annette could have died or been disfigured. Is scarring a symptom of yaws?"

"Yes. We were fortunate that the resort had some penicillin on hand. They were quite underhanded about it, but they did finally administer it."

"Underhanded? How so?" Aislinn asked.

"They saw the outbreak as a way to make some money. There wasn't enough penicillin to go around, so it went to the highest bidders."

Aislinn gripped the phone tighter. "So some of the infected people didn't get the medicine."

"Yes."

"Do you remember how many people were infected?"

"Six. Five girls and one boy."

"And the girls got the medicine."

"Yes."

"Did the boy get sick?"

"Yes, he suffered terribly." A moment passed, then she asked, "Is the young man the person who killed our daughter?"

"That is a possibility. We're not sure at this time."

"Are you going to charge him?" There was rage in the voice now.

Aislinn couldn't destroy whatever hope there might be under that anger by being evasive. "Yes, Mrs. Shelby, if we are certain he's responsible we will find him and charge him."

"Please let us know."

"Yes, of course," Aislinn said, then gave Doris Shelby her contact information in case she thought of anything else. "Also, everything we've talked about today should be kept strictly between us. It's fine to share this with you husband, but no one else. No friends, and certainly not the media. If we think you've spoken to anyone about this, it will make it difficult to share any further information."

"I understand."

The call ended and Aislinn opened her browser and found the contact information for Condovac la Costa Resort in Costa Rica. She stopped by Enrico Sanchez's desk, tapped him on the shoulder and together they headed for the privacy of Westcott's office.

"I might need someone fluent in Spanish," she said as she dialed the number.

She did, and even with Sanchez present the call didn't go well. The manager of the resort shut them down the moment they requested information on guests who had stayed there. Privacy concerns, he said, adding that the files they needed were not on the computers and inaccessible. Aislinn pushed a bit, then closed it off by thanking him for his time.

"Curtis can deal with that," she said to Sanchez after she hung up. "Thanks for trying."

"No problem." He headed back to his desk.

Aislinn stood in Westcott's office for a moment and stared at the picture of Liem Khilt on Curtis's corkboard. "Got you, you motherfucker," she said, then picked up the phone and dialed Westcott's cell.

# CHAPTER FIFTY-FOUR

If Curtis thought Anna Rodriguez drove fast to get to the beach, she pretty much set a land speed record on the trip back. Curtis poured himself out of the cruiser and followed Rodriguez into the building. They found Steve Armitage in his office, scanning some computer printouts.

Curtis sat in a chair facing the LA detective. "The names our guy has used in all four abductions and killings are anagrams. Rearrange the letters in each name and this is what you get." Curtis jotted the three words on a pad and slid it across the desk.

"Shit, we've got a serial killer," Armitage said, staring at the words.

"No, I don't think so." Curtis took a few minutes to rehash Corrine Wheeler's view on the killer's profile, all the while thinking how tired he was of explaining the same thing over and over. "He's specific about his targets, highly organized and precise in his timing and execution. And he's never sexually attacked any of the women. He's on a mission."

"He's a sick, twisted, bastard." Armitage swallowed the last of his coffee and slammed the mug down on his desk. "Fucker."

Curtis's cell phone buzzed and he checked the caller ID. It was Aislinn. "What's up?" he asked.

"I have something pretty damn fine." Aislinn's voice sounded eager.

Curtis sat up, listening intently. "What?"

"We found the link between the women."

"Is it Costa Rica?" Curtis asked in a hushed tone.

"It is definitely Costa Rica. Annette Shelby's mother had a vivid memory of the trip. She knew the dates, the resort, everything, right on the phone. Condovac la Costa Resort, June 15th to 30th, 2000. It turns out Annette Shelby and a few other kids at the resort got really sick with yaws. They were panicking."

"Why? What's so scary about yaws?" He was up and walking about now, holding onto the phone like it was a winning lottery ticket.

"It's debilitating. She said the scarring from the sores can be permanent. And that's not all."

"What?" Curtis asked.

"The resort didn't have enough penicillin for all the kids. Shelby's parents had the money to buy the shots Annette needed. At least one kid went without the medicine."

"Let me guess. A boy." He stopped pacing, his heart still racing.

"Bingo. His parents either didn't have enough money or wouldn't cough up for the drugs. The other kids got the drugs, and he got a full-blown case of yaws."

"Give me the details on the resort again." Curtis motioned to Armitage for his pen and jotted down the information as she gave it to him. "Excellent work, Aislinn."

"I tried to get a list of the guests at the time, but nothing was computerized back then. All their guest records are filed away in some box in a back room. When I asked for them to dig them up and send them to me, the manager wouldn't do it."

"All right. Maybe we can convince them from this end." He switched to another topic. "Anything from VICAP?"

"No."

"Well, not surprising. I'd say our guy is exacting revenge for something that happened eighteen years ago."

"Looks like."

"Okay, keep on it. I'll talk to you soon." He hung up and filled Steve Armitage in on the conversation. "I think we just found our motive."

"Holy shit, that disease must have messed him up bad."

"I guess." Curtis finally sat down. "I need to Google yaws—find out more about it."

"I can do better. We have a Merck Manual in the library," Armitage said, referring to the thick paperback Merck & Company publishes for home use on medical issues. "You want to have a look?"

"Sure do," Curtis said.

Armitage turned to Rodriguez, who was hovering at the door, waiting to see if Curtis needed another ride. "You know where the library is?"

Rodriguez nodded. "Yes."

"The Merck Manual, please."

"You bet." Rodriguez was gone, moving quickly down the hallway.

A middle-age plainclothes officer stuck his head into Armitage's office. "I've pulled the classified ads over the time period you asked, but I'm not finding anything with the key words you gave me."

Armitage did the introductions. Jim Strickland and Curtis shook hands and Armitage said to Curtis, "Maybe it's not there."

Curtis shook his head. "It's there. Remember, this guy is predictable. There's a message somewhere between March 10th and March 24th." He gave Strickland the four names Liem Khilt had used in the different cities. "Try looking for a combination of the nine letters he used to make up the names he used. Watch for the initials, he likes to use those as well."

"Right."

"Take a copy of the interview he had with your detectives when you were working the Moran case. Watch for words he used in the interview."

"Sure," Strickland said, taking the paper and a copy of the interview. He almost bumped into Anna Rodriguez at the door, the Merck Manual in her hand.

"Got it." She handed the heavy, red paperback to Curtis. "Is this what you wanted?"

"That's it." Curtis flipped to the back and found yaws in the index. He turned to page 1099 and read the relevant pieces of the text aloud. "*Yaws begins as a slightly raised sore, usually on a leg. The sore heals, but granulomas erupt on the face, arms, legs and buttocks. Painful open sores may develop…and many other disfiguring growths, especially around the nose may develop.*" Curtis glanced up at Armitage. "He was disguised when I met him in Boston. Facial prosthetics. Now we know why."

"He's disfigured."

Curtis nodded. "Disfigured and pissed off about it." He thought for a minute, then said, "How long would it take you to get a warm body down to Condovac la Costa Resort in Costa Rica? We need to get our hands on the guest logs from the last two weeks of June 2000."

"Not long, there are regular flights from LAX," Armitage said. "We could probably have someone on location and digging through the files by noon tomorrow."

"Can you arrange that?" Curtis asked.

"Sure." He reached for the phone, dialed a local and a minute later a serious looking woman appeared at the door. She was middle-age, heavyset, and wore no makeup. "Rosalinda Garcia, this is Curtis Westcott, Boston Homicide. We need you to take a little trip."

Thirty minutes later, Rosalinda Garcia was on her way to LAX with nothing but the clothes on her back and her credit card. Armitage had been specific with his instructions. Fly into Liberia, get to Condovac la Costa Resort on Playa Hermosa and dig up the guest records for June 2000. Take photos and send jpegs the moment she had them, day or night. She had both Westcott's and Armitage's cell numbers.

The next three hours were spent going back over the interview Khilt had given the LA detectives and trying to make sense of it.

"It's there," Curtis said. "It's just not coming through."

Steve Armitage agreed. "*Rolling wood into the house for the fireplace. Chunks of wood up a hill, from the forest by the lake.* He sure made it look like gibberish." He rubbed his eyes and glanced at his watch. It was almost five in the evening, and dinner with his family wasn't going to happen tonight.

"Anna, you should go home," Armitage said. The young patrol officer had spent the entire day waiting in or around Armitage's office in case Curtis needed a ride.

"No, thanks," she said. "It's not every day I get to sit in on a homicide investigation. I'd rather stay, if that's okay."

"Sure," Armitage said. He turned to Curtis. "Are you getting hungry? I could order some pizza."

Curtis gave him a weak smile. "Sure, you order the pizza, Boston Homicide pays. It's the least I can do."

Armitage grinned. "Deal."

Curtis set the printouts aside while Armitage called in the order. When the big man hung up the phone, Curtis said, "*Remember the past*, that's easy. *Challenge the future*. I wonder what that's supposed to mean."

Armitage shook his head. "That's not what he said. It was more like *the future as a real challenge*."

"I know that," Anna Rodriguez said. Both Curtis and Steve stared at her. "I know that line. *Remember the past. Challenge the future*. I know it." She stood up and grabbed her head in her hands. "Damn it, I've seen that somewhere. Where? Where?" She looked up at the ceiling, frustrated.

Curtis and Armitage didn't say a word for at least two minutes as Anna talked to herself, trying to place where she had seen the line. Then she dropped her hands to her side and a smile crept across her face. "I got it. I know where I saw it."

"And..."

"One of my friends lives in a small city inland from Laguna Beach. It's called Lake Forest. And the city's slogan is *Remember the past. Challenge the future*. I'm positive."

Armitage was at the door in five seconds, yelling for someone to bring him a detailed street map of Lake Forest. It arrived inside two minutes. They spread it out on the table and the three of them poured over it, looking for something, anything, that tied in with what Khilt and his other aliases had given them. Anna Rodriguez spotted it.

"Here," she said, pointing at the map. "Rollingwood Road. And it intersects with Wood Hill Lane. *Rolling wood* and *wood up a hill*. Rollingwood Road and Woodhill Lane. It's an intersection in Lake Forest."

"…*from the forest by the lake*," Curtis said. "Lake Forest." He looked up from the map at Rodriguez. "Damn good work, Anna."

"Thank you, sir."

"Feel like giving me a ride?" he asked.

The young cop grinned.

# CHAPTER FIFTY-FIVE

Rush hour in Los Angeles. Everyone in a hurry and getting nowhere. Cars crawling up the freeways, and everyone on their cell phones. After two minutes of not moving Curtis gave Anna the nod. Rodriguez switched on the lights and siren and the sea of cars jamming the Santa Ana Freeway parted. Begrudgingly. They drove south to the 518, then cut north toward El Toro and Lake Forest. At eight minutes after six, Anna pulled onto Lake Forest Drive and glanced over at Curtis, who was checking their location on his GPS.

"Where to?" she asked.

"Lake Forest to Jeronimo Road, turn right and drive until you see Rollingwood. It'll be on your left."

Rodriguez found Jeronimo, then made the turn onto Rollingwood. They were surrounded on both sides by mature eucalyptus trees, well over fifty feet high. The houses were tucked between a maze of bright white trunks and the tips of the trees formed a canopy over the winding street.

"So this is it," Curtis said quietly, staring out the window. "This is where it all started."

Darkness was setting in now, the thick leaves blocking out the last rays of sunlight. A gentle breeze blew inland from the ocean and the smaller branches swayed about, clicking together softly. He spotted the street sign at the intersection, tucked up against a two-foot high retaining wall that was overgrown with several large shrubs.

Anna stopped and shifted the car into park. "We're here."

Curtis got out of the car, followed by Anna Rodriguez. He stood on the corner, first looking down Rollingwood, then down Woodhill. The streets were narrow and winding and he couldn't see very far down either. He simply stood at the intersection, listening and thinking. Liem Khilt had been here. He felt it. This was the place he had brought Kelly Moran. This was the place he had held her, and where he had killed her. But which house?

Both streets were lined with average, middle-class homes, and door knocking on every house until they found the right one was not an option. Right now the only way to save Renee Charlesbois was to unravel the clues before time ran out. It was a chilling thought. Curtis was used to dealing with murder after the fact, not before. This time he had been given a chance to actually stop a killing.

It was simple, really. If he failed, Renee Charlesbois died.

He refocused on the street. Khilt had led him from Boston to Napa to Chicago to Los Angeles, and now to this intersection. If Khilt had been that precise in his directions, then he had also supplied the last piece of information. It was in the file somewhere. As Curtis pulled his satchel out from the back seat of the cruiser, Steve Armitage pulled up in an unmarked car with a second plainclothes detective.

"Anything?" Armitage asked as he approached the squad car.

"This is it," Curtis said. "This is where he held Kelly Moran." He looked down both streets. "One of these houses."

"Which one?" Armitage asked.

Curtis shrugged. "I don't know." He held up the satchel. "I was just going to look through the file again." He took the Moran interview out and set it on the hood of the car. The streetlights were on, but ineffective for reading. Anna Rodriguez retrieved a flashlight from the car and shone the beam on the pages as Curtis read them again. Armitage stood beside him, going over the interview line by line.

There was little meat left in the paragraph Khilt had used to describe Lake Forest, except for the mention of wood chips. *Wood chips everywhere.* Curtis scratched his head and said, "It's a long shot, but maybe the house has wood chips somewhere on the lot."

"Maybe," Armitage said.

Armitage turned to the detective and Anna, who were waiting for directions. "Each of you take a street and look for a house with wood chips somewhere on the lot. Move fast."

Rodriguez dug out another flashlight and headed off down the street. The two homicide detectives stayed at the car, searching for what else they could get out of the interview.

"This whole thing about the OG is bugging me," Curtis said. "*I try to steer clear of the OG in my personal life and help the people who really need it.* What the hell is that? There is absolutely no reason for him to say that. And why shorten it. Why not just say overly gregarious? And he says it in the same sentence as *personal*."

Armitage shook his head. "I checked with the men working the personal ads in the newspaper. Nothing so far."

"There has to be something," Curtis said, squinting at the writing in the darkness. The sun had set and a vague outline of a crescent moon drifted in the sky, barely visible through the trees. An occasional car turned onto the street, the drivers staring at them as they navigated the corner, but the street was mostly quiet.

"You're sure we're on the right street?" Armitage asked

"Yeah, I think so. There are too many coincidences for it not to be. But why lead us here, then not tell us which house?"

"I could get more manpower here in an hour or two. LAPD or Lake Forest cops. Whatever you want."

Curtis thought about the prospect of cops swarming the neighborhood and shook his head. His preference was to keep this low key and off Khilt's radar in case he was somehow watching. "One hour, Steve," he said. "Let's take an hour and see if we can figure this out. If we can't, we call in the troops."

"Okay," Armitage said as Rodriguez and the other detective showed up, shaking their heads. They'd come up empty. Nothing as obvious as a pile of wood chips to point in the right direction.

They reread the interview, walked the length of both Rollingwood and Woodhill, and talked about possibilities. Nothing. The houses were all different in their style, but similar in their size and how they were set on the lot. There were no distinguishing characteristics to draw attention to any one house, and after an hour Steve Armitage made the call. Five cars from LA and three from Lake Forest were on the move. Curtis and Steve leaned against the hood of the cruiser, waiting.

"You don't think he's in LA, do you?" Armitage asked.

"No, he's in Boston," Curtis said.

"So he's not here, but you didn't want to bring extra bodies in right away. Any reason?"

Curtis shook his head. "I'm not sure. Sometimes I get feelings." He faced Armitage, knowing without the man's help he would have been dead in the water. "It sounds trite, but we've nailed more than one perp on my intuitions."

"I thought intuition was something unique to women," Armitage joked. "I'd be in trouble with the LAPD top dogs if they heard that."

Curtis stopped in mid-breath. "Dogs," he said slowly. "LAPD. Lapdog. LAPD, and add the OG. Lapdog. That's it."

"That's what?" Armitage pushed off the front of the cruiser.

"The personal ads. He had to use them in LA because he had no previous crime to point this direction. And he would have had no idea who would be handling the Kelly Moran case, so he would have to direct any message to the police in general. The LAPD. But he couldn't just stick LAPD in the paper, or it would instantly be noticed. So he uses lapdog, then tells us in the interview to *steer clear of the OG*. Drop those two letters off lapdog and you get LAPD."

Armitage was on his cell phone. Once he reached the right party, he said, "Run a scan across the personal ads using *lapdog* as the key word." He was quiet for a minute, then smiled and nodded, grabbing his notepad from his pocket. He jotted down a few words, then said, "Thanks," and hung up.

"One message. And I think you nailed it." He read it out loud. "*Lapdog. Just like in C R. 120 NE, 20 S. And so it begins.* He said there were no initials."

"Of course not. Putting his initials in would have made it too easy." Curtis rubbed his hand across his forehead and looked around. *Just like in C R. 120NE, 20 S. And so it begins.* The C R is Costa Rica, that's easy, and the numbers and letters are directions, I would guess."

Anna Rodriguez cut in. "That makes sense. They don't have addresses in rural Costa Rica." Everyone was silent, staring at her and she continued. "Addresses in Costa Rica are given by a number of meters from a known point. Might be a store, a large tree, even some things that are now long gone."

"Really?" Curtis said. "You're serious."

"Absolutely."

"The distances are probably from this corner," Armitage said. "It's the starting point he gave us." He glanced up and down both streets. "Should I cancel the backup?"

Curtis was thoughtful. "I think so," he said. "I don't think brute force is the answer, and I'm worried he might have a CCTV camera setup somewhere. He could be watching the street."

"That's what I'm thinking," Armitage said, making the call on the two-way radio.

"How long is a meter?" Curtis asked.

"Thirty-nine inches," Rodriguez said. "Give or take a fraction of an inch." She anticipated the next question and said, "I have a tape measure in the trunk of the cruiser." She moved quickly to get it.

"She's a hell of a cop," Curtis said to Armitage as Rodriguez opened the trunk. "You might want to give her a shot at the detective exams."

"I was just thinking that," Armitage said.

They placed the end of the tape at the base of the street sign and moved northeast on Woodhill Lane until the tape was at thirty-three yards. They marked the spot, then added three inches on for every yard. They repeated the process until they were at 120 meters, then looked south. They didn't need to use the tape measure to know which house it was. There was only one. It was a single-story rancher, about fifteen hundred square feet, with trimmed lawns under a towering eucalyptus. There were no flyers or newspapers on the front porch, and no mail sticking out of the mailbox. The window coverings were pulled shut and no lights shone from behind the thick draperies.

"Looks pretty normal," Steve Armitage said. He turned to Rodriguez and the other detective. "Take the houses on either side. Find out what you can about who lives here." They hurried off, leaving Curtis and Armitage standing on the street, staring at the house.

"We need to get in there," Curtis said.

Armitage started dialing on his cell phone. "I'll get a search warrant, but they take time."

"How much time?"

"We might get one from the night court judge, but my guess is sometime tomorrow morning."

Curtis shook his head. "No way, Steve. I don't have that much time."

"We need a search warrant, Curtis."

Curtis continued to stare at the darkened house. Liem Khilt had brought Kelly Moran back to this house, kept her captive for two weeks, then killed her by sending a massive electrical charge through her body. Then he had moved on to Chicago and Napa, killing two more women while dangling unnoticed clues in front of the police. Then Boston. His city. With murder, Khilt had stepped over the boundaries that civilized society allowed. He had broken a cardinal law and soon he would do it again. Curtis stood unmoving in front of the house.

"I don't think we do."

"You go in there without a warrant and anything you find from that point on will be inadmissible."

"I know, but we have ground to go in without a warrant. We have imminent danger to life." There were a few things that circumvented getting a search warrant, and an immediate threat to someone's life was one. The courts referred to it as *imminent danger to life*, and it was something savvy cops used when pressed for time.

Armitage cocked his head slightly, and said, "How long did you say until he's going to kill her?"

"Fifty hours, give or take."

Armitage was nodding now. "And the warrant will take at least twelve. That delay puts the woman in imminent danger."

"It does," Curtis agreed.

"It's an end run."

"It is."

"I think it'll hold up, at least in California," Armitage said.

"Well, we're in California, so that's what we need." Curtis waited while Armitage made his decision.

"Let's go in."

# CHAPTER FIFTY-SIX

Monday night. Day twelve. Two more days, two more nights. Time was running out for Renee Charlesbois.

Liem Khilt stared at his reflection in the mirror. His face was a mottled canvas of pockmarks, deep and vivid purple. There were no redeeming features to his face, and on the few occasions he had ventured out without makeup, children had pulled back from him, repulsed by the sight. Their reaction wasn't a surprise. He was an abomination, ugly beyond words. And all because of those rich bitches and his spineless loser of a father.

Cold eyes stared back at him as he remembered his father, begging for his life. His mother, that incredulous look in her eyes, refusing to believe until the last second that her son was capable of giving the car the final push. She hadn't made a sound as the car went over the edge. His father, a weak man right to the final seconds, screamed as the car plunged into the wooded ravine. Useless sounds by a useless man. The vision slowly dissipated and he picked up his gun from the dresser and checked the chamber. It was loaded. He tucked the gun in his waistband and headed downstairs. He glanced through the opening in the door and saw her sitting on the bed reading one of the magazines he had given her. She looked up absently as he entered, then refocused on his face.

"No makeup tonight," he said as he closed the door behind him. "Do you like what you see?" She didn't comment and he sat in the chair. "You did this to me. I thought you might like to see what not being wealthy buys."

"I didn't do that," Renee said. "Whatever problems you have with your face have nothing to do with me."

"Oh, that's not true." He leaned the chair against the wall. His right hand stroked the gun barrel, the metal cool to his touch. God, he wanted to kill her so bad. *Right now, right here. Use the gun.* His grip tightened on the handle, but then the moment passed. He released the gun and said, "I want you to think back to an earlier time in your life. Back to 2000. You would have been about sixteen, give or take. Remember?"

"I remember lots of things from when I was sixteen."

"I'm thinking about one time and place in particular. Costa Rica. Two weeks of fun. That's how my mom and dad sold me on the trip. We were going to have the time of our lives. Two weeks at a beautiful resort, with a beach and tropical rainforests. I'll tell you, they did a great job selling it. I was really excited. Pumped up. Couldn't wait to go." His face contorted into a sneer. "I couldn't wait to get to the jungle and ruin my fucking life."

Renee set the magazine on the bed beside her. "I remember the trip to Costa Rica, but I don't remember you."

"Do you recall getting sick?" he asked.

She did, and she sucked in a quick breath. *Yaws.* The disease had really worried her parents and she had wondered why at the time.

He leaned forward, spittle forming at the edges of his mouth as he forced out the words. "You barely remember getting sick. Or getting the medicine. You heartless bitch." His eyes burned with contempt and his hand moved back to the gun. "You got the fucking medicine and you hardly remember. You bitch." He was screaming now.

"I remember," she yelled back at him. "A bunch of us caught that weird tropical disease. We were given injections. It went away." She pushed her dirty hair back off her face, her eyes watching his hand as it stroked the gun.

"You got the injections," he said, calmer now. "You and your bitch friends. But there wasn't enough medicine. Do you remember the weather? Terrible. The winds toppling trees, the roads impassable. There was no way to get out to the nearest town for more medicine. So one of the kids went without."

Renee glared into his eyes. "You."

"Yes." He stared back at her, hate radiating from his eyes. "Me." They were both silent for a minute, then he said, "Do you know what kind of medicine it was?" She shook her head. "It was penicillin. Penicillin for Christ's sake. An absolute nothing of a drug. But the stupid bastards running the resort didn't have enough for everyone. Penicillin. What a joke."

"Yaws," she said quietly. "I remember. It was yaws."

His jaw clenched tight. "Very good," he finally said. "Look what it did to me. Look at my face. My dad told me he didn't have enough money to buy the medicine from the resort doctor, like your dad and all the others outbid him. So I went without. And look at what it did to me. It ruined my life."

Renee sat up straight on the bed, and when she spoke her voice was strong. "*You* ruined your life, not the disease. You didn't have to resort to killing people because they got the cure and you didn't. That's absolute bullshit."

"What?" he said incredulously. "What are you saying? That you didn't fuck me over. That your parents, and my parents, didn't screw me?" His face turned a deeper shade of purple. "You bitch."

"No, you son-of-a-bitch." Something inside her snapped. "You sick asshole. You self-absorbed, pathetic asshole."

Khilt leapt from the chair, the gun in his right hand. He swung his arm in a long arc, driving the butt of the gun into the side of Renee's head. She went down hard, unconscious, blood streaming from the cut. He stood over her, the gun in his hand, his finger on the trigger. He aimed it at her head and squeezed. Slowly, the trigger moved ever so slightly. Then he stopped. He stared at her, lying on the cold earth, her body contorted from the fall. Then he relaxed his finger, and the pressure came off the trigger. He let the gun drop to his side. No, this wasn't the way. She was going to die exactly as he had planned, when he had planned. Khilt glanced at his watch. Ten-thirty.

Fifty hours.

Fifty hours until he tied her hands and slowly sliced off her head. He could wait.

# CHAPTER FIFTY-SEVEN

Curtis walked across the grass and down the side of the house into the backyard. He now knew for sure the house was empty. Rodriguez and the other cop had come back with the same story from the neighbors on either side. The owner had bought the house back in January, lived in it briefly in March, and was now out of the country, working on an offshore oil rig. He'd hired local kids to cut the grass and had paid them in advance. His description matched that of Liem Khilt to a T, complete with the dark-rimmed glasses.

They had found the house.

The backyard was an average size with a two-tiered deck that led to a set of sliding doors. There was an empty swimming pool—the rest of the yard was grass and shrubs. Curtis headed for the deck and tried the patio doors, but they were securely locked. He moved along the back of the house, jiggling the windows to see if any were loose. No luck. He stood on the deck and surveyed the house for the best way to gain entrance. After a minute or two, he decided on the back door. It was an older style wooden one, with an eighteen-inch square window at eye height.

"Do you have your flashlight?" Curtis asked Anna, slipping on a pair of latex gloves.

Rodriguez handed it over and Curtis hit the glass with the butt end. It shattered inward, the sound echoing through the quiet neighborhood.

Curtis knocked the glass fragments from the frame, then reached through the broken window and unlatched the door. He and Steve Armitage entered, cautious of potential boobytraps. Off to their left were stairs leading down.

"I'll take the main floor, you take the basement," Curtis said.

"I hate basements," Armitage said. "Don't know why they build houses with them. All kinds of creepy crawlers live in them."

"C'mon, big tough cop like you," Curtis said. "Remember Kelly Moran was electrocuted. Careful what you touch."

"Right."

Curtis's shoes crunched on the shards of broken glass as he followed his flashlight beam through the rear foyer into the kitchen. If Khilt had killed her inside the house, he could have rerouted the electrical service. If that were the case, he may have increased the voltage coming into the house. If Khilt had somehow tied that voltage to the switches, touching any of them could be fatal.

The galley-style kitchen was small for the size of the house and he crept into the dining room where a maple table and four matching chairs were covered in dust. The dining area connected to the living room and Curtis carefully made his way into the larger room. He stood immobile for a minute, listening and looking at the eclectic mix of furniture. Most of it was older, probably originally included with the house, but there was a newer stereo system and flat screen television. He walked around the furniture to the front window, mindful to keep his hands close to his body. He used his index finger to pull the curtains back a couple of inches. Outside, on the street, Anna Rodriguez and the other cop had moved the cars up in front of the house and were in place to control any people or traffic that happened by. Curtis walked back around the furniture and down the hallway.

There were four doors, all closed. Again, Curtis stood quietly, envisioning the layout of the house in his mind. Three of the doors would likely lead to bedrooms and the fourth would be the bathroom. He started at the door closest to the front of the house, touching the doorknob lightly before grasping it and turning. He pushed the door open and entered. He was in the master bedroom and it was a decent size with a small en suite bath to one side. The bed was made and the pillows neatly stacked against the headboard. An alarm clock was on the night table, set to the correct time. He left the room and walked down the hall, ignoring the door he thought would lead to the bathroom and trying another bedroom door, cautiously touching the handle in case Khilt had wired it.

He had a quick look about the second room, furnished only with a cot and a cheap night table, then moved to the final bedroom, in the rear of the house. When he pushed on the door, it felt much heavier than the first two, and he tensed up. It creaked open and he stood transfixed, staring at the carnage. The room was a prison. The windows were covered entirely with steel plates, screwed into the walls, and the walls themselves were impenetrable. Someone had rebuilt the entire inside of the room with bricks and mortar. The inside of the door was thick metal. But what turned Curtis' stomach was the dried blood covering the floor and part way up the walls. A metal chair sat in the center of the room and a thick electrical wire lay next to it.

Kelly Moran's execution chamber.

A white envelope sat on the chair. Curtis surveyed the room, using the flashlight beam to follow the electrical line back to its origin. The chair didn't appear to be tied into the power supply at any point, and he moved toward it, unbuckling his belt. He stood back a couple of feet, slipped his belt from the loops and snaked it out so it landed on top of the envelope. He pulled and the envelope moved with the belt, dropping to the blood-encrusted floor. He picked it up gingerly with his fingertips. The flap was unsealed and he opened it, holding the edge with his fingertips. Inside was a single sheet of standard 20 lb bond paper. He unfolded it and read the contents.

*She deserved to die, you have to understand that.*

*So do the others. But maybe you can save them. Maybe.*

*Which way would you go if you were a betting man?*

*Think of Jefferson across the water, heading south on Bear City, reading a James Patterson novel, with all his right wing views. Soul food for the starved mind.*

*It's quite simple. You just have to think.*

Curtis jerked slightly at a sound behind him. It was Steve Armitage, at the door with a horrified look on his face.

"Oh, shit," he said. "Looks like this is where he killed her."

"Looks like," Curtis said. He handed the envelope to Armitage. "He left this for us."

Armitage read it and said, "Bit of a load of gibberish unless you know it's not."

"Exactly." Curtis pointed to the door. "Let's get out of here."

They backed out of the room and moved toward the front of the house. Curtis reached for the front door handle, then stopped. He dropped to his knees and looked closely at the bottom hinge. Attached to it, and barely visible even with the light from the flashlight, was a heavy wire. Curtis followed the wire up the edge of the door where it was tucked tight against the jamb. It snaked across and made contact with the door handle.

"Fucker wired it," Armitage said, watching over Curtis's shoulder.

"He certainly did." Curtis took a couple of deep breaths. His hand had been two inches from the handle. If he had touched it, he could easily have been electrocuted. He was shaking now as the realization washed over him, and he stuffed his free hand in his pocket to steady it. "Make sure your men know not to touch anything until it's been cleared by one of your technicians."

"Damn straight," Armitage said.

They returned to the rear door and left the house. It was a quick jaunt around the house and back to the front street where Anna Rodriguez and her colleague were waiting.

"It's the right place," Armitage said, explaining to Anna that no one was to touch anything. "Call it in. Get backup and CSU."

"What's in there?" she asked, dialing on her phone.

Curtis didn't usually take the time to explain things to beat cops, but he felt Anna Rodriguez deserved it. "The bedroom in the back of the house was converted to a prison. It's likely where he killed Kelly Moran."

Rodriguez nodded and started talking, asking for backup and a crime scene team.

Armitage leaned on the hood of the car. "She probably bled a lot when the electrical charge exited her body. It split her feet wide open."

Curtis managed a terse nod. "Yeah, it's a real mess."

"We'll park the crime scene unit on the doorstep and wait for the warrant," Armitage said, reaching for his phone. "With what we know now, getting a warrant won't take long."

"Remind your guys not to use the front door," Curtis said again. Khilt wasn't putting any more people in LA on a slab.

Armitage called in the request for the warrant, and when he was finished he pointed to the envelope in Curtis' hand. "Let's have another look at that."

Curtis carefully slipped the paper out of the envelope while Armitage retrieved a clear plastic evidence bag from the car. They slipped it in, sealed it and took a minute to reread it.

"These are clues to the Annette Shelby case in Chicago," Curtis said.

Armitage shook his head in frustration. "If you didn't know Chicago was the city, you'd have no idea what to do with this."

"You wouldn't have a clue." Curtis used his phone to snap a picture of Khilt's letter. "That's the thing. Every time our guy killed one of the women, he left clues to bring us back here, to his starting point. Now we have the clues that lead forward."

"Chicago, Napa, Boston?" Armitage asked.

"I think so."

Steve Armitage had a grim look on his face. "There's no time."

Curtis instinctively glanced at his watch. Eight o'clock on Monday night. Fifty-two hours until the clock ticked over to Thursday morning. Forty-nine if you corrected for the time difference between LA and Boston. Two days to follow what was likely a horribly convoluted trail from Los Angeles to Chicago, then to Napa and finally back to Boston. The word *impossible* slipped through his mind and he filed it in his mental garbage bin. The reality was clear though, he was running out of time.

# CHAPTER FIFTY-EIGHT

The trip to LAX was noisy, with Curtis and Armitage either talking to each other or on their phones exchanging information with their teams. Curtis took a call from Aislinn Byrne as they crossed Sepulveda Boulevard and neared the airport.

"There are a few reasons why Peter Moran's Seattle-based business failed," she said. "But the main one was a call on his demand loan by the bank."

"Was Moran in financial trouble at the time?" Curtis asked, watching the LA lights fly by as the terminal materialized ahead.

"No, and that's the strange thing. Nothing had changed. Moran's construction company was doing well, and his holding company was also in good financial condition. There was no reason for the bank to pull the loan."

"Then why did they?"

"I managed to speak with one person from the bank, but they were in a junior position and couldn't answer the tough questions."

"Like who had a hate-on for Peter Moran and influenced the bank manager to call the loan," Curtis said. This one wasn't rocket science. Someone had forced the bank's hand.

"Exactly."

"Find out," Curtis said. "I want answers by tomorrow morning. Threaten them with a federal subpoena if they don't cough up whoever made this happen."

"Okay, boss."

Curtis cut the connection as they pulled up to the doors for United Airlines. He grabbed his bag from the squad car, shook Anna Rodriguez's hand and thanked her. Steve slipped out of the back seat and accompanied Curtis into the terminal. The flight to Chicago departed in twenty-seven minutes, and Armitage used his badge to get Curtis through the queue and up to the departure gate in record time.

"Good luck," he said. "Keep in mind that we'd like a piece of this guy when you get him."

"He's going to be in jail somewhere for the rest of his life," Curtis said. "Chicago and Napa are going to file charges as well."

"Well, it'll be nice to close the books on Moran's murder. I really appreciate your efforts, Curtis."

"Not a problem. Closure feels good."

"I'll call ahead to Kevin Shipton in Chicago and let him know when your flight is scheduled to arrive," Armitage said.

They shook hands and Curtis moved quickly down the ramp and onto the plane. He pulled out his copies of the interviews with Khilt at the various police precincts before stowing his briefcase. He thought ahead to the next city. Chicago. The second stop for Liem Khilt on his revenge-fueled mission. When the plane was airborne, he flipped down the table and laid out the interview from LA. Alongside, he set his list of words from the different interviews. He stroked off *chopping*, *OG* and *personal*. They were specific to LA. Then he eliminated *Chicago, five after five*, and *five-nineteen*. He knew the city Khilt was referring to, and the times were simply the dates Annette Shelby had been abducted and killed. He was left with two names.

*Patrick Stewart* and *Alex Haley*.

Neither name needed to be in the text. Both felt forced. Curtis was certain Khilt's message was in those two names. But what was the message? There were only so many ways to rearrange the four words that comprised Patrick Stewart and Alex Haley. He jotted them down and there were eight other combinations. One of them was a clue, and the remaining seven were nothing but a jumble of names. Nothing came to him, and after a while he set the list aside and opened the photo of the letter from the Lake Forest house.

*She deserved to die, you have to understand that.*

*So do the others. But maybe you can save them. Maybe.*

*Which way would you go if you were a betting man?*

*Think of Jefferson across the water, heading south on Bear City, reading a James Patterson novel, with all his right wing views. Soul food for the starved mind.*

*It's quite simple. You just have to think.*

The first two lines were nothing but pomp. Khilt was puffing out his feathers, strutting like a proverbial peacock. *Jefferson.* Thomas Jefferson? What did Thomas Jefferson have to do with Chicago? Nothing was ringing a bell. *Across the water. Bear City.* Directions? But from where? He needed a starting point. Khilt had given them the exact location in Lake Forest, and directions from the intersection. The same must be true for Chicago. Khilt was proving too methodical to deviate. At least, that's what he was counting on. If Khilt *did* decide to change his MO, they were dead in the water.

He put his phone down and looked at the page on the top of the pile. It was the Napa interview. *Five after five, Chicago, Alex Haley.* There was nothing new there. Still, he must be missing something. He gathered up his papers as the flight attendant came down the aisle, serving drinks from the cart. He asked for water and sipped it slowly, lost in thought. *Bear City?* The Chicago Bears were the city's NFL franchise, but why would Khilt care about pointing to Chicago again. It was repetitive, and that didn't fit. *Across the water.* Christ, did he mean across Lake Michigan? Why even start in Chicago if that was the case? What was on the other side of the lake? He didn't know, he didn't care. If Khilt was throwing out generic clues, they were in trouble. The more he thought about it, the more he was convinced the phrase had nothing to do with the lake. Consistently, Khilt had dropped precise clues in the interviews. They were designed to lead the police to a specific city, and a starting point inside that city. Then the clues from the previous murder scene, or the newspaper ads, gave the exact location of the next crime.

That was the premise Curtis had built his investigative procedure on so far, and he wasn't going to start deviating now. Somewhere inside the letter he had found in Lake Forest was the exact location of where Khilt had kept and killed Annette Shelby. He reread the letter, but there were no sudden flashes of brilliance, just an ocean of muddled grey.

The plane began its descent into Chicago and Curtis packed up his phone and papers and slipped them back in with his laptop. They touched down at O'Hare and he found Kevin Shipton waiting for him at the exit from the gate. They talked as they walked and Curtis showed Shipton his copy of the letter from the Lake Forest house. Shipton had a puzzled look on his face after he read it.

"What the hell does it mean?" he asked as they exited O'Hare to a waiting unmarked car.

"I was hoping you could tell me."

"Well, his reference to Bear City is probably Chicago. That's our NFL franchise."

"Yeah, that much I figured out."

"But *Jefferson? James Patterson? Soul food for the starved mind.* What the hell is that?"

"No idea."

"Heading south. That sounds like directions."

"Probably. But south from Chicago? South in Chicago? Across what water? We need a starting point, Kevin. Without it, we're at a standstill."

"What did you have from the interviews that could be of help?"

"Two names. Alex Haley and Patrick Stewart. We need to run all combinations of the two names through the computer."

"Okay. I'll call it in. How you doing for tired? It's almost three in the morning."

"Getting by. I'd like to try and sleep a bit."

"We have a room with a cot at the precinct," Shipton said. "It's okay in a pinch."

Curtis did the math in his head. Forty-five hours until Renee Charlesbois' appointment with death. "It'll have to do."

# CHAPTER FIFTY-NINE

The room was dark, but outside the door he could hear a flurry of activity.

Curtis sat up on the cot and rubbed his eyes. He had slept, and it had been refreshing and without the dreams that haunted so many of his nights. He sat for a minute, getting his bearings. A strip of light under the door was the only illumination, and as his eyes slowly focused he remembered where he was.

Chicago. In the small room at the precinct where Kevin Shipton and his colleagues often caught a catnap. He glanced at his watch, the hands glowing soft green in the darkness. He had finally bedded down at about six o'clock Tuesday morning, and it was now almost ten. Thirty-eight hours until Thursday and Khilt's deadline. Thirty-eight hours until Khilt killed Renee Charlesbois. Curtis stood up and walked shakily to the door.

The hallway was a buzz of people moving about with purpose. He worked his way through the throng to the washroom, then found a coffee station with a full pot. He poured himself a cup and headed for Kevin Shipton's office. The homicide cop was in and on his phone. He waved for Curtis to enter.

Shipton hung up as Curtis sat in one of the chairs facing the desk. "Steve Armitage called and left a message. They managed to get a search warrant from the night court judge and the CSU team has been inside the house for about five hours now. He wants you to call him."

"Okay." Curtis sipped the coffee. It was really good, freshly brewed and not too strong. "Did you get anything more out of the letter we found in the LA house?"

Shipton shook his head. "We passed the letter around the precinct and gave everyone a shot at it, but nobody came up with any original ideas. The reference to Jefferson is confusing. Does he mean Thomas Jefferson? Or maybe Jefferson Street? We're not sure."

"Well, the letter sounds like he's giving us directions," Curtis said. "He might be referring to Jefferson Street. Where is it?"

Shipton spread a map of Chicago on his desk and pointed. "North Jefferson Street originates near the rail tracks that abut the river, right underneath the Grand Avenue overpass. It runs south and ends at the South Branch of the Chicago River."

"Does it ever cross the river?" Curtis asked.

"No. But it does run parallel to Halsted, which was one of the streets he mentioned in his interview with John Abbot after Annette Shelby was abducted."

Curtis brightened. "That's good. We can work with that."

"Maybe," Shipton said, running his hands through his hair. "Halsted is a main street, and it continues north across the river. The location he gave for his house is about three-tenths of a mile north of the starting point for Jefferson Street. I'm not sure how you're going to tie that together."

"I'm getting a bit confused," Curtis said. "I don't know Chicago very well."

"Let's shift to the room where we can spread out the map. Give you a better look at the layout of the city."

They moved into the boardroom and poured over the map together, using every word Khilt had given them. *Jefferson. Patterson. Bear City. Right. Soul food. Starved mind.* Six detectives joined them and the room was noisy with chatter when Curtis excused himself and found a quiet spot to call Steve Armitage in Los Angeles. He had the man's direct line and Armitage answered on the second ring.

"Your guy tried to be careful," Armitage said, "but he left us some trace evidence. We found a couple of hairs on the pillow and a few pubic hairs under the sheets on the bed in the master bedroom. Semen on the sheets as well. No sign of any other fluids, so we're guessing he jerked off. You find this guy, Curtis, we can easily tie him back to the house by matching his DNA to what we found."

"Excellent work, Steve," Curtis said. "Now we just have to find him. Any word from the detective you sent to Costa Rica?"

"Rosalinda Garcia. Not yet, but she'll be on the ground by now. I expect to hear from her soon."

"I need the list of guests. We need more than one avenue of attack on this guy. We're stalling here in Chicago. I can't get a grip on what he's trying to tell us with that letter we found in the house. What we need is for Rosalinda to get her hands on the guest list for June 2000. Then we need to connect a name on that list to the investigation."

"Okay. I'll forward you whatever she finds the moment I have it."

"Thanks."

Curtis put a call through to Aislinn, but got her voice mail. He left a message, then returned to the boardroom. The detectives were still hunched over the map, pointing and talking. Maybe they had something. His spirits rose as he entered the room.

Kevin Shipton glanced up and the look on his face quickly dashed any hopes he might have had. He shook his head. "We can't make anything work, Curtis," he said. "Nothing comes together. Not even forcing it."

"You won't have to force it," Curtis said. "When we hit the right spot, it'll fall into place. He's methodical, organized, and detail oriented."

"Then we don't have it," Shipton said. "We need to look elsewhere."

Curtis nodded. "Any ideas?" He scanned the room, locking eyes with each of the detectives and getting nothing in return. "Okay," he said. "Can you keep working on it?"

Shipton was quick to answer. "We're on it until we get this guy."

"What about the two names I gave you? Patrick Stewart and Alex Haley? Did you find anything there?"

"I have two officers working that, but the number of hits on both the computer and the Internet are astronomical. I'll give it another hour, then shift another couple of guys over to help them if we don't have any breakthroughs here."

"Good. What about the personal ads in the newspaper? Did you find anything that might be our guy talking to us?"

Shipton shook his head. "Sheer numbers are against us, Curtis. The hits run into the thousands. And since most of those ads are in code or abbreviated, it's taking us forever to sort through them."

Curtis managed a grim smile. "You're working all the angles," he said. "I appreciate it."

"This is as much for us as it is for you. Annette Shelby's murder was high profile and it generated a lot of press, all of it negative. Getting her killer behind bars would really help."

"We'll get him eventually." Curtis rubbed his temples as a headache threatened. "Renee Charlesbois is my problem, and you guys moved on it like it was in your own backyard. So no matter what you say, I still appreciate what you're doing."

Kevin Shipton grinned. "Okay. Encouraging words. I'll take them." He looked around the room at the other detectives. "*We'll* take them."

Curtis' cell phone rang and he excused himself and retreated into the hallway to take the call. It was Aislinn. "What's up?" he asked.

"Stan's working with VICAP on narrowing down this guy's MO in case there were other victims before Kelly Moran in Los Angeles. I've managed to dig up a bit more on why Peter Moran's business crashed and burned."

"What did you find?"

"The loan was called in by a bank executive named Frank Harris. He's a few rungs up the food chain from the manager of Moran's branch. Harris is based out of San Francisco, and I have a contact in the San Fran PD who agreed to have a chat with Harris today. We should know more later."

"Keep on that, Aislinn. Whoever forced Moran's hand could be our guy, and if he is, that would give us his real name. The more we've got on him the better chance we've got of tracing his movements inside Boston."

"I'm on it," Aislinn said.

"How's the shit-hitting-the-fan level in Boston these days?" Curtis asked.

"Not bad. I've talked with the mayor twice, but he's being pretty accommodating now that Jacques Charlesbois is reined in."

"So Charlesbois isn't making waves?"

"He's quiet. Still calls a couple of times a day to find out what's new and I keep him in the loop. He knows you're on the trail and getting close."

Curtis sighed audibly. "I wish I felt that confident, Aislinn. We've run into a brick wall in Chicago. The letter he left at the house in LA isn't making any sense. Somehow, we're missing what he's giving us."

"You'll get it," Aislinn said. "You always do."

Curtis forced a laugh. "Yeah, sure. I appreciate the boost, but this is getting frustrating."

"Well, frustrating or not, you'll be glad to know we haven't had a single homicide since you left. It's a sign."

"Yeah, a sign that you guys are under-worked and over-paid."

"Bye," Aislinn said.

"Later." Curtis slipped the cell phone in his pocket and stood in the hall, leaning against the wall and oblivious to the people streaming by. Aislinn was right, he *was* close. He had caught the word association between Chloe's party and the interview at BPD. Then he had recognized that Khilt was leaving no clues to the current crime, but mapping out his previous and his next murders. Following that logic, he traced the killer's movements back to the origin—the house in Lake Forest where he had killed Kelly Moran. Curtis didn't know the man's true identity yet, but he knew why the women were dying. He had motive, Modus Operandi, and a lengthening trail of valuable clues.

He allowed himself a grim smile. Aislinn was right. They would get this son-of-a-bitch. They had come too far to fail now.

He took a couple of deep breaths and returned to the boardroom. They needed a break in the case and he meant to find it.

# CHAPTER SIXTY

Rosalinda Garcia deplaned at the International Airport in Liberia, Costa Rica, and headed straight for the taxi queue. She moved down the line of waiting taxis, locking eyes with every driver until she saw what she wanted—an honest man who would get her to the hotel in the least amount of time. She saw him, slipped into his cab and waved. The man jumped in and pulled away from the curb, despite the objections of the other cab drivers who were ahead in the queue.

Garcia had grown up in a family of cops. Her dad was a cop, her brothers were both cops, and now she was a detective in the homicide division. She hadn't gotten there by accident. Her ability to read people was almost legendary in the precinct where she worked, and the brass always brought her in on the toughest interviews—the ones with the psychopaths. The dead eyes, Steve Armitage called them. No one could read them like her. She could see behind the veneer and flush out the tiny pockets of humanity left in their souls. For Rosalinda Garcia, finding a good cab driver in Costa Rica was child's play.

"Condovac la Costa," she said in Spanish. "Please hurry. I need to be there quickly."

"Yes, of course," the man replied, stepping on the gas. The Honda surged ahead as he navigated the congestion of cars and buses parked outside the terminal.

"How long is the drive?" she asked.

"Forty minutes," the driver said. When they reached the main road he turned left, away from the city and toward the coast.

Rosalinda called Steve Armitage's cell and gave him her ETA, then settled back in the cab and watched the scenery flash past. It was in the height of the rainy season and the vegetation was brilliant green. Overhead, giant Guanacaste trees rose to eighty feet, their massive trunks twisted and deformed, yet beautiful. The hills rose behind them as they left the jungle rainforests and their shrouds of mist that kept the jagged, volcanic mountains lush throughout the year. Ahead of them, where land met the Pacific Ocean, black sand beaches fringed the rugged coastline and the hills were scorched brown. They reached the turnoff to Playa Hermosa and her driver cut west toward the coast.

The road was bumpier here, with potholes and sharp curves, narrowing to a single lane over an occasional bridge. Young, well-dressed children with inquisitive eyes watched from the porches of a steady stream of small, colorful houses that dotted the sides of the road. The driver turned onto the road for Playa Hermosa and drove another ten minutes on a very rough track. Ahead, as the coast returned to view, was a sign for Condovac la Costa.

The cab pulled into the resort and Rosalinda jumped out, telling the man to wait. No problem there, she hadn't paid him yet. She found the lobby and asked for the hotel manager, then had a look around as she waited. The resort was a series of hillside bungalows, all facing the calm waters of the Gulf of Papagayo. The hills were steep, and shuttles whisked about the resort, ferrying tourists to their rooms, the swimming pool and restaurants. The air was quiet and warm and the sun felt hot on her skin. After about five minutes, a diminutive man with short dark hair and very brown skin appeared through one of the doors leading out to the resort. He looked anxious as he approached. Not many of his guests dressed in pantsuits.

"I am Eduardo Fernandez," he said in English, extending a tiny hand. "Can I help you?"

She answered in Spanish. "Rosalinda Garcia, Los Angeles Police Department. Homicide. I need your cooperation on a murder investigation, Senor Fernandez."

The look on Fernandez's face changed from anxious to confused. "Los Angeles police? Homicide? What could you possibly want from our resort?"

Garcia took a couple of minutes to give the hotel manager enough details to justify him opening the books, but nothing more than he needed. When she was finished, he pursed his lips and a very concerned look blanketed his face.

"Allowing you access to our guest registry would be highly irregular, Ms. Garcia. Even for records from back in 2000. I'm not sure I can allow it. Perhaps if you were to bring something from the local court, I would comply. Otherwise, I don't think so."

"Senor Fernandez." Garcia led the man by his elbow to a grouping of chairs on the patio overlooking the ocean. "I'm going to be very open with you here and tell you more than I should, so you understand how important it is that I get this information today. Not tomorrow or next week. I need it today."

Garcia gave the resort manager what she knew about the case, emphasizing the position of power and wealth that the kidnapped woman's father held in America. She finished and sat back in her chair, the midday sun baking her in the pantsuit.

"This man, whose daughter has been kidnapped, he was one of the guests back in 2000?"

"Yes. It was when he and his family were at the resort that the problem originated. Your doctor prescribed doses of penicillin to five girls, but did not have enough to treat the boy. We believe he's the one who has been kidnapping and killing these women. I don't imagine I need to tell you how angry this woman's father is going to be if his daughter dies because you resisted helping with the investigation."

"What about this man who is killing these women? He sounds dangerous. He may come down here looking for me if I give you the information you want."

Garcia shook her head. "No chance. There is no doubt at this point that this man will end up in jail. That's a fact. What we don't know at this point, is whether we can save the rich man's daughter."

Fernandez was hesitant. "I'm not sure."

"What about the doctor?" Garcia asked. "Perhaps I could speak with him."

Fernandez shook his head. "I'm afraid not. That would be Dr. Enrico Hamdi. He died about five years ago."

Rosalinda Garcia sat quietly, reading the man's eyes. He was scared, terrified even. But she knew she had him. She waited, her body relaxed in the chair, sweating but not giving him even the slightest hint of weakness. After about ninety seconds, he licked his lips nervously and nodded.

"Okay. But just the records for June of 2000."

"That's all I need, Senor Fernandez," Rosalinda said.

She followed him back into the hotel and down a hallway to a locked room in the rear of the building. He selected a key from a ring and opened the door to a file room. It was unbearably hot, and Rosalinda peeled off her suit coat and set it on a rickety card table leaning against one wall. She watched as Fernandez scanned the cabinets, by holding his finger out in front of him as he read the labels. Finally, he pulled out a drawer packed tight with files. Again, he scanned down the folders with the finger, then pulled one out. He looked through it, then passed it over to the LA cop.

"This is June of 2000," he said.

Rosalinda Garcia opened the file and let her eyes run down the list of names. She stopped on Moran, then again on Shelby and Klein. Finally, near the bottom of the registry she saw Charlesbois. All the other woman's surnames were there as well. She quickly counted the number of entries on the pages. One hundred and seventy-four. There was no way to discern which of those guests were the boy's parents. She needed to get the list back to LA.

She gave Fernandez a hint of a smile. "Well done, Senor Fernandez. Now I need to use your scanner."

# CHAPTER SIXTY-ONE

The valley was heating up and shimmering waves rose off the pavement, distorting Brandy Eagleson's vision as she drove. She pulled into the parking lot of the local grocery store, intent on picking up some junk food. It was Tuesday, her day off, and what better way to spend it than snuggled up on the couch watching a couple of movies. And for that, she needed some snacks.

She used to head into San Francisco when she wasn't working and spend time in the city. That was back when she had a husband and all the baggage that goes along with a rotten marriage. It had been a disaster from minute one, and she had burned four long years trying to make it work. Being single again wasn't so bad. She was lonely, but at least her days weren't consumed trying to please another person who couldn't be pleased. She pushed the memories from her mind and walked into the store.

Brandy knew the clerk and they talked for a couple of minutes before she headed for the potato chip aisle. She bought three bags and drove home. She powered up her television, went to Netflix and started browsing. Curtis Westcott crossed her mind as she flipped through the categories. He was handsome, with his olive skin and curly, black hair. She wondered if Boston cops could all wear their hair that long, or if he was a department head who got to set the rules. Whatever the reason, it suited him. He seemed like a nice guy with an honest soul and she briefly wondered why he had chosen to work in homicide. She shook him out of her mind and focused on the movies.

Comedy was out. She didn't feel like laughing today. Most of the movies the studios said were comedies were either stupid or simply not funny. She went to action and adventure and scanned the titles. She'd seen quite a few of them, and the ones she hadn't picked in the past still looked bad. There were so many Kung Fu movies, and she wondered who watched those things. She finished in the action section and tried drama. One with Alec Baldwin on the cover looked good, but when she read the blurb she realized she'd already seen it. Maybe there was a new release.

Ten minutes later she hadn't found anything interesting and was out of the new release section. She dug around a bit, then stopped on one of the covers. It was an older movie, a strange one that she had watched a number of years back. *Apocalypse Now*. Francis Ford Coppola was the director, and she had never really understood what he was trying to tell his audience. Why was this sticking in her mind? She stared at the title, her brain churning through the mud, trying to remember. *Apocalypse*. Where had she heard that word?

Then it hit her. Curtis Westcott. It was in the transcript from the Napa interview. The man Curtis was looking for had used the word. How? What was the context? She racked her memory, trying to remember. Something about the good and bad years of the Napa wines. Erica Klein had likened the bad ones to the apocalypse. That was it. She stared at the cover. She realized what he was saying. Westcott was right, the man was giving them a message and she had figured it out.

Brandy grabbed her purse and rifled about for Westcott's business card. It was tucked in one of the side compartments and she held it up so she could see his number. Hands shaking, she dialed.

"C'mon, Detective Westcott, be there" she said as the phone rang.

# CHAPTER SIXTY-TWO

Curtis sat on a rickety chair in the Chicago station and watched the fax machine slowly spit out the pages. It had been years since he'd seen a fax and he didn't miss the technology in the least. Nowadays, homicide cops took pictures on their cell phones, but the weak Internet signal at the resort in Costa Rica had derailed sending an email, and Rosalinda had taken a different tack. Despite the slower pace, the data they needed was arriving.

At the top of the page was the insignia of the Condovac la Costa, in Costa Rica. Immediately below the resort's logo was the date. June of 2000. Noted below that, in Spanish, was the guest registry for that particular month. The fax finished and beeped. Kevin Shipton pulled out the final page and handed it to one of his detectives, who returned a minute later with a handful of copies. She distributed them about the boardroom, then sat at the table with her own copy.

"One hundred and seventy-four registered guests," Shipton said, reading the number from the bottom row. "It's been almost nineteen years since these people stayed at the resort, and all we have are their names and the city they're from. No phone numbers, not that it would matter. Most of them would have been landlines back then, and they'd probably have cell numbers by now." He set the pages on the table. "This is going to take some time."

Curtis scanned the list again. He used a pen to stroke off the women Khilt had already killed. Then he looked for anyone with a New York City address and hi-lighted them. There were only three names.

"Adamson, Gregory, and Zulkowich," Curtis said. "One of those three may be the next victim. From the clues he dropped in Boston, the trail went back to Napa and ahead to New York. Could you get one of your detectives to check and see if any of these families had a child in his or her late teens in 2000. Find out if they came down with yaws while they were on vacation."

Shipton nodded to the woman who had made the copies. "Angela, it's yours, but don't panic them. If Curtis is right, they're not in danger quite yet."

Curtis wasn't so sure. "If he's already killed Renee Charlesbois, he may be on his way to New York. I doubt it, but better to err on the side of safety."

"What should I tell them?" Angela asked, already moving toward the door.

Shipton cut in. "The daughter will be in her mid to late thirties now. Ask her if she could stay home tonight. I'll have Frank Chorney from the Bayview precinct visit her. Frank's a good guy. I'll fill him in and he'll know how to handle it."

"That helps," Curtis said, nodding. "But it doesn't get us any closer to who this guy is." His eyes wandered up and down the list. The bastard was on there somewhere, but which one? Names were names, and none stood out. There were no clues. His phone rang and he checked the caller ID. It was a California area code. When he answered it, he heard Brandy Eagleson's voice. She sounded excited, almost breathless.

"What's going on, Brandy?" he asked, leaving the room and finding a quiet place in the hall.

"Detective Westcott, I think I've figured out what the guy you're looking for was saying."

"What's that?" Curtis asked, his ear pressed tight to the phone.

"He used the word *apocalypse*, remember?"

"Yes. What do you think it means?"

"The winery just across Highway 29 from Frog's Leap is Niebaum-Coppola. And Francis Ford Coppola directed *Apocalypse Now*."

"And Coppola owns the winery?"

"A portion of it, yes. He's been involved in winemaking in Napa for years. I thought it was too much of a coincidence."

"Yes, you're right. It's brilliant, Brandy. You may have it. Tell me, are there any old wine cellars on the property? Someplace he could have kept Erica Klein for two weeks without anyone noticing."

"Absolutely. Some of the older wineries in the valley are laced with abandoned caves. I know for sure there are lots of them at Niebaum-Coppola."

Curtis took a couple of quick breaths. Niebaum-Coppola Winery. Brandy had likely found the starting point for Napa, but without the directions from wherever Khilt had kept and killed Annette Shelby in Chicago, they didn't have enough to work with. They needed to find the Chicago location. And they needed it fast.

"Do you know the area well?" he asked.

"Very well. We used to play in the caves when I was a kid. They're really creepy."

"Is this your cell number, in case I need to call you. I still have to figure out what happened in Chicago, but I might need some help in Napa. Are you okay with that?"

"This is my cell," she said. "Call anytime."

"Thanks," Curtis said. "Don't forget to keep your phone turned on and with you. We don't have a lot of time here."

"Okay."

"Good work. Talk to you later."

"Later." The line died.

Curtis returned to the boardroom. "We have most of what we need to find the location where he kept Erica Klein in Napa Valley, but we need to figure out things here, in Chicago."

Shipton glanced at his watch and shook his head. "Noon. Thirty-seven hours. Not much time."

Curtis rubbed his forehead and dropped into a chair. Shipton was right, they were pretty well dead in the water. He considered booking a flight to San Francisco, but he didn't know when, or if, they would solve the Chicago problem. Booking a flight was impractical. Even with commercial flights working almost perfectly, he was in trouble. Simply getting to all the cities was going to be tough, let alone having enough time to work the case once he was there.

Shipton saw the distressed look on Curtis's face and asked, "What's wrong?"

"Time is what's wrong. I don't think I can get from Chicago to Napa to Boston with what I have left."

"You could give the Napa police what you've got and let them run with it," Shipton said. "Same with your guys in Boston. And you're already here, in Chicago."

Curtis gave the idea some thought. It had crossed his mind, but he had dismissed it. Brent Keely already had the wrong man in custody, and Curtis knew that until he had absolute proof that Arnold Baker wasn't their perp, the Napa police were not going to respond well to a request for help. That was two strikes against looking for help from Keely. Which meant he had to return to the valley once he had the clues from Chicago.

*If* he got the clues from Chicago.

That left Boston. He had a good team in place, and he knew Stan and Aislinn would move fast once they had the necessary information. Still, nothing Khilt gave them was solid, and while they might have the nuances, sorting out what Khilt was leaving them would take time.

"I don't know," he said. "Involving Keely in Napa is the worst case scenario right now."

Shipton shrugged. "Then you need a private jet."

Curtis laughed. "Do you guys have one kicking around. I know we don't in Boston."

It was Shipton's turn to laugh. "Funny guy. We have to fight for pens and pencils. No movie stars or rich people here."

Curtis sat straight up and grabbed for his phone.

Shipton gave him a curious look.

"Very rich," Curtis said. "That works." He dialed Stan's cell number and tapped his fingers on the table, waiting for him to pick up. It rang four times, then Stan's voice came through the line.

"What's up, boss?"

"Stan, call Jacques Charlesbois and see if he has access to a private jet. I'm running out of time and I can't rely on the commercial airlines."

"You want him to send a private jet to Chicago?"

"Yes."

"Okay, I'll call him."

"Let me know."

"Immediately."

"How is Aislinn doing with finding out what happened to Peter Moran's company?"

"I saw her in the hallway about fifteen minutes ago. She's working on some Harris guy in San Francisco."

"Yeah, I know that much. Nothing else?"

"I don't think so."

"Okay, call me back about the jet."

Curtis touched the end button on his phone and grinned at Kevin Shipton. "Good idea, that private jet thing."

# CHAPTER SIXTY-THREE

Seven o'clock Tuesday night. They still had nothing that pointed them to where in Chicago Khilt had kept Annette Shelby before slicing her up and dumping her body on the golf course.

Kevin Shipton rubbed his eyes. They were bloodshot and tired. "Christ, Curtis, there is just no way these directions make any sense. We've looked at it from every possible combination. This isn't working."

Warm bodies were arriving as the shift change got underway and the room was getting busy. They nodded to Shipton as they passed and a few had comments on how terrible he looked. One woman went to her desk and came back with some Visine. Shipton put a couple of drops in each eye and blinked away the excess.

"I feel like shit," he said. A box of donuts showed up and he pilfered a couple, which he and Curtis attacked with gusto.

"That was awful," Curtis said when the donut was gone and washed down with a coffee chaser.

"No wonder I'm so fucking fat," Shipton said.

Curtis stared at the table. It was covered with maps of every description—municipal, topographical, transit and el routes, parkways, bicycle paths, legal descriptions, even the canal systems. No stone left unturned. Shipton was right, their approach wasn't working. They were out of options.

The rush of the shift change had ended and only two detectives from the day shift were left in the room with them. Shipton told them to head home to their families. "Make sure your cell phones are on," he added as they left.

Shipton glanced over as an older man, with graying hair and a badly stooped back, entered the room pushing a janitor's cart. Shipton gave the man a quick nod as he moved slowly about the room, emptying garbage cans.

"Hey, Samuel," Shipton said. "Everything good?"

"All's fine. Wife still lets me come home after work."

"Don't know if mine will after this."

"All nighter?" Samuel asked.

"Yeah, got a tough one."

"It's here somewhere," Curtis said quietly as Samuel put a new bag on his cart and dumped the full one next to a nearby desk for pickup later. "Somewhere in all this mess is the key."

"We've looked at it from every possible angle, Curtis," Shipton said. "It's not here."

Curtis glanced at his watch. "Thirty hours until the day he'll kill Renee. Thirty hours and we can't find him. God damn it."

Shipton was silent for a minute, then he said, "If I were a betting man, I'm not sure which way I'd go on this one."

"*Which way would you go if you were a betting man?*" Curtis said, reiterating one of the lines from the letter Khilt had left in the Lake Forest house. "Which way."

Samuel's voice cut in. "I sure as hell wouldn't stay in Chicago."

"What?" Curtis said in a tired voice, turning slightly. The old man was leaning on his broom, staring at him. Curtis turned to face him directly. "Why would you say that?" he asked.

"Because you can't gamble in Chicago. Got to go outside the city to play the tables or the slots. If I were a betting man, and I have been known to drop a few dollars on the odd occasion, I'd be in Joliet."

"Joliet?" Curtis asked. He glanced at Kevin Shipton, who was now looking very awake.

"Sure," Samuel continued in his slow drawl. "The casinos are in Joliet, not Chicago. There are two of them. The Empress and Harrah's. So, if you're a betting man, get out of town. Head for Joliet. But I wouldn't be going there for any other reason. It's a grey sort of place. Prison town, man."

Shipton had a map of Joliet on the table in less than two minutes. Two interstates cut through the city, the 56 and the 80. Stateville Correctional Center occupied a huge tract of land beside the residential area of Crest Hill. And just west of the prison was the river. Crossing the river, was Jefferson Bridge.

"Jefferson." Shipton pointed at South Center Street, a few blocks south of Jefferson Street. "Patrick Haley Mansion," he said, looking up from the map. "Alex Haley and Patrick Stewart. Patrick Haley."

Curtis could feel his heart beating fast. "Okay, we got Patrick Haley, Jefferson, then across the water on the bridge." He traced his finger east to Chicago Street. "Bear City," he said, poking the map. "Chicago Street."

Shipton's eyes were already scanning ahead. "Look, here, off Chicago Street. Patterson Road. If you turn right, it runs along the south side of the river."

Curtis wet his lips and managed a smile. "Got it," he said. He grabbed the janitor by the shoulders and looked the startled man in his eyes. "You may have just saved a life." He snatched the map of Joliet from the table and with Kevin Shipton leading, jogged to the front door of the station house. "What about the mention of *soul food for the starved mind*. Anything ring a bell there?"

Shipton was already working his cell phone, getting his detectives back from their short visit with their families. "I have no idea, but let's get down to Joliet and drive the route. The last road he mentioned was Patterson, so that's the first one we try."

They jumped into Shipton's unmarked ride and the Chicago cop found the nearest on-ramp to the 57. Traffic was moving at well above the posted speed so he left the siren and flasher off, traveling in the fast lane. At the Mascouten Reserve they cut onto the 80. The fast lane was clear and Shipton opened it up. Their speed was over ninety miles an hour when they entered Joliet.

*Prison town.* It was how Samuel had described Joliet, and Curtis looked about with intense interest as they took the 132 exit and slowed to the posted speed. There were few trees along the streets, and most of the houses were small and in varying states of disrepair. Old Chevys lined the curb, their bodies eaten with rust and their windshields cracked or broken. Curtis glanced over at Kevin Shipton.

"This place is kind of ugly," he said.

Shipton shook his head. "It's not all like this. The area on the east of the river is pretty rough, but once you get across the bridge the west side is okay. It's actually quite nice off the 55."

"I'll take your word for it," Curtis said as Shipton made the turn off Chicago Street onto Patterson Road. Shipton took it down to twenty miles an hour and Curtis said, "You watch the left side, I'll take the right?"

"Sounds good."

The road twisted about as it followed the river. The left side of the street was covered with shrubs and wildflowers, with gravel drives leading to clapboard houses. There were large gaps between the houses and more decrepit cars and trucks littered the front yards. The other side of the road was different. The trees along the riverbank were flourishing and blocked out any view of the water. The houses were larger on this side, and sat on expansive lots. Still, many of them were ill kempt. Some were dark and a few boarded up. They passed an open lot, covered with gravel, and Curtis tapped Kevin Shipton on the arm.

"Check it out," he said.

Shipton stopped and stared. Next to the vacant lot and barely visible through the overgrowth was an old, abandoned brick building. The sign on the front, still readable despite the peeling paint, read, *Bobby & Mamie's Soul Food.* Curtis opened the door and stepped out into the quiet evening air. He walked slowly toward the old restaurant, his mind whirling. This was it. While the entire city of Chicago read the newspaper accounts of her disappearance, Annette Shelby had been held captive in this nondescript building. Then he had killed her. And the city had grieved with the family. A senseless and brutal murder. A city outraged.

Now he stood in front of the place she had died. He turned to Kevin Shipton and the expression on the Chicago cop's face told it all. Hate, mixed with failure. That Annette Shelby's fate had been in his hand and he had missed the signs.

Without speaking, the two men walked toward the building.

# CHAPTER SIXTY-FOUR

Curtis was fifty feet from the empty shell that once housed Bobby & Mamie's Soul Food Restaurant when his cell rang. It was Stan Lamers. Curtis stopped, still facing the abandoned building and answered the call.

"Did you get me a jet?" Curtis asked.

"Don't you ever say hello?" Stan shot back.

Curtis grinned. "Okay. Hello."

"Hello, LT. Good call on the plane. Charlesbois' company has a time-share on a Gulfstream. The pilot is already on his way to Logan, and they're filing a flight plan for Chicago. They should be there in less than three hours."

"Jesus, Stan, good work. Your timing is perfect. Shipton and I are standing outside the building where Khilt kept Annette Shelby for two weeks."

"Seriously? Thought you said things were looking bleak."

"We caught a break," Curtis said. "Once we had the starting point for Khilt's directions the rest fell into place."

"So what now?"

"We're going in. By the time we're finished here, the plane should be at O'Hare. Tell them to file a flight plan for San Francisco."

"Done."

"Did Aislinn get anything on Moran's corporation?"

"Oh, that's a great story," Stan said. "Aislinn had a buddy of hers from SFPD visit Frank Harris, but midway through the Q & A, Harris begged off to hit the bathroom and when he came back he had a lawyer with him."

"What?"

"Yeah. Apparently Harris started sweating like a nervous drug mule and tried to play dumb, but that didn't last long. Whoever was behind the collapse of Peter Moran's business has this guy scared. He's totally lawyered up right now and we're not likely to get anything out of him for a while."

"Well, we know what Khilt's capable of," Curtis said. "Maybe Harris does too. If he does, then refusing to talk isn't that unbelievable."

"We're close to figuring out who this guy is, LT."

"Yeah, Stan, we are. Keep me in the loop. Things are looking good here, too."

"Okay."

Curtis killed the call and walked toward the abandoned restaurant. Kevin Shipton was standing at the front door, reading a posted notice. He pointed to it as Curtis approached.

"Good news. The building is slated for demolition," he said.

Curtis felt a tiny bit of the weight come off his shoulders. They didn't need to use *imminent danger to life* to circumvent getting a warrant. "No expectation of privacy," he said. "No warrant required to enter." It was a much stronger reason to enter without permission.

"Precisely."

Shipton was already circling the building, looking for the best way to enter. Curtis had filled him in on the booby trap he'd found on the front door of the Lake Forest house, and Shipton was being cautious. Curtis followed him around the building, to where it backed onto the river. The trees were all overgrown and the river was barely visible through the foliage. It was quiet except for the sound of water flowing, and Curtis pushed his way through the dense shrubs until he was next to Shipton.

"What do you think?" he asked.

Shipton shook his head. "I don't get down here often. Joliet has their own police force. I don't know the area at all."

"Shit." Curtis shook his head. It was important to have a local with you on something like this.

"I can call for back-up," Shipton said.

"No. It's getting dark. We need to get in that building before there's no light left. It doesn't look like there's power inside."

"Okay." Shipton brushed a bug off his face. "I think one of the lower windows in the back is best."

Curtis resurveyed the building. It was brick-built, sturdy, and the doors were solid. The windows on the front and the upper sides might be rigged somehow, but some of the smaller windows near the ground were completely hidden by the undergrowth. They were likely the safest.

"Let's try one," Curtis said. Shipton handed him some gloves and he put them on.

They found a window they thought would work and peered through the dirty glass. Shipton slipped a credit card in the crack between the frame and the jamb and worked the clasp. It snapped open and the window popped out an inch. He pulled it open carefully and shone his flashlight inside. The floor was strewn with garbage and the odor was strong and unpleasant. Shipton pinched his nose and breathed through his mouth for a minute, then released his nostrils and crawled through the window. He dropped to the floor, squashing a plastic bottle with his foot as he landed. Curtis followed and together they stood in the expansive basement, surveying the room.

The walls were concrete and the ceiling about eight feet high. It was a large space, about a hundred feet wide by one-twenty long, with little sunlight filtering through the small, greasy windows. After a quick look about, Curtis pointed to the stairs.

"Let's check out the main floor while there's still a bit of light."

"Okay." Shipton led the way to the wooden staircase in one corner of the basement.

The stairs were solid, but creaked with every footstep. Shipton un-hooked the clasp on his pistol, but left it in the holster as they reached the top of the stairs and opened the door. It was quiet, and both men stood without moving, taking in the room. It had been a restaurant and the tables were still there, along with a host of broken chairs scattered about. Most of the hanging light fixtures were smashed and the soft-wood floor was dirty. At the back of the building was a set of swinging doors leading to the kitchen.

"Nothing here," Curtis said. "Let's try the kitchen."

The sun was setting as they pushed through the doors. There was a central island that served as the prep area, two grills with overhead ventilation units and a set of sinks with broken plumbing. Any items which could be removed without a blowtorch or a bulldozer were gone, leaving just the skeleton. In the far corner was a separate room with a heavy metal door. The freezer. They glanced at each other and Curtis walked over and pulled on the handle. The door swung open and he shone his flashlight beam into the room.

"Jesus Christ," he said quietly.

Shipton took two steps in and stood beside Curtis. "Aww, fuck."

The room was the scene of a bloodbath. Spatters of blood had shot across all four walls, likely the result of a severed artery. The floor was dark brown and caked with dried blood. On one wall was a hook, which had been anchored to the wall with four lag bolts. On the hook was a set of handcuffs, also encrusted with blood. A few dinner dishes were stacked neatly in one corner. Next to the dishes was a scalpel.

"How did I miss this?" Shipton's face reflected the horror he was looking at.

"C'mon, Kevin, you know it was next to impossible."

Shipton stood immobile, transfixed by the scene. "She died here."

"Yeah, she did." Curtis glanced over and saw the wetness in Shipton's eyes.

Curtis swallowed hard. He'd been exactly where Shipton was right now—missed the clues and let the bad guy slide away—and it was an ugly place. He scanned the room for what he knew would be there. The clues to what happened in Napa. Nothing was obvious at first, and except for the hook with the handcuffs, the walls were completely bare. The air conditioning unit, which cooled the room, was on the exterior.

The cool air entered the room through a heavy grill, but it was firmly secured with eight large screws. That left the dinner plates.

"That's unlike him." Curtis slowly walked across the room to the pile of dishes. "Always so clean, and now he leaves a stack of dirty dishes."

He pulled a pen from his pocket, squatted down and poked at the dishes. He used the pen to gently lift the top plate, then the next and the next. Between the second last and last plate was a slip of paper. He gripped it by the edge and pulled it out slowly, careful not to rip it. Then he set the paper on the floor and Kevin Shipton directed his flashlight beam on it.

*Too many Japanese. That's the problem. But once you get by them, it's easy going.*

*Are you really with me? I doubt it.*

*Look in the caves, always the caves. But be careful, they can be dangerous.*

*The oldest ones are the most interesting.*

*Don't forget to bring a deck of cards. A game of crib perhaps. It's all in the counting.*

Curtis gingerly handed the paper to Kevin Shipton, who pulled an evidence bag from his pocket and slipped it inside. They returned to the main restaurant area and Curtis took a picture of the note with his phone.

"What now? Napa?" Shipton asked.

"Yeah. Napa and then Boston. We're getting close."

"Did you get what you needed?"

Curtis nodded. "It's confirmation that he kept Erica Klein in one of the abandoned Niebaum-Coppola wine cellars. And if Brandy Eagleson is right about the extent of the cave system, we're going to need every scrap of information we can get to find where he was holding her."

They hurried to the front door and checked for boobytraps. Once they were sure it was clear, they exited the old brick building and walked back to the car. Shipton hit the flashing lights and the siren, then rocketed out of the parking lot, heading for O'Hare and Jacques Charlesbois' private jet. Curtis sat in the passenger's seat, quiet, deep in thought. He was absolutely sure he could find Liem Khilt. Now the question was, could he find him in time to save Renee Charlesbois.

# CHAPTER SIXTY-FIVE

Liem Khilt sipped herbal tea and hummed a Beach Boys song while he waited for his computer to boot up. He couldn't remember the name or the words, just the melody. The tea was hot and stung his lips but he barely noticed. He had other things on his mind.

It was nine o'clock in Boston. Three hours from the calendar flipping over to the final day of Renee Charlesbois' life. There was no doubt in his mind about two things. Renee Charlesbois would die in precisely twenty-seven hours—allowing her to live even an hour longer was dangerous. And Curtis Westcott, despite his tenacity, would not find her in time. That put a cruel smile on his face.

His computer was ready and he entered his password and went to his email. His fingers froze on the keyboard. There was an automated email from the remote system he had installed at Bobby & Mamie's Soul Food Restaurant in Joliet. Someone had broken a tensile steel trigger, thin as a human hair, between two of the plates in the freezer. That activated a motion sensor in the main restaurant area attached to a tiny camera. Any motion in the room would now switch on the camera and generate an attachment with a ten second video.

He opened the file and double clicked on the attachment. A small window appeared on his screen. He positioned the cursor over the play button and started the video. The screen came to life with grainy images swathed in pale green light. Walking through the main area of the abandoned restaurant were Kevin Shipton and Curtis Westcott. They weren't searching, but moving quickly, which meant they had found the note embedded between the two dirty plates. The video stopped about four seconds after they reached the front door. Long enough for Khilt to notice them looking closely at the door before opening it. They had likely found the electrical wire attached to the door handle in Lake Forest.

Khilt watched the video three more times, trying to read something from the men's facial expressions, but the images were too poor. He killed the email and sat back in his chair, the tea still in his hand. Mentally, he was doing the math. Chicago was one hour behind Boston, making it eight o'clock pm, but Westcott would be heading for Napa, where the time was only six in the evening. That gave him plenty of time to visit the Niebaum-Coppola winery. But the time differences didn't really matter. It was Eastern Daylight Time that counted. Even if Westcott found the Napa clues, he still had to get back to Boston and find Renee Charlesbois. Which meant he would lose three hours to the time change. The bottom line was, Westcott had just under twenty-seven hours.

Khilt used the computer to access the airline schedules for flights from Chicago to San Francisco and San Fran to Boston. He printed off all the pages and hi-lighted the results. Another smile crept across his disfigured face. Only three flights worked. The ten-eighteen out of Chicago and then either the eight-sixteen or two-forty out of San Fran. The only chance Westcott had of making it to Boston in time was to catch the ten-eighteen to San Fran, solve the Napa case in less than ten hours and fly back on the two-forty. That put him in Boston at almost ten in the evening, giving him two hours to arrive at the front door.

It simply couldn't be done.

Khilt shut down the computer, picked up his gun and headed down the stairs to the basement. He glanced through the hole in the door to see where the woman was, then entered and sat in the chair by the door. She lay curled in the fetal position—a mess. Her hair hung in greasy strands and her face and hands were smeared with dirt. She had tried to keep clean at first, but after ten or eleven days, had given up. Now she simply lay curled in a ball, staring at him with unbridled hate in her eyes.

"Curtis Westcott's an extremely intelligent man," he said in an upbeat voice. "He's very close to finding you."

She was silent for a minute, then said, "You don't seem too worried." Her voice was raspy, almost non-existent.

Khilt leaned back in the chair until the front legs were off the ground and the back scraped the wall. "Not worried at all. In fact, quite confident that things will go well." She didn't respond and he continued. "Special night tomorrow. It's your choice of whatever you'd like to eat. Sky's the limit, don't think small."

He was still smiling when she came at him. Her legs pushed hard against the wall behind her and she shot off the bed, her hands grabbing at the chair legs. She locked onto one leg and pulled, yanking the chair out from underneath him and sending Khilt crashing to the floor on his back. The gun skittered across the floor and she rolled toward it, her fingers inches from the barrel. She felt a vice-like grip on her leg and her body was dragged back across the hard-packed dirt. She rolled onto her back and viciously kicked out her free leg, catching him in the face and breaking his nose. Blood gushed from both nostrils and he screamed, a primal roar that was deafening inside the small room. Renee flipped over, diving again for the gun. This time her hand closed on cold steel. The barrel. She had to get her finger on the trigger. She clutched clumsily at the gun, turning it and grabbing the handle, all the while rolling away from her captor. She smashed into the wall and came up with her arms outstretched, the gun pointing, her finger on the trigger. He was only a few feet away, diving at her, his arms aimed at her head. She centered the gun on his head and pulled the trigger.

Nothing happened. The safety was on.

A split second later, Khilt's body hit her and the impact drove her head back into the wall. She was stunned. His fist was coming straight at her face, then it all went black.

Liem Khilt stopped hitting her in the face and stared. She was covered with blood, her nose broken and one cheekbone smashed in. Her jaw was askew and he suspected he had broken it as well. His own blood was still dripping from his nose, pooling with hers. He stood up, leaving her in a heap on the floor.

"You stupid bitch," he said, touching his nose and wincing. It hurt. She had really nailed him with her foot. He kicked her in the ribs, but when she didn't respond he stopped. No sense hurting her if she couldn't feel it. "Tomorrow, you will pay for this. Tomorrow, when I slice off that piece of beat up pulp you call a head, I'm going to do it slowly. So slowly. You'll die a hundred times before I'm finished."

Khilt picked up the gun and left the room, locking it securely behind him. He wiped at the blood streaming from his nose, his face battered and sore. The realization hit him that she had come within a fraction of an inch of killing him. He stopped at the bottom of the stairs, breathing through his mouth and tasting the blood. Westcott was not going to stop and there was little doubt now that he would eventually peel back the layers that Khilt had used to protect his true identity. Still, he had killed three of the women and Renee Charlesbois would die tomorrow. He could slip out of sight once she was dead and wait for things to cool down, then go after the woman in New York. He had enough money to disappear after all five were dead. His spirits buoyed a touch as he thought of a new life on a beach somewhere. He would miss the meticulous planning and the exhilaration of the kill, but he had always known it would end. Right now, all that mattered was staying on his timeline and slicing off Renee Charlesbois' head. A little over twenty-four hours, then her two weeks were over. Thirteen days, fourteen nights, just like the two weeks in Costa Rica that had ruined his life.

"Vacation's almost over," he said as he trudged up the stairs. "Hope you enjoyed it."

# CHAPTER SIXTY-SIX

Curtis saw the Gulfstream the moment he walked out of the executive terminal at Logan. It was a magnificent plane, shimmering silver in the bright halogen lights. The reason he knew for sure it was the right plane, was because Jacques Charlesbois was standing on the tarmac at the foot of the stairs. Curtis strode across the cool asphalt toward him. When he was a few feet from the man, he said, "What are you doing here?"

"She's my daughter." Charlesbois' voice carried easily above the din as another private jet moved past them into the takeoff queue. His tone had changed, no longer aggressive. "I'm coming with you."

Curtis stood four feet from him, reading the angst in his eyes. He was already down, and there was no upside to kicking him. "You're an observer, nothing more. Understood?"

"Understood," Charlesbois said. There was no smile, no hint that he had won a small battle.

"Did the pilot file a flight plan for San Francisco?" Curtis asked as they moved up the stairs and into the plane.

"Done, and we're fueled. We can leave anytime."

"Good." Curtis headed for the cockpit. He poked his head in and nodded to the two men in the seats. "Let's get this thing in the queue."

"No need," one of the pilots responded. "Someone with the police department called in and we're cleared as number one for takeoff when we're ready."

Kevin Shipton had pulled some strings.

"We're ready," Curtis said.

He left the cockpit as the pilots began their preflight check and he headed back into the main cabin. The interior of the plane was beautiful, with luxurious leather seats and highly polished wood tables.

"Where's economy?"

Charlesbois, seated at one of the groupings of four, managed a glimmer of a smile. "You look like shit."

"I haven't slept in two days. Barely had time for food." Curtis sat opposite Charlesbois and closed his eyes for a minute. It felt wonderful.

"What can you tell me?" Charlesbois asked, leaning forward, a hopeful look on his face.

"Everything," Curtis said. "I can tell you everything."

The first half hour of the flight was spent with Curtis talking and Charlesbois listening. When Curtis had finished bringing Renee's father up to speed, including the final message they had found in the abandoned restaurant, Charlesbois shook his head in disbelief.

"You mean this whole thing is over some vacation in Costa Rica twenty years ago? That's absolutely crazy."

"Not to him. He's still insanely angry."

"Obviously. He's killed three women and has Renee."

Both men were quiet. Finally, Jacques Charlesbois said, "Christ, I've been an ass."

"You have," Curtis agreed.

"I can't believe you managed to figure this out."

"We're not quite there yet." Curtis opened his eyes and took a deep breath. "The only thing that matters is finding Renee. That's the end game."

"Right." Charlesbois sat for a minute, staring at his hands in his lap, then he looked up. "I'm responsible for what happened because of the reward I offered."

"Yes, you are," Curtis said. "We'll deal with that later."

A few moments passed, then Charlesbois said, "So, as I understand it, he's left us a clue somewhere in the Niebaum-Coppola winery. That clue will give us the location where he's holding Renee. We need to find it and then get back to Boston."

Curtis nodded. "Precisely."

The in-flight telephone rang and Charlesbois answered, then handed it over. "Looks like call forwarding your cell phone worked. It's for you."

"Thanks." Curtis shifted a bit in his seat so the phone cord reached. "Hello."

"Curtis, it's Kevin Shipton in Chicago. I've got a forensics team at Bobby & Mamie's place and we've found something you should know about."

"What?" Curtis asked.

"They found a trip wire in the dirty dishes. Extremely thin and virtually unnoticeable. When you moved the plates it snapped and activated a motion sensor in the main part of the restaurant. Once the motion sensor was live, it turned on a miniature video camera when we entered the room. It has a wireless connection to the Internet."

"So he filmed us leaving the restaurant?"

"Yup. Then sent the images to his computer. First look at the system shows no email address. He had a program in place to wipe out where he sent it."

"So he knows we were in the restaurant."

"If he's turned on his computer and checked his email, then yes. He knows."

"Shit," Curtis said. "He's going to know we're close. He might panic." He thought for a second, then said, "Kevin, see what else you can get out of this. Maybe he's not as smart as he thinks he is."

"We're on it, Curtis. I've got my best CSU team working the scene. I'm on my way back to the building now. Almost there."

"Thanks," Curtis said. He handed the phone back to Charlesbois who replaced it in the holder.

"Problems?" There was a mixture of fear and anxiety on Charlesbois' face.

Curtis shook his head. There was no upside to telling Jacques Charlesbois what the video clip of them leaving the restaurant might mean. That the killer could decide his time frames are too liberal and cut them by a day. That his daughter might die sooner because they hadn't found the trip wire in the dishes. No, there was definitely no upside to that.

"Everything's fine. We just need to get to Napa. Nothing's changed."

# CHAPTER SIXTY-SEVEN

Napa Valley. It should be the last stop before heading home to Boston.

Two people were key in Napa—Brandy Eagleson and Brent Keely. While he viewed Brandy as an asset, Keely was more of an unfortunate necessity. The tight time frame required getting into Niebaum-Coppola winery in short order. They had tried contacting the owners, but they were on a ship in the Antarctic and unreachable. That meant they needed Brent Keely on side and opening doors. The Napa homicide cop was quiet as Westcott informed him he was on his way back to the valley, but didn't take it well when Curtis told him they had the wrong man in jail. Once Curtis finally got Keely to agree to meet at the winery, he hung up. There wasn't time to bring Keely up to date on the details of the case, and it would be better to deal with the man face to face.

Charlesbois had instructed the pilots to change the flight plan to land at a small airstrip close to Napa, and they arrived just after midnight. They drove through town, the traffic almost non-existent. When they pulled up in front of the gates to Niebaum-Coppola, three cars were waiting. Brandy Eagleson's Toyota, Keely's unmarked car and a police cruiser. Curtis could see Brandy sitting in the driver's seat of her car. She didn't get out when they arrived. That was probably not a good sign. Keely was outside his vehicle, leaning against the hood, his arms crossed on his chest. That was definitely not a good sign. Curtis parked and approached him, Jacques Charlesbois at his side. Three uniformed police stood nearby.

"Good evening, Detective Keely," Curtis said in a steely tone.

"What's going on, Westcott? You're here working a case we've already solved."

"Cut the shit, Keely, you've got the wrong guy." Curtis was in no mood to have his access to the caves blocked by an incompetent cop exercising very poor judgment. "Arnold Baker had nothing to do with Erica Klein's death." Curtis's tone was threatening. He took less than a minute to bring Keely up to speed with Khilt's MO and why they were convinced he had killed Erica Klein.

Keely's arms remained crossed. "The owners of this winery hardly need this hassle. I don't want them upset because you have a crazy idea that Erica Klein was kept in one of their caves."

"Crazy idea?" Curtis moved closer to the man, until he stood about four feet away. "Are you telling me you're not prepared to give us access to the wine cellars?"

"You need a warrant. Good luck getting one at this time of night."

Curtis's face went a blistering shade of red. "I need to get in those caves, Keely. Every scrap of evidence I have points to them as the place where the murderer kept her." Aside from the chirping of crickets, the night was deathly quiet. Curtis studied the man's face in the pale moonlight. "There'll be hell to pay, Keely."

Charlesbois moved forward, standing next to Curtis. "He has my daughter, Detective Keely. And he's going to kill her in less than twenty-four hours. We can't find her unless we get in those caves." His voice was emotional but firm.

Keely remained unmoved. "You need a warrant."

Charlesbois looked like he was going to explode. His teeth were grinding together and his mouth started to open, then he stopped. He closed his lips and simply stared at Keely. Then he turned and walked back to the rental car, pulled his cell phone from his pocket and dialed a number.

Curtis wasn't finished trying. "Keely, we're going to get into those cellars one way or the other. We have a stack of evidence exonerating Baker. Cut your losses and admit you've made a mistake."

"No fucking way."

Curtis was furious. "You're not doing yourself any favors here by keeping us out, Keely."

Keely was about to respond when Jacques Charlesbois rejoined them. He held the cell phone loosely in his right hand and his demeanor had changed. He was calm as he handed Keely the phone.

"For you," he said.

Keely didn't move for a few seconds, then reached out and took the phone. "Hello," he said.

"Is this Detective Brent Keely?" the voice asked.

"Yes. And you are?"

"Detective Keely, this is Reginald Bassinger. I'm the governor of Massachusetts. I understand we have a problem with access to a potential crime scene."

"With all due respect, sir…" Keely started.

"Keely," the governor shot back immediately. "One thing I can tell you with absolute certainty is that I can have the governor of California on the phone in under a minute if you don't cooperate. If I make that call, tomorrow will be a vastly different day for you than today."

Keely took a long, deep breath. "I understand, sir." He handed the phone back to Charlesbois and turned to Curtis, venom in his eyes. "It's all yours."

Curtis walked quickly to where Brandy sat in her car. When she saw him approaching she opened the door and slipped out into the night air.

"He told me to stay in the car," she said as Curtis came within earshot.

"I figured as much. Thanks for coming, Brandy."

"It's okay," she said.

"We need to get inside the caves and find whatever clue he's left us that leads to Renee's location in Boston. Here's what we got from

Chicago." He pulled out the notes he had made in Bobby & Mamie's. She read the entire script, then focused on the first line.

"The first part is easy," she said, pointing to the road leading into the vineyard. "The trees bordering the access road are Japanese plum. I'd say he's telling you to head up the road, past the trees."

"Confirmation we're at the right place. That's good. Do you have a flashlight?" he asked and she nodded. "Okay, then let's take your car."

"Sure."

Curtis waved at Charlesbois to join them and the three piled into the car. Brandy started up the long, straight drive, her foot heavy on the gas pedal. Trees flashed past in the translucent moonlight, evenly spaced and wonderfully symmetrical. *Too many Japanese. That's the problem. But once you get by them, it's easy going.* Clues, always pointing the way. Curtis wondered what kind of person would take such elaborate measures to perform such horrific acts. Serial killer or not, Liem Khilt was a sadistic bastard. He glanced behind them. Brent Keely and the car full of uniform officers were following.

Brandy drove by the main house at full speed, but Keely's car slowed and stopped at the house. They were alone on the massive estate, solitary headlights cutting through the darkness. The road changed once they were amongst the vines, twisting and weaving its way up and around the natural undulations in the landscape until they finally entered the oldest section of the vineyard. The vines were bent and gnarled, and created grotesque shapes that reminded Curtis of long, twisted fingers reaching from the grave.

"The oldest caves are on the southernmost part of the estate," she said. "Probably best to start there, given the message he left you."

*The oldest ones are the most interesting.*

"Good idea," Curtis said. "A moment later he asked, "How extensive are these caves?"

"Unbelievable. This winery's been here since Gustave Niebaum finished construction in 1887. And right from minute one they were building wine cellars. There are probably three or four miles of caves and tunnels on this estate. Once you're inside, it's like a labyrinth, but with a bit of order. The main tunnels run north-south, deep under the hills. The problem is, there are hundreds of branches off the main routes, sort of like a fish skeleton."

"Then we need to look very closely at what he gave us. He's habitual. The answer will be there, it always has been."

Brandy pulled up in front of a small wooden building built into the side of a sandy hill. It resembled an outhouse with no back. She killed the engine and said, "This is the oldest part of the cave system."

They got out of the car and walked the last few feet to the structure. Curtis reached the door first and tried the handle. It was locked. Before he had a chance to say or do anything, Charlesbois stooped over and picked up a nearby log. He aimed it at the handle and used his weight and size to deliver a shattering blow on the metal. The wood surrounding the handle splintered and the door cracked open a couple of inches. He dropped the wood and gave the door a solid kick, sending it crashing to the ground.

"They can send me the bill," he said.

Curtis leading, they entered the caves.

# CHAPTER SIXTY-EIGHT

The stagnant odor and cool temperature of the caves hit them the moment they entered. Brandy had a sweater with her and she slipped it over her shoulders. Curtis went first, lighting the passageway with the flashlight. The walls were mostly earth, interspaced with timber shoring to keep the tunnel from collapsing. The floors were hard-packed dirt and slightly uneven, making progress slow at best. Other than the flashlight, it was pitch black.

The first passage moved directly south, deeper into the hill. Off this passage were numerous branches, each identified by small numerals set into the thick, wooden posts. The main tunnel was 7, and the branches started at 7-1 and increased as they traveled farther into the maze. Curtis stopped when they reached 7-5, opened the file he had brought with him and shone the light on the notes he had made in Chicago.

"The first part, about the Japanese trees, we've figured out. But the rest is still Greek." All three of them concentrated on the words.

*Too many Japanese. That's the problem. But once you get by them, it's easy going.*

*Are you really with me? I doubt it.*

*Look in the caves; always the caves. But be careful, they can be dangerous.*

*The oldest ones are the most interesting.*

*Don't forget to bring a deck of cards. A game of crib perhaps. It's all in the counting.*

"*Are you really with me? I doubt it*," Charlesbois read the line aloud. "Is he baiting us?"

Curtis responded. "It's more like he's wondering if whoever found the note in the dishes is the right person. It may be in there in case some passerby picked it up. *Look in the caves* is easy. We're in them. The remark on them being dangerous might mean he's rigged up some sort of surprise for whoever ends up on his trail."

"We're in the oldest ones on the winery grounds," Brandy said. "So we're probably where we should be."

Curtis nodded. "There's the mention of the deck of cards. Nothing this guy says actually *means* what he says. That line is in there for a reason, and it's not about a deck of cards."

"Counting is important in crib," Brandy said. "Do you play?" Both men nodded and she continued. "Then you know that after you discard to the crib, you peg. The object is to make 15 or 31, and to create runs or play the same card as the previous one, like a seven on a seven."

Charlesbois cut in. "When you count your hand, you say 15-2, 15-4, 15-6, then add your runs and pairs. Twenty-nine is the highest possible score, nineteen is impossible."

"15-2," Curtis said. "And we're at tunnel 7-5 right now. That could be the answer."

"Do you know where the 15 series of tunnels are?" Charlesbois asked Brandy.

She shook her head. "Not off hand, but if I remember correctly, the main tunnels increase as they move east."

"Do the branches interconnect the main tunnels?" Curtis asked.

"Yes. Most of them. We should be able to turn left down one of the branches and eventually find the 15 series."

"I think that's the plan," Charlesbois said. "Curtis?"

"It makes the most sense," he agreed. "Let's try it."

The still air in the tunnel system was cooler and damper as they moved deeper into the hillside. Brandy buttoned her sweater to the top, and both Curtis and Jacques were shivering. Old barrels, most broken or smashed, sat against the walls, and at the intersection of main tunnel

9 and branch 6, they found an old kerosene lamp. The base of the lamp was filled with liquid, and Charlesbois tried his lighter on the wick. It caught, throwing a bright yellow glow against the walls and floor. Curtis switched off the flashlight to conserve the batteries.

An hour later, they reached tunnel 15. They gathered at the crossroads, looking up and down the passageway. It looked similar to the rest of the tunnels, about six feet across with a seven-foot ceiling. A small alcove where the two tunnels met was filled with twenty or thirty casks in varying stages of decay. Curtis held the lantern up so it shone on the rotting wood.

"This is 15-6. It could be anywhere around here," Charlesbois said.

Curtis nodded. "We're going to need to move these barrels around to see if he's left us anything. But be careful, he warned us they could be dangerous."

"We're looking for a single sheet of paper?" Brandy said, glancing about. "It'll be like looking for a needle you-know-where."

Curtis set the light on one of the barrels and began carefully shifting the wood about. The other two joined in and after fifteen minutes disappointment hit. Khilt had left nothing for them at this intersection. They moved back to the intersection coded 15-4, and repeated the process. Then 15-2. Still nothing. Curtis checked his watch.

"It's almost three-thirty here, six-thirty in Boston. We're not getting anywhere."

Charlesbois looked tired and disappointed. "You're sure it's here, Curtis?" he asked. "We're not off target somehow?"

"I'm positive, Jacques," he said. "This is where he kept Erica Klein before he killed her."

"What about blood? Shouldn't there be a lot of blood about? You described the other crime scenes as being quite bloody."

"He strangled her. She never bled out like the other two women. This crime scene is going to be subtler, with less physical evidence."

"More difficult to spot," Charlesbois said, sitting on one of the intact barrels in the alcove they had just searched. He took a long drink from the water bottle they were sharing and wiped the back of his hand across his mouth. "Did you have this much trouble with LA and Chicago?" he asked.

Curtis ran back through the two cities and what it had taken to solve each case. "Very similar. The only difference is that it was more difficult to find the starting points, and easier to locate the clues he left once we knew where he wanted us to look. Here, the difficulty is in finding the clue itself. The starting point, Niebaum-Coppola winery, was easy once Brandy nailed what he meant when he used the word apocalypse."

"I can't believe you managed to piece this together," Charlesbois said. "We're so close."

"Close doesn't count." Curtis laid his notes on the top of another barrel. He handed Brandy the light and she held it so the pages were well illuminated. This time he scanned back through everything—his original notes from Boston, then Napa, then Chicago and LA, and then back to Napa. Everything Khilt had given them with planted clues. He stared at one name for a full minute. Al Stoogs. Weird spelling. And why give the name in the first place if it wasn't important? Al Stoogs.

Charlesbois was up and moving about, double-checking before they moved on to ensure they hadn't missed anything. Curtis gathered up his papers and started stuffing them back in the file. The list of names from the hotel in Costa Rica caught his eye and he absently glanced down the row of names. Beside each name was their city of origin. There were a lot of Canadians, a few Germans and a number of Americans. Los Angeles was one of the most popular exit points for Americans. A few were from Texas and one from Montana. Just as he was about to place the page back in the file, he noticed a city that hadn't clicked the first time he saw it.

Los Gatos, California.

The letters jumped off the page at him. Al Stoogs. Los Gatos. He crossed each letter off the name of the city as he jotted them on the page, forming the name. It fit. It fit perfectly. There was no uncle. The name was simply an anagram for where the killer lived. Los Gatos. It was just like the anagrams he had used in the police interviews. He looked at the hotel's records, line-by-line until he saw Los Gatos, then glanced at the registrant's name.

*William and Betty Roberts.*

The parents of a multiple murderer.

Curtis began stuffing papers back in the file while he opened his cell phone. He tried dialing, but there was no response. He checked the signal strength. Nothing. They were too deep into the hill. He glanced at his watch. Almost four in the morning. Seven in Boston. He looked up to see both Brandy and Charlesbois staring at him. Brandy's eyes locked on his for a second, then she glanced at his left hand. He looked down and realized why they were staring. The sheet of hotel guests was crushed into a tiny ball, with just the edges sticking out between his fingers.

Curtis held up the crushed ball of paper. "Got him," he said, motioning for them to head toward the exit with him. He needed to get Aislinn or Stan on the phone. "I know who the son-of-a-bitch is."

# CHAPTER SIXTY-NINE

Curtis reached the entrance to the tunnel system and hit the send button on his phone the moment he was in the open. The eastern sky was beginning to lighten and the morning air was still and warm. It felt good after the damp and cold of the caves. A groggy Aislinn Byrne answered after six rings.

"Shit, LT, it's the middle of the night."

"Wake up and run a couple of names for me. William and Betty Roberts. They lived in Los Gatos, California eighteen years ago. They might still be there."

"Eighteen years ago. Are they Khilt's parents?"

"I think so."

"Were they on the list from the resort in Costa Rica?" Aislinn said, perking up.

"They were. Remember Al Stoogs?"

"Sure, Khilt's uncle."

"It's an anagram for Los Gatos. William and Betty Roberts were from Los Gatos. Get me everything you can on them, but concentrate on their son. He would probably have been in his mid to late teens, which would make him thirty-three to thirty-eight, give or take. Then get his name out to every law enforcement agency in the country."

"Should we bring the bureau in on this right away, or wait?"

"I especially want the FBI on this. Dredge up every scrap of information you can on the son. Concentrate on real estate purchases or leases. Maybe his name will show up on some recent lease or purchase document in Boston. If it does, I want you there in record time. He's keeping Renee somewhere close by. If you get any hint of where he might have her, I want warrants in place in minutes, not hours. Make sure you call me and keep me up to date in real time."

"Okay. I'll call when we get a positive ID on this guy."

Curtis checked his battery and closed his phone. He'd been plugging it in every chance he had, but the charge was almost gone. Brandy's car was nowhere close. Neither was an electrical outlet. He pocketed the phone and hoped it would still be working when he needed it. Jacques Charlesbois and Brandy were sitting on a rock just outside the access door to the tunnels. Their eyes were bloodshot and Charlesbois' face looked haggard with stress and worry.

Curtis glanced at the horizon and the stark outline of thousands of twisted vines. Daybreak. Renee's last chance. He glanced again at Jacques Charlesbois, who had put his faith in him, and felt buoyed for a moment. He had come such a distance, but there was one leg of the puzzle left to solve and it was a seemingly impossible one. Somewhere in the miles of caves was a clue. A solitary clue that would lead to Renee Charlesbois. His decision earlier in the night to keep the crime scene intact by limiting the manpower was looking like a poor one. His moment of hope was fading quickly. He punched Brent Keely's number into the phone and hit send. The Napa cop was on the line in seconds.

"Where the fuck are you, Westcott?" he yelled.

"Entrance," he leaned over so he could read the numbers on the side of the wooden building. "Nineteen."

"I'm on my way. Don't move an inch."

"We need more people, Keely," Curtis said through gritted teeth.

"You get what I decide you get," Keely snapped and hung up.

"You dumb motherfucker," Curtis whispered as he slipped the phone into his pocket.

Curtis stretched his arms over his head and wondered what was going through Jacques Charlesbois' mind. Hate, fear, horror, helplessness. All that and probably more. He closed his eyes, realizing he understood what Charlesbois was feeling because the same emotions were churning inside him.

# CHAPTER SEVENTY

"Here's a bit more on our guy," Aislinn said as she walked into Stan Lamers' office. She handed him a few sheets of paper, fresh off the printer.

Stan scanned the new pages with tired eyes. He'd been up since Aislinn called him just after four in the morning, and now it was almost noon. "Andrew Roberts, thirty-five, resident of Los Gatos, California. Worked at a tech startup until he inherited eight million when his parents died in a car accident. He was twenty-seven at the time. Used the insurance payout as seed money to build a Silicon Valley software firm specializing in online games. Sold it for thirty-seven million about sixteen months ago."

"Games," Aislinn said. "What sort of games?"

Stan read through the text until he found the list of games the company had developed, then read it out to Aislinn. "Pretty violent shit."

"Grand Theft Auto on steroids." Aislinn said.

"Yeah, good description." Stan put the papers down and shook his head. "He had it made. What was he thinking?"

"Talk about carrying a grudge," Aislinn said.

Stan flipped through more of Aislinn's findings on Andrew Roberts. "Check this out." He stabbed his finger at one of the pages. "There's a police report in here on the accident that killed his parents. The cops suspected that their deaths may not have been accidental. Something about the speed that the car was traveling when it went off the road."

"I read it," Aislinn said. "Then I put a quick call through to Carmel and talked with the detective who ran the case. He was convinced the kid killed the parents. They had circumstantial evidence, but nowhere near enough to convict. In fact, the insurance company offered to foot part of the investigative bill, but there just wasn't enough evidence to proceed."

"You can buy a good investigation for a lot less than eight million dollars," Stan said.

"They could hire me for the rest of my life," Aislinn said.

There was one grainy picture of Andrew Roberts in the file. "Is this it for pictures?"

"That's it. Just his driver's license, and it's pretty bad. The guy was a veritable recluse. It's obvious he didn't like his look after yaws chewed up his face."

"You want to call Curtis or should I?" Stan asked.

"I'll call," Aislinn said, reaching for the phone.

The reception on Curtis's phone was poor when Aislinn's call came through, but improved as Curtis hurried back to the cave entrance. He listened to Aislinn's summary, then said. "So Liem Khilt is Andrew Roberts. Good work. Alert the Los Gatos police and have them stake out the house. Ask them not to move in until we resolve things in Boston. Kicking in the front door of his house is only going to let him know that we're onto him, and he might panic and kill Renee on the spot."

"Okay."

"What about leases? Did you find any real estate transactions in his name anywhere in or around Boston?"

"Nothing yet," Aislinn said. "We have the real estate board working on it, running his name through their computers. Land titles office as well. All our extra manpower is working the phones with the leasing companies, since they're not tied to any database. It's slow going, but we'll know in a couple of hours." Aislinn checked her watch. "It's noon here, so give us until two or three."

"Okay. My cell battery is almost dead and there's nowhere to plug it in. Try Charlesbois' cell phone or call Keely's number in Napa if you can't get through to me."

"No problem. How you doing out there? Find anything yet?"

"Nothing. I'm sure we're at the right place, but unless we can figure out what he's telling us in the letter we found in Chicago we're dead in the water."

"What was in it?" Aislinn asked.

"I'll take a picture and text it to you." Curtis hung up, then found the photo he'd taken while in Chicago and sent it to Aislinn's cell phone.

Curtis slipped the phone back into his pocket and reentered the caves. Brent Keely had brought eight warm bodies with him to assist in the search, but Curtis suspected what Keely really wanted to do was keep tabs on what he and Charlesbois were doing. He returned to where he had left Brandy and Charlesbois, working all the narrow branches that spun off the number 19 tunnel. He'd picked that because 19 was the only score unattainable in a single hand in cribbage. Charlesbois was meticulously checking some smashed barrels when Curtis arrived. He looked awful, his hair matted with sweat and his face and hands covered with streaks of dirt. His manicured fingernails were broken and caked with mud.

Charlesbois looked up. "Did your men ID him?"

Curtis nodded. "His name is Andrew Roberts. He's a Silicon Valley millionaire. His parents died in a suspicious motor vehicle accident a few years back. The Carmel police suspected him but couldn't prove it."

"Paying back his parents for not outbidding us for the medicine," Charlesbois said.

"Is that how it was?" Curtis asked. "I mean, the incident in Costa Rica."

"Yes. I remember it now." He sat on the dirt next to a barrel and leaned against the earthen wall. "When Renee and the other kids contracted the disease, the doctor used some scare tactics on us. He told us the kids could be disfigured or possibly even die without the medication. So when we were faced with the choice between paying an exorbitant rate or taking our chances, we paid."

"Andrew Roberts' parents didn't have the money?"

"If the price was reasonable, or if the resort had more penicillin, they would have been fine, but that wasn't the way things played out. The price kept going up until they backed off. The girls got the shots, the boy didn't."

Curtis was intrigued. "Do you remember how much you paid?"

"It was five or ten thousand dollars—I can't remember exactly. My wife decided Renee was going to get the shots, so no matter what the cost, we would have paid it."

"Why didn't the doctor send someone for more medicine?"

"The weather was so bad no one could make it to the nearest town to pick up more penicillin. The wind was unbelievable. It tore trees out by their roots and the highway, which was awful to start with, was totally impassable."

Brandy finished checking under the last few pieces of a cask and sat beside Curtis. She shook her head. "Nothing," she said.

Curtis gave her a small smile. She looked worse than Charlesbois. Her hair was wet and hanging limply over her shoulders. Dirt was firmly embedded under every fingernail and her normally white teeth were coated with dust and grime. She had been digging to free broken slats from the hard-packed earth and pushing and pulling old barrels around for hours, just as he and Charlesbois had. Without so much as a whimper.

"You've been a lot of help today," Curtis said.

She tried to smile, but it wasn't there. "Erica Klein was a fine woman. She was kind and there was no reason for her to die. Just as there's no reason for Renee Charlesbois to die. I'll do whatever I can to keep that from happening."

Charlesbois' eyes were moist. "Thanks, Brandy," he said.

They were the two most emotional words Curtis had ever heard.

# CHAPTER SEVENTY-ONE

Eleven o'clock in the morning on the west coast. They were almost at the point of no return.

It was Boston time that counted. Curtis had allowed for the three-hour time difference, then added four and a half hours for the flight to Boston and another half an hour to drive to the airstrip where the Gulfstream was parked and waiting. He figured that by noon on the west coast, maybe twelve-thirty, their time was up. Which meant they needed results within the hour.

Curtis glanced up and down tunnel 31. They had tried every variation of cribbage scores and commonly used numbers. They still had nothing tangible to work with. Both Charlesbois and Brandy were exhausted. None of the three had slept in over twenty-four hours and the combination of sleep deprivation, numbness from the constant cold and backbreaking physical work had taken its toll. There had been no word from Aislinn or Stan, which meant their killer had taken extra precautions when renting or purchasing the place where he was holding Renee. That didn't surprise Curtis.

*Don't forget to bring a deck of cards. A game of crib perhaps. It's all in the counting.*

Why cards? For that matter, why cribbage? With all the possibilities surrounding the game of crib coming up empty, Curtis began thinking along new angles. A deck of cards had four suits of thirteen, totaling fifty-two. Was it that simple? Had they been fooled by the smallest red herring in the school? Fifty-two. Curtis dragged out the schematic of the cave system, which Brent Keely had dredged up. The highest cave number was 50. Beside the thin lines detailing cave number 50 was a note in tiny printing. He struggled to read it in the ambient light.

*Auxiliary caves.*

That was it. Nothing more. Auxiliary caves. What the hell did that mean? He leaned over to Charlesbois and said, "Maybe crib isn't the answer, Jacques. Maybe he means fifty-two cards. Tunnel 52." He pointed at the diagram. "It says there are auxiliary tunnels beyond 50. What do you think?"

Charlesbois was already getting to his feet. "Anything is better than sitting still." He grabbed a light Keely's men had supplied and started down one of the cross tunnels at a brisk pace. Curtis and Brandy fell in behind him and they made good time, reaching tunnel 50 in less than half an hour. The caves were even older here, and in terrible condition. The ceilings were low, about five feet, and Charlesbois and Curtis had to hunch over to avoid hitting their heads. Water dripped down the walls and clumps of dirt and rock lay on the floor where they had fallen. The rocks were slippery and wet, the footing treacherous, and all three of them slipped at least once and ended up on the ground. They stood in a close group at tunnel 50 and used the lights to illuminate the dank cave. It was so cold they could see their breaths when they exhaled.

"If tunnel 52 exists, it should be straight ahead."

"Right. Let's go," Curtis said.

They crept ahead carefully, using the walls to steady themselves. The cross tunnels had mostly ended, and they continued east along the main line. There were no markings at the first crossroad after tunnel 50 and Curtis simply said, "51," and kept moving as they passed through. The intersection of main tunnel 52, perhaps fifty feet further, was a complete disappointment. There was no alcove, no barrels, nothing where the killer could have hidden a message at the crossing point for the two tunnels.

Charlesbois started down the cross branch but returned in about ten seconds. "Dead end," he said. He tried the other direction and rejoined the group in less than half a minute. "Same on that end. This tunnel is the only one that intersects with number 52."

Curtis leaned against the wall with his knees bent to take the pressure off his back. "This is all wrong," he said.

Charlesbois knelt on a dry patch of rock. "What do you mean, all wrong?"

"If Andrews kept Erica Klein here for two weeks, he had to feed her. There's no way he could make his way through these tunnels every day with food. The autopsy on Erica indicated she had been well fed, like all the others. Can you imagine coming in through this series of tunnels every day? I don't think so. Somehow, we've missed the clue."

Jacques Charlesbois ran a dirty hand through his hair. "Well, there's fifty-two cards in a deck, and that's where we are. Tunnel 52. And there is nothing here."

"That's not quite right," Brandy said.

"What?" Charlesbois asked. "What's not right?"

"Technically, there are fifty-four cards in a deck. Fifty-two plus two jokers."

All three of them glanced at the narrow opening where the tunnel continued. It was little more than a crack in the damp, cold earth. The tunnel didn't appear to be supported by any sort of beams or braces, and it was readily apparent that venturing into the dark opening was extremely dangerous. Curtis tried to shine the flashlight through the hole, but the beam illuminated nothing but more rocks, then darkness.

"Brandy might be right, Jacques," Curtis said. "Remember what he wrote. *Don't forget to bring a deck of cards. A game of crib perhaps. It's all in the counting.* The part about crib may mean nothing. But the segment about counting might mean, *count the jokers.* And that would be fifty-four."

"I don't know if I can make it through that crack, it's too narrow," Charlesbois said. "One thing's for certain, if I have to turn around, I'm stuck."

"I was thinking the same thing," Curtis said. "Christ, what now?"

Before either man could move, Brandy shone her light into the crack and slipped between the two walls. In seconds, she was too far in for either man to grab her.

"What the hell are you doing?" Curtis yelled. "Get back here, Brandy."

She ignored him and pushed deeper into the fissure. "I'm small enough to turn around if I need to. I'm going to check it out. I'll call for you."

Her light was already dim, partially blocked by her body and growing fainter every second as she sidestepped along, her feet scraping on the rough earth as she tried to find some sort of traction. A few seconds later the light was gone and the scraping noises barely audible. Curtis glanced at Charlesbois and he just shook his head in disbelief. They waited, hardly breathing. Then they heard her voice carry back through the crack.

"There's a small clearing here, and a door. I'm going to try it." There was a hint of a squeaking noise, then she yelled, "Curtis, Jacques, get in here. Quick."

Curtis dove into the crack, pushing through with his shoulders at right angles to his body. The rocks were very slippery, but falling was all but impossible with his body wedged so tightly between the two walls. He kept moving ahead, his flashlight illuminating the way. He could hear Charlesbois coming behind him, but couldn't turn to see how he was faring. After about two hundred feet, the crack opened into a small cave with ten-foot ceilings and small stalactites and stalagmites formed by dripping water. Curtis stepped around the calcified mounds and through the open door directly ahead. The beam from Brandy's flashlight lit the room, and a few seconds later Charlesbois came bursting in. Both men stared at the scene in front of them.

They were in a rectangular room, about fifteen feet by twenty. There was a closed door directly across from them, no windows, and an eight-foot wooden ceiling with a single recessed light. The walls were hard-packed clay. A metal bunk sat against one wall. On the opposite side of the room was a single folding chair, the kind that was often used with portable card tables. A bucket, half-filled with what appeared to be human waste, sat next to the bed, and two or three feet from the bucket was a stack of dishes.

Liem Khilt. Andrew Roberts. Whatever name he went by, this was where the monster had kept Erica Klein before killing her.

Curtis walked across the room to the other door, gave the handle and door jamb a close inspection, then tried opening it. The handle turned easily and the door swung open. Beyond it was a steeply inclined stairway, about twenty feet long by four wide, leading to another door. Curtis jogged up the stairs to the second door and tried it. At first it resisted opening, then as he put his weight behind it a crack appeared and sunlight flooded in. Another push with his shoulder and the door opened. He walked through and looked about. It was a desolate stretch of land up behind the Niebaum-Coppola winery, and Khilt had piled dirt against the door, making it hard to open from inside and almost impossible to see from the outside. Curtis walked a few feet to the crest of the nearest hill and peered over. At the bottom of the hill was a dirt road. That explained how Andrew Roberts got food to Erica Klein every day. He returned to the room and found Charlesbois and Brandy huddled over the pile of dishes.

"Don't touch them," Curtis said quickly.

"We already discussed that." Charlesbois stood up and let Curtis in to have a closer look. "We figured this is where he may have rigged up some sort of booby-trap."

Curtis dropped to his knees and shone the light into the stack of dishes. There were seven plates stacked atop each other, then two mugs and numerous plastic utensils resting on the top plate. Curtis shone his light deeper into the pile. He tried to see if there was anything hidden behind the dishes, but they were placed too tightly against the wall. Then he peered closely between each dish. In the center of the pile, barely visible, were the edges of a piece of paper. It was what they had spent hours searching the cold, inhospitable caves for, and it was within his grasp. He lay prone on the floor, concentrating the beam on the plates. Then he saw it.

A tiny glint of light reflecting off a piece of metal. He focused on it until he could make out what it was. His hand was shaking from holding the flashlight steady, and he finally rolled over onto his back and looked up at Charlesbois and Brandy.

"There's a very thin steel wire attached to the plates. It runs vertically from the floor to the plate sitting on top of the piece of paper. The wire isn't much thicker than a human hair and lifting the plates will snap it. Whatever he's connected to the wire is probably set to go off when the connection is broken."

"Can you bypass it somehow?" Charlesbois asked.

"I don't know. I'd need something metal, like a pin or a needle. Either of you have something like that?"

They shook their heads, then Brandy said, "Why don't we just go to the other side of the room and throw a rock at it. Hopefully he doesn't have too much explosive stuff attached to it."

Curtis shook his head. "Even if the blast was small, it would still destroy the paper. And we need whatever's on it to find Renee."

"What about calling Brent Keely?" Charlesbois said. "He could send one of his men up with a pin."

Curtis shook his head. "If we call Keely now, we'll end up waiting for a bomb disposal unit. They will have to come up from San Francisco. If we involve Keely now, we're finished."

They stood in silence, all staring at the dishes. Close enough to touch, yet seemingly unattainable.

"Bastard," Charlesbois growled.

The single word summed it up for them all.

# CHAPTER SEVENTY-TWO

Renee was famished.

There had been no breakfast, no lunch, and no dinner. In fact, since their skirmish, there had been no sign of her captor. After the brutal beating he had laid on her, she likely wouldn't be able to eat even if he did show up with some food.

She suspected her jaw was broken. Just touching it sent shockwaves of pain to the back of her brain. But she was more worried about the orbital bone just under her eye. He had smashed it, and a constant piercing pain originating in her eye made every movement sheer agony. Even laying on her cot with her eyes closed was almost intolerable. She had ventured from the cot once that day, to use her toilet, and was unsure if she could get up again. Strong-willed or not, she had her limits.

She sensed her ordeal was coming to an end. Her captor had been acting differently the last couple of days, and now she was terrified of his arrival. Her sixth sense was in overdrive, tingling and telling her that time was growing short. That had fueled her attempt to overpower him—a desperate measure by a desperate woman. She had actually gotten her hands on the gun. If he had taken off the safety before he entered the room, he would be dead. And she would be free.

Renee thought about her parents. Her mother, so fragile and gentle. Her father, an emotional man under that rock-hard exterior. They must be completely distraught. Especially her mom. Renee knew she would never survive losing her daughter. Part of the push to stay alive was that she couldn't let that happen.

Yet, what control did she have over the outcome? In reality, none. She had tried to escape and had failed. Now, with her injuries, she was completely helpless. She was totally reliant on others to find her and save her. She knew they were out there, doing everything in their power to get her out of this prison. They were coming. They were close. She could feel it.

She drew on her father's strength, and his will for her to live soaked into her body.

"Godspeed, father," she said.

# CHAPTER SEVENTY-THREE

Brandy Eagleson pulled her cell phone from her pocket and hurled it against the stone floor. It exploded into fragments. Both Jacques Charlesbois and Curtis Westcott jumped at the sudden, violent action. Brandy dropped to her knees and began picking up the pieces.

"There's got to be something in all this mess that we can use to bypass that circuit," she said.

Curtis and Jacques joined her, plucking the shards of the phone from the ground. Brandy held one up and said, "Look at this. Do you think it'll work?"

Curtis took the tiny piece from her outstretched hand. It was a thin strip of metal about four inches in length, attached to broken pieces of plastic at both ends. It was what gave the strength to the phone's frame. Curtis stripped off the remaining bits of plastic and nodded. It was perfect. Now the trick was getting it into position. He moved back to the corner where the plates were stacked and set his flashlight on the ground so the beam shone on the pile. Jacques Charlesbois hovered above him, pointing the beam of his flashlight on the narrow gap between the dishes and the wall. Curtis hunched over and took a few deep breaths.

"God knows what sort of device is attached to the wire," he said quietly, more to himself than anything else.

"God and Andrew Roberts," Brandy said.

He glanced up at her and couldn't help smiling. He wondered if her face would be one of the last things he would ever see. With that thought the smile faded.

Curtis looked back at the plates and slipped his fingers into the gap, the thin piece of metal in his fingertips. The lights Jacques and Brandy were shining on the plates weren't much help now. He was running blind and everything was by touch. He could feel the wire on the edge of his index finger as he slowly lowered his hand. The rough surface of the wall scraped his knuckles, and beads of sweat formed on his forehead and dripped on the top plate. The tip of his middle finger reached the ground, his index finger still in contact with the wire. He kept the two fingers pressed tightly together, the small piece of metal from Brandy's smashed phone between them. Slowly, he dragged his middle finger across the ground, millimeter by millimeter. He felt the object the wire was attached to. He recognized the shape he was touching.

"It's a blasting cap," he said quietly. "It moves when I touch it, so I don't think there are any explosives attached to it."

"You're not sure?" Brandy asked.

"No." He maneuvered the metal strip into place by touch. "I'm not sure."

"So if the blasting cap detonates, dynamite could go off as well?"

"Perhaps," he said. "But I doubt it. He's rigged this to destroy the paper if someone lifts the dishes. A blasting cap is probably sufficient."

He secured the metal strip from the phone as best he could to the top of the blasting cap by pressing it gently into the contact point. Then he positioned the strip against the wire near the top plate and pressed. The bypass was in place.

"Jacques or Brandy, hand me a rock. I need one just big enough to jam between the plates and the wall."

"To keep the metal strip in place?" Brandy asked as she scoured the room for a suitable stone.

"Yes."

Charlesbois found a good one in a corner and handed it to Curtis. He angled his hand to the side, still holding the metal, and carefully slipped the rock into place. It felt like it should hold. Then he said to Brandy, "You've got the smallest fingers. I want you to pick up the plate just enough to slip out the paper. Then set the plate down exactly as it was. Okay?"

"I'll try," she said, getting on her knees and reaching for the plates.

"No," Curtis said sharply. "Lie on the ground, arms in front of you. Keep your face in the dirt and feel what you're doing with your hands. If you're staring at the dishes and the blasting cap goes off, your face will be shredded by the exploding glass."

She looked scared. "I'm not sure I can do this, Curtis."

He gave her a hint of a smile. "If there's one thing I'm absolutely sure of, it's that you can do it. Just lie on the ground, get a grip on the plate with one hand and the edge of the paper with the other. Then lift a bit and gently pull."

"Okay."

She did as he said, and once she was in position, she began to lift the edge of the plate. Curtis kept a constant pressure on the metal as he felt the pile rise. He knew that without the bypass in place and the pressure from both his hand and the rock, the wire would have snapped. She continued to lift as she gently tugged on the edge of the paper with her other hand. Then she stopped lifting.

"It's moving," she said.

"Good, now pull it out real easy. No sudden motions."

There was just silence, but he could see her hand slowly moving back, the paper coming into view. It was just about free when Curtis felt the pressure on the wire release. It had snapped. He had to keep exact pressure on the bypass and not let it slip on either end. The slightest mistake now and both he and Brandy were severely injured or dead. She finished pulling on the paper and gently set the dishes back in place.

"Got it," she said.

"Good. Now, both of you get out," Curtis said. "Right out of the caves, into the sunlight. Do it."

"But…," Brandy started.

"Now," Curtis said, sweat forming quickly on his brow as he struggled to keep the pressure constant. "Don't argue with me. Get out of here."

Charlesbois grabbed Brandy and the two of them retreated from the room, taking one last glance at Curtis, in the corner, his hands absolutely still, his face covered with sweat. They disappeared into the passage that led to the surface.

Curtis looked down at the pile of plates the murderer had rigged to kill or maim whoever came looking for him. There was one thing he hadn't told Jacques and Brandy—he suspected the soft lump the blasting cap was embedded in was some sort of explosive. C4 likely. It wasn't much, but even a small amount would likely kill him. If it didn't, the explosion would certainly cause the tunnel to collapse. He was in an almost impossible situation.

He had no choice but to finesse the bypass so it would hold on its own for a few seconds. Yanking his hands back as quickly as possible and rolling away from the blast was not an option now that he was sure Khilt had attached C4 to the cap. He needed to use the rock to pin the metal strip in place, then slowly remove his hands and hope for the best.

He was beginning to shake from the exertion of keeping the right amount of pressure on the metal. He needed to make his move before exhaustion set in. His fingers were cramping as he struggled to reposition the metal strip against the wire. He could feel the edge of the blasting cap and the wire, and he slowly applied more pressure so there was good contact between the cap and the wire. The pain in his fingers was excruciating and spreading through his hands to the rest of his body, which was twisted at an awkward angle. His back muscles were seizing up and he had to let go. He slowly released the pressure on the metal. It was holding. He slid his hand out and backed off until he was three or four feet away. Then he tipped onto his side and rolled over a few times, putting more distance between himself and the explosive. Once he was at a safe distance, he scrambled to his feet and ran out the door. He was halfway up the corridor that led to the exit when the blasting cap went off and the C4 exploded.

The blast roared up the tunnel behind him, a wall of compressed air, rocks and dirt. Ahead of him, Brandy and Jacques were at the exit, staring in as he ran, his legs pumping as fast as he could. The surge hit him and knocked him flat, only a few yards from the exit. Dirt and rocks pummeled him, and above, the ceiling began to collapse. Huge pieces of dirt rained down and pinned him to the tunnel floor. He couldn't breathe or see and panic set in. *Christ, I'm going to die in this tunnel.* He struggled against the weight of the dirt, but could barely move.

Then he felt a hand on his arm and immense pressure on his shoulder socket as Charlesbois dragged him through the dirt and rocks toward the exit. Inch by inch he kept moving ahead, his body screaming in pain as he slowly emerged from the rubble. Charlesbois got a grip on his other arm as well and continued pulling. Then his shoulders were out and Charlesbois got his massive hands under Curtis's armpits and yanked. He came free and Charlesbois dragged him the final few feet to the exit. They tumbled out the door and hit the grass, Curtis on top of the big man. He rolled off and stared at the sky. It was vivid blue, with one puffy cloud.

Brandy's face appeared and she started brushing the dirt off him, away from his mouth and nose. He didn't move, just stared in her eyes. He'd noticed how blue they were the first time they met, but now he realized they were translucent. They were, perhaps, the most beautiful eyes he had ever seen.

Above Brandy, framed against the midday sun was Jacques Charlesbois.

"Thanks," Curtis gasped.

"No problem," Charlesbois said. In his hand was the single sheet of paper they had risked their lives to find.

# CHAPTER SEVENTY-FOUR

Curtis could barely breathe. He rolled onto his side and coughed out a mouthful of dirt. He was shaking almost uncontrollably, fully realizing he was a dead man if Charlesbois hadn't pulled him out from under the dirt and rocks. He looked again at the paper in Charlesbois' hand, then at the man's fingers. They were torn to shreds from digging, one nail torn out and blood dripping from the cuts and tears. Curtis wiped his face and sat up.

"Jesus, Jacques."

The big man knelt down. "Yeah, that was close."

Curtis reached out and took the paper and scanned the contents. It was short and disappointing.

*Charles Westcott? Is it you? Wouldn't surprise me.*

*North, in the horseshoe.*

*Can't miss it.*

Curtis reread the text four times, then let it drop to his side, on the dusty earth. He had risked his life for this? There appeared to be nothing of value in the note. Yet he knew the message had to be there. Curtis closed his eyes, the sun warm on his face. It was such a simple thing, but if it hadn't been for Jacques Charlesbois, he would never have felt the sun on his skin again. Now, even with the note in their possession, it was looking like Khilt might be successful in killing Renee Charlesbois. Her life rested in the hands of a man so tired and burnt-out he could barely string together two coherent thoughts. He opened his eyes. Both Jacques and Brandy were staring at him, waiting, hardly breathing, for him to open his mouth and tell them what the words meant.

He didn't have a clue.

"Jacques, is your cell phone still working?" he asked.

"Yes." He handed it over.

Curtis wiped a splotch of blood off his hand, then dialed Stan's cell. His detective picked up immediately. "Did you find it?" he asked.

"Yeah, get Aislinn and I'll read it for you." A minute later Stan put the phone on speaker and Aislinn said hello. Curtis recited the words, clearly enunciating every one, then stopped.

"Next," Stan said.

"There is nothing more. It's only those three lines."

"What? That's it? Two of the three lines are totally useless. The second line is the only one that might give us a location."

"I'm not sure," Curtis said slowly. "He's given us everything we need to this point. I can't see him stopping now."

"Shit," Aislinn cut in. "This tells us nothing. Nothing." There was frustration and anger in her voice.

"Anything on the real estate angle? Did you find any purchases or leases in his name?"

"Not one. We've checked with every property management firm, the real estate board, land titles, and the short and long-term rentals in the newspapers. We ran the searches using Andrew Roberts, Liem Khilt and every other name he used in the previous cities."

Curtis stood on shaky legs and began walking back toward Niebaum-Coppola Winery and Brandy's car. He was still on the phone and Brandy and Jacques fell in behind him. "Well, guys," he said to his detectives, "you've got what we've got. That's all he left us. The answer is in there somewhere."

"Okay, LT, we'll get every spare body we have on it."

"Check your call display. I'm on Jacques Charlesbois' cell. Call me on his number. My cell's dead."

"Right. Are you heading for Boston?"

"Yeah, but it's going to take us five hours or more to get there." Curtis glanced over at Charlesbois and asked if he could have a car at the Boston airport. He nodded. "Charlesbois will have a car waiting at Logan. I'll ride with him. You and Aislinn stay on your phones."

"Will do."

"And Stan, Aislinn, if you get anything you want to move on and I'm in the air and unreachable, use your judgment. If it's good, go for it. We're out of time."

"Okay. See you in a few hours."

Curtis handed the phone back to Charlesbois. "Let's run," he said.

They reached the cars in ten minutes. Brent Keely and six other Napa police were waiting there. Keely had a pissed-off look on his face and the other six looked like they wanted to go for their handcuffs.

"What the hell happened to you?" Keely asked.

"Cave in."

"Where were you?" Keely's tone was anything but civil. "We've been all through those tunnels trying to find you."

"Fifty-four," Curtis said. "There's an entrance on the south end. Hike back up the way we came and you'll find it. He kept Erica Klein in a room up there that linked into the tunnel system." Curtis held up the paper they had found in the room. He was holding it by the upper corner. "He left this. You can keep it for evidence. I took a picture of it with my phone."

Keely motioned for one of the men to get an evidence bag, and when the paper was securely locked inside, he read the contents. "What's going on?" he asked. "Is this Charles Westcott supposed to be you?"

Curtis shrugged. "I have no idea. He knew in advance that he was going after Renee once he killed Erica, and it wasn't a stretch to figure that this file would end up on my desk. So, maybe he does mean me."

"Fucker didn't even get your name right. Dumb-ass."

Curtis ignored the comment and turned to Brandy. "Can Jacques and I get a lift back to our rental car?"

"Sure," she said.

"Westcott, we need to debrief first."

"Maybe another time, Keely. Right now, I simply don't have the time."

He slammed the door and they were gone, leaving Keely and his cops in a large dust cloud. Brandy drove fast through the estate, past the Japanese plums to the junction with the main road where they'd left the rental. All three of them got out and Charlesbois took a minute to thank Brandy. They ended up hugging each other. It was a long, emotional hug that neither seemed willing to break. Finally they parted and Jacques cradled her head in his hands.

"If you ever need anything, Brandy. Anything. You call me. You want to talk over coffee, you want to start a business. Anything. You've got it. You understand?"

"Yes, but right now the only thing I want is for you to get Renee back safe and healthy."

He hugged her again, the tears cascading down his cheeks. Then he let go reluctantly and sat in the passenger seat of the car and waited for Curtis.

"I don't have much time," Curtis said to Brandy, taking her hand. "There's no real way to thank you. Without you and everything you've done, we wouldn't have had a chance. If we find Renee in time, a large part of our success belongs to you."

Her face was streaked with dirt and her hair was swept back and slick against her scalp. Tired and bloodshot eyes said it all. She managed a smile and squeezed his hand. "Find her, Curtis. Save her."

"I'll try."

He pulled his hand from hers and slipped behind the wheel of the car, ignoring the pain that shot through his body. He kept stiffening up, and every time he stretched a muscle it was agony. Sitting was no exception. He took a few deep breaths and slammed the car into gear. Seconds later they were en route for the private airstrip.

Charlesbois called ahead to the pilot and had him file a flight plan for Boston, then gave him their ETA so he could set their position in case there was a queue for takeoff. Curtis drove fast, weaving through the traffic, his speed hovering around eighty miles an hour. They slowed as they entered Napa, where the traffic was thicker but still made good time. It was precisely eight minutes after one on the west coast when they parked and ran to the waiting plane. The pilots had made a good estimate of when they would be entering the queue and the tower had given them priority for takeoff. At one twenty-two the Gulfstream lifted off, en route for Boston. Twenty-five minutes later they settled in at a speed of five hundred and sixty miles an hour at forty-one thousand feet. Their ETA was ten-seventeen in the evening, Boston time. Curtis and Jacques washed up in the bathroom, then they sat facing each other with a polished wood table between them. Curtis wrote the message they had found in the Napa wine cellar on a piece of paper and laid it on the table. Both men studied it intently.

"*Charles Westcott*," Curtis said. "He doesn't make mistakes like that, Jacques."

"*Charles* is the first seven letters of my last name," Jacques said as he carefully wrapped bandages around his fingernail and the host of other cuts on his hands.

"That's what I'm thinking, but where does that get us? We know he's kidnapped Renee. We don't need any additional information to figure that out. We need her location. That's something he's given us in the past. Why change now?"

"So we're undecided on what he means by *Charles*. But *Westcott*, that's you."

Curtis nodded. "It was pretty predictable from the onset that your daughter's abduction wouldn't land in Missing Persons. Homicide has the best resources, which means I would likely be involved. *Is it you? Wouldn't surprise me.* I think he's put that in the note in case I managed to follow this back to Napa from Boston."

"It's a compliment," Charlesbois said.

"Well, if it is, he can take his compliment and shove it up his ass," Curtis said. "The third line, *Can't miss it*, indicates once we get close we won't have to look hard. We just need to be looking in the right spot."

"So it shouldn't be as difficult as the caves," Charlesbois said.

"I sure as hell hope not. So that leaves, *North, in the horseshoe*. Do you know anything in Boston shaped like a horseshoe?"

Jacques Charlesbois was quiet for a couple of minutes. Then he said, "No. Nothing. Not one thing."

Curtis nodded. "Me neither. Nothing."

"What about the clues he left when the police interviewed him in Napa?"

Curtis pulled that page from his file. He read aloud the portion of the interview that dealt with Boston.

*It was getting on, and I had just glanced at my watch before another guest I was talking to introduced us. She was a very interesting woman, from a long line of vintners and well traveled. We talked at length about lots of things, but ended up spending a bit of time on Boston, as the fellow who introduced us was from some suburb just outside the city. Anyway, he was a bit of a jerk. Made a stupid remark about one of the wines and Erica moved on. As did I. He moved around the room like a chicken with its head cut off, and ended up talking with a couple of shady looking characters. Rather a motley crew for such an upscale tasting.*

Curtis set the text on the table. "I've spent hours staring at this, and the key words I can see are *Boston, some suburb just outside the city, chicken with its head cut off, shady looking characters, upscale* and *motley crew.*"

"Okay, *Boston* is easy. So is *some suburb just outside the city*. But which one. There are a lot."

"Exactly. It's a needle in a haystack. But he's made it clear that he's not keeping her in Boston."

"*Chicken with its head cut off?*" Charlesbois asked.

Curtis didn't respond and Charlesbois repeated the line. Finally, Curtis said, "He's been consistent in telling us how he plans to kill the next victim."

"He's going to cut off Renee's head?" Charlesbois' face turned deep crimson. Curtis kept his eyes focused on the singular piece of paper that sat on the table. "Motherfucker. I'll fucking kill him."

Curtis didn't say anything, just threw Charlesbois a sideways look.

They sat in silence for a few minutes, listening to the low hum of the jet engines. Curtis broke the quiet. "I have no idea what he means by the last three remarks, other than *upscale* may indicate a suburb with high property values. That's just a guess."

"Lot of guessing going on," Charlesbois said.

For the next four hours the men alternated between working on the puzzle together or taking time by themselves, trying to understand what the killer was telling them. They taped a map of Boston and its neighboring suburbs on one of the seats and referred to it every time they had an idea. When the pilot announced they were fifteen minutes from landing at Logan, they still had nothing. Curtis checked his watch. It was three minutes to ten. Two hours until Renee Charlesbois' execution.

He glanced out the window. Boston was aglow, its streetlights and buildings a mass of twinkling dots directly below them. The pilots were making a left-hand approach to the airport, and out the right window and ahead he could see the lights terminate where land met Quincy Bay. The lights beneath him were constant, save for the parks and a long, irregular slash through the city that was the Charles River.

Everything stopped.

His mind focused on one thought. The river. Its natural path through the city had many curves.

A horseshoe?

Despite the turbulence as the plane made its final approach to Logan, he unbuckled his seatbelt and changed seats, taking the one that faced the map pinned to the seat. He reached across and traced the Charles River with his finger. From where it spilled into the Boston Inner Harbor, through Cambridge and Watertown, then Waltham and along the southern edge of Newton. The river narrowed after Cow Island Pond and headed due south. Next to Brookdale Cemetery it turned again, this time to the northwest. His finger slowed then stopped.

"Got you, you son-of-a-bitch," Curtis said as the Gulfstream's wheels touched down.

# CHAPTER SEVENTY-FIVE

Curtis was stiffening up. His shoulder was throbbing from being yanked out of the dirt, and he was covered with scrapes and bruises. He ripped the map off the seatback as the Gulfstream taxied to the terminal and laid it out in front of Charlesbois.

"Here, Jacques." He set his finger on the bottom section of the map. His finger was resting on a short section of the Charles River, immediately north of Motley Pond. "When he said *Charles*, he meant the river, and the reference to a *motley crew* was to Motley Pond. And due north of the pond is this."

The river curved back on itself, creating a natural horseshoe. "Oh, God," Charlesbois said. "Renee?"

Curtis nodded. "North, in the horseshoe. We've got her, Jacques." He glanced at his watch. Ten twenty-three. An hour to drive, give or take. "We should make it before midnight. I'll call Aislinn and Stan and get backup in place. It'll take them the better part of an hour to get that far south. Or we could call it in to central dispatch and have some cruisers sent out."

"Which is best?" Charlesbois asked.

"Not sure," Curtis said. He was on his feet and moving as one of the pilots exited the cockpit and opened the plane door. They breezed by the man, thanking him for getting them cross-country in such good time, and into the terminal.

Charlesbois pointed to one of the doors. "My car's this way."

They ran through the terminal, Curtis limping but keeping up to Charlesbois, and across the parking lot to a sleek, black Porsche Carrera. Jacques jumped into the driver's seat, Curtis slid in on the passenger side.

Jacques started the car and hit the gas. "You're not sure whether to call it in or not?"

"I'm damn sure I know where he is." Curtis buckled up and held on. "We're going to be tight for time, but we know who we're looking for and how he thinks. If we call it in, the uniform cops who get the call will know nothing about what they're walking into. There's a risk factor there, Jacques. They could easily underestimate this guy, maybe even spook him."

Jacques nodded. "I get it. If they spook him, he could hurt or kill her."

"Possibly, but there's a downside," Curtis said. "Time. We're going to be cutting it close."

The Porsche slid sideways on the pavement as Jacques raced out of the parking lot and onto the main drag leading to Sumner tunnel. He floored it and the car shot ahead, pinning Curtis against the seat. "What's the route?" he asked.

Curtis checked the GPS on Charlesbois' phone. All possible routes looked clear, traffic flowing fine. "Get on the 9, go south down the east side of Jamaica Pond, then Center Street to Veteran's Parkway. Then High Bridge Street south. Take the exit to Northeastern University."

"I know it," Jacques said, increasing his speed. He got into the open for a few seconds and glanced over at his passenger. "How do we do this, Curtis?"

There was no right or wrong call. Either way held a high degree of risk. "I think it's your call, Jacques," he said. "She's your daughter."

There was no hesitation. "We'll take him. I'll get us there in time."

"Okay," Curtis said. He dialed Stan Lamers' cell phone. "Stan, we have the location. You, Aislinn, and two senior men. Nobody else. Stay off the radio. No sirens or lights as you get close. If you get there before we do, stay quiet." He gave his detective the location.

"Jesus, Curtis, that's a long drive."

"So get moving." Curtis killed the call and put the screen back on the GPS.

Curtis watched the city speed past as the Porsche cut through the still night air. Millions of people all having another normal day. Nothing special. Maybe a young girl would meet a nice boy tonight. Maybe someone was celebrating a promotion at the office. Maybe a man and a woman would fall in love. To most people in the city, today was just another day.

To Curtis and Jacques, it was Renee Charlesbois' last chance.

Curtis stole a glance at the dashboard clock. Ten fifty-one.

One hour and nine minutes.

It was close.

Too close.

# CHAPTER SEVENTY-SIX

Andrew Roberts looked at the name on the police report documenting his interview after Renee Charlesbois' disappearance.

*Liem Khilt.*

Jesus, they were stupid. Every one of them, falling all over themselves to hold court with him, listen to his words, yet they didn't have a clue what he was really saying. He had given them everything they needed to find him, but they had failed. He stood at the kitchen counter, repeatedly drawing the edge of the carving knife along the sharpening stone. A clock hung on the wall, just above the stove.

Eleven forty-two. Eighteen minutes.

He had done it. He had stayed to his self-imposed schedule despite the efforts of the Boston police. Curtis Westcott had come close. He had actually figured out what was happening, and had made it as far as Chicago. But that left Napa Valley, and finding the room tucked away in the abandoned Niebaum-Coppola caves was next to impossible. Westcott was stalled—a sailboat without wind.

The minute hand on the clock moved slightly. Seventeen minutes. He tested the blade and decided it was sharp enough to easily slice through Renee Charlesbois' windpipe and then the muscles and tendons in her neck. Her spine would be a bit of a test, but that was what this was all about. A game without a certain degree of risk and effort was not worth playing. And this game was more than worth playing.

It was a killing game.

He set the knife on the kitchen table and readied the rest of his equipment. A plastic body bag sat on the table, neatly folded. Her torso would fit in it nicely, and he could throw her head in as well until he got to where he wanted to dump her, then the head would get some special treatment. The bag would keep the blood in his vehicle to a minimum, but that wasn't really important. The vehicles were all disposable afterwards. This one would end up in the ocean, under a few hundred feet of water.

He glanced at the clock. Twelve minutes.

A set of plastic coveralls was lying in a pile on the kitchen floor and he put them on, securing the seals with the Velcro tabs. They felt bulky and odd, but without them, he would be drenched in blood. The carotid artery, just under her ear, would spit blood all over the room. There would be no escaping it.

He checked the clock one more time. Nine minutes.

It was show time.

# CHAPTER SEVENTY-SEVEN

At eleven-thirty at night, High Bridge Street was usually wide open and flowing freely. It came as a total surprise to Curtis and Jacques when a night crew had one lane shut down. There was a line of red tail lights as far as they could see, and because they were in the Porsche they had no flashing lights or siren. They were stuck.

"Shit," Charlesbois yelled. He got out of the car and jumped onto the hood.

Curtis was on the phone. "Stan," he screamed over the sound of the squad car's siren. "Where are you?"

"Coming up behind you," Stan yelled back. "I can see the traffic jam. You should be able to see our lights."

"Jacques." Curtis stuck his arm out the window and pointed behind them. "Do you see lights?"

Charlesbois turned and started nodding vigorously. "Yeah, and coming up fast." He jumped back to the pavement and slipped into the car. "That your guys?"

"Yup," Curtis said, then spoke into the phone. "We're in the Porsche at the end of the line. Who's with you?"

"Aislinn's in the car behind me."

"We'll slip in between you two," Curtis said.

"Got it." The siren was loud now. "We're here."

The cars started pulling onto the curb and Stan drove up alongside them. He waved and kept moving. Charlesbois merged in with Aislinn tight to his bumper. The road ahead of them was a sea of parting cars and they were moving well now.

Curtis checked his watch. It was too tight. He dialed Stan's number.

"Stan," Curtis said when he answered. "Do you have the phone number for Andrew Roberts' house in Los Gatos?"

"I do."

"Give it to me," Curtis said.

Stan read it off, starting with the California area code. He tossed the phone on the seat when Curtis killed the line.

"I'm going to try and patch a call through to the guy who's got Renee," Curtis said as he dialed the California number. A man picked up on the second ring.

"The Roberts' residence," he said.

"Andrew Roberts, please," Curtis said.

"Mr. Roberts is not here right now. Can I take a message?"

"You can do better than that. Conference him in on this call, and do it immediately. Tell him Curtis Westcott of the Boston Police Department is on the line."

"I'm sorry, but that is quite impossible. Mr. Roberts has asked not to be…"

"Make it possible," Curtis said curtly. "Or I'll have the Los Gatos police at your door in ten minutes and you'll be charged as an accessory to murder. Do it. Get your boss on the phone so I can talk with him."

There was a moment's silence, then the man said, "Hold, please."

"What are you doing?" Charlesbois asked as Curtis waited on hold.

"Getting Khilt on the line and buying some time." Curtis took a quick glance at the dashboard clock. Eleven fifty-six. "We're about five minutes out. We don't need much."

A voice that Curtis instantly recognized came on the line. "Lieutenant Westcott. What can I do for you this evening?"

"You could stop this insanity right now," Curtis said. "Before you dig yourself in any deeper."

"Oh, I think you and I both know I'm already in fairly deep," Roberts said. "Why stop now? I mean, it's obvious you know who I am."

"Massachusetts could keep you on kidnapping charges, Andrew. If you kill Renee, the charge goes to first degree murder."

"Six of one, half a dozen of another." Roberts' voice was calm, almost emotionless. "You have to understand that at this point, I really don't care what the charges are."

"You should. It could mean the difference between life in prison or the death penalty."

"Come now, detective. We both know the death penalty was ruled unconstitutional in Massachusetts in 1984. Don't play games with me." There was a pause, then he asked, "How did you figure it out?"

"You know exactly how. You left the clues. I simply pieced everything together."

"Very impressive, detective. I never thought that would happen."

"Well, it did. Give it up, Andrew. We know who you are. You can never return to the life you had. You're finished. Give it up and let Renee Charlesbois live. There's nothing to be gained by killing her."

"In my mind there is." Another pause, then, "Hold on for a minute. I'll be right back."

"What's going on?" Jacques asked when the conversation stopped. His eyes were wide with fear.

"I don't know. He put me on hold."

Stan's car stopped at a narrow drive on the right side of the road. Charlesbois pulled alongside, and Stan pointed up the winding road. "This is it."

"Turn off your headlights," Curtis said.

The sky was clear and there was enough light from the moon to show the way. Charlesbois cut his lights and the sports car crept slowly through the darkness, the two cruisers following close behind.

The thick underbrush on both sides of the private drive shielded the Porsche from view. As they got closer, they could see a solitary light through the trees—the rest of the large bungalow was dark. Charlesbois steered the Porsche around the last turn then stopped. Beyond that point was open ground with no cover. If they made a move on the house they would be completely exposed.

"Leave it here?" Charlesbois asked, his knuckles white on the wheel.

Curtis nodded. He was about to speak when Andrew Roberts came back on the line.

"Well, aren't you the tricky bastard," Roberts hissed.

"What do you mean?" Curtis reached up and smashed the interior dome light with the butt of his flashlight, then opened the door and stepped quietly onto the gravel drive. Aislinn and Stan came up from behind, quietly, guns drawn.

"I checked the location of the cell tower your call is coming from. You're in Boston."

Curtis was caught off guard. "We knew our time was up, Andrew, so we came back."

"Don't bullshit me, Westcott," the killer yelled. "You found what you needed in Napa, now you're trying to buy a little extra time. Fuck you." The phone went dead.

Curtis glanced at the house. He saw a figure flit through the lit room, then disappear. Roberts was on the move.

Curtis whispered to Aislinn to take the rear of the house, and for Stan to cover the patio doors at the side. Aislinn handed Curtis a spare service pistol and he chambered a round. He told Charlesbois to stay put, then started across the open expanse of grass toward the house. He had a minute, maybe two, to get inside and find Renee. His legs pumped hard as he ran toward the house, his breath coming fast.

Renee's executioner was coming for her.

# CHAPTER SEVENTY-EIGHT

Curtis slowed as he started up the stairs to a wooden porch that ran the length of the house. He was at the front door when he heard a noise behind him. He whirled around, raising the pistol. Jacques Charlesbois was a few feet behind him.

Curtis wagged his finger at him. "Jacques, this is police business. Get back to the car."

"No chance. My daughter is in there. I'm coming with you."

Arguing with him wasn't going to help Renee.

"Stay behind me," Curtis said. Charlesbois nodded.

Curtis grabbed the door handle and turned. It was unlocked. He pushed it open and entered the house, the gun outstretched, his finger curled around the trigger. The foyer was dark and his eyes flicked back and forth, watching for Roberts and checking the floor so he didn't trip and stumble.

Curtis could see into the living room. It was sparsely furnished, but there was no sign of Roberts. Beyond the living room was a long hall, leading to the rear of the house. Curtis focused on the corridor, searching for traces of light coming from beneath a door. Nothing. He stuck his head around the corner and looked into the kitchen. It was lit by a fluorescent tube and the artificial light gave the wood cabinets a strange orange hue. He moved quickly through the empty room to the back entry. There were three stairs leading down, then a small landing.

He slipped off his shoes and tiptoed to the landing and took a quick glance around the corner. More stairs, leading down to darkness.

He took a deep breath. Which way? Back into the rear of the house or down to the basement? Roberts had kept Kelly Moran on the main floor of the house in Lake Forest, but that was LA, where houses didn't have basements. It would be much easier to keep Renee captive in the basement than on the main floor. He started down the stairs, the gun pointed in front of him, Charlesbois behind, shoes off and moving quietly.

Curtis counted the risers. Houses with normal eight-foot ceilings usually had fourteen. When he reached the fourteenth his foot touched rough cement. They were in a dark hallway and Curtis kept moving, feeling the floor with his toes before planting his feet. He kept his left hand on the wall to keep himself centered in the hallway until he reached a corner. There was a hint of light in the intersecting hall, and Curtis took a quick look around the edge. At the end was a door with a small opening at eye height. The light in the corridor was coming from the room, and he could hear muffled noises. Then a distinct voice. Renee's.

"No, please. No." Her voice was barely audible. Pleading.

Curtis turned and grabbed Jacques Charlesbois as he began to surge ahead.

"No," he whispered, then released his grip and tiptoed down the hall toward the light. Charlesbois' breathing was heavier now, more audible, and Curtis began to worry that Roberts would hear. He reached the door and peered through the opening.

The room was well lit, and Curtis could see a man dressed in some sort of plastic suit near the far wall, hunched over a cot. The bottom part of a torso and a pair of legs were visible, but the upper part of Renee's body was hidden from view. Curtis grabbed the door handle and burst into the room, his gun leveled at Roberts' head. The man spun about and Curtis saw the carving knife in his hand, blood spatters on the blade. His face was mottled purple, his eyes feral.

"Drop it, Andrew," he yelled. "Drop it right now."

Renee shrieked as Roberts grabbed her by the hair and yanked her onto her feet. He spun her so she was between him and Westcott, the knife at her neck and cutting into the flesh. Charlesbois lunged for Roberts, but Curtis threw his shoulder into the big man and blocked him. Silence settled in except for the heavy rasp of Renee's labored breathing.

"It's over," Curtis said, his gun aimed at Andrew Roberts' head.

"But how does it end, detective? Does this one live? Does she die? I don't think it's quite over yet."

With only a couple of inches of Roberts' face visible, Curtis didn't have a clean shot. "Why kill her? She had nothing to do with you not getting the medicine."

"*He* did." Roberts' eyes briefly flicked at Jacques Charlesbois.

Curtis could feel Jacques tense up behind him, ready to rush Roberts. "Why didn't you go after the people at the resort? They were the ones who wouldn't give you the medicine."

"Are you trying to deflect things, detective? It's not going to work." A hint of a smile crept onto his face and his grip tightened on the knife. It cut deeper into her flesh.

Jacques Charlesbois made his move, blowing by Curtis and grabbing for the knife. Roberts' hesitated for a split second, and that tiny sliver of time was enough. Curtis fired. The bullet streaked by Renee's ear, hit Roberts in the eye and tore a hole in the back of his head. The knife clattered to the floor.

Renee's knees buckled, but Charlesbois had her in his arms before she collapsed. He held her close for a minute, then gently laid her on the cot. Her throat had a shallow slash mark and she was bleeding, but it hadn't cut deep enough to nick her trachea or an artery. Her eyes were open and alert. She was struggling to breathe, but managed to force out one word.

"Dad."

"Shush," Charlesbois said, cradling her head, his tears welling up and running down his face. "Quiet, Renee. You're safe. It's over."

Curtis dialed Stan's number. "We've got her," he said when Stan answered. "Get EMS here right away. She's alive, but bleeding and in pretty rough shape."

"Got it. Where are you?"

"In the basement. I'll turn on some lights."

"Aislinn's on her way down."

Curtis stood in the center of the room and looked about. So this had been Renee Charlesbois' prison for two weeks. It was a horrific thought. No light, no fresh air, no idea of what would happen every time the door opened. Day after day, holding on to hope. Praying someone would find her.

The killer's body lay on the floor in a heap, covered with blood, half his head missing. Liem Khilt. Tim Kehill. Keith Mill. Mike Thill.

Andrew Roberts.

The monster was dead.

Aislinn arrived and began securing the crime scene. "So that's our bad guy." She stared down at the body. "What a waste of skin."

Jacques Charlesbois looked up at her. "Detective Byrne." The tears were still flowing. "Thank you."

Aislinn knelt down and Renee grasped for her hand and squeezed hard. The two women stared at each other for a long moment, then Aislinn gave her a quick smile, stood and went back to working the scene.

Curtis put the safety on his pistol, then walked back up the stairs and out the front door into the evening air. Outside on the lawn, Stan was waiting for the long line of cars and people who were on their way.

"Close one," Stan said. "You okay?"

Curtis sucked some of the fresh night air. Exhaustion was setting in. "Yeah, tired to the bone though."

Stan grinned. "Ahh, you're just getting old." He headed into the house to help Aislinn.

Curtis stood in the welcome silence, the adrenaline rush fading. Every bone, every joint, felt battered and beaten. He pulled out Jacques Charlesbois' cell phone and dialed a number. Brandy Eagleson answered.

"Hi," he said. "It's Curtis. I thought you'd like to know we got him."

"Is Renee okay?" she asked.

"Yes. She's in pretty bad shape, but she'll make it."

"Oh, thank God."

"Yeah," Curtis said. "Thank God." He was silent for a moment, then he said, "I'll call you in a few days. Give you an update on how she's doing."

There was no pause. "I'd like that."

Curtis smiled. "That's good." He glanced back at the house. "I need to go now. I'll call."

"Okay. Good night."

He hung up and slid the phone into his back pocket. He looked up at the sky, so full of stars. A warm feeling washed over him. He thought about his parents' check on his fridge, knowing that's where it would stay. There was no ego in admitting to himself that without his involvement, Renee Charlesbois would have died.

A slight breeze rustled the leaves and a shiver ran up his spine. He brushed his hair back from his face, still staring at the stars. Had something guided him through Andrew Roberts' maze? If it had, he was glad for it.

He closed his eyes, and for that single moment, his world was right.